THE SCOUT

ERIC TOZZI

The Scout
Copyright © 2013 Eric Tozzi

Cover design by Eric Tozzi

Printed in the United States of America

ISBN: 978-0-615-91404-6

PROLOGUE

I T AWOKE GRADUALLY, POWERING UP one system at a time, as the computer program switched from flight to atmospheric entry. The journey had been long, though time seemed of little consequence inside the womb-like darkness of this thermally tuned environment. It was the distance—tens of billions of miles in the vacuum of interstellar space—that presented considerable risk to the flight and ultimately the mission. But this phase of the journey had been successful and was nearly finished. Each system ran diagnostics that confirmed complete health across the board. Everything was in the green. All systems were stable. The risk shifted to the next phase of the mission, one of the most challenging.

All of it began with an idea that evolved into a long-term project requiring ages of remote sensing aimed deep into the very heart of the galaxy. Candidate worlds were carefully surveyed for detailed information regarding surface composition and mineralogy, major surface modification processes, ages of surfaces, gross physical characterizations and atmospheric conditions. But only a finite amount of data could be obtained remotely. Advanced surface operations were the only way to be sure that a world—any world—would be a fully viable candidate for the project.

An alarm sounded in the dark, signaling a lock on the target planet ahead. The entry, descent, and landing sequence program loaded flawlessly. Everything was happening just as expected. And very soon, in just a few days, surface operations would begin on this candidate world that orbited a small, yellow-white star.

CHAPTER 1

THE MOMENT JACK MCALLISTER HEARD his phone ring, saw that it was his father Richard calling and answered, he knew he'd made a mistake.

"Hey," Jack said.

"Jack," his father replied. "Got your email last week. I suppose congratulations might be in order."

"*Might* be in order?"

"You know what I mean."

"Not sure that I do, Dad. Maybe you should clarify."

Richard fell silent and Jack felt the air in the room sour. Normally appareled in quiet confidence and steady optimism, undergirded by a six-foot athletic frame, Jack slouched, pushing his fingers through thick ebony hair out of nothing more than irritation. He glanced out the window of his apartment where soft afternoon light was turning salmon beneath an impending, inevitable dusk. The drive from Pasadena to Big Bear would be three hours minimum. There was still enough time. Barely. Jack moved from the bedroom to the kitchen in an effort to keep his momentum.

"This must be very exciting for you," Richard said.

"It is," Jack replied. "It's a big deal."

"I suppose. I'm sure it will impress some people. Women mostly. Since you're not entangled with what's-her-name anymore, you can start dating the Hollywood types. If you ever went back to school and got that Ph.D., then I'd be impressed."

Jack reached the refrigerator, grabbed a cold water bottle from the door, fumbled, and dropped it on the floor. *Shit.*

"Her name was Jamie. And I'm sorry the bachelor's in mechanical engineering wasn't good enough, Dad."

Richard began to push, much as Jack expected he would.

"I still don't get it, Jack. When you turned thirty, it's like you hit the gas, let go of the wheel and flew straight off the cliff. I suppose none of that matters now, since your success is in fiction, not reality. Perhaps the work was too hard for you. Maybe I was expecting too much."

Jack felt anger pooling inside, and he knew he'd have to either climb out of the ring, or drive in with a couple of jabs and a strong right hook. He transitioned to the living room, gathering his wallet and car keys.

"How's Mom?" he asked. It would steer the conversation down a very short road.

"Marion's fine," Richard said briskly.

She's not fine, Jack thought.

"Is she saying anything?"

"She talks a little. She's not walking as much."

All part of the disease.

"I worry that she..." Richard took a long, deep breath. "I worry for her."

Richard's voice was heavy, his words leaden with premonitory grief. Jack stopped short of the front door. He had every intention of terminating the call with his father and leaving the apartment. But instead he waited there.

Motionless. Feeling the dull thump of his heart in his chest. Something was off.

"What's going on there? You and Mom still have help?"

"Yes, the ladies are around. Cathy's a good cook and makes sure we're taking our medications. I just had a feeling today that—"

It was Richard's abrupt silence that unsettled Jack.

"A feeling about what?"

Richard's voice resurfaced from the quiet.

"I was just thinking about how...things have changed. It's inevitable, I guess: life, the world...it all changes. There's just no stopping it."

Jack eased himself onto the couch, quietly placing his car keys back down on the coffee table. It was disturbing, the sudden turn in the conversation, his father's tone so dark and weighted. If Jack could accuse the man of anything, it was being critical and callous, but this—this was something else.

"Dad, is there something you want to tell me?"

"It's nothing. Not a big deal. I'll let you get back to whatever it is you're doing. What are you doing?"

Richard was returning to his old self.

"I'm driving up to Big Bear to watch the meteor shower," Jack said.

"Really. I'm surprised. I assumed you'd given up on real science."

"You assume way too much, Dad."

Jack loudly scooped up his keys and rose from the couch. It was time to leave.

"I better get going here."

"Sure, Jack. Have fun. Oh, wait...have you talked to your sister recently?"

"Amy? Couple weeks ago. Why?"

"I called her earlier and left a message. She hasn't called me back."

Jack glanced at the Tag Heuer on his wrist: 5:53 p.m. Traffic on the freeway would be unkind. He had to leave.

"Dad, she's probably getting her kids to bed. Give her some time. She'll call you back."

"Okay," Richard said. "Take it easy, Jack. I worry about you."

"Don't," Jack said, and hung up.

———

By the time Jack crawled up the onramp and shuffled into the right lane, the entire freeway was throttled with cars. After two hours of pumping the brakes, idling a few feet at a time, accelerating softly before pumping the brakes again, he reached the mountain road that jagged off the elbow of the freeway. The cloudless sky purpled and darkened above him as he climbed seven thousand feet closer to it. Normally Jack played music in the car, but not this time. Instead he was replaying in his mind the conversation he had with his father. And the more he replayed it, the more he was troubled by it.

It's inevitable, I guess: life, the world...it all changes. There's just no stopping it.

Those words were cryptic, foreboding, and unusual for Richard's normally practiced and narrow lexicon. But Jack decided it could be chalked up to old age and a whisper of dementia he'd subtly noticed occurring in his dad over the last year. It was nothing close to what he saw his mother go through, however. She was locked away in another world behind a door marked Alzheimer's. Jack glanced down at his right forearm, at the tattoo of the Phoenix he'd gotten years earlier, the great bird lifting dramatically from a mountain of ash, bound for a limitless sky. He frowned.

The phone rang suddenly. It was Richard calling again. Jack's heart sank. He couldn't take another round.

Not now, Dad.

And he turned off his phone.

Jack found a place to park off the north shore of Big Bear Lake where he now stood beneath an open night sky so clear it seemed an illusion, a fantasy created by some visual surrealist. The deepness of the black was so great that Jack felt for a moment he could fall into it, as though he were hanging upside down over an abyss into which entire galaxies could evaporate. A cold breeze skimmed the lake and rolled over him, and all at once it became clear: his father would never understand him, never approve of his son's chosen career path that seemed a blasphemous departure from his own. Richard was not unlike the blackness Jack found himself staring into: a cold, empty vacuum.

The first meteor was subtle, like a strand of softly glowing hair in broad daylight. The next few were more obvious and brilliant. For an hour they came a few at a time, super accelerated, falling diamonds grazing an oily black heaven.

Jack heard his father's words again. Softly.

Life, the world…it all changes. There's just no stopping it.

Realizing that the shower was over, Jack drifted back toward his car, and turned his phone on. It chimed instantly from three unheard calls, all from a familiar area code: Indiana. *Dad.* But Jack didn't recognize the number.

Before he could dial back, a call came in from the same number, and Jack answered immediately.

"Hello?"

"Is this Jack?" said a woman, her voice low, knotted with anxiety.

"Yeah. Who is this?"

"It's Cathy. I've been trying to reach you and your sister for the last few hours."

"Is everything okay there? Is it Mom again?"

"No, honey...it's your dad. He collapsed in the kitchen tonight. It was very sudden, a heart attack. We called the paramedics and they worked on him for almost an hour. I'm so sorry...but he didn't make it. He's gone."

CHAPTER 2

THE SKY WAS TRANQUIL OVER Merriweather, Indiana, on the evening that *it* arrived. The non-presence of atmospheric activity was unusual for May as with regularity the sky was a full motion canvas of cumuli, and on occasion, explosive supercells. But from east to west there were only a few gauzy clouds dusting the atmosphere. The sun was still aloft, bathing the timbered horizon in a warm, pineapple glow. A quiet breeze kissed the town, which rested snugly in the middle of a vast forest—a man-made island in a sea of towering trees. Those who were out walking their dogs around the block or playing with their kids on rambling front lawns savored it. And none of them had any idea what was heading toward them from that wide-open sky.

Jack drove slowly down East 5th Street, ignoring all of it. He wasn't in a hurry. In fact, had he been able to flip a U-turn in the middle of the street and go back the way he came, he would have. Gladly.

This is not happening, he thought. *This cannot be happening!*

He tightened his grip on the steering wheel, pushing against it to straighten himself in the driver's seat. He felt perspiration forming on the small of his back, soaking into the black dress shirt he'd bought the day before. It was humid here, and hot. When he'd gotten off the plane in Indianapolis just three days earlier he'd noticed it immediately, like walking into a spa.

Jack glanced at the tape deck in the dash. Weren't those extinct? He vaguely remembered cassette tapes when he was a kid, but compact discs invaded like a military force and did away with them. Richard still had cassettes back at the house, though. Boxes of them. And Jack would have to go through them all, every last one. It hurt just to think about it. But of course it wasn't just relic bits of forgotten media—it was an entire lifetime of personal items that he would have to sort piece by piece. It was overwhelming. There would be time for all of that later. It would have to wait.

Focus, Jack! Minute by minute, one thing at a time, he thought.

It was all he could deal with now. Minutes. If he were to think in terms of hours and days, it would produce an emotional tsunami, a devastating force that would efficiently bulldoze every last quarter of sanity left in him. And he couldn't let that in. Not now. Minute by minute. One thing at a time. And the only thing he had to do now was make it to the funeral home without having an accident.

Jack's phone rang. It startled him, even with the ringer volume turned very low. It wasn't like him to be this unhinged. But in the wake of Richard's sudden death, everything that seemed fixed and familiar had fallen away.

He glanced at the name on the small screen: AMY HILL. Jack tapped the screen to answer.

"Hey," he said evenly.

"Hey," she replied. "We're running a little late. Are you there yet? Have you seen him? Have you seen Dad?"

He glanced up ahead on the left side of the road. The large, dark, A-frame of the funeral home loomed into view a half mile out. Jack felt his stomach turn reflexively.

"Not yet. I'm almost there," he said.

"We'll be on our way in twenty-five minutes," she said.

"I'll see you then," Jack replied, and ended the call.

He slowed his dad's Mercury, and pulled left into the parking lot of the funeral home. Save for what was presumably the funeral director's car in the very corner of the lot, and another that likely belonged to the secretary, it was empty. Jack drove toward the front of the building, slotting into the space directly facing the entrance. He turned off the engine and let the quiet sheath him.

He stared ahead at those double wooden doors and thought about what it was going to feel like when he finally saw his dad in the casket he had picked out just forty-eight hours earlier. He glanced at his watch and took a very deep breath, thinking he could wait here in the car for Amy and her family to arrive and they could all walk in together, or he could cross through those doors now and have a few minutes alone with his father. Slowly, he unfastened his seatbelt and got out.

Jack locked the car and stood immobilized. In just a matter of moments, everything that had happened in the last five days would become irrevocably real; no more denial, no more wondering about how it all happened and why. Jack lifted his chin, steeled himself, and started toward the entrance. Above him, the faint light from distant stars began to freckle the pale evening sky. Jack ignored this, unaware that one of those stars was *moving*.

The alien craft resolved from the quiescence of space and the backdrop of a billion shining stars like the round fired from a gun. Approach speed of the vehicle as it screamed toward the blue gradient of the Earth's atmosphere was an unflinching twelve thousand miles-an-hour. The craft was of simple design: a black metallic cone, eighteen feet wide with a convex armored front. It deftly adjusted its implacable course by firing small thrusters in sequence: two shorter bursts—pause—then a third. A trajectory correction maneuver complete, it suddenly, violently made contact with Earth's upper atmosphere.

Friction applied to the front of the vehicle produced a contact heat as great as the surface of the sun. It exploded savagely into a trail of super-heated plasma as the brute force of aerodynamic drag began to slow the craft down. The armored front of the vehicle, which was in fact the heat shield, held strong. This peak heating period went on for several minutes before the vehicle had cleared Earth's invisible defense and was now falling toward the surface with nothing to stop it. Tons of metal falling...falling.

There was a pyrotechnic blast from the rear of the craft, and a black, webbed form deployed, stretching and expanding into a parachute. Nine G's of force pulled against the vehicle, and it decelerated through the sound barrier, issuing a basso, tactile, sonic boom. Hidden descent engines fired in sequence, slowing the craft even more, steering it toward the forest canopy below, and the pre-determined target area in a small clearing.

It remained in the sky a few moments longer before it plunged with sheer finality into the trees beyond the horizon of the town. What few people thought they saw that night was a meteor. The sonic boom they heard bumped the town like dull thunder, rattling windows and causing the ground to quiver. While there were some who marveled at the experience and thought it was "cool," a few were frightened and dialed 911. No one knew where it landed, or if it even had. And most had forgotten all about it within a few hours.

CHAPTER 3

JACK FOUND HIMSELF IN THE foyer of the funeral home, standing at the entrance of the chapel where, beyond those dark doors, his father's open casket waited inside.

"You may go in whenever you like," the funeral director said in a warm, rehearsed tone. It was a canned invitation—template—as was everything Jack had heard in the last few days. He didn't blame the guy. He believed his sincerity, but couldn't help think about the fact that he had probably said the exact same thing in the exact same way a thousand times before.

"I did some more research on your father," the man said.

Jack turned to him. "Really?"

"Yes. He not only worked on the Voyager mission, but the Mars Viking landers. What an extraordinary accomplishment!"

Jack warmed and felt something genuine in that bit of praise.

"He was at the console at JPL the day it landed on Mars and first images came back," Jack said, remembering fondly.

The funeral director grinned ear to ear. "Wow. Incredible!"

Jack nodded.

"And you," he said, "I didn't realize you were a writer."

Jack grew quietly uncomfortable.

"I suppose since your books are science fiction and all, it's not as serious as what your father did. But I'm sure he had a huge influence on your work. And there's certainly no reason to feel like he might have overshadowed you with his amazing career," the man said, endeavoring a conciliatory smile.

What a thing to say, Jack thought, his expression becoming aluminum.

"I'm going to go inside now, and I'd like to be left alone."

Taking the cue, the funeral director took one huge step back and nodded.

"Of course. If there's anything you need—anything at all—please just let us know."

Jack nodded. The man pivoted neatly on his dress heel and walked off toward his office. Jack was alone, hearing only low classical background music, feeling his heartbeat as it gradually accelerated, becoming more tactile in his chest. He drew a deep breath and pulled open the doors, stepping into the rear of the chapel. He looked immediately right, toward the front of the room, and saw his father's unmistakable profile there, visible just above the edge of the coffin. It was the stillness of the face that struck Jack immediately. It was mannequin-like, hollow, with no evidence of life present or past. Finality.

Jack felt himself dropping into a space that existed between moments—into the surreal—unable to move. But he gathered himself and walked closer, one step at a time.

Closer. His father's facial contours resolved more clearly as he approached.

Jack reached the casket and stared straight down at Richard. *It's him, but it's not him anymore.* It was the first thought that struck Jack as he hovered there. He understood now what people meant when they said the body was just a shell that, upon death, emptied. All at once Jack felt it, the full weight of it, tearing all the bolts and beams free from what had been a familiar edifice. *Dad was gone.* His shell was the only thing left, surrounded by the silk softness of the casket.

"Dad," Jack said softly, "I wish you would have…"

He had every intention of finishing the thought, but couldn't. He choked, and for the first time in several days, allowed the sorrow to come. It crashed through him just like a tidal wave, inevitable and unstoppable, sweeping violently through his senses, lifting him, carrying him away like collapsed building detritus. Jack cried. He didn't fight it, didn't try and resist. He let it take him. He put his hand down into the casket to touch the breast of his father's burial suit.

And that's when he heard a distant sound like thunder, but not quite the same thing. It was a single, staccato, low frequency boom. The old glass of the funeral home chattered in the panes like castanets. Jack pulled his hand back quickly, startled. He scanned the room to see if anything was moving. If it had been an earthquake of any significant magnitude, chandeliers would swing and pictures might shift on the wall. Nine months earlier, Indiana had experienced a 4.1 temblor that had people shaken and local news in a veritable swarm. But as Jack further surveyed the room, it was clear that no such manifestation was there.

Amy crept into the chapel, her husband close at her side. She turned and saw Jack standing over the casket that held the remains of their father.

She wept.

———————

Sheriff Clifford Hawkins was comfortable in his chair, watching the clock on the wall as the minute hand approached the hour. He found himself doing it all the time now—watching that clock. It had started six months earlier when he began thinking about retiring early. He stood up and decided it was time to go home when an evidence tech named Jeremy cut the corner to his office door and leaned in.

"Hey, we're getting calls about a meteor...or something," Jeremy said.

Hawkins was tired. Weary, actually, from a month of overseas travel that was supposed to be a vacation and a time of rest. But as it happened a brisk schedule of stops across Europe on a tourist package from AAA had proven to be more demanding than rewarding. All he wanted to do right now was to go home to his wife, his dog, a hot dinner, and a carefully chilled bottle of Oliver Wine. Those were the kinds of evenings he favored more and more as he crested the peak from age fifty-nine to sixty.

"Meteor?" he asked.

"Yeah, I guess. Shook some folks up," Jeremy said.

"Did it hit the ground?" Hawkins asked, even though he didn't care.

"Not sure," Jeremy said.

"Anything about it on the news?"

Jeremy knew where this was going. Nowhere.

"No, sir. Not yet."

Hawkins nodded and gathered his wallet and keys from the top of his desk.

"Put in a call to Grissom or the Naval Division over in Ridgewood County. See if they had any tests going on, or if they tracked anything."

Jeremy nodded, "Sure."

He held a moment in the doorframe to make sure that was it. Hawkins verified with a watered down smile and deft little shrug that settled his blazer evenly across his shoulders.

"Call me if anything comes up," Hawkins finally said.

Jeremy went back toward his office around the corner and that was the end of it. *Okay*, Hawkins thought, *down the hall, out the side door—done deal.* He turned off the humming fluorescents in his office and started down the hall. His shoes clicked loudly on the old linoleum as he went, and for some absurd reason he felt not unlike a teenager trying to sneak out of the house without making a racket. He had almost made it to the door when Deputy Linda Craig swung into his path from the fax room.

"Hey," she said, "I made calls to Grissom, Terre Haute, and Indianapolis. Charlie Bennett's an air traffic controller there. I went to school with him. I hear anything worthwhile, I'll let you know."

"Thanks, Deputy," he said, and winked kindly.

Without another word, he slid through the side door and out into the parking lot. Hawkins strode to his car without a care in the world. He knew damn well that if Linda said she made the calls and would get the information, it would get done. She was, by far, the brightest and most competent deputy that he had. She would go far no matter what she decided to do with the rest of her life, and this town was damn lucky to have her on watch.

Hawkins dropped into his car behind the wheel and closed the door. He started the engine, but hesitated before putting it in gear when he noticed them—a small group of people on the sidewalk, heads titled back, looking into the sky. One of them pointed and traced an invisible line across the horizon. A few of them shrugged. Another began illustrating, dramatically with his hands, something he'd seen just about fifteen minutes earlier. Hawkins watched this go on for another moment before putting the car in gear and driving slowly away. As he turned toward home, he glanced upward into the bare evening sky. *It's nothing,* he thought, and put his eyes back on the road, his mind already at home.

Linda breezed down the corridors of the Hills County Sheriff's Office in an organic sort of rhythm. She was something of an anomaly: at 25 years of age she was overflowing with a confidence and infectious hope that every single day she was there, she was making the city, and indirectly the world, a much better place. This rang dissonant with some of her peers who saw the world and their job through a much different lens: hazy and dim, patently bleak. Adding to her peculiarity was the fact that she embodied, and at the same time transcended, the quintessential appearance of the girl next door—easy to fall for. She had lightly freckled cheeks and chartreuse, peregrine eyes that stood out beneath long, bright, coppery hair. Having run track in high school and college she earned an athlete's physique and, despite the unflattering uniform she was required to wear on the job, she made the thing look good. Damn good.

She glided into her office to deposit a field report on her desk when the phone rang. Without missing a beat, she grabbed the receiver and answered.

"Deputy Sheriff Linda Craig," she said. It was Charlie Bennett from Indianapolis Airport.

"Hey, it's Charlie," he said. "Regarding that meteor. I've got something for you."

CHAPTER 4

J ACK, AMY, AND HER HUSBAND Dean, had remained in the chapel for three hours as visitors came to see, and to say goodbye to, Richard McAllister. During the first hour there were only a few who came: neighbors, friends, and a nice elderly couple that were regulars at the local cafe where Jack's parents would eat breakfast four times a week. Then, abruptly, the visitors stopped coming. And it was probably just as well, Jack thought, because it was time for Marion McAllister to arrive and see her husband. It was a moment among many that Jack was dreading, having no idea how she would react, or if she would react at all.

Nine years earlier Jack had gotten on the phone with his father for what he assumed was going to be another plebeian conversation that would run the rim of all the familiar topics and faux pleasantries: How are you, what's new, read any good books lately, and when are you going for that masters of science in applied mechanics, son?

"Hi, Dad."

"Hi, Jack," his father began that night. "How are you doing?"

The greeting had all the familiar sentiment of a hundred conversations they had over the previous year. But this was unlike any of the other conversations by simple virtue of the time. The kitchen clock read 9:00 p.m. in Los Angeles where Jack was, which meant it was midnight in Indiana. Jack's father never called this late. Never.

"I'm fine," Jack said. "It's late there, isn't it? Everything okay?"

The line went empty for a long moment. He could faintly hear the sound of his dad's breath, low and heavy in the earpiece.

"Sure, Jack, we're both fine." There was that break again, that abrupt emptiness.

"Dad, you sure?"

It was another several moments until Richard spoke.

"Jack, listen...it's about your mom."

Jack's pulse quickened instantly. He had been standing in his kitchen, but moved to the living room couch to sit. The lights were dim in here.

"Yeah?"

Richard said, "Jack, we had some tests done recently, and...your mom's been diagnosed with Alzheimer's."

And there it was, shoved out in the open. Despite the initial jolt, Jack had anticipated as much, and the shock was short lived. Not five years prior to this conversation, Jack had noticed some troubling things about his mom. It began with growing vines of non sequiturs in almost every conversation with her, no matter the subject. Serious memory lapses started to occur after that. In the span of a ten minute drive to the grocery store, Marion would ask a total of five times where they were going. And then it was eight times. It became involuntary and unremitting.

She began compulsively doing loads of laundry that consisted of nothing more than a few hand towels at a time. Sometimes there were no towels, just a washing machine full of water and soap. Then she began speed walking through the house, doing laps around the living room, dining room, and kitchen. She became more and more belligerent, more and more confused. Lost. It was out of control. And once, at 2:30 in the morning, she had gotten out of bed to make coffee, overfilling the tank and spilling scalding hot coffee grounds all over the kitchen counter.

Jack and Amy had reviewed those things with each other privately while Richard pretended, intractably so, that they weren't really happening. Hearing his father finally say it on the phone was, in its simplest form, an admission and a resignation.

"Dad, I'm sorry," Jack said.

"Look, I know I haven't always been frank with you when it comes to our health, but the last thing I want is for you and your sister to worry," Richard complained.

Jack was offended. *Worry?* And if Richard or Marion died suddenly while hiding a serious illness, that would somehow make it all easier? Just so long as Jack and Amy didn't worry and lose a night of sleep? It was bullshit. Jack decided it was time to set the man straight on a few things. But instead, he didn't. The heaviness Jack heard in his dad's voice grieved him on a sub-level of emotion he didn't even know he had. That was nine years ago, and Jack had not forgotten it. It became a marker on that long, tortured road that his father was going to have to walk. Jack and Amy would traverse it with him, however more indirectly. Nevertheless, it was a heartbreaking journey for all of them.

Samantha, the evening caregiver, led Marion McAllister into the chapel with the utmost care, sensitive to her physical state in which she could hardly walk anymore, but merely shuffle a foot at a time. Jack studied her as she approached, hardly recognizing his mom anymore. Once so ebullient, she was now somber and frail. Her skin had thinned so that every muscle, tendon, vein, and in some cases bone had a pronounced imprint on her features. Her lower jaw was crooked, bent into a cross-bite that made her look like she was angry or frustrated. Perhaps she was and her body was simply manifesting those things outwardly. She was slow to react to anything or anyone and had stopped speaking almost altogether.

Jack and Amy helped her shuffle the rest of the way to the casket. She put her hands on the edge of it for balance. Son and daughter flanked her, watching her closely. She stared down at the body of Richard McAllister, her husband of thirty-five years. Jack felt his heart in this throat, watching her.

"That's Richard. That's your angel man," Amy said, putting her warm arms around Marion's brittle frame.

"He's with the angels now," Amy said, through a sob.

Marion looked directly down at Richard. She nodded. And for a moment it seemed as though she formed a smile despite her taut, crooked jaw. But whether it had really been there, or whether Jack simply imagined it, it was gone now. Marion's face was an empty visage set with unblinking, unreadable, glassy eyes. They stood there with her another few minutes, then walked her back to the front pew in the chapel, where they very carefully helped her sit down.

Others came to pay their respects over the next two hours, many of them students from the university that had studied physics with Richard who was their professor. After years of work as a mechanical engineer at Lockheed Martin and then Jet Propulsion Laboratory, Richard McAllister went into teaching. He became a professor at the university and that's what he had been doing faithfully the last thirteen years of his life. Jack was struck by the sincerity of everyone who came to see his dad and how much Richard had inspired all of them in some way or another. At just around 7:45 p.m., the visits stopped and they all left the chapel without saying a word.

Coming out into the foyer, Jack looked briefly for the funeral director to reconfirm the schedule for the burial the next morning. He was nowhere to be found, and the building seemed a dimly lit cavern now, eerily quiet and still. Jack caught a glance of the man outside, noticing that he was standing in the parking lot, looking into the night sky. Staring. *Weird,* Jack thought. He strode over to him, intent on making this brief.

"We're finished here," Jack said. "What time tomorrow?"

The man didn't respond. He was trance-like on the horizon, which was now bathed in the ashen light of dusk. Watching.

"Meteor," he said in hushed awe. "I think that's what it was."

"What time tomorrow," Jack pressed.

"Ten o'clock," the man said absently. "We'll see you here at ten."

As if they had never spoken, the funeral director walked back toward the building, through the ingress and inside. Jack turned for his car and pulled open the door. He glanced up momentarily, and that's when he noticed it for himself: a long, tubular cloud, gnarled and distended like large intestine, linking the timbered edge of the world to a sudden, noticeable surge of storm activity in the sky. It wasn't a tornado, but it was a sign that the local atmosphere had been disturbed. And it left Jack vaguely unsettled.

CHAPTER 5

THE LIGHTNING BURST LIKE A million flashbulbs triggering all at once, throwing long shadows from furniture dissonantly across the walls and floor. There was an earsplitting crack chased by a rolling, low frequency wave that shook the wooden bones of the house. Had an old, dilapidated office hi-rise been brought down to earth in a teeming concrete pile by explosive charges next door, that is surely what it must have sounded and felt like, Jack thought as he lurched upright on the sofa in the living room where he had fallen asleep watching TV. The set was dark as was everything in the house. The power had been amputated. He planted his feet on the carpet, muscles taught.

"Shit," he said out loud, and felt his heart pound against the inside of his rib cage. He stood slowly, cautiously, as though his very presence might somehow induce what was presumably another close proximity lighting strike. Jack feather-stepped barefoot to the window, warily brushing aside the gauzy chiffon curtains to have a look outside. The night was an inky void that made it impossible to see anything at all. But he could hear the wind scolding the trees, their branches and pine needles hissing in dissent.

Jack had seen enough documentaries to know that in conditions similar to this, monsters could be spawned out there in the dark, monsters in the form of tornadoes—EF3s, EF4s, and even EF5s—capable of obliterating a town as efficiently and dreadfully as an atomic bomb. And no one would realize they were coming until it was too late to do anything but kneel and pray.

He stepped quickly down the hall, past the kitchen, listening intently to the groans of the house as it resisted the winds. He didn't hear anything coming from his mother's bedroom, but decided to check on her in case the thunder had frightened her. He took the corridor briskly while each step uttered a faint creak under his feet. He passed three doors, arriving at the fourth.

He gently turned the old knob and eased the door open. His eyes attuned to the dimness, and he could make out the shape of his mother's hospital bed. Marion had been unable to sleep in a standard bed for over a year. She had to be in a fixed position at night with the added precaution of side rails to prevent her from possibly rolling off the bed and falling. In her condition, even a very small drop like that could shatter a brittle hipbone or crush ribs. Jack glided up toward the edge of the bed to peek at her. To his surprise and relief, she was still asleep.

Not wanting to disturb her, he eased himself back out of the room and carefully shut the door. And that's when he heard the built-in generator at the side of the house throttle up, resurrecting the power. Small lights from kitchen appliances seemed suddenly, boorishly bright. The sound of the television upset the quiet and Jack bolted quickly, albeit gingerly, back down the hall, past the kitchen, and into the living room. He reached the remote and mashed the volume button under his thumb. The sound fell to a whisper. Jack let out a long, hard sigh and settled back on the couch.

He grabbed his phone from the coffee table and touched the screen, noting the time as 3:37 a.m. In less than four hours the morning caregiver, Cathy, would arrive to wake Marion, get her cleaned up, dressed, and fed. Jack would get himself ready and they would all drive back to the funeral home, have the memorial service for Richard, and then drive out to the cemetery where they would bury him.

Heavier still on Jack's heart was the indelible realization that for the next few weeks—possibly months—he would have to go through every last corner of the place for the express purpose of preserving important items, discarding the trash, and ultimately reducing it all to an empty house that could be sold. Marion could not stay there any longer. She would have to be placed in a proper facility where she could be cared for around the clock. And she would have to be close to someone in the family, be it Jack in Pasadena or Amy in Tampa. Presently, neither one of them could get to her in under twenty-four hours if something happened.

Topping it all off was a hard dose of financial reality: in-home, around-the-clock care was unsustainable. Mercifully, Richard had managed to accrue a decent retirement and make a little something through more conservative investments. There was enough for the funeral and enough to get Marion situated somewhere else. Jack decided it was time to stop thinking. He had to get some sleep before the funeral, even if it was only a few more hours.

The winds outside had begun to settle into more benign drafts and the thunder rang duller and more distant.

Relieved, Jack began to settle back into the sofa and was preparing to shut off the TV, but saw something and nudged the volume up to hear it.

Local anchors were throwing each other the late stories of the day. The word, METEOR, with a question mark, floated in the little box over the makeup-dusted anchor's shoulder as Jack heard him say:

"...what appeared to most people as a meteorite that dramatically appeared in the sky over Hills County this evening. Some nervous calls to 911 had emergency operators busy, but others watched curiously and then went back about their business."

The camera threw back to the other anchor, and a new story about a local charity began. Jack shut the thing off, dropped the remote on the table, grabbed his shoes at the foot of the sofa, and very slowly made his way back down the hall toward the guest bedroom where he would in fact sleep for the next few hours. And wade through a forest of dark, unsettling dreams.

CHAPTER 6

THE MORNING OF THE FUNERAL came and Jack felt it all happen in a strange, fast-forward sort of way. He recalled getting up and saying a few words to the half-full chapel, then remembered being one of the pallbearers, feeling the weight of his father in the casket as he and the others walked it carefully to the waiting hearse just outside. He rode in the back of a big Lincoln Town Car limousine with Amy, her husband, and their two small children. No one said a word as they drove along the two-lane highway that needled through the verdant, grassy countryside. It was only when they pulled off the main road and crept past the iron-gated threshold of the cemetery that Amy said cryptically, "My God."

Jack felt something spider up his back, the hairs on his neck lift. They drove in slowly, passing all the headstones. There were rows and rows of them, going back over the hill as far as they could see, each one imprinted with only a few words that summed up a person gone, a life lived over a finite period of time. They arrived at the spot where Richard was to be buried, where he would stay indefinitely with a stone scarcely worded to summarize his own life. The rectangular pit had been dug, the rig for lowering the casket carefully placed. A small tent had been erected to keep them in the shade.

Jack felt everything begin to move in fast-motion again as they said their goodbyes over and over, cried, held each other for some measure of comfort, and then walked to the town car for the ride back to the funeral home. As they crawled past the leaden gates and back onto the main road, Jack felt as though a door were suddenly closed and sealed behind him. And it was at that very moment that he felt, literally and proverbially, the world become a larger and emptier place than he had ever known.

Later that evening they met back at the house for an early dinner with Marion, after which Jack and Amy went for a walk around the neighborhood. The impulsive glitter of lightning bugs danced ballets beneath the pooling shadows of dusk. The fresh air and overture of insects were soothing as they drifted down the circular street. It struck Jack—the stillness out here, the absence of noise endemic of a world that was spinning way too fast. *No wonder Dad loved it here so much,* he thought.

Amy said, "Jack, if I could stay right now I would."

Jack replied, "I know. We've all got a lot on our plates. I'll get started here. You find a place for Mom in Tampa. After that, you can come back and help get her moved."

"I will."

"We'll do this tag-team over the next few months between us," Jack continued. "I think we can get it done by

September. Most important thing is securing a new place for Mom. That's the priority."

Amy agreed in silence.

"What about you? Aren't you supposed to start a new book?"

Jack said, "I'll get it done. Somehow."

Amy fell silent, pensive now as she shortened her steps until she stopped walking all together.

"Jack...you don't have to prove anything, you know," she said.

Jack was puzzled.

"I don't know what you mean," he said.

"Dad," she said.

Jack looked away to a far off point in the deep evening sky.

"I'd say that's irrelevant now. He's gone."

She gently put her hand on her brother's shoulder.

"Dad was in his own world most of the time...or on another world. I always felt like I had to earn his approval somehow."

Jack said, "I gave up a long time ago, Aim."

"Jack, please...don't lose yourself. You don't have to prove anything. Mom needs you."

They walked the rest of the way in silence, circling down another street, then coming back around to the house where Amy's kids could be heard playing inside. They went in and Amy promptly diverted to the living room to check on her kids who were giggling and clacking plastic toys around. Jack drifted slowly through the kitchen, down the hallway to the back of the house, toward the very last door on the right. Intended as a third bedroom, Richard had converted it to an office. There was a bulky wood desk crowned with a sleeping computer. Two full bookshelves butted against each other, fighting for what little space was left on the far side of the small room. A cabinet with a half-dozen drawers and a color printer on top squatted nearby. Jack could only imagine how much paperwork was burrowed inside all those drawers.

He became overwhelmed at the thought, and was preparing to leave when he noticed something edging subtly out from beneath the computer keyboard. Jack stepped quietly to the desk. He nudged the keyboard aside and felt a strange trepidation when he saw a sealed envelope with one word scrawled across the front. In messy blue ink was his name: JACK.

Open it. He held it in his hand, considering it. Based on the last conversation with his father, he had an impending sense of dread that inside the envelope was probably a letter…or more likely a rant of some sort wrapped around a rebuke, marinated in a father's disappointment of his only son. Quickly he pulled open the top drawer of the desk, dropped the envelope inside, and shut it.

CHAPTER 7

J ACK OPENED HIS EYES SLOWLY, or rather forced them open, only then comprehending that morning sunlight had managed to penetrate the tiny window of the guest bedroom in spite of the brown plastic shutters that hung canted over the top of it. He could smell the blunt aroma of strong coffee brewing in the kitchen. There were low voices and footsteps as Cathy began the routine with Marion that included helping her to the bathroom, cleaning her, changing her Depends, getting her dressed and out into the dining room for breakfast.

Jack stared up at the vintage, cottage cheese texture on the ceiling and sighed, wondering where in the hell to start: the garage, Dad's office, the living room, the bedrooms, closets? He decided that paperwork would have to come first. Dad's office. That's where he'd begin. Right after coffee and breakfast.

Now dressed, Jack came into the kitchen, said "Hi" to Cathy and gave Marion a kiss on the forehead.

"Hey, Mom," he said, and smiled kindly at her. She responded with a look that was a blend of bewilderment and gratitude. He gazed into her eyes a moment longer, patted her affectionately on the shoulder, and then made his way toward the kitchen for a cup of coffee.

The doorbell rang, the sound sharp in the morning calm.

Cathy hurried to the door. "I'll get it. Probably the nurse come to check on your mom. Gotta keep an eye on her Coumadin."

"Oh, right," Jack said. He grabbed the coffee, poured it carefully and reached for the creamer.

"Jack...someone here to see you," she called from around the corner.

Probably someone who didn't make the funeral and wants to offer condolences, he thought.

Jack quickly stirred in the cream and then a careful teaspoon of sugar. Satisfied, he took a big sip and went to the door. He was still feeling dull, but became instantly clear when he realized that the man standing lofty in the doorway was the Sheriff. Hawkins slid off his semi-reflective sunglasses and folded them carefully. Jack sized him up as the guy who used to pound the streets, now likely close to retirement, hence the small tire around the waist. His salt and pepper hair was still thick and had an almost windblown look to it.

"Jack McAllister," Hawkins asked. "You Richard's son?"

"That all depends," Jack replied almost derisively. It was an attempt at humor for a moment in which Jack felt incredibly awkward. *What the hell was this about?*

Hawkins put out his hand for a shake, his expression somber.

"I am so sorry about your father. I saw him frequently at the diner in the mornings with your mom. Spoke with him on many occasions. Fascinating man. Good man. Please accept my condolences," he said.

Jack shook his hand, taking it firmly.

"Thank you."

"Look, I know you've probably got a million things to do. If there's anything I can help you with at all, please let me know."

Jack nodded.

"I'm also here to see if perhaps there is something you can help me with," he added.

Jack was immediately perplexed.

"Really? What could that possibly be?"

Hawkins looked him straight in the eye.

"Wondering if you could help me find a meteor," he said.

CHAPTER 8

J ACK HAD NEVER BEEN IN a police car—had no intention of
ever being in a police car for *any* conceivable reason—
and yet here he was, riding shotgun with the Sheriff
through town, and he figured since he wasn't in the back
seat with cuffs on, the whole thing was only somewhat
bizarre.

Hawkins asked, "Did you see it?"

Jack had been thinking about everything he had to do
and was becoming vaguely uneasy about riding with the
Sheriff out to a spot in the woods to look for an alleged
meteor. In hindsight he should have politely excused
himself from this little excursion, stayed at the house and
started going through Richard's files in the office. But it was
too late now. He was belted neatly into the front seat, about
to cross the last intersection of town before heading into
the wilderness.

"I'm sorry. See what?"

"The meteor. Did you see it?"

"No, I was at the funeral home," Jack said.

"Of course," Hawkins replied. "Well, some people saw it—or thought they saw it—and we got some spirited calls as a result."

Jack said, "I saw a quick blurb on the news."

Hawkins nodded. He flipped on the blinker, pulling left off the street, accelerating up the onramp and onto the highway that stemmed neatly from two lanes to four.

Hawkins said, "Look, Jack, I didn't know who else to go to. I heard you write books and since your dad was a scientist, I figured...well, you get the idea."

"I do," Jack said. "But perhaps I should clarify that I write science fiction books and I'm not a scientist."

The air in the car changed and a painful beat of silence followed. Hawkins straightened up in his seat and with well-practiced ease, cracked his neck loudly.

"Oh, I see."

Jack felt uncomfortable; foolishly idle just sitting there. *Better say something.*

"Look, I know my dad was the scientist, but growing up with him I learned a lot. I made a lot of friends in aerospace over the years. And I did earn a bachelor's in mechanical engineering. Guess that counts for something."

Hawkins finally said, "Well, Jack, I don't think you need to worry. You're talking to a man who flunked grade school astronomy. In my opinion, you're Alfred Einstein."

"Albert," Jack said.

"See," Hawkins smirked.

They drove for ten more minutes before Hawkins slowed and pulled off the highway, turning down a small, nondescript trail that swept them away from the asphalt and into the primordial span of the forest. Sunlight stabbed the windshield intermittently through the thick wooded canopy. Up ahead, parked in a small clearing, was another squad car.

"Reinforcements," Jack asked.

"Volunteer," Hawkins replied. "No one else wanted to come all the way out here today."

Jack smirked and tried to put himself in the shoes of the poor sap in that car. The guy probably wanted to stay at his desk, check emails, go to lunch at one of the regular places, drive the rounds for a few hours and then punch out and go home. And now he was going to have to hike around out here, looking for a meteor, or rather evidence of a meteor impact. And the odds that they would find any such thing were slim to nil. Actually they were worse than that. They had a better probability of encountering, photographing, and soliciting an autograph from Bigfoot than finding an impact site with a small meteor in it.

Hawkins didn't mind so much. Being out here kept him away from the office, the phones and the noise. Plus it would help kill a few hours. He parked neatly behind the other vehicle and alighted from his side. Jack got out and was awed by the woods and how vast they really were. The trees themselves were massive, reaching heights over sixty feet, towering individually in the midst of tens of thousands of others in what could only be likened to an ocean. Looking from left to right, Jack was confronted by two seemingly mirrored, densely wooded infinities.

The door to the other vehicle popped open and Linda climbed out from behind the wheel. Jack noticed her immediately—her striking features, that fiery mane of red hair tamed into a ponytail and those green eyes. *Whoa,* he thought, but played it cool.

She approached and smiled directly at him.

"Deputy, this is Jack McAllister. Jack, this is Deputy Sheriff Linda Craig." It was subtle, but Jack noticed that Hawkins had emphasized the *Deputy Sheriff* portion of the introduction. Jack smiled kindly in return and extended his hand for a shake.

"Very nice to meet you, deputy," he said. She shook his hand and he noted the firmness of her grip. It was immediately obvious this woman worked for a living out here.

"Good to meet you too, Jack," she said, quickly taking in his handsome features and his muscular build. It was the unusual amount of warmth, the alien softness in her voice that cued Hawkins it was time to get down to business. He cleared his throat a little too loudly, she noticed. She also noticed the tattoo on Jack's right forearm.

"Nice tattoo. Is that a Phoenix?"

"Yes, it is."

Hawkins asked, "The city?"

"Mars lander, actually," Jack said. "Something my dad worked on."

"It's cool," Linda said.

"Thanks."

Hawkins broke in, "Okay...so we've got several eyewitnesses that say a meteor fell somewhere out here in this direction."

Linda added, "Yes, and we called Grissom Air Reserve Base and the airports to see if there were any tests going on, or if maybe someone had tracked it."

"And what's the story?" asked Jack.

Linda began, "Well, the military says there were no tests, no flights, nothing going on in that airspace. Spoke with a friend of mine at Indianapolis Airport," she continued, "and he tells me they did see something on radar two nights ago, but it was probably a glitch, not a meteor."

"Really? Why did he say that?" Jack asked.

"Well, because the signal went in and out for a minute and the object apparently slowed down."

Jack began to process what she had just said: the signal was in and out for a minute and the object in question slowed down.

Okay, Jack, don't jump the rails here, he thought. *No science fiction.*

Very small meteorites lost velocity when entering Earth's atmosphere and had been known to drop below the speed of sound as they descended, which would kind of fit what Linda had just described. Except for the part about the signal going in and out.

Linda added, "He said they also caught some kind of a smoke plume on the Doppler."

"Huh," Jack said. Now it seemed perhaps it didn't fit. A very small meteorite would not produce a smoke plume that Doppler would easily read. Perhaps the advanced radar found at Cape Canaveral might pick up on something that small, but not the larger wavelength national instruments radars that the meteorologists used. In that case it would have to be a larger object, something bigger than 50 kilograms or just over 100 pounds perhaps.

But something that large would not slow down as much as smaller objects. So they were now talking about a large object that decelerated measurably over just a few minutes time. No matter, Jack thought. If a meteorite had fallen out here, it was highly unlikely they would find it, especially on foot, just the three of them.

"Based on photographic records alone, it's estimated some thirty thousand meteorites larger than a quarter of a pound fall to Earth every year," Jack said, "and only a handful are actually collected and made known to the scientific community."

It elicited a prompt and synchronized, "Wow," from both Linda and Hawkins.

"Not that I want to rain on this parade, but our chances of actually finding a small meteorite out here are extremely low," Jack said.

Linda and Hawkins traded stares.

"And what if it were a larger one?" she asked.

"Still tough to find on foot," Jack replied. But something was bothering him and he couldn't shake it.

"If a large meteoroid had made it through the atmosphere and impacted the ground, there would be widespread destruction out here."

Linda said, "Right. Wasn't there something like that in Russia a long time ago?"

Jack was impressed. "Yes, the Tunguska event in 1908. A large meteoroid burst in the air and caused catastrophic damage to a whole forest. The explosion itself was probably a thousand times stronger than the Hiroshima bomb."

"Jesus," Hawkins said.

"But if it was a large object that we're talking about, it's strange that it would slow down so drastically and that the signal would drop in and out." Jack was thinking out loud and found himself face to face with a theory that, if verbalized, might brand him crazy with present company. But what the hell—he was out here for what was going to be a very short hike anyway. After this he would have to go back to the house and start the long, terrible process of putting the family estate in order. Sounding crazy at this point mattered very little, and Jack figured that any ignominy he might suffer would be minimal.

Jack proceeded, "It's strange because it sounds like an EDL."

They stared at him intently.

"What's an EDL, Jack?" Linda asked.

Jack said, "Sorry, let me explain: It's an Entry, Descent, and Landing. It's how you get a vehicle that's traveling at extremely high speeds down to a soft landing on the surface of a planet in a very short amount of time. It's sometimes known as reverse rocket engineering."

And that was it. The cat was out of the bag, so to speak. Here he was, a science fiction writer talking about the entry, descent, and landing of a spacecraft with local law enforcement simply looking for a meteorite. Jack briefly envisioned himself being asked to do a field sobriety test after which possibly being handcuffed.

"A vehicle," Hawkins said, deadpan.

"How does it work exactly?" Linda asked.

Jack took brief inventory of their expressions, their body language, and to his surprise they appeared genuinely interested. Or was it amused?

Jack said, "Let's take the Mars missions as an example: A vehicle we send to Mars will use the atmosphere of the planet to slow itself down as it approaches at very high speeds. It produces an incredible amount of friction on the capsule, so it loses most of its incoming velocity. Once it gets through the atmosphere, it slows down even more with a hypersonic parachute that deploys from its aeroshell. Now it slows to the point that the vehicle can cut itself loose from that aeroshell, engage its descent engines and land at only a few miles an hour on the surface."

Hawkins glanced down at his hand as he picked at a piece of dead skin on his thumb. *Not a good sign,* Jack thought. Linda however was more engaged, those emerald eyes touching his. Although Jack figured it could have been to see if he was making all of this up. The eyes were, as the expression went, a window to the soul, and anyone in law enforcement was trained to spot the telltale signs that someone was less than forthcoming by observing eye movement.

Jack said, "I'm using that as an example. I'm not saying that something landed out here." The pause that followed grew pregnant with unease.

Linda said, "Well, how about we take a look around— maybe a mile or so that direction." She was pointing south from their current location that, as far as Jack could tell, led straight into the deep woods. "If we come up empty, we call it a day," she said. "Besides, you look pretty fit there, Jack. A mile should be easy for you."

She smiled at him, and Jack felt warmth bloom in his cheeks. Was he blushing? He grinned at her and finally broke a smile.

"You seem the athletic type yourself," he said.

Hawkins grunted audibly. Linda shot him a knowing grin.

Finally he said, "Okay, how about you two take that mile, come straight back. I'll take a look around here."

Linda smirked and collected Jack softly with a glance.

"Okay, let's do this," Jack said.

They started off south, getting smaller and smaller in the middle of the forest that seemed neverending.

———————

Jack and Linda walked close together, carefully stepping through the undergrowth, scanning the environment around them for any signs of an impact or something out of the ordinary. There was nothing out here. Jack thought it was a waste of time looking for something that, in reality, was probably very small, had likely vaporized in the atmosphere, and had been scattered dozens of miles in every direction. But Jack thought—on the other hand—that getting a chance to talk with Linda was not a waste of time.

Linda said, "Jack, I wanted to tell you that I appreciate you coming out here today. I heard about your father and I'm very sorry. Must be incredibly hard for you right now."

Jack felt a sudden surge of grief piling up behind his eyes, but he quickly muscled it back down.

"Thank you," Jack said stoically. "It was sudden, unexpected. Not sure that it's sunk in yet. All I can think about is having to go through the house and sort it all out and find my mom a new place to live."

"How is your mom doing?"

"She's late stage Alzheimer's. Very late."

"I'm so sorry," Linda reflected.

"We explained to her what had happened. She came to the funeral, saw him there in the casket. But it's hard to tell anymore what she's comprehending and what she isn't."

Linda became very solemn.

"My grandfather had Alzheimer's, so I know where you're coming from."

Jack nodded, not looking ahead anymore; not looking for anything. The thoughts of Richard and Marion drowned everything else.

"Jack," she said, "if you need any help, support, whatever it may be while you're here in town, I'll do what I can. Even though I'm not sure what that would be exactly."

Jack said, "Thank you. I'll keep that in mind."

Leaves and twigs popped lightly under their soles as they trudged on. Being out here like this pilfered Jack's awareness of time, and not just in an immediate sense; without all the familiar sounds of the world—phones, cars, radios and human voices—time became nonlinear. Jack could imagine them now walking through a forest that might as well have existed tens of thousands of years ago. It unnerved him. He took a glance back over his shoulder, no longer able to discern where they had come from, and stopped walking.

"Do you think we should head back?" he asked.

Linda scoured the woods on both sides and came up empty. While she had initially been optimistic and perhaps even a little excited about the prospect of actually finding a meteorite, the apparent futility of this search on foot was fast becoming a drain.

Linda said, "I suppose we should, since—"

A growl of nearby thunder truncated her thought. It rolled through the woods, echoed east to west, then settled into the ground with a tactile vibration. Jack looked up to see just how awful the sky might be, but noticed something else that quickly drowned his anxiety over aberrant weather. He wondered how he could have missed it for the last hundred yards. Linda hadn't seen it either. She was fixed on her phone, attempting to find a signal strong enough to give them a current Doppler map of the area.

"Coverage is dicey out here. TV said there was a chance for thunderstorms today. Guess they were right," she smirked, and gave up on her phone. It was only then she noticed Jack staring straight up, focused on something overhead. She threw her attention to the forest canopy high above them—or rather, what was left of it.

"Whoa," she said, taking a sharp, indrawn breath.

"Any chance that lightning strikes did that," Jack asked, already knowing the answer.

Linda shook her head. "No way."

The tops of the trees had been decapitated in a straight line for a hundred yards, a coulee cut savagely through the top of the woods. Some of the treetops were still there, but had bent and snapped like mere twigs by some hideously powerful force, hanging precariously now above them like giant sleeping pendulums. Most were missing entirely. Jack came to the sudden, inexorable conclusion that something had in fact crashed through this part of the forest at high speed. Something very big.

CHAPTER 9

THEY WERE LOPING ADROITLY, SENSES sharp and alert as they pressed on, bearing straight beneath the gaping wound in the forest canopy, mindful of the debris that littered the ground ahead of them. They were driven now by physical evidence that, if followed carefully along its path, could lead them to the source of this indisputable event. And whatever it was, Jack guessed, there would be no mistaking it once they came upon it. They had stopped briefly to snap pictures of the injured trees on their phones, hoping to achieve some sense of scale, and then pressed on.

Linda said, "Jack, do you think a satellite crashed through here?"

A very remote possibility, Jack thought. But what the hell else did they have to go on? It wasn't a large meteoroid impact—of that he was certain.

Jack said, "Not sure. I suppose it is a possibility. It might explain why—"

Abruptly the damage above them ended just twenty yards ahead, and what was left was a deadfall of gashed, mutilated flotsam and compressed brush. Whatever tore through here was probably in the area, very close to them. *It had to be*, Jack thought. He swept the ground like a bloodhound, his focus enormous, looking for something inorganic, something—*there!* Littered in the dirt all around him were toothed, metallic fragments. Dozens of them. *From a larger piece somewhere.* He bent down for closer inspection.

"Look at these here."

Linda hurried over and knelt beside him. Jack reached down carefully, touching one of them lightly. It was cold. He picked it up, handling it between his thumb and index finger dexterously like he would a big shard of broken glass, noticing immediately that it was blackened. Burned. Nothing around them on the ground was burned. So it was heat-related prior to reaching the ground.

Atmospheric entry, he thought—only then realizing he was hurtling onward through bewilderment into something much more unsettling.

Maybe a satellite did crash out here.

Linda picked up another piece, scrutinizing it, turning it over and over in her fingers.

"Looks burned," she said. Jack nodded.

"Yeah. It fits with what happens during atmospheric entry. But if this were a satellite, why didn't we hear anything about it on the news?"

Linda shrugged. Jack stood up and happened to glance to his left, toward a pile of crushed wood and gaggled branches. There was something sandwiched in the debris, a massive, circular edge protruding through the damage. He moved toward it, achieving a better angle that caused it to appear saucer-shaped. But it was shattered and crescent-like, eighteen feet across at its widest point he guessed. He crept toward it, his form small beneath its looming edge.

"Jack, be careful," Linda said.

"I will."

Getting closer he noticed what looked like interlocking pieces—*were they tiles or plates*—forming a protective layer on one side. They were all blackened.

"I don't believe it," he said.

"Jack, what is it?"

"I can't be completely sure, but it looks like...maybe these are heat tiles of some kind."

"Heat tiles," she echoed.

Jack grabbed one of the large branches and pulled against it. It wouldn't budge.

"If we could clear some of this debris, we could get a better look at it."

Quickly, she joined him and the two of them pulled together. Even with both of them exerting everything they had, it became swiftly obvious it wasn't going to dislodge.

"It's pinned in there real tight," she said.

Jack grabbed his phone and photographed the edge of it, then the tiles, and then a wider angle of the entire shape. There was a whip-crack of thunder, an ensuing low frequency growl.

"I know this sounds crazy," Jack stammered, "But I think this might be a heat shield."

"Do satellites have heat shields?"

"No. None that I'm aware of."

"So, what does this mean?" she asked.

Jack knew what it *could* mean, but it seemed irrational. It was the kind of thing he would dream up for one of his books. And yet here it was right in front of him—dwarfing him—a massive piece of something that convincingly resembled flight hardware. And Jack seriously doubted that it had come from any known spacecraft on Earth.

Jack said, "We should take some of the small pieces back with us."

Linda replied, "I've got some evidence bags back at the car."

She watched him then, closely. Jack was pensive. Baffled. Troubled.

"Jack," she insisted, "what do you think this means?"

He fought—fought hard against the surety of what was in front of him. It seemed crazy. *It was crazy.*

"I think...something may have landed out here. Not a meteor, or a satellite, but something else. A spacecraft of some kind. And that means there will likely be more pieces of it around—somewhere."

The forest lit up explosively then. A shotgun blast of thunder pounded the wilderness, slapping off the trees, rocks and earth. The ground trembled.

"Shit," Jack shouted, "that can't be good."

"We'd better get the hell out of here," Linda said and they both started off, but not before grabbing a few of the smaller pieces they had found. Quickly they left the site and headed back for the cars. Neither one of them said anything as they walked the first quarter mile. Soon, however, they were running as rain began to curtain down around them, announcing the arrival of one of the worst storms Hills County had experienced in months.

The rain came harder, the wind pushing it through the forest in horizontal, slashing waves. Jack and Linda were at a full run now as the storm opposed their every step, soaking them, spraying them in the face. They sprinted now, footslogging through the muddy ground, a spray of chocolate-brown water trailing them. The world around them brightened as if God had taken a photograph. A terrible, bone-shaking clap of thunder detonated above them.

And now those drops of rain turned to stone. It was hailing. Jack became more and more persuaded that he was going to die out here if they didn't reach...

The cars came abruptly into view through the trees, not far ahead. Hawkins stood under an oversized black umbrella, waving them in frantically.

"What the hell happened out there?" Hawkins roared over the storm.

Jack shouted, "We found something! It's—"

Linda cut him off. "We can't stay here! Let's meet back at the station! Jack can ride with me!"

Hawkins agreed and they dove into their cars, yanking the doors shut. Jack and Linda took deep, labored breaths, steadying themselves as the wind-driven hailstones punished the outside of the car, lashing the windshield, drumming loudly against the roof like automatic gunfire.

Jack said, "God, it came in so fast! Is that normal out here?"

Linda's hands were visibly shaking. She found her keys and fumbled them, hearing them drop below her seat.

"You don't get those back in LA," she asked.

"Not even close." Jack let out a long, deep breath.

"That was bad," she said. "But I've been out in worse."

Jack shook his head, unable to comprehend such a thing. She fished for the keys, finding them on the floor mat. Her hands steadied. Slowly, carefully, she started the car. She dropped it in gear and pulled a hard turn, steering them back onto the highway where they accelerated through the falling hail and back toward town.

CHAPTER 10

A S JACK AND LINDA DROVE toward the station, the storm broke. The hail softened back into rain that eventually thinned into a tender mist. Jack had been quietly processing what it was they had just discovered in the forest, and if any possible spacecraft that he knew of would carry such an enormous heat shield. No matter how he evaluated it, nothing seemed a match. Was it possible that a secret Department of Defense project might require such a large heat shield? Jack just couldn't swallow it.

Linda finally said, "Jack, I know you've got a million things to do. I feel terrible about keeping you any longer, but could you give us a few minutes of time when we get back to the office? I think you can better explain this to the Sheriff than I can."

Jack would oblige, but keep it short.

"I'll do what I can," he said.

She thanked him and they kept driving. The edges of the town surfaced behind a large grassy hill and they exited off the highway, heading back into the grid of downtown, cutting through the one-way streets, taking an alley and arriving neatly behind the police station. Linda carefully took the pieces they had collected from the undergrowth and placed them in sealed plastic evidence bags.

Minutes later they were in the Sheriff's office where Linda gently closed the door for privacy. Hawkins dropped into his chair behind his desk and rubbed his brow pensively.

"So what exactly did you find out there?"

Linda carefully put the evidence bags on his desk where Hawkins got abruptly lab-intense, examining the contents.

Jack said, "Well, I can't be completely certain without some lab tests and a visual confirmation from someone in aerospace, but I think we may have found a heat shield from some kind of spacecraft."

Linda quickly drew her phone and pulled up the pictures she had taken.

"The top of the forest out there was torn up," she said. "There were tree tops missing and debris on the ground...like something crashed down from the sky at very high speed."

She handed it over to Hawkins who slipped on his glasses and fingered through each shot carefully. His brow pinched downward and he was breathing loudly through his nose.

"You get any pictures of it—the actual piece?"

Jack handed over his phone and Hawkins skimmed the shots of the large, crescent object. After a moment he handed it back.

"I know what that is," Hawkins said, settling deeper into his chair.

Jack and Linda shared bewilderment as Hawkins interlocked his fingers and dropped his hands neatly behind his head, a man resolved and confident.

"That is an engine cowling from a large jet."

Jack looked at his photos again. *No way,* he thought, but he decided to indulge Hawkins anyway. "Really?"

Linda said, "I saw it, too. Didn't look like anything from a plane."

"Well," Hawkins grunted as he leaned back over his desk, "that's exactly what it is."

Jack asked, "Just curious here—how are you so certain about that?" then realized how he must have sounded. Adjusting his tone, he said, "What I mean is...what makes you think that...exactly?"

Hawkins focused on Jack, his eyes unflinching and austere.

"Because six weeks ago an inbound 767 encountered some bad weather and lost an engine cover on approach to Indianapolis International. The FAA went apeshit looking for it. They never found it."

Linda nudged, "I thought they located that? Wasn't it about five miles southwest near Greenwood Park?"

Hawkins shook his head, "That's not what I heard." His tone was ice. She recognized it almost instantly—the rigidity, the conceit. The apathy. It had crept into him over the last eighteen months and Linda guessed it was a limpid precursor to his retirement. She decided not to challenge him, especially in front of Jack. Jack picked up on it also, however more indirectly, and decided it was time to go.

"Well, then I guess that settles it," he said unpersuasively.

Hawkins said, "You've been a tremendous help to this department today, and for that you have my gratitude."

Hawkins stood and shook Jack's hand firmly.

Jack nodded. "Sure thing. Now I just need a ride home."

"I'll get you home," Linda said.

"Thanks," he replied.

Without another syllable they left the room and Hawkins sank back down in his chair, his gaze falling to the wall clock that labored beneath the weight of every passing minute. He sighed, then glanced at the evidence bag on his desk and the jagged, dark pieces inside. *Nothing but trash,* he thought, and slipped the bag into the bottom drawer of his desk.

Linda started the engine and Jack had no sooner fastened his seatbelt than she asked, "You want coffee? We can hit the drive-thru on the way back to your place."

"God, yes," he said. "That would be great."

"My treat," she said, grinning warmly at him. She pulled her ponytail free, letting that red hair fall. It spilled past her shoulders and around her cheeks, bright and coppery like silk. She grabbed hold of it, and in one deft move, refitted it in a more precise ponytail than before.

"There," she said. "Better."

Jack wondered if she had simply done it because the ponytail had lost its integrity from their near-death run in the woods, or if she was showing it off for him in an attempt to flirt.

"You have beautiful hair," Jack said.

"Oh, thank you," She said. Putting the cruiser in gear, they started back through town. The rain continued innocuously as Jack watched all of the homes drift by, in a state of near disbelief over how wide open each property was. Front yards out here seemed like public parks as Jack compared them to neighborhoods back home in Pasadena.

"Can't believe how much space there is here. No wonder Dad loved it so much," Jack said.

"Not like that back in LA?" she asked.

"Not really," he said.

The road opened from two lanes to four.

"So, what books have you written?" she asked.

"Just one so far. It's a science fiction thriller set on an alien world."

Linda edged up on her seat.

"Well...what happens?"

"You'll have to read it when it comes out," he chuckled.

"I definitely will," she said. "It sounds very cool! I'll bet your dad was proud."

Jack thought about that and sighed. "Not so much."

Linda said, "Oh."

Jack finished, "He had...other plans for me. Doesn't really matter now."

Linda straightened in her seat.

"Well, it sounds like you've worked very hard," she said. "I could never write an entire book. You should be proud of yourself."

Jack replied, "Thanks. It requires long days and nights. There comes a point when you give up a social life entirely to reach the finish line."

"So how does your wife or girlfriend manage with you being so busy?" she asked, not looking at him as they crossed a set of railroad tracks, mumbling down a street of ancient, disheveled pavement.

Okay, she's fishing here, Jack thought. *No doubt she's already noticed the absence of a ring on the finger, so now she's included a girlfriend as part of a catchall question.*

Jack grinned and said, "She doesn't mind because she doesn't exist at the moment. When I meet her, I'll let you know."

The truth was, Jack had been single for a while, more precisely six months. Before that, he had dated several women over the years, finally connecting with a pretty blonde law student at UCLA named Jamie. But things fell apart when she decided to move to New York, closer to her family. It became non-negotiable—an ultimatum—and short of transplanting himself to the east coast just for her, he'd run out of incentives.

And there was also the girl here in Merriweather that he had a short fling with about ten years earlier while visiting his parents. She was a student at the university and was studying broadcast journalism, if he remembered correctly. *She was a wild one*, Jack thought. He hoped he had simply thought all of that and not said it out loud. Jack decided to return the serve.

"So, how about you? What's it like being a deputy sheriff?"

Linda said, "It can be tough, that's for sure. My ex-husband didn't care for me being gone odd hours and decided that he wanted something a bit more normal. That's what he wrote on the yellow post-it-note the day he packed up and left—*normal*."

Jack said, "Sorry. Must have been difficult."

Linda said, "Not one of the better chapters of my life."

She suddenly giggled.

"Guess I just made a pun," she said as they pulled into the parking lot of the Starbucks and slotted into the line for the drive-thru.

Jack was amused, "Good one."

He was enjoying her company, her smile and her warm, cute sense of humor. Her honesty.

"Look," she said, her tone taking an abrupt turn, "I'm sorry about what happened back at the station."

"The sheriff, you mean," Jack said.

She nodded.

"I think—we all do in the department—that he's wearing the clock down and missing a few things along the way."

They pulled forward as the car ahead of them glided to the window to order.

"Jack," she said, "is there any chance that he's right? That it's just an engine cover out there?"

Jack was feeling quelled now, adrift and distant.

"I suppose anything's possible, but...." He shook his head. "Didn't look like any engine cover to me."

He was looking right at her, his eyes unclouded and certain, and Linda knew someplace deep inside that he was right, and that this was not over. The car in front of them pulled away and they ordered. The conversation post-caffeine was harmless banter about music, movies, and food. It was just a few minutes later that they pulled into the driveway at Jack's parents' house. Linda kept the engine running.

"Jack, thank you so much for the help today."

"Sure," he said. "Thanks for the coffee."

She hesitated.

"You said earlier that if this were a piece of a spacecraft of some kind, that there would be other pieces."

"Well, yes," he said. "A heat shield is only one component of a landing system. So it would follow that there are more pieces that would make up the entire thing."

Then she said, "So…in your opinion…what might be inside such a landing device?"

That was the shadow hanging over them, Jack realized. It could be anything…it could be nothing.

"Honestly," he said unblinking, "I really don't know." Then, "If you need anything else, please call me."

"I will," she said, somehow knowing that's exactly what she'd be doing.

CHAPTER 11

J ACK WAS HUNCHED OVER THE bottom drawer of a cabinet in
Richard's office. It had been four hours since he had
begun removing all the papers from hanging folders,
thumbing through them and starting two separate piles on
the floor, *save* and *shred*. So far, the latter was double that
of the former. Jack was astounded at the sheer volume of it
all. He came to a moment of clarity sometime in the
previous hour that his father had in fact saved every single
receipt from the last twenty, thirty, perhaps forty years.

There were statements for insurance, both home and
auto, bank accounts, retirement accounts, and
investments. There were cancelled checks, bound into little
bricks with taut rubber bands—hundreds and hundreds of
them—thousands potentially hiding deep inside any
number of boxes out there in the garage. There was a soft
knock on the door.

"Jack, dinner's ready," Samantha called from the
hallway.

"Okay, thanks," he said.

He dropped the pile of papers he was weeding through and left his dad's office, shutting off the light as he pulled the door closed behind him. He made his way into the dining area and found Marion already seated at the table. She was gazing vacantly at her placemat, but looked up as Jack entered the room.

"Richard," she said. Her face lit momentarily with a vague sense of recognition.

"No, Mom. It's me, Jack."

She held onto him with a look of bewilderment, struggling to resolve his face with broken pieces of memory, unsorted and adrift behind her eyes. Jack forced himself to smile for her sake, though inside his heart was breaking.

"It's okay, Mom. It's going to be okay," he said, even though he knew things would not be okay. Samantha brought dinner to the table and they ate in silence.

CHAPTER 12

D AN GREEN OPENED HIS EYES when he heard the noise again. It was noticeably louder and clearer, but vague and elusive in terms of direction. Perhaps it was the metrical beating of rain against the outside of the tent that was throwing him off and making it hard to identify the sound. In his mid-thirties, Dan was a confident and skilled hiker, backpacker, and camper. He'd heard it all in the wild during more than a decade of experience. He had been able to quickly identify the sounds of a wide variety of animals—large, small, frisky, curious, and predatory—with his eyes closed. Literally. And that's what he had been trying to do for the last fifteen minutes.

He was growing more and more uncomfortable and shifted in his sleeping bag, inadvertently bumping his girlfriend, Monica. She grunted, rolled, and stretched her legs. She would be annoyed that he woke her.

"What's wrong?" she muttered. Dan held his breath, listening again, struggling to filter out the tapping of the rain.

"I heard something. It woke me up," he said, his voice just topping a whisper.

Monica rolled over on her side, now facing him, eyes slit and groggy.

"Well, what is it? Some kind of animal?"

"Not sure."

"What time is it?"

Dan didn't want to know. It didn't matter what time it was. Time had nothing to do with anything out here. Nevertheless he began to calculate the hours that had passed, leaping back to 3:30 p.m. when they had started off the main trail that had already deposited them 2.3 miles into the forest. They had hiked through the afternoon, probably another few miles, and then had decided to make camp where they were now. It afforded them time to sit and enjoy the stillness before nightfall. Light rain was likely and arrived on schedule after dark. It was nothing that they couldn't handle.

Flashing forward in his mind, they climbed into the tent and started snuggling around 11:45 p.m. and had fallen asleep not long after. Dan himself had probably slept a few hours and that's when he became vaguely aware of a sound out there—*a sound he had never heard before.* It lured him out from sleep, and he had spent the last fifteen minutes lying very still as not to wake Monica, listening for it again. It was vexing him.

"I don't know what time it is," he said, though he guessed it to be just after 2:00 a.m.

"Can't you check your watch?" she asked. She was pushing him.

"Doesn't matter," he replied. "It's late."

He refocused on the sounds around them, and the only thing he could hear now was the tap, tap, tap of large drops birthed from water tension on the towering tree limbs above, falling sixty or more feet, bombing the taught, nylon skin of their tent. Dan decided that perhaps he had imagined the other sound. He closed his eyes again and relaxed, issuing a long sigh.

He had no sooner done this than he felt something in the ground beneath them. It was a *vibration*. Short. Subtle. And for a moment, Dan thought he heard that sound again. Autonomously, his heartbeat accelerated. *What the hell is wrong with me,* he thought. *Calm down, it's nothing.* Tap, tap, tap spoke the raindrops.

The ground shivered, more pronounced this time. Dan threw open his eyes. That sound again. Louder. He wasn't imagining it. It sounded...*mechanical*. Was that possible? *Out here?* It didn't make sense, but the more he listened, the more he was certain that it was...

The ground trembled, and Monica stirred instantly.

"Did you feel that?" she asked.

"Yeah," he replied, keeping his voice low behind his teeth.

The sound began again, louder still, and more defined. It was mechanical. But like nothing he had heard before. Monica sat upright, un-bunching her oversized sweatshirt, her eyes sharpening.

"Dan, what the hell is that?"

The ground shook, then settled. It was much stronger now. *An impact tremor,* he thought, feeling his heart break a trot. He pulled himself out of his sleeping bag and grabbed the new LED flashlight he had brought with them. Monica slid out of her bag and got on her knees, pushing her long hair back behind her ears. The sound started again, much louder now—which meant that whatever was out there producing it was getting closer.

"What the hell makes sounds like that?" Monica trembled.

As quickly as it began, the noise extinguished, leaving only the light metronome of raindrops. Dan climbed to one knee, planting his other foot on the ground. He reached for the zipper to open the front of the tent. Monica seized his arm, her grip strong with adrenaline.

"Dan, don't go out there," she pleaded.

"We can't just sit here like this," he said. "I've got to take a look."

Dan unzipped the entry and crawled through it to the outside where he immediately felt the dull pecking of the raindrops on the crown of his head. He stood motionless in the iron darkness, listening intently. He clicked on the flashlight, which unsheathed a blinding white beam that pierced the dark like a blade. Methodically he began sweeping the woods that encircled them, panning the walls of the forest foot by foot. Spotlighted now were the ankles of towering trees, brush, the wide-empty gaps in between...and nothing else that the light could touch. Dan was teeming with an ambiguous sense of dread that at any moment the light would pass over *something* out there...something dangerous. *Get a grip,* he thought loudly. *Christ, get a grip on yourself!*

Monica's voice came softly from inside the tent behind him.

"Dan, what is it?"

"I don't see anything," he whispered. Monica climbed out from the tent slowly like a woodland creature emerging from its lair.

"Dan, I think maybe we should—"

The woods quaked from the impact of hidden tonnage nearby, and a mechanical growl rose in the air around them. There was an ear-splitting crack, then the squeal of twisting, tortured wood. Large branches, invisible in the darkness above them, broke loudly, and Dan quickly realized that a full-sized tree was plummeting earthward, directly down on top of them. Monica screamed. He heaved her out of the way as all five hundred tons of it plunged diagonally through their camp, crushing solid rocks, splitting and splintering smaller trees and eating their little tent. A violent gust of hard air took them to the ground like a fist as the earth undulated, wavelike. The flashlight spilled from Dan's grasp, tumbling away, still cutting the dark with its sharp beam.

Dan struggled back to his feet. The world was swimming around him and he caught a hazy glimpse of Monica lying on her back, her long hair splayed like a fan on the dark ground. He reached for her, frantic, fumbling, finally grabbing her hand. He steadied himself and pulled her up. She stood, disoriented, shaking her head. Dan felt it, too: dizziness, a ringing in the ears, and a rolling sense of nausea. The impact of the tree had generated not only a sound of tremendous decibels, but also a physical shockwave that had momentarily stunned both of them. The mechanical sound grew louder still, impossibly so. And now, despite the suffocating darkness of the woods, they saw it for the first time: an enormous moving form materializing into what was left of their campsite. The thing, whatever it was, moved on multiple limbs, hideously insectile and fast considering its sheer mass. It loomed ponderously over them—massive—closing on them, crushing the ground in front of them.

"Oh, my God! It's coming!" Monica screamed. "Run! Run!"

A metallic howl gashed the air like a thousand razor-sharp blades in rapid motion. It was the last thing either one of them remembered before they began running for their lives, hearts throbbing from gushing rivers of adrenaline in their bloodstreams. A cloud pursued them, a dark mist of tiny moving particles that swarmed thickly in the air as they ran. The sound crescendoed in their ears, bellowing, drowning out Monica who was still screaming.

"It's coming! Run! Run!"

Mike Smith glanced over at the clock in the dashboard of his pickup. It anemically glowed the time—2:17—to which he groaned. He was tired and bleary-eyed from his shift at the bar near the college. He glanced at the speedometer, the needle pinned at 67. Speed limit out here on the highway was a firm 50. *Shit.* He eased off the gas, not wanting another ticket.

He sighed loudly, confronted by a metaphorical fork in the road ahead. He could go home, watch some TV, crash, or stop by this alleged party that was unfolding at Dave Meyer's place on the other side of town. He had all but decided to go home when he heard the familiar chime of an incoming text message on his cellphone.

He picked up the phone and tapped the screen. The text read: *R-U COMING BY THE PARTY?? I'M HERE* ☺*!* It was from a girl named Carrie Regan—the very *hot* Carrie Regan. Over the last few weeks he had just begun to crack that shell of hers while he mixed drinks for her at the bar. Once he got her to laugh at his jokes and smile at his juvenile antics behind the bar, he knew he had a better-than-snowball's chance with her. No way in hell he was going to let the opportunity—

Something slashed the highway in front of him, a running form exploding into his headlights.

"Shit!" he yelled, mashing the brake pedal against the floor. There was a sickening impact against the bumper as something struck the hood. It rolled and cracked against the windshield, the glass spider-webbing violently. In that fraction of a moment, Mike was almost certain that he heard a woman's scream. The airbag deployed, bursting into his face, and everything went suddenly dark.

CHAPTER 13

J ACK WAS SETTLING IN THE guest bedroom, his body sinking into the mattress, his head into the pillow, sensing a warm embrace of stillness that promised real sleep for the first time in several nights. He felt himself getting lighter, his thoughts more muted and distant. He was about to sail into a very deep and quiet—

A loud pounding struck the hollow wood door of the bedroom. Instantly Jack felt himself thrown from that place of peace, back down into the full weight of consciousness. His heart jumped in his chest. Samantha's voice was on the other side of the door.

"Jack? Jack!"

"Yes," he replied, unnerved.

"There's something wrong with your mom! Call 911!"

Jack sprung from the bed and threw on his T-shirt. Samantha was already running back toward Marion's room at the end of the hall as Jack emerged with his phone. He raced after her until he stood at his mother's bedside. Her appearance was alarming. Her skin had turned ashen grey and she was bathed in sweat that soaked her nightgown and the bed sheets completely through. Her breathing was labored. She was mumbling something unintelligible. Samantha took her pulse at the neck and gently turned Marion's face toward her.

"Marion? Marion, honey can you hear me? Can you wake up?"

Marion's eyes were locked shut.

"She's not responsive at all. I've never seen her like this, Jack!"

Jack punched in 911 and got the operator. As he relayed what was happening, he could hear Samantha in the background, pleading over his mother.

"Marion, can you hear me? Wake up, sweetheart. Wake up!"

Within five minutes there were bright flashing lights in the driveway, strobing through the windows of the house, lashing the walls in a bloody red glow. Moments later, paramedics were single file glide-stepping through the house and inside the room with Marion. They were methodical. Cool. Step by step. But no matter what they did, she was unresponsive. In the next sixty seconds they had her off the bed and were rolling her outside to the ambulance.

Jack was grabbing his keys, wallet, throwing on his shoes when the ambulance driver told him not to follow them too closely through town. Jack acknowledged and piled in the car with Samantha. They stayed behind the ambulance a distance, but Jack found himself pushing hard on the gas, blowing through yellow lights as they neared the hospital.

In fifteen minutes they were bedside in the hospital room with Marion, who had been revived in the ambulance. Color was coming back to her skin, and her eyes were open and clear. The doctor who examined her had no definitive explanation for what had happened, but hypothesized that it was arrhythmia of the heart. They would run more tests, but for the moment Marion seemed stable.

Jack felt a wave of relief. Driving in the car, he feared losing his mother. And he wondered what it was going to feel like if he had to bury them both in the same week.

Jack approached her bedside, noticing that she was staring straight up into the overhead lights as if locked with something beyond the lab equipment and ceiling tiles. It wasn't until he was directly at her side that she turned her head weakly toward him, her eyes touching his. She looked so fragile, as if at any moment she could go. And then she stuttered something, her voice low in the back of her throat.

Jack said, "Mom, what is it?"

This time the words surfaced, weak and staccato, but clear enough for him to understand.

"It's coming. It's coming."

Jack felt a cryptic foreboding in her words, and his mind raced back to that derelict heat shield in the woods.

"Mom, what is it?" he asked.

She clenched her jaw, unable to talk. She was speaking with her eyes now. She was telling him something. Warning him? It only lasted another moment before she turned her head, her eyes going back to that infinite point beyond the ceiling.

The phone rang loudly at Linda's bedside and she was instantly awake, the small screen of her iPhone bathing the room in low ambient light. She grabbed it quickly, sitting upright in one reflex motion. It was Hawkins, and it was

3:45 a.m. Last time she got a call like this from him it was for some serious shit—a coked-up gunman had holed up in a bar that led to a tense standoff that lasted for hours. That was four years ago. She answered swiftly.

"This is Linda," she said.

"Linda, it's Clifford. Better get dressed. Meet me five miles south on the highway. There's been an accident involving pedestrians."

"Pedestrians? All the way out there?"

"Yeah. Get there as soon as you can. Medics called in and said one is DOA."

"I'm leaving now," she said and hung up. She was putting on her uniform, checking her belt, radio, gun, all the while her mind turning furiously like a centrifuge in an attempt to analyze what she had just been told. How did pedestrians get all the way out there...unless perhaps they were camping. But if they were camping, how the hell did they end up getting struck on the highway at this hour with almost no traffic? *Damn.* She grabbed her keys and within seconds was out the door.

CHAPTER 14

WHEN LINDA PULLED UP TO the scene of the accident, troopers had already shut down the highway in both directions. Two ambulances were flanked by four more squad cars and a dozen blazing road flares. Highway patrol officers stood around a blue Toyota pickup truck that had taken a direct hit on the front end. The bumper had collapsed in a V-shape and the hood had accordioned down its own length, now cratered in the center. The windshield was dust. Blood was painted from the bumper, to the hood, around the window and over the rooftop. And ten meters behind the truck was a black body bag. Linda spotted Hawkins, examining the scene from a distance, grim faced and pacing around the perimeter.

Linda parked and alighted from her car, walking evenly toward him. He didn't make eye contact when she approached, instead keeping his gaze on the truck and the edge of the woods just beyond the pavement.

"What happened here?" she asked.

"Follow me," he said, and walked toward the back of the first ambulance where paramedics were working on Mike

Smith's face, which had been lacerated by projectile glass. He was shaking. Hysterical.

"I didn't see them! They came right out of nowhere! I swear I didn't have time to stop!"

Linda looked him in the eye.

"Sir, have you been drinking tonight?"

Mike shook his head fiercely.

"No, no, I told them—I only *work* at the bar! I'm a bartender, I never drink at work!"

"Were you on the phone? Were you texting?"

"No, I—" He hesitated, blinking rapidly.

"You were texting," she continued, "or you got a text and read it. Did you take your eyes off the road at any point?"

Mike imploded, his eyes brimming with tears. He bit into his lip, battling to regain his composure.

"I got a text, and I looked—*but it was like a half second, I swear to God!* They ran right out in front of me!"

Hawkins said, "Alright, take it easy. Calm down."

He urged Linda to follow him and they walked toward the second ambulance where Monica was sitting up on a gurney, a blanket wrapped around her. She was saying something under her breath, rocking herself lightly back and forth, eyes wide open, unblinking. They approached the medic who was tending to her.

Hawkins said, "I need to speak with her."

"She's in shock," he replied. "I wouldn't recommend it."

Linda said, "Let me. Do we know her name?"

"Monica Wells," he said, handing her driver's license to Linda. She glanced at it, that smiling face in the picture. Local girl.

"Monica, my name is Linda, I'm a deputy sheriff. Can you tell me what happened tonight?"

The girl was mumbling and it was hard to make out exactly what she was saying. Linda squatted, attempting to make eye contact with her. Anticipating a vacant stare in those sunken eyes, Linda was startled when she came face to face with raw, primordial terror.

"Monica, can you tell us what happened here?"

She erupted in a shriek so sudden and so loud that it sent Linda falling backward. She hit the asphalt hard. Hawkins reached down quickly and pulled her back on her feet. Monica's scream rang inhuman in the night air.

"Oh my God, it's coming! It's coming!"

In all the years Linda had been a deputy sheriff, she had never felt such a tangible presence of terror as she did now.

"It's coming! Run! Run!"

"What's coming?" Linda asked. "What is co—"

Monica vomited explosively. Linda jumped backward as the waste dumped loudly onto the asphalt, steaming instantly against the cold, wet ground. The girl collapsed back on the gurney, her eyes rolling up into her head. The medics charged in, checking her pulse, slapping an oxygen mask over her face. They loaded her into the ambulance and within seconds they were pulling away, sirens howling, engine screaming with sudden hard acceleration.

Linda turned away, feeling a violent wave of nausea splash inside her stomach. But she closed her eyes, took slow deep breaths and steeled herself, fighting it. Slowly then, it passed. Hawkins inspected her.

"You going to be okay?"

She nodded. "You ever see anything like that before?"

Hawkins said, "No."

He walked to the lip of the asphalt and stopped, standing now at the very edge of the wet grass that grew evenly to the forest wall. Linda joined him there.

Hawkins said, "Any guess how far it is from here to those trees?"

It didn't take her long to calculate.

"Looks like twelve...maybe fifteen yards," she said.

"And what does that suggest?" he asked.

Linda had already been thinking about it. There was clearance of at least thirty-six feet between the edge of the forest and the highway, which meant that...

"No pedestrian in their right mind could inadvertently run from there to here and not have more than ample time to see and hear an oncoming vehicle," Hawkins said.

"Unless they were crazy, trying to kill themselves...or running for their lives from something," she added.

Hawkins glanced at her, his stare sharp.

"What exactly did you see out there yesterday with Jack?" he asked.

Linda hesitated, but decided now was not the time to be subtle.

"It wasn't from an airplane. It had plating, like armor on one side, and it had been burned."

"Burned on one side," he added.

"Yes."

Hawkins had been the sheriff of Hills County for twenty years. Before that he was a deputy and before that a Marine. What he felt at that moment was foreign and bordered on the irrational. It was a growing undercurrent of trepidation that carried with it an almost supernatural awe. Because Hawkins was actually starting to think that something did land in the woods out there—*something not from Earth*. And whatever it was, it had just scared two young, vigorous, people so much that they dashed like uncomprehending deer into a four-lane highway and an oncoming vehicle. What the hell could inspire that kind of panic?

Hawkins finally said, "Maybe you should call Jack in a few hours and see if he'd help locate the rest of that...spacecraft...or whatever the hell it really is."

Spacecraft. Linda heard it correctly and she caught herself glancing about nervously, the woods feeling suddenly dangerous and alive. Watching them.

"You okay?" he asked.

Linda pulled herself together.

"Yeah. I'll take care of it," she said.

Hawkins nodded and walked back toward his car. Linda looked into the sky: no stars, low cloud ceiling. She launched the weather app on her phone and shook her head when the saw the forecast. SERIES OF SEVERE STORMS DUE! She scanned the details. They'd have a window of time to go looking for the rest of this thing before the first storm hit. And if predictions held any truth, the first one would be very bad.

CHAPTER 15

J ACK FOUND HIMSELF BACK IN the house he grew up in and it was almost exactly as he had remembered it as a child. He was on the second floor along with his mother, his sister, and his father, standing near a big corner window that overlooked the Pacific Ocean and the limestone bluffs that hugged the tender curve of the coastal beaches of Southern California. It was here, in this brief moment, that Jack felt a sudden rush of warmth and comfort.

The house began to shake and sway, the ground rolling beneath them. It was an earthquake, and the waves were getting stronger. The joints of the house began to split horrifically, separating under the prodigious force of unstable, moving earth. The drywall tore apart like paper. Windows bulged and burst, glass dumping out and away from the house as the entire structure began to slide toward the edge of the bluff.

"We have to get out of here!" Jack screamed at his family. The floor suddenly dropped from under them as the second story pancaked down on top of the first. Jack tumbled, frantic for some sense of orientation. The entire house was about to slide off its foundation and drop into the ocean, which was teeming with furious white caps and skyscraper-high swells that slammed into each other and against the coast with apocalyptic force. The house slid further, the room achieving a strong, sudden tilt. Jack felt himself starting to fall backward. He desperately reached for his sister's hand, and in one awful moment everything came apart.

The house plunged, falling through open air, down toward the stygian sea that was possessed of hell itself. The house hit the surface of the ocean with a sickening, loud crack. Jack felt the impact, followed by the motion of the sea, throwing the structure at will as if it were a child's toy. There came the spray of cold ocean water, the tilting of the house as it bobbed helplessly between mountainous swells. A wall of water one hundred feet high rose over the house, curling horrifically into a wave about to break over them. Jack closed his eyes and tensed, preparing for the bone-crushing impact of a million tons of seawater.

All at once the dream ended, and Jack found himself waking in a tangle of bed sheets. It was still dark outside. He sat up and took a few deep breaths, trying to settle down and lose the images in the dream that were playing back in his head. He leaned over and grabbed his phone from the nightstand. It was 6:45 a.m. Jack decided he would not fall back asleep for fear of rejoining the nightmare at the point from which he had just been mercifully evacuated.

He got up, slipped on his jeans, T-shirt, and shoes. Getting dressed helped motivate him. He decided he would slip quietly into the kitchen, brew a strong pot of coffee, and then go back to his father's office where he would continue to sort paperwork. Or he could check his dad's emails, notify some of his contacts what had happened, and maybe go ahead and close the account.

Jack made the coffee extra strong, and as he nursed it, he began looking through his dad's emails. There were friends and colleagues whose names kept appearing in the inbox for Richard. *So apparently Dad kept in touch with most everybody he worked with over the years,* Jack thought. He began checking the subject lines of each one. There were a lot of forwarded jokes, articles, and other amusing anecdotes, most under a banner subject line that read: *THOUGHT YOU MIGHT ENJOY THIS,* or *THIS IS FUNNY!*

Jack scrolled down the inbox, now going back a week, then two weeks, then three, examining the subject lines that all seemed to be trivial until he saw one that read: *MRO-HiRISE IMAGE COMPARISON, THARSIS REGION.* Jack held on this one and reread the subject line. MRO stood for the Mars Reconnaissance Orbiter, a robotic satellite currently mapping Mars with a high-resolution camera called HiRISE. The Tharsis region was a volcanic area of the planet with a distinct geology and a number of extinct volcanoes that were nothing short of marvels, among them Olympus Mons, a shield volcano that rose 89,000 feet above the surface of the planet. To put that in perspective, it was three times the height of Mount Everest.

Jack opened the message. It was from Stephen Hunter at the Jet Propulsion Laboratory. Jack remembered Stephen. Nice guy. And if Jack recalled correctly, he worked in the image processing lab which not only stitched together large mosaics from smaller images that came back from the twin rovers, but also created true 3D terrain projections from orbiter data that allowed them to produce true-to-life animations and flyovers of select features on the surface of Mars.

Jack began reading the message: "*Interesting. I would agree, but there's no way to be certain without verification from the ground. Too bad Opportunity can't just whiz over there for a look!*"

Opportunity was one of twin Mars Rovers sent for ninety-day missions back in early 2004. To NASA's and the world's amazement, it had lasted over eight years and had driven more than twenty miles on the surface of the planet. Its twin sister, named Spirit, had also outlasted her original projected lifespan by a factor of twenty. But Spirit had gotten her wheel stuck, which destroyed her mobility, and the brutal cold of the Martian winter did the rest. Ironically, Spirit's operation had been declared finished and her obituary penned just a few weeks before Richard passed away.

Jack scrolled down the length of the message to the beginning of the exchange. It had begun: "*Hi Richard, hope all is well in Indiana. I'd like your opinion on something. Scratching our heads here on this one. MRO caught this image last month. There was a subsequent pass a few weeks later and…it's peculiar. Not sure what to make of it.*"

Jack scrolled up to his father's reply: "*Stephen, thanks. I'll take a look, though I'm not sure how much good that will do. Eyesight's not what it used to be, ha, ha! Give me a few days and I'll get back to you. Say hi to Gail if she's still in Dr. Logue's office.*"

There was a link to a secure site where Jack's father could view the images in question with the proper password. *Okay*, Jack thought, *he did presumably view these images on the JPL secure server. But had he downloaded them to his machine?* Jack was more than curious. He wanted to see the images himself. He read on, finding his dad's response: "*Stephen, I've looked at the images. Very strange. Maybe we should talk by phone. Give me a call at 812-555-2776.*"

Jack said to himself, "What was so strange, Dad?"

There came a distant peal of thunder. *Not again*, he thought. He began to all the more appreciate the very predictable weather of Southern California, even though some argued it was dull. Jack took a long swallow of coffee when his phone rang. It was a local Merriweather number, but Jack didn't recognize it. He answered.

"Hello."

"Jack, it's Linda from the sheriff's office."

Her voice was warm, if not uniform and perhaps official sounding.

"Oh, hey," Jack said.

"I have to start by apologizing for even asking, but...something's happened and we could use your help again."

"What's wrong?" he asked.

"May I come and pick you up in about an hour?"

CHAPTER 16

J ACK COLLECTED HIS WALLET, KEYS, and phone. He caught a glimpse of himself in the mirror, noting the sunken dark circles beneath his eyes. Samantha stood in the kitchen, busy preparing Marion's medication that would need to be carefully ground into powder and mixed with her breakfast.

"Morning," Jack said.

"Good morning," She answered. "Out for a busy day?"

Jack said, "Yeah. I'll be back later. If something comes up, call me."

The doorbell rang. Samantha automatically started for the door, but Jack cut in front of her.

"It's for me. I'm getting picked up," he said.

"Oh...okay," she said, surprised. Jack paid her a cheap grin and made for the door and opened it. Linda stood motionless, her whole expression weighted and tired. This was not the same woman he'd met the day before.

"Hello, Jack," she said.

"Hey. What's happened?" he asked.

Linda noticed the faint, dark circles rimming his eyes.

"You get any sleep?" she asked.

"What?"

She motioned semi-circle around her eyes with one finger.

"Oh," he replied, catching on. "Took Mom to the ER middle of the night. Thought we lost her. Didn't sleep much after that."

Linda put her hand on his shoulder—just briefly—a reassuring touch.

"Sorry about all this, I'll explain on the way to the station. We'll meet the sheriff there."

They started toward her squad car parked at the end of the driveway just as Cathy pulled up in her two-door Subaru. Her eyes grew when she saw the squad car and Jack about to get in it. She rolled down her window.

Cathy said, "Hi, Jack. Is everything okay?"

Jack forged a smile that was borderline theatrical.

"Hi! Yeah, everything's fine. Be home later today. No worries." He waved at her and then dropped into the squad car with Linda. Cathy rolled toward the garage door to park while Linda and Jack pulled away. She watched them warily in her rearview mirror before getting out of her car, tracking them as they pulled out of sight down the street.

Jack glanced back toward the house as they drove away.

Linda said, "I should have had you meet me at the station rather than picking you up. It looks suspicious."

Jack said, "Yeah, you may be right. So what's happened?"

Linda started, "We had a pedestrian hit and killed on the highway last night. It was a boyfriend and girlfriend camping—at least we think they were camping. Seems they ran a couple miles then dashed straight into the highway like wild deer fleeing a predator. Boyfriend was hit by a pickup truck and killed. The girlfriend was hysterical—kept screaming, 'It's coming, it's coming, run!'"

Jack listened quietly, a confluence of astonishment and trepidation pooling inside.

"Jack, I've seen folks who are hysterical out of their minds, but never like this. These people had been running for their lives from something."

It's coming.

Jack said, "Linda, I know this is going to sound crazy...but that's what my mom said last night when we took her to the ER."

"What?"

Jack continued, "When my mom was in the hospital room last night, she looked right at me and said, 'It's coming.' And she said it as if it was urgent. Life and death."

Linda didn't respond because she had no idea what to do with it. Coincidence? Had to be. *It had to be!*

Jack said, "So what do you need me for?"

Linda said, "The sheriff asked if you could help us find the rest of...it, whatever it is out there."

Jack said, "It's no longer an engine cover, is it."

She faced him squarely.

"No, it isn't."

Had Hawkins not received the call himself about a domestic disturbance and not heard the name Ronnie Talbot, he would have met Jack and Linda at his office on time. Instead he was miles away from downtown, pulling up a driveway unfit for a mule. He rolled toward a desultory A-frame house that looked as though it had been painted a hundred years ago. Next to it was a corral with a tired looking horse that maundered back and forth. Near the corral on the west side of the property was a tortured old barn, and encircling the property was the forest.

Hawkins parked and turned off his engine. He reached down and touched the butt of his Glock, sleeping there on his hip. He took a deep breath and very slowly got out of the car, keeping the tips of his fingers on his weapon. He had no sooner set the sole of his shoe on the muddy ground than he heard a man bellowing from inside the house.

"I don't care! It's a goddamned nuisance!"

There came a woman's voice in reply. Much lower, and agitated.

"Ronnie, I'm sayin' maybe it's just them working on the roads..."

The man's voice grew even louder.

"No one's working on the road that late, for shit-sake! What are you, stupid?"

The woman countered.

"Don't talk to me like that!"

Hawkins was walking on eggshells toward the house when the front door exploded open on its geriatric hinges. Ronnie Talbot, a veritable brick shithouse of a man in stained overalls and white T-shirt tromped out onto the porch, spun, and caught Hawkins in his sight. *Keep him calm*, Hawkins thought loudly.

"Hello there, Ronnie. Nice morning."

Ronnie had large, dark eyes that sat deep in his head beneath a brow like a window awning. It afforded him all the charm of a young Boris Karloff playing Frankenstein's monster. Those eyes dilated and darted back toward the house where Hawkins guessed instinctively that a loaded shotgun was probably just inside, leaning against the frame of the front door.

"Sheriff, what the hell is going on out here?"

Hawkins said, "Ronnie, I'm not sure what you m—"

"I'm talking about the noise! It started after that meteor or satellite crashed out there! What do you know about that, Sheriff?"

Hawkins said, "Ronnie, it was probably nothing more than a very small meteorite, no bigger than a golf ball."

The giant man replied with an untrusting stare. Finally, he said, "Well how in the hell do you explain all them noises out there?"

Hawkins asked, "What kind of noises?"

Ronnie drew back a long snort and spit the resulting mass over the edge of his deck.

"I dunno...like machinery...but it wasn't a tractor or anything I've heard."

Machinery? Hawkins was bemused, but played it cool for the sake of keeping Ronnie cool, otherwise there was no telling how bad things were going to get.

"Ronnie, I don't know what to tell you. We haven't had any other complaints out here, and if I had any idea what it might be, I'd offer an explanation. Sound carries sometimes, you know. Plays tricks on all of us. It's possible you heard something that was clear out at the Hills Airport. In fact that's probably what it was, Ronnie—an airplane throttling."

Ronnie narrowed those big, cold eyes.

"I know what an airplane sounds like, Sheriff. This didn't sound like an airplane!"

Hawkins opened his hands in front of himself, a conciliatory gesture.

"Ronnie, I'm sorry. I wish I had a good answer for you, but I don't."

He thought quickly, then said, "I tell you what, I'll look into this for you—check with the airport, department of transportation, some of the neighbors—see if I can come up with something. How does that sound?"

Ronnie began shifting on his feet, glaring at Hawkins, analyzing him with a built-in bullshit meter. Finally, he said, "Okay, Sheriff. Okay."

"Sure, Ronnie. That's what I'm here for."

Hawkins turned and strolled back to his car, his movements cool and even. He slid behind the wheel, started the engine, and waved at Ronnie through the windshield. The big man didn't wave back. Perhaps he didn't see the gesture? *Didn't matter*, Hawkins thought. The situation had been diffused and it bought him some time. He turned the car around and idled carefully down the driveway and back out to the main road. It was only then that he let out a long, deep breath.

His phone vibrated loudly as a text message came in from an officer named Mitch. He was young, twenty-two, and new to the department, having only been there a year. He was also new to adulthood and still proficiently adolescent. The text read: *Found the campsite. Holy shit! Sending you location. May take a minute—coverage sucks out here.*

Hawkins read it and could only imagine what 'holy shit' actually meant, although he guessed it to be an overstatement, since Mitch had been prone to blowing things out of proportion on the job. He once described a small dumpster fire as a—what was it—oh yeah, *blazing hot inferno*. The phone vibrated again as a map arrived with a location pin fixed in the center of it.

Hawkins went back to the text and typed: *No drama, Mitch. How bad is it—really?* He waited. Mitch answered back, this time with a photo attached. It shouted: *THIS BAD...*

Hawkins opened the picture and pinch-zoomed in. Instantly he realized that the kid wasn't overstating the situation, not at all. In fact, what he saw in the picture was worse than 'holy shit.' It was on a whole different level. Hawkins quickly dialed Linda's number.

Linda was in her office with Jack looking at the Doppler map on her computer. There was an 80-mile-wide band of green with an eye made up of yellow and red—a lot of red. It was just starting to bulldoze through the corner of Kentucky and was moving northeast, directly toward them. On its current course, it would hit in just six hours. And there was another system, maturing fast, cuing up behind the first one; green also, but growing angry in the center.

The severe weather warnings were explicit and all but promised worse case scenarios. Twisters were almost guaranteed, with some counties in Oklahoma already reporting multiple funnel clouds and golf ball-sized hail. And someone had reported what they feared was an EF-3 on the ground outside of Tulsa, disemboweling the countryside.

Jack said, "Are we going to have enough time?"

Linda bit her lip against impending anxiety.

She said, "Looks like it's coming in waves over the next few days. Which means we're going to be playing a game of chicken with Mother Nature if we want to locate this thing."

Jack said, "Maybe we should wait until these systems have passed."

Linda said, "I think you may be right. But we've got to investigate the campsite of our victims from this morning, otherwise we could lose any physical evidence to the weather. We have to be certain about what happened out there, especially if it turns out this was a criminal act and unrelated to our mysterious piece of spacecraft."

Linda's phone vibrated as the pinned GPS map from Hawkins arrived. At first glance, she was puzzled. Then the phone rang. She tapped to answer. Hawkins cut her off before she could utter a syllable.

"That's the GPS for the campsite. Meet us there."

Linda said, "There's a severe storm front coming straight at us. We've got five, maybe six hours tops."

Unflinching, Hawkins said, "The site is bad, deputy—very bad. You'd better leave right now. And hurry so we can beat this storm."

Linda said, "Okay." She hung up and grabbed her car keys. "They found the campsite. Jack, I'm having second thoughts. Maybe I should take you back to your house."

Jack stood. "No, I'm with you on this. Let's go."

CHAPTER 17

S UMMER REYES HAD JUST FINISHED typing her script for the story she was producing for the 6:00 p.m. news. It included her on-camera introduction, her narration, B-roll footage, and her wrap-up. All she'd have to do now is go to the police station and get an on-camera interview with someone in the department who knew what the hell really happened to a couple of pedestrians on the highway early that morning. With a few good sound bites she could make it work. She saved the document and closed the lid on her laptop.

She rose from her desk, stretched and glanced over at her gym bag, which rested half open on a chair by the door to her office. She could see her workout tights peering at her from the opening. She wondered if she had time to go to the gym before her idiot cameraman, Kyle, got back with some additional footage for another piece she was supposed to finish. But since he'd have to capture the footage into the computer and do a rough assembly anyhow, it would afford her time to do whatever the hell she wanted. It was settled, then—she'd go to the gym.

Because no one told Summer Reyes what she could and couldn't do.

Summer was a girl who began awkward in grade school and junior high, but suddenly, dramatically transformed in high school as if some fairy godmother had anointed her with magic dust from a wand. Once she started community college, Summer was a stunning, exotic beauty who quickly learned that her potent sexuality could be used as a weapon.

Her past was a veritable trophy case full of people she used as objects and then conquered. Her future was, in her mind, already settled: she would do one more year here at the local station, then go to Indianapolis and get anchor. Then she'd move to Atlanta and score a job at CNN. Beyond that she could see herself becoming the next Katie Couric...except, of course, a much sexier version. She could see it, smell it, and taste it. But in the meantime, she had to finish this piece about some pedestrian who got himself killed in the middle of the night on the highway, way the hell out of town. It didn't make any sense. The guy must have been drunk or on crack.

There was a light knock on her doorframe that announced the sudden presence of Walter Smith, the station manager. Walter was the distant side of fifty and a somber fixture at the station. He never smiled. Even Summer's sexual power seemed to have little effect on him, which Summer chalked up to a severe lack of testosterone and clinical depression. Because no man with even a nominal level of hormones could be so dark around her. He dumped a newspaper unceremoniously on her gym bag.

Walter said, "There. I'm finished."

Summer smirked. "Thanks for the leftovers, Walter."

She snatched up the paper and tossed it on her desk.

Walter said, "I want to see your piece on the highway thing by five, no later. We'll run it at six if it's any good."

God, she hated it when he tried to order her around.

"You'll have it when it's done, Walter. Come off it. *It's me we're talking about here.*"

Walter bristled. "That's why I need to see it before we air."

Summer bled him a half-smile that had all the charm of a rainforest viper.

"Don't worry yourself. You'll have it," she said.

Walter coughed loudly and then left, his shoes clacking down the old linoleum hallway. She heard the door to his office close.

"Frigid asshat," Summer steamed under her breath.

She snapped the newspaper off her bag and glanced at the front page. Seeing nothing of any interest to her, she began sifting through the rest of it. She was ready to toss it away, when she saw the name Richard McAllister mentioned in the obituaries. She scanned it, finding the list of surviving family, notably Jack McAllister. That was a person she had not thought about, or seen, in a long time.

For a moment, albeit a fleeting one, Summer felt a blend of sadness and compassion. *He must be in town,* she thought. *I should pay respects and give him a quick call.* Just a quick one.

Summer pried open the lid of her laptop and launched her web browser. She landed on the Internet white pages and found a local number for Richard McAllister. Easy. Jack was probably staying at the house, putting things in order she reasoned. She grabbed a pen and blasted down the number quickly. She was all set to dial when she put her fingers back down on her laptop and flew to Google's main page. Carefully, she typed in the name Jack McAllister. The results were instant and Summer was surprised when she saw the result: science fiction author.

When Summer had met Jack years ago, while she was still in school, he was rowdy, fun—a party boy—in no way striking her as someone that was destined for success, especially in the literary world. He was just a great looking guy with an amazing body, looking for some fun and adventure, resisting pressure from his father to become an engineer.

"Good for you, Jack," she said out loud. Now she was going to *have* to call him, talk, reconnect and see what ten years had done to him. Hopefully, he still had those lifeguard good looks and hadn't let himself turn into a fat honkin' slob.

Summer dialed the number and waited. Not three rings later a woman answered.

"Hello, McAllister residence," Cathy said.

"Yes, hello. Is Jack there?"

"No, I'm sorry, he's running errands today, but he should be home later this afternoon. Can I leave him a message?"

"I'm Summer, an old friend of Jack's. I was so sad to hear about his father's passing. I only just found out about it today. Do you have his mobile number by any chance? I would love to give him a quick call and personally give him my condolences."

Cathy said, "Sure, just give me a moment." Summer waited while Cathy found Jack's number, returned to the phone, and gave it to her. Summer thanked her and hung up. She tapped in the number and dialed. It went straight to Jack's voicemail. She cleared her throat, waiting for the little tone, which came after the warm digital voice instructed her on when exactly to leave a message. Finally the tone came.

"Hi Jack, this is Summer Reyes calling. It's been a very long time. Um, I'm calling because I just found out about your father, and I am so sorry for your loss. If I had known sooner, I would have come to the memorial. Anyhow, if you get this, and you have time to talk, please call me at 812-555-9909. Okay, Jack, take care—and again, please accept my condolences." She hung up.

He would call her back—unless he was married now. But even so, she figured he'd still call her. After all, she gave him one hell of a wild ride all those years ago. And he was pretty damn good, too. So good they ended up breaking her futon, if she remembered correctly. Yes, either way Jack would be returning her call. Summer stood, snatched up her gym bag and strode out of the station, owning the space with every step she took.

CHAPTER 18

WHEN WE GET TO THE site, we'll only have a few hours to look around before that storm lands on top of us," Linda said as she drove them out toward the scene of the crash. Jack noticed the speedometer creep from 70 to 75.

He said, "I don't know if that's going to be enough time to locate the other pieces of the craft. Depending on its incoming velocity and how many pieces there were, they could be near each other, but they might be spread out. There's just no telling."

Linda said, "I understand. We'll have to cover as much ground as we can before that system lands. After that we won't be able to get back out here safely until tomorrow morning—and even then it's going to be dicey with that other storm brewing in the south."

She held quiet a moment, then said something that surprised even her.

"Jack, I'm not superstitious or anything, but it's weird. Weather's been clear the last few weeks, and all of a sudden this thing lands and we can hardly get near it. It's like some force is opposing us. Like whatever this is...doesn't want to be found. Sounds ridiculous, I know. I'm letting my imagination get the best of me. Freaking myself out a little bit."

Jack was about to respond when he felt his phone vibrate on his pocket. He pulled it out, noticing a missed call and a voicemail. *Damn.* Coverage was spotty out here, he noticed. Calls would sometimes fall straight to voicemail. Email came in spurts, some messages held prisoner in cyberspace for hours before being emancipated. What if the call was regarding Marion? What if something happened while he was gone?

Jack felt guilt climb on his shoulders—*he should not be out here.* He should be back at the house. He should not be part of a search party looking for something that may, or may not be real. He should be looking for life insurance papers, making phone calls, opening old boxes, sorting and shredding. He should be keeping an eye on Marion, even though the caregivers were doing just that. He took a deep breath and dialed into his voicemail.

Linda said, "What is it?"

Jack said, "Not sure. Got a voicemail. Hoping it's not about my mom."

Linda tripped into a moment of total clarity. What the hell was she doing towing Jack all the way out when his father had just died and his mother was losing the battle with a cruel disease?

She said, "Jack, I don't feel right about this. Maybe I should take you back home."

Jack motioned her that he was about to listen to the message. The greeting began, and Jack recognized who it was. The voice had changed, deepened a little, but there was no mistaking it—the voice belonged to Summer Reyes.

An MTV-style montage of memories played in his head, the finale including Summer in bed, thrusting up and down on him like a piston. It all ended as he caught the part where she left her phone number. Jack checked the missed call log to make sure her number had registered in the display. It had. Okay, he thought. He could call her back later. He finished and put the phone in his pocket.

"Everything okay?" Linda asked.

"Huh? Yeah, just an old friend giving their condolences," Jack replied, feeling suddenly awkward.

Linda said, "Oh. Look, Jack, I was saying I don't feel right about this."

"About what?"

"About dragging you out here. You should be at home with your family, taking care of your mom."

Jack knew she was right. But he also knew they were almost at the spot where they could hike into the woods and perhaps find this thing, whatever the hell it was. Linda would have to do it whether he came along or not, and turning back now would pilfer what little time was left before the storm hit. And the thought of Linda by herself out here made him uncomfortable. Yes, she was tough, resourceful, bright—yet he was still uneasy about it.

Jack said, "I appreciate that, I really do. But we're just too close to turn around. Let's keep going."

"Okay, Jack. Okay."

Linda pushed their speed to 80 until they arrived at the scene, which was occupied by a half-dozen police cruisers. There were two officers at the side of the highway that had set up a temporary closure of the shoulder. Across the highway from them was a news truck. A cameraman was there shooting video from a distance.

They exited the car and Linda asked one of the officers there if the others, including Sheriff Hawkins, had come back from the site yet.

"No ma'am, not yet," one of them said. Jack glanced back at the cameraman for a moment. Linda came to his side, urging him out of view.

"Local news," she said. "I'd rather not have you showing up on the evening broadcast."

Jack nodded, and slowly they took their first steps into the woods, dissolving into the growth, gone from view in a second.

CHAPTER 19

B Y THE TIME JACK AND Linda had arrived at the
campsite, or rather what was left of it, Hawkins,
Mitch, and the others were examining the site,
none of them any less awestruck than when they'd first
come upon it. One of the deputies was photographing the
site with his attention on the fallen tree, and more
precisely the base of it that had been snapped clear
through. The tree itself had fallen diagonally through the
area like the tail of an angry brontosaurus and flattened
everything beneath it. A tiny bit of fabric from Dan and
Monica's tent was reaching out from under the bulk of the
tree—mangled, pathetic. Gnarled pieces of tubular metal
were all that was left of two camping chairs.

Linda took it all in and was immediately anxious. There
was no lightning last night, no strong winds or twisters, she
thought. What the hell was powerful enough to break one
of these trees, and only one of them so precisely? *Whatever
was inside the spacecraft.* The thought came—separate from
her own thoughts—as if someone else had whispered it to
her. She understood now how it was that Dan and Monica

could have run mile after mile, ending up in the middle of a major highway, not even realizing they had before it was too late.

Jack was sizing everything up against the heat shield they had found the previous day and he was doing everything he could to find the incongruence; the part of the equation that would prove they were unconnected. But there was just no way in hell he could deny the link, however intangible it was. Whatever landed out here did this. And whatever it was, was one large and very powerful son of a...

"Twister did this," Mitch declared. "I have no doubt in my mind. Probably an EF2."

Linda said, "I don't think it was a Twister, Mitch. There was no hail last night, no winds, no funnel clouds, only light rain."

Mitch clenched his boyish jaw, his fingers tightening on his belt.

"Well, I've seen a lot more twister damage than you have, darlin'! Okay? No disrespect."

"No disrespect," Jack said out loud, holding Mitch's eye line. "I have a hard time believing that."

Mitch glared back at him.

"Excuse me. Who the hell are you, anyway?"

Hawkins took several long steps until he was face to face with Mitch, and he quickly morphed from Sheriff to Marine Sergeant.

"He's a specialist in this area and my guest. And don't you ever speak to my deputy like that again. We clear, son?"

Mitch folded beneath Hawkins' iron tone, swallowing hard, his eyes darting uncomfortably away.

"Sorry, Linda. I mean, deputy."

Linda nodded, deciding to let it go. She'd had a few run-ins with Mitch before. He seemed a terminal adolescent, so she chalked it up to that.

"Specialist in what area?" Derek Smith asked. Derek was sporting fully reflective sunglasses and furiously masticating a large wad of gum. Jack threw a look at Hawkins for a save, since he wasn't about to tell them his specialty was science fiction.

Hawkins said, "Aerospace."

They all glanced at each other, half-amused.

"Aerospace," Derek asked. "You mean like NASA? Rockets?"

"Yes," Hawkins said.

They were all very quiet, examining Jack who did his best to look worthy of his new bullshit title, *aerospace specialist*. Especially with the Phoenix tattoo on his forearm, which Derek noticed instantly.

"Do all rocket scientists have tattoos now?" he volleyed, hovering on the edge of being patronizing.

Jack said, "My father, who just died this last week, had been involved in engineering the Mars Polar Lander, which never made it safely to the surface of the planet due to an improperly terminated descent engine. They built the Phoenix lander based on his original architecture of the polar lander with some modifications and it landed flawlessly," Jack said. "Victory from ashes."

All of them got quiet a moment.

"So then," Derek stumbled on, attempting to save face, "does all of this here have anything to do with the meteor that crashed?"

"It wasn't a meteor," Hawkins said.

Mitch spent a long hard look on him.

"What was it, then?" he asked.

Hawkins silently threw the question to Jack who cleared his throat.

"It's a...well, we *think* a spacecraft landed out here."

Mitch snorted. "A spacecraft?"

"What kind of spacecraft?" Brett Carpenter asked. Brett was a guy in his late twenties who had joined the police department after one year of community college. He'd earned the nickname, Rooster Boy, based simply on the fact that he was unusually tall and narrow-framed with a long, rooster neck. His senior year picture captured him sporting long hair parted down the middle of his head. Nearly everyone at the station had Brett pinned as a former, full-time stoner.

Mitch guessed, "Military?"

Jack said, "No, not military."

Mitch said, "Satellite? One of them XM Radio satellites—"

Jack cut him off. "Not a satellite of any kind. A spacecraft. Probably not from Earth, *from somewhere else.*"

It took several seconds for this to sink in. Mitch rolled his eyes.

"Is this some kind of a friggin' joke," he said.

"Stow it, Mitch! Right now," Linda said, her voice raised, strong, hard as brass. "This is not a joke!"

Mitch glared at her, then looked at the ground and bumped a small rock away from his shoe. He was starting to feel about two inches tall.

"Yes ma'am," he said. "Sorry."

Jack walked over toward the base of the tree to have a closer look. It had been split by some hideously powerful force leaving what looked like a wide-open mouth, full of long, lethal fangs of unexposed, blanched wood. Linda arrived next to him.

"Careful, Jack," she said. "You fall on one of those, you're impaled, and we're a long way from the ER."

Jack could only imagine what it would feel like to have one of those foot-long spears punch clear through him and out the other side. That grisly thought alone caused him to take a cautious step back. Linda noticed something and said, "Whoa. Look at this."

Jack saw it, too—a hole that entered the side of the tree at the base. It was a perfect circle, deep enough and large enough for Jack to put his fist inside it until half his forearm had vanished. He pulled it back out and peered carefully inside.

Jack said, "It looks drilled out."

Linda's gaze floated until she noticed another, this one in the ground just a few yards away.

"Jack, there's another one."

He joined her there, examining a perfectly made hole in the ground. Linda bent down, made a fist, and lowered it inside until her forearm was completely gone up to her elbow.

"It's deep," she said, finally pulling her arm out.

Hawkins and the others circled them, staring.

Hawkins asked, "What do you make of that, Jack?"

Jack said, "Looks like something drilled these holes."

They heard Mitch call out, "Hey, there's another one over here!" He was thirty yards away, squatting close to the ground. They all arrived as he too put his fist down into the hole, this one swallowing his arm all the way to his shoulder.

Mitch said, "Damn, I can't even feel the bottom of it!"

Derek said, "Only thing I can think of that could make a hole like that is a power auger."

Brett said, "No way someone's bringing one of those out here."

Derek countered. "What makes you so damn sure, Rooster Boy?"

Brett said, "Don't call me that."

Linda said, "Hey, guys—chill!"

It's like being on a hike with grade school children, Jack thought. Everyone fell silent and the ambience of the woods murmured around them.

Jack said, "Okay, it looks as though whatever came through here and made these holes came from that direction, which would be…"

"Northwest," Linda said.

"I think if we go further that direction, following these holes, I'll bet we can find the rest of the craft."

Hawkins asked, "What exactly might we find?"

"An aeroshell and a parachute," Jack said. "Maybe."

He glanced at the others. It was obvious they had no idea what the hell he was talking about. Rather than stand there and try to explain it, Jack decided to take the lead, and started walking carefully on a straight path northwest. One by one, they followed him.

CHAPTER 20

AS THEY FORGED ON, THEY discovered broken twigs, weeds, compressed grass, and more of the same large holes. Jack was vacillating somewhere between apprehension and outright trepidation at the thought of locating the remains of a spacecraft that may have come from someplace far beyond Earth. He began quietly exploring scenarios and outcomes—the slippery slope of "what ifs."

What if there was some radioactive material present in the craft? What if there was an alien substance in the capsule that they were in danger of inhaling? What if the occupant, or whatever it was that made the holes and pushed over the tree, was back there right now...waiting for them? What if they were walking into a trap? But...what if this turned out to be nothing more than a freak storm, an absurd "act of God," with no further viable explanation? What if they were wasting their time and there was no spacecraft? What if the damn thing they found yesterday was an engine cowling and nothing more? Shit.

A distant, muted roll of thunder unspooled over them. And—oh, yeah—what about the monster storm that was ever so slowly, yet so surely creeping up on them from the southwest?

Linda stopped walking. She was standing close to a tree, leaning into it, examining the bark carefully.

"Hey, have a look at this," she said.

Jack and the others gathered in a tight gaggle around her. Jack wasn't noticing anything, but Mitch and the others did almost immediately.

Mitch said, "Whoa, what is that?"

They were looking at a patch of small dimples in the bark rimmed with very fine, powdery detritus. There were hundreds of them.

Brett said, "Hey, over here."

He was examining the low hanging branches of another tree with the same tiny, precise holes in the leaves. After checking more trees, more branches and even some of the long grass that skirted the area around them, they found that nearly everything had been peppered with these tiny perforations.

Mitch said, "Did aphids do all of this?"

Brett said, "Termites, maybe?"

Hawkins moved out ahead of them, but stopped abruptly when he noticed something in the treetops move. He kept his voice very low as he spoke.

"Up ahead, eleven o'clock—something's moving."

They all fell in around him, eyes wide and fixed. What Jack figured to be fifty yards ahead of them, a purling black mass shifted high in the trees.

"Oh, shit! Did you see that?" Mitch said, his voice loud with adrenaline. Hawkins glared razor blades at him.

"Shut up! Everyone keep your voices low," he said in a harsh, dangerous whisper. Linda carefully stole a few feet closer to him. Jack crept in behind her, the others ever so slowly catching up. The movement occurred again, amorphous and fluid. Faintly they heard a flapping sound that accompanied the motion. It happened once more, and then stopped.

Jack crept out ahead of them, edging behind the trees for a better look. He saw it move again, hearing the same sound. *Was it...?* He'd have to get closer to be sure, and he'd have to hurry—the earth was darkening under a ceiling of clouds with bubbling underbellies. *Atmospheric instability.* He started off quickly.

"Jack, wait..."

He could hear Linda behind him, urging him back, then felt her gently touch his arm in an attempt to slow him down.

"Jack, we're almost out of time here." He remained fixed on the point in front of them. And there it was again: the shifting of shadow like a dark dance above them, a low muffled flapping in concert.

Jack said, "You see that?"

"Yeah, I do."

"I think it's part of the spacecraft, but I need to get a closer look."

Linda said, "I'm starting to get a really bad feeling about this."

As of a week earlier, Linda had been certain that she could handle just about anything the world threw at her. She chalked any premonitions, raised hairs on the back of the neck, bumps in the night—stories about ghosts and monsters—to hysteria, hyperactive imaginations or perhaps hallucinogenic drugs. Any inexplicable feelings she might encounter on the job were rooted in where a bad guy might be hiding if they were in a foot chase. What she was feeling now transcended all of that.

Jack looked into her eyes. Normally made of green steel, they were weakening, vulnerability that Jack had not seen in her before.

Jack said, "I know. But let's get this done. Let's find out what this thing really is."

She rallied slowly and nodded. Hawkins slid in beside them while the others hung back, now half camouflaged by the tall grass and low hanging branches.

Hawkins said, "Jack, I can't let you go any further. I'd be putting you in danger and it would be gross negligence on my part. You wait here, I'll go check this out."

Jack felt the strong urge to protest, but relented and acknowledged with a nod. Hawkins rose and started away from them in even steps, the sound of moving grass and small twigs the only evidence of his passing. And it was mere moments until they could no longer see or hear him. It was the first time the forest fell into a broad silence. Linda gripped the handle of her gun spontaneously. She tensed, listening, straining to see ahead into the forest where Hawkins had vanished.

"Jack," Hawkins called back, his disembodied voice small out in front of them, "you'd better come look at this."

They uncrouched from their spots and cautiously weaved through the growth for thirty yards until they reached him. Hawkins was glaring straight at it, there in the trees.

The alien craft parachute hung high in the canopy top of the forest, a bulky black mass, draping the trees like theater curtains, gently flapping in response to an evenly pitched breeze. It glistened, even in the dullness of the storm-choked daylight, not like silk, but like organic tissue one might observe on a sea mammal.

Jack said, "That looks like a parachute."

Coupled to the chute were dozens of long fibrous strands, hanging like downed power lines, slithering in the breeze, slapping gently against the bark. They spiraled downward toward the ground, the ends vanishing away into a curtain of brush and tree branches. They were still linked to something—most likely another component of the spacecraft, Jack thought. He could dimly see a big, conical shape through small openings in the growth—a motionless hulk. *Aeroshell.* Impulsively, he tore away from the group and climbed through the obstruction of branches and brush, coming face to face with it.

And *my God*, he thought—*it was huge.* Jack guessed it to be eighteen feet across at the bottom of the cone, which was facing away from him, steeply tilted, the lip of it propped against a large tree it had crashed into upon landing. The whole thing tapered back into a snug fitting where the strands of the parachute were still attached to it. Looking up, Jack saw the hole in the forest canopy where this part of the spacecraft had neatly punched through almost vertically. This was consistent with atmospheric entry descent and landing: as the parachute throttles the incoming velocity, it brings the craft to a more vertical descent rather than an unrestrained, horizontal one. This was textbook detritus from a carefully engineered EDL.

Jack heard a disturbance of branches behind him and Linda suddenly materialized through the obstruction. She took a sharp, indrawn breath when she saw it. It reminded her of a flying saucer. *No bullshit,* she thought, *that's exactly what it looks like.* Had she seen it in a movie she would have scoffed at the almost cliché resemblance—but here it was, confronting her sense of reality, dwarfing her beneath its own fantastic shadow.

Jack inched closer to it, examining the gloomy, metallic surface that appeared to have no rivets or bolts whatsoever, as if the entire piece of the spacecraft had been fashioned from one piece of material. Hawkins called out from the other side of the brush.

"You okay in there? Find something?"

Jack called back, "We found the aeroshell. It's here."

Jack moved carefully around its side, inching for a better look at the front end. He crept further along the hull, now discovering scorch marks, pitch black in long slashing patterns across the surface. Extreme heat damage. Jack reached the edge of the giant shell and peered beneath its rim to look inside. It was hopelessly dark underneath there.

Linda said, "Jack, be careful."

Jack said, "I will. It looks empty."

He craned his neck in further.

"Can I borrow your flashlight?"

He extended his hand toward her, palm open. She grabbed her flashlight and approached him.

"Maybe I should look first," she said.

"I got this," Jack said. His hand held open space until finally she passed him the flashlight. He took it, feeling the weight of it, and ducked back under the rim of the capsule. He could nearly stand upright as he clicked the flashlight on. A strong focused beam speared across the surface, exposing dark material that looked like insulation of some kind. There were also small panels dotted with dead electronics, but like nothing Jack had seen before. The whole thing was a peculiar, mechanical womb.

Linda drop-crouched underneath the side of it and leaned in near where Jack was.

"Jack, we don't have much time left, the storm is…"

From the dimness close to them came a sudden, inhuman grunt and the snap-crack of crushed timber. Jack whipped the flashlight haphazardly across the cavernous space, slashing the beam downward where it momentarily spotlighted a set of large, black eyes that glistened and then blinked. And suddenly, those eyes charged at them.

CHAPTER 21

EFORE HE KNEW WHAT WAS happening, Jack spilled
backward, crashing against Linda, who was unable
to keep her balance, and fell with him. A shadowy,
rushing form barreled past them, slamming up against the
derelict hull of the aeroshell as it bulleted out into the
forest, branches breaking in its wake. Jack was turned all
around, struggling for some sense of orientation. Linda
rolled and came back up on hands and knees, carefully
climbing to her feet. Jack captured his balance and stood,
now spotting it. It was twenty yards away, watching them
with huge, doll-like eyes; a mature stag with long, jagged
antlers. Its ribcage was ballooning up and down rapidly
with panicked breath.

"Shit," Jack said, collecting himself.

The deer glared at them another moment, its head
snapping left, then right, those marble-black eyes sizing
them up. It finally leapt away, springing adroitly through
the trees until it was gone.

Linda said, "Okay, so if this thing is empty, what should
we conclude?"

Jack said, "That whatever was inside probably separated from this capsule, came down the last thousand feet on descent engines of some kind, survived landing, and is somewhere out here."

Hawkins had climbed through the growth and was examining the hull of the spacecraft.

Mitch followed him in, his gaze starting on the parachute, falling to the aeroshell. He was shaking his head, a faint smirk appearing on his mouth.

"Sheriff, can I...talk to you a sec?"

Hawkins approached and they stepped another ten yards away from the group. Linda noticed.

Mitch kept his voice low as he spoke.

"This isn't a spacecraft, Sheriff."

Hawkins glared at him.

"Really? Then perhaps you'd like to tell me what it really is," Hawkins asked.

"My brother-in-law is Air Force, okay...I've seen stuff kinda like this here. It's..."

Linda drifted softly toward them and Mitch dialed his voice down to a whisper. With Hawkins and Linda listening intently, he continued.

"It's an airborne cargo delivery system, Sheriff. They use these kinda things for supply drops in the field. I seen 'em once at the base."

"Are you sure?" Linda pressed.

"Damn sure. Look, there's an airborne training facility fifty miles west of here. They do tests all the time on these new parachute systems."

Linda glanced back toward where Jack and the others were, and she began to wonder if perhaps Mitch was right. Hawkins touched eyes with her and quietly agreed.

"If my brother-in-law was here, he'd tell you the same thing I'm telling you. This thing is Air Force, not some spaceship from another planet."

"Then how do you explain the damage back there, the tree, the holes in the ground?" Linda pressed.

"Lightning."

Jack turned in their direction, noticing Hawkins, Linda and Mitch huddled, speaking softly. Linda made eye contact with him, and then averted her eyes.

What the hell is going on? Jack thought.

Hawkins gazed skyward, those bulging clouds beginning to turn olive green. Mitch noticed it, too.

"Shit. Sky's going green."

The heavens unloaded a horrific, white hot flash and an almost immediate crack of thunder, like a million pounds of dynamite exploding. They all crouched low. Jack's ears rang.

Hawkins yelled, "All right, we've stayed too long! Everyone back to the highway, now! Back to your cars! Let's go!" None of them gave it any thought, or argued. They moved instantly.

They humped it back along the way they had come, passing back through the wreckage of the campground. There was another flash and a simultaneous explosion of thunder. A strong wind came. The entire sky was green. Supercell clouds were exploding outward, churning, angry, bulging like malignant tumors.

Jack began to run, as did all of them. None of them slowed down or spoke. They ran for their lives beneath storied trees that were coming to life under the power of the wind. The white oaks leaned and swayed, their gnarled and massive branches swirling like the muscular arms of giants reaching for them, swooping over them, attempting to grab them with huge, twisted fingers.

Linda had achieved startling speed as she bombed through the forest. She was only vaguely aware of the others as she could see them in her periphery, and she was almost certain that it was Jack who was just out in front of her, running like a bat out of—

All at once her foot caught in the dense undergrowth, and the ground sprang up toward her. Her right shoulder made full contact with a large stone, the sound of the impact a pronounced and horrible crack. The pain was immediate and explosive. Linda saw bright stars and screamed. Jack heard her and pivoted quickly. He sprinted back to her and carefully turned her over. The pitch of the wind grew, a sudden inflow of warm air howling past them. She looked up at him, his outline faint and blurry. He held the back of her head carefully in one hand, supporting her neck. Hawkins dropped next to him, looking into her eyes.

"Linda," Jack shouted, "are you okay?"

Her vision cleared and she dove through another crashing wave of pain. She nodded at him, "I think so."

Hawkins said, "Can you walk?"

She nodded, even though she wasn't entirely sure. Carefully they eased her to her feet. She stood, feeling adrenaline blasting through her veins, shoving the pain out, banishing it, locking it away until later.

"I'm okay," she said. "Let's get the hell out of here!"

They arrived back at their vehicles at the side of the highway, out of breath with small cuts and welts from branches they had blindly slashed through. The winds had grown stronger, the sky a more bruised tone of purple-grey. And there was visible rotation above them—the storm was organizing. They piled into their cars, cranking the engines to life. Linda and Jack were the last to get situated as the others began pulling out. She felt a gruesome burst of pain from her shoulder as she reached for the steering wheel. She hissed and groaned, stabbing the ignition with the key and cranking it over to start the engine.

Jack said, "Maybe you should let me drive." Linda thought it over, and while it made perfect sense, she was hesitant. She couldn't let the pain control her. It was a lesson she had learned many times on the job. The pain could wait until later.

There was a crack against the windshield that startled both of them. Then came another one, followed by a loud impact on the roof. There was another. And another. CRACK, CRACK, CRACK, until it became a percussion line, a snare drum salvo. It was large hail, and it was falling faster. Lemon-sized balls of ice were pounding the car, dimpling and denting the hood, cracking the windshield like blows from a hammer.

Linda said, "There's no time! Hang on, Jack!"

She pinned the gas hard, pulling on the wheel in defiance of the pain that pounded her shoulder like those hail stones pounding the car. They spun, the rear tires lifting, gliding as though on newly waxed marble. Jack grabbed the door handle for stability. They hydroplaned another few feet until the tires bit into the asphalt and they stopped. Linda pulled quickly onto the northbound fast lane behind the other cars that were already accelerating out ahead of them. She mashed down the gas, the V8 growling under the hood, struggling against the gale that was opposing them.

In the distance ahead of them, at the very edge of town, came the howl of a tornado siren. Linda swept the sky horizon to horizon out in front of them—nothing there.

"Shit! Is that what I think it is?" Jack said.

"They don't sound unless there's one on the ground somewhere," she replied.

Jack looked down at the passenger side mirror. A dark, rope-like finger emerged over the woods behind them. "There it is," he shouted.

Linda stole a glimpse in the rearview mirror of the twister as it swelled into a perfectly formed cone the width of a football field, vacuuming the earth, spewing dirt, stones and grass from its base, throwing it all into the sky in a centrifugal rage. It roared like a hundred freight trains, clawing the ground, eating it, tearing the world apart. Jack watched in total awe. Nothing that he had ever seen in documentary footage prepared him for the unbridled destruction he was witnessing.

Linda crushed the accelerator under her foot, the car lurching forward, the speedometer reaching 90, 95, 100. The highway was wet ahead of them, and the car was dancing precariously on the blacktop, arguing for purchase with every yard. Jack turned to look through the back window. The twister had formed directly over the highway and bulldozed straight into the east side of the wilderness. There was an explosion of green treetops and wood as it mowed through the forest like it was short grass on someone's front lawn. Swiftly then, it began to break apart, the bottom lifting serpent-like, dissolving in a vaporous slashing vortex. In just a few short moments, the monster was gone.

"It just ended," Jack said. "It just ended!"

Linda eased off the gas and they decelerated back to 70. She glanced in the rear view mirror and saw the empty, molested horizon behind them. Feeling a shotgun burst of pain, she hissed loudly.

Jack noticed and said, "We should get you to the ER."

Linda said, "I'm taking you home first."

"I should stay with you."

"I appreciate it, Jack, but I can't let you do that. This was a bad idea. I almost got you killed out there. I was stupid."

"Linda, it wasn't your fault."

"Your mom needs you, Jack. *She needs you.* We're not doing this anymore."

Jack fell silent. He felt the sharpness in her voice. She wasn't giving him an option, or friendly advice. She was giving him a rebuke—and ultimately, she was giving it to herself.

Jack said, "We still have the pieces of a spacecraft back there..."

"Maybe not," Linda said. She hesitated. "Mitch thinks...it's Air Force. A parachute delivery system of some kind."

Jack said, "He's wrong. It's not Air Force. If it was, there would be markings identifying it."

Linda said, "Jack, we're backing off. The weather is going to be bad for several days. This thing is dead. We won't be going back out there."

Jack said, "I think you're making a mistake. It's not Air Force."

"Jack, you don't know that. You're a very smart guy, but you don't know everything. Let it go. It's over."

Her words stung deeply.

"If my dad was here and this was happening, he'd go back out there and find it himself. He wouldn't buy the Air Force story."

Linda fell silent and winced. She took a deep breath.

"Jack, I'm sure he would have. But he's not here. Leave this alone. It's nothing supernatural. We'll take care of it from here."

———————

They pulled into the driveway at Jack's place fifteen minutes later. The pain in Linda's shoulder had steadily become more intense; heat was radiating into her upper back and she could feel swelling in her right arm. It had become more difficult to steer the car and she was beginning to feel a ripple of nausea. She was going to have to get the nearest ER fast.

Jack unbelted himself and pulled open the door.

"Maybe we should..."

Linda said, "I don't think so."

The pain was eating her alive.

"If you need me to..."

"I don't."

Her tone was broken glass. Jack nodded and climbed out from the car. Not looking back, he went to the front door, unlocked it and went inside, closing it firmly. Linda was teetering on the edge. She'd make things right with Jack later, but now she was going to have to race to the ER. She began feeling light headed. *Shit.*

She put the car in reverse, backed out of the driveway, and pulled away fast, blowing through a stop sign until she reached the main road. Once clear, she roared out, slashing a hard left, heading west toward the hospital. She was clipping along, twenty over the speed limit. Dizziness started to come on her. She fought it and turned on her siren, which she figured would get people out of her way and maybe keep her conscious. The rains started again, blowing in diagonally on the face of the winds that were gaining strength with every second. Small hailstones began falling, ticking against the body of the car. Linda's vision began to darken on her periphery, small spots appearing in the middle.

Jesus, help me, I'm going to black out.

But she managed, her body arguing every moment, to pull into the hospital parking lot, climb miserably to her feet and lurch into the red-painted entrance of the ER. And not a few steps further, when a nurse spotted her coming, her vision tunneled deep black, and she collapsed right there on the floor.

CHAPTER 22

J ACK FOUND MARION IN THE living room, comfy in her recliner, watching a rerun of *I Love Lucy*. Her expression was glassy and vacant. It seemed she was ever so slowly emptying, her soul leaving in small pieces, day by day. Text from the National Weather Service crawled at the bottom of the television declaring the tornado warning for Hills County officially over. But it also cautioned that further storms, some capable of producing large hail and strong winds, were possible through the rest of the afternoon. Steady rains were all but guaranteed through the night as expected. All the more, Jack missed Southern California days.

"Hi, Mom."

She didn't respond.

"Mom?"

Marion sat unmoving, her lips now pursed in a blend of cautious curiosity as Lucy got herself into and out of another slapstick jam on the TV. Standing in the room just a few feet from her, it was as though Jack didn't exist—as if nothing beyond the pale glow of millions of pixels existed.

He decided not to try and capture her attention by saying something. Instead he pulled up a chair so he could sit next to her. Reaching for her hand, he touched it gently. There was a severely delayed response, but one nevertheless. Marion finally turned her head and looked at him. Her eyes seemed unusually large behind her glasses, and Jack could almost see the corrosive effect of the dementia in her pupils.

She said, "Oh."

He smiled at her and squeezed her hand lightly. In the same amount of time it might take water to boil on a stove, Marion formed a smile that was scarcely discernable. But Jack noticed, and it was enough for him.

"Hi, Jack. Is everything okay?"

Cathy had just appeared from the back of the house where she had been refitting Marion's bed with clean sheets.

Jack said, "Sure. Yeah."

"I was just a little worried when I saw you in the sheriff's car this morning."

"That was a deputy, not the sheriff."

"Oh, I see. But is everything okay?"

Jack was not in the mood for twenty questions, but decided he better say something.

She's not stupid, he thought. *She knows something is going on. I'll just tell her that we've found an alien spacecraft in the forest outside of town and the occupant, whatever it is, had already terrorized and kill someone. Other than that, everything's great.*

"Yeah, everything's fine," he responded evenly, then thought, *I sound just like Dad—everything's always fine.*

He added, "They just needed some advice on that meteor thing the other day."

Cathy said, "Oh, yeah. I saw it on the news."

Jack said, "They figured with my dad being in his field—me being his son—I could help them out."

Jack was uncomfortable and decided it was time to steer this conversation down another avenue, quickly.

"How is Mom doing today?" he asked.

"She did pretty well this morning. Ate most of her food. She's a little constipated, so we're going to have to keep an eye on that," Cathy said.

"Has she talked about Dad? Has she mentioned him at all?"

"No, she hasn't."

"Are there any other changes that you've noticed?"

"She's not talking as much. And she's having a harder time walking."

All at once, it hit him—a dark, foreboding truth—he was looking at a ticking clock. Alzheimer's was a disease with an irrevocable fate. There would be no cure, no magic pill or procedure that would afford Marion a deferral from the inevitable. The changes Cathy had described were part of the disease. Sometime soon, Marion would be unable to walk at all. She would stop speaking altogether. And then she would be unable to swallow food or liquids. Breathing would become increasingly difficult for her and, if she didn't leave her body by her own will somehow, she would eventually suffocate if she didn't starve to death first.

It's inevitable: life, the world...it all changes. There's just no stopping it.

Suddenly those words, spoken by Richard just a week earlier, adopted a whole new meaning. Life, his family, the world—it all felt dangerously frail. Everything had changed, and nothing was certain anymore. Not even tomorrow.

Snap out of it, Jack. Get busy and do something, he thought.

Jack carefully let go of Marion's hand and stood. She didn't notice.

Jack said, "I think I'm going to get to work in the garage and start to look through some of those boxes out there."

Cathy said, "Sure, Jack. Let me know if you need any help."

He said, "I will," even though he had no intention of doing any such thing.

Jack stepped into the garage from the kitchen and pulled the door closed behind him. He was alone. Save for the incessant tapping of rain on the house, it was quiet in here. He had a look around. There was Dad's maroon tinted Mercury sleeping in the center, a lawnmower and snow blower cuddling in the far corner next to some old furniture that had never been donated or sold. There were bookshelves, antiquated pieces that no one born in the last thirty years would want. A crush of unmarked cardboard boxes throttled most of the space, quietly jeering at him.

I can do this, he thought. *I have to do this! Even if it's one box at a time!*

Jack walked around the car and came to a short stack of them. He opened the top of the first one revealing nothing but old paperwork inside. He could see the edges of receipts in there, hundreds of them from years long buried and forgotten.

Dammit, he thought loudly beneath a gathering cloud of anger and despair.

He grabbed another box and pulled hard on the top, the old cardboard tearing like sheet paper. Expecting more yellowed paper detritus, Jack was stunned when he found himself staring down at a framed photograph of his parents. They were young. Marion was in a hospital bed, bundled in a warm blanket, smiling, reaching up and touching Richard's face tenderly as he stood by her bedside, staring passionately into her eyes. Jack remembered that photo. It was taken the day he was born.

He closed the top of the box and then broke down. The sobs came relentlessly as he felt himself imploding, dozens of pieces of childhood memory appearing, then all being swept away by an image of Richard in the coffin—frail, hands folded over each other, eyes sealed shut.

Pull yourself together, Jack, he thought. *Pull it together! How the hell are you going to get through all of this if you can't even make it through one friggin' box!*

Jack took long, deep breaths and wiped the tears away with his palm, settling. His mind started to churn again and he found himself thinking about Linda. The pain she was feeling seemed to be extraordinary and Jack hoped she hadn't broken her shoulder. He grabbed his phone and pulled up her number, but didn't send the call. *She's probably in the ER right now getting x-rayed and checked head to toe.*

Then he thought about how she had given him the boot and told him he was no longer needed in the field with them. It soured him, even though he knew she had a damn good reason for doing it. Jack decided he would call her later.

And what about Summer Reyes? She had called him, left a message and a number. She was here in town apparently, and Jack supposed she had never left since college. He went back to his voicemail and listened to her message:

"Hi Jack, this is Summer Reyes calling. It's been a very long time. I'm calling because I just found out about your father, and I am so sorry for your loss. If I had known sooner, I would have come to the memorial. Anyhow, if you get this and you have time

to talk, please call me at 812-555-9909. Okay, Jack, take care—and again, please accept my condolences."

Jack considered everything—mostly the fact that he was falling apart right there in the garage. Everything was so totally screwed up, so insane. Nothing made sense.

Maybe a phone call to Summer—*ah, ah, Jack, remember, she was wild...unpredictable...and not always in a good way.*

But people change. And besides, this wasn't a date. It was a phone call and nothing more. A slice of normalcy wrapped in a conversation.

Jack stopped thinking, retrieved her number from the log and hit SEND. The line rang. Rang. Rang. *Shit, it's going to go to voicemail,* Jack thought, and he considered hanging up, when suddenly a voice answered—a velvety woman's voice.

"Hello, this is Summer."

"Hey, Summer, this is Jack McAllister returning your call."

There was a long pause on the other side of the line and some shuffling.

Summer said, "Hey Jack! Sorry, I was trying to get my headphones in. How are you? I am so sorry about your father."

Her voice was warm and soothing. Jack could feel himself untightening.

"Thanks, Summer, I appreciate it. It happened very suddenly and was totally unexpected."

Summer said, "That's awful! And how is your mom dealing with it?"

Jack said, "Mom is late stage Alzheimer's and in pretty bad shape now. We're going to have to find her a new place to live, probably a care facility out of state."

Summer said, "Very sorry to hear that, Jack. I'm sure this is all so hard right now. You've probably got a mountain of work and responsibility on your shoulders."

"Yeah. It's a bit overwhelming."

"Well, if there's anything I can do to help—or if you just want to talk—call me. I'm a reporter on the local news team so my hours can be a little strange, but I'm around if you need me."

"Thanks, Summer. That's really sweet of you. Things are just...shit. Sorry. Guess I'm a little over-stressed here."

A pause fell, Summer allowing it to linger before she said, "You need a break, don't you."

Jack said, "Yeah, I think I do."

Summer held back, waiting for him to move.

Jack said, "You available to meet up later? Maybe get a bite at the old spot—the Italian place with great pizza."

"Well," she began, "let me think—perhaps after seven, since my story airs at six. The weather's still bad, but we might have a little break from the rains then. No more hail."

Jack said, "Okay. Just let me know."

Summer said, "Tell you what...let's plan on seven-thirty. If something comes up and I can't make it, I'll let you know."

"Okay, see you then."

"Sure Jack. It'll be nice to see you. I gotta go."

And she hung up. Jack put his phone away and felt a tide of normalcy splash over him. Dinner and a conversation—*how much more normal could you get?*

But Jack's thoughts drifted, as if by their own will, back to the aeroshell and the parachute in the forest. The decimated campsite. Those strange holes in the ground. And his dad's email exchange with Stephen Hunter at JPL:

I've looked at the images. Very strange. Maybe we should talk by phone.

I have to find those images, Jack thought. *I have to see them.* For some reason, as yet unrevealed, Jack began to think that perhaps—somehow—there might be a connection between those images and what they found in the woods. *Thin, Jack. Very, very thin.*

Yet he quickly left the garage and headed back into the house, back down the hall toward his father's office as the sound of rain climaxed to a roar.

Summer had just hung up with Jack when she flipped to another number in her smartphone and dialed quickly. It rang twice, and the weary voice of Kyle Beck answered.

"I'm almost there, Summer," he said.

She could hear the knot of exhaustion in his voice. Good, she thought. *Keep him stressed and he gets shit done.* Kyle seemed to thrive on stress, even though he pretended not to like it. Summer knew him better than he knew himself after two years working together in the field. He was a good cameraman and easily bossed around.

"Hurry up, Kyle. You've still got to give me a cut I can show Walter by five."

"I'm aware of that."

"That leaves us less than thirty minutes on location to get my sound bites. That's not a lot of time, Kyle. Especially in this shit weather."

She heard a loud huff on the other side of the call. *What a baby.*

Kyle said, "Okay, I'm almost there."

Summer said, "Chop-chop, Kyle," and hung up.

She removed her smartphone ear buds and glanced across the street at the police station through the glossy rainwater on her windshield. The sheriff agreed to talk to her, albeit briefly. Apparently that chick deputy, Linda, wasn't available for some reason. Usually she gave her some pretty good on-camera bites if she needed them. The sheriff was just plain boring on camera. But he would have to do. She needed something to get this piece finished, even though she knew damn well the only thing he was going to tell her was that it would be 'an ongoing investigation,' which really meant 'we're not going to tell you jack shit!'

Lumbering around the corner and crawling down the street opposite her was the news truck. Summer glanced into the rear-view mirror to check her makeup and hair. Not bad, but the crappy weather and the brick façade of the police station wouldn't make a very flattering backdrop for her. Oh, well. She just needed to shoot this segment, get to the station and cut it, hand it to Walter, and then go home and tidy up before meeting Jack for dinner. Summer grabbed her umbrella, opened her door, and carefully stepped out into the downpour.

Jack's concentration was enormous as he sifted through his father's computer files. Hours had passed since he had hung up with Summer and the rains had come in waves the entire time, heavy, sheeted downpours followed by lighter and more even showers. Half the time, Jack didn't really notice it so much. Either it was due to the fact that he was actually getting used to the storms or his focus on finding these mysterious Mars images was drowning them out.

Jack had just finished checking all the document folders, pictures, movies and miscellaneous and had come up empty. It seemed that the images from JPL were not on his computer at all. So either Richard had simply viewed them online, or he had downloaded them and deleted them.

Or....

Jack pulled open his father's desk drawers one at a time. The top drawer came open, and he immediately spotted the envelope with his name written on it in ballpoint pen. *Read it.* Jack held very still, uncertain, and yes, afraid—afraid of what might be in there—what Richard may have written for him—about him. *Not now.*

Jack closed the top drawer and moved on to the next one. Eventually he found a spindle of blank CDs. Except as Jack pulled it out and began looking at them more closely, he realized they weren't blank at all. *Backups maybe.* He put the first disc in the drive and waited for it to load. *This could take hours,* he thought, and glanced at the time. It was 4:45 p.m. already.

Summer glanced at the clock on the wall in Edit Bay 2—it was almost 5:00 p.m. Kyle was hunched over his keyboard, intense, clicking his mouse while moving video clips around the project timeline in Final Cut Pro. Summer knew he was almost done based on what she saw in the timeline, but she decided to push him anyway. Fire under his ass would get him to sprint the last few yards and she could get this thing to that old fart-bag...

"Is it ready?"

Walter was leaning in the doorway, his seemingly dead, apathetic face hovering there.

Summer said, "Yes, Walter, just finishing it up now."

Kyle snorted. "I still need to adjust audio levels here."

Walter said, "Just play it for me."

Kyle started the piece from the beginning. They all watched it together and Summer glanced occasionally over at Walter to try and gauge his reaction to it—which was almost impossible being as dark and dull as he was. She glanced back to the screen and noticed something.

"Hey, Kyle, did you drop in some new shots here?"

Kyle said, "Yeah, these are better establishing angles."

They were shots of the highway from later that morning with police cars pulled off to the side of the road, a couple of officers standing by, and another police cruiser arriving in a close up. Deputy Linda exited the driver's side, and there was someone exiting the passenger side—*a man not in uniform.* Civilian. He turned semi-profile toward the camera and Summer exploded.

"Stop. Stop right there!"

Kyle hit the spacebar and paused the video. "Look, Summer, these shots will work because earlier we cut back to—"

"Shut up, Kyle, the shots are fine. Just shut up for a moment."

Kyle ground his teeth privately and deflated back into his chair. Walter bristled.

"Can we get on with this," he growled.

Summer knew the face. The hair had changed—it was shorter now—but she knew it was Jack McAllister on the screen in front of her. He had been in the car with Deputy Linda Craig and they were getting out at the scene of the accident. *What in the hell was he doing out there with the deputy? Why would they involve him?*

Summer said, "Let me see the raw footage of this right here."

Kyle sat back up in his chair and in a few brisk keystrokes pulled up the raw footage. He performed a *match-frame* function, which took them to the frame they were looking at now. He played it from there. On the screen Linda said something to the other officers and then she and Jack walked into the woods together.

"Can we please just get on with this," Walter hissed.

Kyle said, "What is it, Summer? I can replace that shot if you don't like it."

"No, it's fine. Leave it. You can finish playing it now."

Kyle tapped the spacebar on his keyboard and they watched the rest of the piece. It concluded with Sheriff Clifford Hawkins on camera. He was stiff and predictable.

"We still don't have a clear picture of what actually happened, except to say it appears to be a tragic accident."

The last clip was Summer in front of the police station under her umbrella with the station microphone in her hand, a semi scowl on her face.

"Now I'm told by the sheriff's office that there will be an ongoing investigation into the bizarre accident that brought a young couple's camping trip to a very tragic end this morning. I'm Summer Reyes. Back to you in the studio."

Walter said, "It's fine. Burn it to tape." He turned and evaporated from the doorway.

Kyle said, "What was that all about?"

Summer said, "Nothing, Kyle. Absolutely nothing." And she got up from her chair and stalked out of the room. Kyle knew Summer well enough to know that was bullshit. Something was wrong. He went back to the clip and the moment of her reaction. It was the guy in the shot with the deputy. It had something to do with him.

Jack had been going through CDs and was starting to feel the futility of it. He was coming up empty and it was getting late. He glanced at his watch: 6:45. He was supposed to meet Summer at 7:30. Shit, he still had to freshen up if he was going to make it there in time. He'd have to come back to this later.

And that's when he noticed the disc at the very bottom of the spindle had black marker written on it that read IMAGES. Jack grabbed the disc and dropped it into the drive. A moment later it appeared on the desktop. He clicked it open and found a folder labeled MRO IMAGES. Mars Reconnaissance Orbiter. *This is probably it*, Jack thought. He opened the folder and found 3 TIFF images, labeled THARSIS ANOMALY IMAGES 1–3.

Jack double clicked the first image. The view was typical of an orbiter—vertical perspective looking straight down on the surface of the planet. He had seen thousands of these as a general topic of interest over the years. Jack looked closely at the image and right away he saw the anomaly. A dark, black object had impacted the butterscotch-colored terrain and had cratered the surface, upturning darker soil normally concealed.

There appeared to be a sprawled-out shape, like a pitch-black fan, close to another object that was round. Jack looked closer and noticed very fine strands linking the two pieces together. *It looks just like a parachute and an aeroshell*, he thought. And then it hit him inside—a feeling of absolute certainty, pronounced and articulate like a voice—

just like the one you found in the woods today. Jack shivered in disbelief. How the hell could that be?

He opened the next image and saw another object, perhaps a quarter mile from the other pieces. It was hard to make out any absolute detail at this pixel resolution, but from what he could discern, it appeared to be hexagonal with some sort of attachments at the sides. It too was pitch black and the more Jack looked at it the more it reminded him of an insect.

"What the hell is that?" Jack muttered to himself.

He opened the third and final image. It was the same view as before, the attached parachute and aeroshell still there, but that third object, the one that reminded Jack of an insect, had *moved*. It was now a hundred yards or more from its original spot. And behind it were—*could it be possible*—rover tracks? No. Not like a rover. They were different. Jack was absolutely still, edgy and intent.

There was a loud knock on the door of his dad's office. Startled, Jack half-jumped from the chair, banging his knee against the underside of his dad's colossal wooden desk.

"Jack, I'm about to give your mom some dinner. Do you want any?" It was Samantha. He hadn't heard her come in. He hadn't heard anything in the last few hours.

Jack said, "Uh, thanks, but no. I'll be out tonight."

"Okay," she said. Jack could hear her footsteps as she walked back down the hallway to the kitchen. He looked at the clock and hissed. It was 7:15 p.m.

CHAPTER 23

J ACK DROVE GUARDEDLY AS THE rain fell. The old wipers were dull and of little help, whining metrically as they drug back and forth over the windshield. Headlights from other cars grew into large optical flares through the watery glass, partially obscuring his view of the iron cold street. He was half looking for his turn, half thinking and desperately trying to process the images he had just seen on his dad's computer. There was a generous balance of uncertainty about what exactly it was. But one thing was certain—the same kind of mechanism that they had found in the forests outside of town had apparently landed on Mars a few months ago.

Jack made a right turn, then an immediate left. He drove past squatting small shops that fit snugly together like shoeboxes then saw the neon sign for the restaurant up on the right. He pulled into the parking lot and to his surprise, found only one available parking space. Apparently the weather hadn't dissuaded people from venturing out for a meal. He turned off the engine and glanced at his watch. It was 7:33 p.m. Not bad. Summer was probably already inside, waiting. Jack was about to grab his umbrella and make for the front door, but he hesitated and considered the evening ahead.

This was just dinner and conversation. Nothing more, nothing less. This was a dose of normalcy. There would be no talk about the spacecraft in the woods, the extraordinary images from the Mars orbiter, or, perhaps more importantly, reminisces of old times that included partying and sex marathons. Clear, Jack thought. *Crystal.* Satisfied, he clutched the umbrella, exited the car and darted toward the warmth of the restaurant.

In a blue Toyota Prius at the far end of the parking lot, Summer watched from the obscurity of night and a rain spotted windshield as Jack trotted into the restaurant. She would wait another ten minutes before going inside. It would give Jack time to wonder where she was. It would make him anxious perhaps, and that's exactly what she wanted. She would find out why he had gone with the sheriff's deputy to the scene of the accident on the highway, because it didn't make any sense. Why the hell would they involve *him?* He's a science fiction writer, *not a real scientist.* It couldn't have anything to do with the alleged meteor. *Or could it?* No matter what the real story was, she would get to the bottom of it. Because Summer perceived that something was there, a story shrouded in the silence...a very big story.

She checked herself in the small, lighted vanity mirror. Her makeup and hair were near perfect. She admired her image a moment longer, then closed the mirror and stowed it. *Time,* she thought. And then she thought about where the evening might lead...how far she'd be willing to go with him if it meant getting essential information. She decided to improvise and adapt. And who knew—if things ushered them to the mattress, perhaps they'd revisit some of their favorite positions from all those years ago. *Perhaps.* She grabbed her umbrella and slid serpentlike from her car, deploying her umbrella in one deft move, walking slowly toward the lighted entry of the restaurant.

Jack decided to go ahead and get a booth. Whether Summer made it or not, he was going to have to eat something. And besides, it was getting very—

There she came, striding toward him, a catwalk grin on her face. She wore very tight, low-rise jeans that transitioned seamlessly into designer boots with long, spiked heels. A fitted, short leather coat stayed snug against her. She still had that long dark hair, those almond shaped eyes and long eyelashes. Jack thought she looked really damn good. Better than that. She was—

"Hey, stranger. It's been too long," she purred.

Jack stood and they embraced as most long lost friends do. But this was different. She pressed against him, connecting her hips firmly with his. She was holding him around the waist and then kissed him on the cheek with those full, soft lips. And in an instant, it triggered Jack's memory to the first time they had met.

It was Halloween a decade prior. Jack was visiting his parents in late October after having been laid off from a job he didn't like, and a breakup from a girlfriend he did like. Richard had just started the job at the university and Marion had not yet been diagnosed with Alzheimer's. Jack remembered his dad say, *"Jack, lighten up a little. Life's too short. Come for a visit. We'd like to see you. You can spare us a couple days, can't you?"*

Jack was at a party at one of the dorms by the college. He had been invited by one of his dad's students if he recalled correctly. The music was loud and nearly everyone was in costume. It was about an hour into the party that Summer, dressed as a black cat, entered the room and owned it. She glowed in a lycra bodysuit that fit her like second skin. A convincing feline tail hung playfully behind her hourglass hips and she had tiny cat ears peeking through that full hair. Her deep, dark eye makeup caused her eyes to glow. And those eyes were staring at Jack. Fastened on him as though he were Serengeti prey. And then she smiled, and things got started.

Jack came back into the moment as Summer slid into the booth. Jack dropped into his seat across from her. An overhead lamp threw a cone of warm orange light over them and a red glass candle fluttered playfully off to the side. She shed her leather coat, revealing a tight fitting red silk blouse with buttons undone right down to the top of a black, lace bra.

"So, Jack...how are you holding up?"

He was going to have to work here and not stare at her chest with which he had become intimately familiar all those years ago.

He said, "There's a lot of work to do and I'm not sure where to start. And mom is..."

A waitress arrived and Summer ordered a glass of Chardonnay. Jack ordered a Cabernet.

"You want to split a pizza?" Jack asked.

"Sure. Last time we were here it was...hmm...I don't remember." The fact was, she did remember. But this was a test.

"White with grilled chicken," Jack said.

So, he remembered after all this time. Interesting, Summer thought. They ordered and it wasn't long before their drinks arrived.

Jack said, "You look great. Really great."

She smiled dangerously at him.

"You're so sweet. You're looking great too, Jack. Still muscular. Still handsome."

He grinned.

Summer said, "So...sounds like you've been very busy. What did you do all day?"

He hesitated and took a sip of his wine.

"Oh, you know...spent the whole day going through boxes, papers, computer files."

Summer said, "From the first thing in the morning until this evening, huh? Must be exhausting. No wonder you needed a break."

"Yeah," he said, and took a long sip of wine.

You're lying, Jack.

"So, what's been going on with you in the last ten years?" he asked.

Summer decided that she would do the talking—for now. It would give Jack more time to drink his wine and loosen up. She would need him to be loose so she could ask him some questions about how he ended up on the highway with the deputy sheriff. He wasn't a suspect was he? Didn't look like he was being treated as one in the footage she saw. She gracefully sipped her chardonnay and began.

"Well...ten years...let me see if I can summarize for you."

CHAPTER 24

Y OU'VE SUFFERED A HAIRLINE FRACTURE in your right
shoulder. It'll heal on its own, but you're going to
have to give it time and keep it immobile as much
as possible. No stress on the joint and no workouts."

Linda sat up in the hospital bed as the doctor glared
dispassionately at her, his eyes hazy from a fourteen hour
day.

"I'm giving you a prescription for the pain. It's strong
stuff, so don't go operating any heavy machinery."

Linda regarded her arm that hung limp in a soft sling.

"That's the first thing I was planning on doing," she said
beneath a derisive grin. She took the prescription from him
and got to her feet.

"You need a note or something for work?"

She collected the last of her things from the chair by the
door.

"I'm not missing work," she said, and left the room.

Linda walked back down the fluorescent soaked hallway
toward the entrance of the ER. It was a long walk over old
linoleum. She trotted carefully through the parking lot in

the rain until she reached her car and quickly dropped in behind the wheel. She pulled the door closed and sat still for a moment beneath the thrumming of the rain on the roof and windshield. She grabbed her keys and then realized she would have to use her left hand to start the car. Things she normally took for granted would be a challenge, at least for a while, until her shoulder healed. *Damn,* she thought, *I don't have time for this!*

And then she thought about Jack. She had drilled him a new one and he was just trying to help. They had pulled him into this whole mess in the first place. His father had just died and his mother was probably not far behind, and they were dragging him out into the wilderness, involving him in something that—

Linda grabbed her phone to see if perhaps...no, he hadn't called. God, she felt terrible. She would have to at least smooth things over with him and apologize. Not for any ulterior motive, but because he deserved it. She was about to dial his number when the pain in her shoulder sprouted, causing her to freeze. She bit down on her lip and exhaled loudly. She was going to have to get the prescription right now. She couldn't think straight like this. She'd have to call Jack later. Besides, he was probably already in bed half asleep from sifting through a deadfall of paperwork at the house. She would call him in the morning and make things right. But right now, she needed to get to the pharmacy.

By the time the pizza had arrived, Jack had already finished his wine. Summer still had more than half a glass left since she had been doing most of the talking. *Okay,* she thought, *he's had a glass of wine and he's about to have pizza, which is mostly carbs. He'd likely order another glass of wine. That, plus the food, would relax him.* And she needed him to be relaxed.

"So, Jack, your turn. Summarize the last ten years of your life."

"It's been a wild ride."

"Care to elaborate?"

"Went from earning a science degree, like the good son of an aerospace engineer, to getting a book deal as a science fiction author."

"Really? Any bestsellers yet? Movie deals?" *Another careful sip—still feeling sharp.*

"Not yet," Jack said. "I may be writing a script for a producer soon. And I've got to get started on another book as soon as things get sorted out here."

"And what's the storyline going to be for that one, Jack?"

"Not completely sure yet. I'm outlining a few ideas."

"Are you open to some suggestions?" she said.

"You mean a pitch? You want to pitch me an idea?"

"Sure. You game, Mr. Author?"

Jack was amused. "Okay. Thirty seconds or less," he said.

"Thirty seconds? That's it?" She giggled.

"Yeah, time is money. I've got a meeting with J.J. Abrams after this, so I'm in a big hurry! Whaddaya got? Hit me."

Summer leaned in playfully, dropping her hands on the table.

"Okay, um, how about a robot bear breaks out of a secret government lab and terrorizes the city?"

Jack snorted. "What?"

"Yeah, a robo-bear," she said.

He laughed. "Terminator meets Gentle Ben? I don't think so. Try again. You got twenty seconds."

"Geez, you're stingy with the time. Okay, um...vampires..."

Jack shook his head playfully, "No, no, no. No vampires."

"How much time do I have?" she asked, snickering.

"About ten seconds," Jack said, and took a sip of wine.

Summer cleared her throat and steepled her fingers for what Jack could only imagine would be another outrageous concept.

"How about," she started, "a meteor falls out of the sky over a small town, and presumably crashes in the woods, except it's not really a meteor but something else. Maybe a government spy satellite or maybe...from outer space."

The warmth of the food, the wine, the atmosphere, sublimated instantly. Jack felt a bump in his heart rate. Something wasn't right about what she just said. It was too close to home. What was going on here? *Did she know about what they had found that morning? Was that possible?* Jack summoned a snake oil grin and took a shallow sip of wine. *Okay, step slowly,* he thought, *put the ball back over the net.*

"So, what is it—the thing?" he asked. "Come on. You're doing the pitch."

"I don't know, you tell me—you're the author. *What is it?*"

That was a pointed question. Precise. Jack dug down deep for some tips from an acting class he had taken years ago with an ex-girlfriend. Time to play the unimpressed, unmoved publisher listening to just another pitch from some young hopeful at a conference.

"I have no idea because it's your pitch," he said. "Besides, I might go with a time travel story."

Summer noted the elevated tone in his voice, the sudden and slight unease with which he was handling his glass. She didn't want to scare him off, so she grinned playfully and twirled her hair in her fingers to ease his nerves. She quickly gulped the last of her wine and broadened her smile. *Think I may have hit a nerve.*

"It's okay, Jack. I'm not an author and have no clue what would make an interesting science fiction book. Although time travel could be a lot of fun...if you know what I mean."

She reached across the table and touched his hand very lightly. He had forgotten how soft and smooth her skin was. His eyes linked with hers and she stared at him through those long, dark lashes.

"We had some good times, didn't we?" she said, her voice smoothing, softening.

"Yeah," Jack said. He was still feeling off balance. Concerned. Tense. But ever so slightly, the sound of her voice, her gorgeous features, calmed him.

"You know, Jack...I was really sorry to see you go ten years ago."

"You were?"

"Yes."

"I wasn't sure. The way things ended, it seemed pretty defined."

"I was...immature, and a bit insecure at the time. Maybe we both were."

And then she leaned forward, carefully adjusting her posture so her breasts were pushing against her bra, that silk blouse tightening against her firmness.

"What do you think about...this? We're both adults. People change."

For a moment, Jack thought she was joking. But the look in her eye assured him she wasn't. This was crazy. He felt something telling him that this was wrong, that he should politely excuse himself, pay the bill, and get the hell out of there. But he was flooded with memories of them together all those years before—the flirting, the long walks, the kisses, Summer tangled playfully with him in her black silk sheets. There was no way in hell was he saying...

"Yes. God, yes."

CHAPTER 25

I T WAS STILL DARK OUTSIDE when the phone rang loudly at the side of the bed, and Jack kept his eyes shut, not wanting to open them. He felt Summer roll over beneath the sheets, reaching for her phone, grunting. She answered softly.

"This is Summer."

Jack heard a tiny voice mumbling on the other end of the call.

Summer replied, "Walter, can't you send someone else to cover that bullshit story?"

More tiny mumbling, then Summer answered sternly, "Fine. Yes. Okay."

She dropped the phone back on the end table. Jack heard her unleash a long, aggravated breath. He slit his eyes open.

"What's up?"

"Ugh," she said. "I have to go to Indianapolis for a live shot outside the Convention Center. It's the expansion— they're almost finished—cutting a ribbon or something. As if anyone cares."

She slid out of bed and grabbed her red satin chemise off the end of the bed where it ended up during the first five minutes of sex. *Just like old times,* Jack thought. She slipped it back on, then glided into the bathroom, shutting the door behind her.

Jack felt himself beneath the sheets, naked. It was completely surreal being back in bed with Summer. And in another way, it felt completely normal, as though they had never missed a beat since they parted ways ten years ago. Everything that had happened last night was familiar. The foreplay and all the positions were completely intuitive.

We're both adults. People change.

Jack heard the toilet flush and then water running into the sink as Summer washed her hands. She opened the bathroom door. Jack could barely make her out as she lingered there.

"Jack," she said, "I'm sorry to do this, but you're going to have to leave. I have to get dressed for work and be out of here in fifteen minutes."

Jack propped himself up on his elbows, finally able to see her more clearly as she strode to her dresser, grabbing panties and then toward her closet for everything else.

"I understand," Jack said.

"Thanks."

Jack pulled himself out from under the sheets and began collecting his clothes that had been littered on the floor around the bed. *What a mess. And what the hell time was it?*

Suddenly he felt Summer's body against him, the whisper of her lingerie across his skin. She wrapped her arms around him from behind. He stood upright, preparing to turn around and face her, but she held him tight enough that he couldn't. She kissed his back, then pressed her breasts into him so he could feel them. Jack felt himself respond instantly to her and he was prepared for what was surely going to be a wild, sexual sprint. But instead she spoke to him, her tone low and even, an eerily disembodied voice in the dimness.

"Jack, I know you were on site after the accident out on the highway with the deputy sheriff yesterday morning."

Jack's arousal waned, evaporating, and he was absolutely certain he had made a dreadful mistake by coming home with her last night. *Some people don't change.*

She continued, "Not that I blame you because, from a purely shallow position, deputy Linda is pretty hot. Maybe that's why you were out there with her—maybe you're just trying to charm her into bed."

Jack said, "Summer, I don't know what you're—"

Swiftly she reached down and grabbed him, her hand now cupped around his jewels. And though she was gentle, Jack knew that if she chose to squeeze, even a little bit, he would be seeing stars and vomiting.

Wow—ironic, he thought, *she literally has me by the—*

"Jack, the sheriff's department doesn't allow just anyone to hang out during investigations like that."

Jack tried to loose himself from her, but she ever so slightly tightened her grip on him, and he felt a sudden, warm pain down there that stopped him instantly.

"Ouch! Summer listen…"

"No, Jack, you listen to me! Something is going on out there that only you could help them figure out. And based on your father's lifelong career and your current one, I'd say it's related to that meteor. *Or whatever it really is.*"

With a fresh dose of cortisol, Jack grabbed her wrist and pulled himself free from her grip. He broke from her arms like a shot and spun, his muscles taught, ready for anything.

Summer said, "Whoa, Jack, you're still really strong! You can take it easy, though. I think you just answered my question. So do you care to comment on the record?"

Jack stared at her, his eyes now adjusted to the room. She stood with her arms crossed, hips cocked to one side.

"Is that what this is all about? You brought me home last night for this...this game?"

"No, I brought you home because the thought of having you again severely turned me on."

Jack said, "You've got this thing all wrong, Summer."

"I don't believe you, Jack. I think you're lying to me. And I don't like liars."

Never taking his eyes off of her, Jack collected his clothes and began to dress. She didn't move, but only watched him. Jack hurried now, throwing on his pants, shirt, socks and then finally his shoes, lacing them up faster than he ever had in his life.

"Jack, you don't want to be on the wrong side of the fence here. I can be your friend, your protector—or I can be the one that makes your reputation and your life pure hell."

Jack felt a tide of anger roll in.

"What the hell are you talking about? You threatening me, Summer? Is that what you're doing? Let me tell you something, you can't do shit to me. Get it?"

Summer planted fists on her hips that she now cocked in the other direction.

"Jack, if I weren't being serious, I'd find your response and that guttural anger behind it pretty sexy. But I am totally serious. Media is power, Jack—you can make people, or break them. Even the most clean cut, church-going, goodie-good everyman can be destroyed by a story that is, let's say, carefully worded."

Some people don't change.

So this was it, Jack thought. This is what she's become. She had exhibited some of these tendencies so many years ago. *Control.* She had to be in control, to have leverage in every situation, every relationship. She had to have the winning hand because for Summer, life was a war, and if people weren't useful idiots, they were obstacles to be shoved out of the way or destroyed. It was about power. *It all boiled down to power—her power.*

She continued, "Jack, a guy in your profession, newly successful, but not quite where he wants to be...should be very cognizant of his reputation and his image."

Jack said, "I know people, Summer."

She scoffed, "I know people too, Jack! People in your industry! Don't think so? Try me and find out."

Jack began to think the situation through. He would have to put the anger aside, because it would cause him to slip up, to say or do something he would regret. To what end and how much damage Summer could actually do to him was uncertain—*maybe none at all*—but Jack decided that it would be foolish to underestimate her at this point. He had to start out-thinking her which he could probably do as long as anger wasn't fueling his decisions. His first order of business was to get the hell out of her house, or as it might be referred to more aptly, *her lair.* Jack turned and walked out of the bedroom, heading down the narrow hallway back toward the living room.

He was halfway down the corridor when he heard her barefoot steps behind him on the carpet—following him. And a thought popped into his mind. *What if she's coming up behind me with a gun or a knife?*

He moved faster then, still hearing her dull, carpeted footfalls. He saw the front door and rushed toward it. He unlocked it quickly, pulled it open and dashed outside. He took five long steps toward the sidewalk, out into a light rain and turned to look back.

Summer stood in the doorway in her lingerie, staring down the walkway at him. She folded her arms again, leaning against the doorframe.

"Jack, come in out of the rain and tell me what's going on out there in the forest."

"Summer, it was a very small meteor. Okay? The damn thing vaporized in the atmosphere and the little pieces that fell went who-the-hell-knows-where. I told them it was a waste of time because the odds of finding such a small piece are nearly impossible. But they wanted to look anyway, just to make sure. They thought maybe it had something to do with the accident on the highway, but it was a theory, and a lousy one at that. I took a long walk with them and saw a whole lot of your lovely forests and got a generous dose of your shitty weather. You are being paranoid, Summer! And I don't have time for this shit! I've got more than I can handle right now!"

She held her spot. Unmoved. Unpersuaded. Committed.

"Jack, I'm going to be back by lunch today. I suggest we meet somewhere and then, as they say, we can do this the easy way or the hard way."

A roll of thunder came suddenly, and Jack knew it was time to go. There was nothing more to be said. He gave her one last look, trying to x-ray that poker face she was wearing. But in the rain, it was impossible to read. She turned to go back inside, then glanced over her shoulder at him.

"Thanks for last night. You were amazing, Jack." Summer went inside and shut the door.

Jack raced toward his dad's car and fumbled for the keys. He was distraught, his mind running over everything that had happened since the phone had woken them. He reached the car and was nearly soaked by the time he dug the keys out of his right front pocket. He unlocked the door and jumped behind the wheel. He started the car, flipped on the wipers and the headlights. Only then did he take a quick glance back at Summer's house. Jack felt anger surfacing again. He wanted to tell her where to get off and what a power-hungry narcissist she really was. *Subhuman,* Jack thought. *But very smart.* She knew exactly what she was going to do before she walked in the restaurant for dinner. The whole thing was a web, a trap. And dammit— he had just waltzed right into it without a second thought.

Jack pulled away from the curb and started back toward his parent's house. It was decision time. There were but a few options that he could see, and Jack went over them quietly.

Option 1: Shut off his phone, pretend none of this happened, and get to the business of the family. Simply vanish and play dumb.

Option 2: Call Linda and explain what happened. *Really?*

He could just imagine his side of the conversation. It would go something like this: "*Hi, Linda. I slept with an old girlfriend who is now a reporter and she suspects a cover-up with the whole meteor story and, well...she's threatening to blackmail me unless I tell her everything. Just a little FYI, deputy.*"

No, Jack. Very bad idea!

Revising that one: He could call Linda and give her a heads up that an old "acquaintance" in the local media was getting suspicious and asking a lot of questions. Better.

Or...option 3: Now that he had seen images of this thing on the surface of Mars, and knew what he was looking for, he could go and find it himself.

Why? Because it's what Dad would do, he thought. *Dad would want to know what this thing is and why it's here. Dad would understand that this was a history-tipping moment.*

Jack could go and locate the thing, document what he found, and then pass it along to Linda and Hawkins. They'd know then what they were dealing with and could take it from there. But the obvious trouble with that plan was it left Jack alone in the forest with that thing—whatever it was. He saw what it was capable of, as the detritus from the camping site bore witness. If he was alone out there, and the thing killed him, no one would know until long after the fact. *Not such a good idea.* In fact it was idiotic, reckless and would end up tearing his family further apart.

Perhaps there was another option, something in the middle of it all.

Jack pulled into the desolate parking lot of the Forest Mall and stopped. He grabbed his phone and found Linda's number. Before he could think himself out of it, he hit SEND. No more time for games.

It rang several times and then a few more times. Nothing. *It's going to go to voicemail,* Jack thought. He'd leave a—

"Hello? Jack, is that you?" She sounded groggy. Her words slow and dilated.

Jack kept an even tone while he spoke.

"Linda, I've got new information about the spacecraft and what's inside it. I know what to look for. I've seen pictures of it. It's not Air Force."

"Wait, Jack...pictures? How is that possible? What exactly are you talking about?"

"There's something else," he said carefully. "Someone in the TV media here is getting very suspicious and asking questions. They're going to start digging around and likely push a story about some kind of cover-up."

Linda fell quiet for a moment.

"Where are you now?"

"I'm going out there to find it. This morning. Now. There's no more time."

"Whoa, Jack, you can't...I mean, it's not safe to do that."

"I know what to look for and probably where to find it. I called because I'm going to need someone to come with me. I know you're injured, so maybe one of the other deputies could do it. Any suggestions?"

Dead silence. Jack waited for a response, and every second seemed like minutes. She was quiet. Was this another mistake?

"Jack...I'll go with you."

"But your shoulder—"

"I'm fine. It's just a fracture and I've got good meds. Trust me, I can take care of myself. I want to do this. But you've got to explain everything—especially concerning the media. Deal?"

Jack hesitated, hearing something in her voice he hadn't before, and he was not entirely certain that he liked it. But he was backed in a corner now. No way out of this but through.

"Deal. Meet me off the highway. We can hike back in the way we did before."

"No. We should go in another way. Drive past the spot we were before a half-mile and pull deep into the shoulder and under the trees there. Got it?"

Jack said, "I got it. I'll be there soon. I may need to go back to the house for some dry clothes before I head..."

Shit! It had slipped out.

"Back to the house," Linda asked. "You're not at home? What happened, are you okay?"

Damn! He'd have to come clean about what happened with Summer. All of it. But not on the phone. Not now.

"I'll explain when I see you. I gotta go."

"See you then," she replied.

Jack ended the call and closed his eyes, listening to the sound of his own intense breathing and the rain, which continued to fall, drumming a white noise symphony on the hide of the car. *The weather.* They were going to be up against this weather. There were a hundred good reasons for him not to do this, but Jack knew a line had been crossed, and, as he saw it, he no longer had a choice in the matter.

CHAPTER 26

THE NEWS VAN STARTED TO drift into the shoulder of the northbound highway. It was only then Summer realized that Kyle was about to fall asleep at the wheel and kill them both.

"Kyle!" she said loudly. "Watch it!"

Kyle's neck snapped upward, his eyes exploding open. He pulled on the wheel and the rear of the van drifted out from under them. The world spun past the windshield, the horizon tipping as they lost balance.

"Turn into the skid—no—the other way!" she shouted.

Kyle recorrected—a half spin back on the wheel—and miraculously the van righted itself, despite the glossy wet blacktop. The rains had softened since they left the station a half-hour earlier, but continued with no promise of respite, keeping the asphalt slick. Summer felt the anger pumping through her and struggled to collect herself. Not for her sake, but for Kyle's—because she was moments away from punching him in the side of the head. Kyle glanced at her, gauzy-eyed, and yawned.

"Shit. Sorry. I'm okay."

"Maybe I should drive," she said.

"Don't stress, I got it."

He yawned again and slouched. Summer glanced at the speedometer. It passed 70...then 74...76. The van began to float softly, the tires losing contact with the road. Kyle's eyes sank half shut like a cat preparing for a long nap on a fluffy, mountainous afghan. His head began to tip over slowly, slowly...slowly...

"Pull over. I'm driving from here."

"Summer, you never drive."

"I don't care! Pull over now!"

Kyle huffed and straightened up. He glanced in his side mirror and began decelerating, pulling off onto the paved shoulder. Finally, they came to a stop.

"Hazards," she growled.

Kyle slapped on the hazard lights.

"Summer, I'm totally fine."

"Bullshit," she said. "Move."

Kyle unbelted himself and climbed into the rear of the van as Summer transitioned from the passenger to the driver's seat as modestly as her barely-modest skirt would allow. Once she was settled, Kyle climbed into the passenger seat and inaudibly fastened his belt.

She's pissed, Kyle thought. She was always pissed about something. Sometimes she was pissed about nothing. Summer was a living, breathing antonym, her name about as opposite from her personality as humanly possible. Summer was more like winter. Nay—*a very bad winter.*

She grabbed the steering wheel and closed her eyes, taking long, deep

breaths to calm herself. Recalibrated now, she checked her side mirror, put the van into drive, and pulled back out on the highway, accelerating gently to an even 60. Satisfied

ERIC TOZZI

that they weren't going to crash and meet their wet and bloody deaths, Summer spoke.

"Why didn't you sleep last night?"

Kyle cleared his throat.

"Who says I didn't?"

"Kyle if we're going to work together I have to be able to count on you twenty-four-seven. That's how this business works. Get it?"

"Of course. Sorry."

"Don't be sorry, just be awake. What the hell were you doing last night? Were you up all night playing Xbox or editing that film of yours? Or were you looking at porn?"

Here we go again with the porn thing, Kyle thought. She teased him about it because invariably he reacted every time. He was such a sucker. For her it was like shooting a goldfish in a Dixie cup.

"Shut up, Summer! Not every single guy looks at porn! I was cutting my film, okay? I gotta chop another two minutes out if I'm going to make the shorts festivals! They're very strict about run times!"

Summer thought, *Yep—another wannabe Spielberg with delusions of grandeur that a mini-micro budget film with shit acting, lighting and sound is going to launch an A-list Hollywood career.* Pathetic. And amusing. Is that why she kept him on? Perhaps. But Kyle was a good cameraman—very good in fact—though she made sure not to let him know that. Otherwise he might get a big head and leave. Summer liked that he was a skilled editor, too. Most of all, she liked that fact that he was easily controlled. That's why she kept him on. He would do anything for her if properly motivated. Hell, he'd probably take a bullet for her.

But he was getting pissed. She could tell. Maybe she was pushing him too far. She decided that, for the moment, she would stroke his ego just a tiny bit—get him to talk about his film. It would loosen him up for what she was going to ask him to do later.

Summer said, "So how's it going? Did you get the cut finished?"

Kyle was puzzled. Summer never asked about his film or what he was doing outside of work.

"No, it's not finished," he answered cautiously. "I still need to cut some time off the front end. Pace is too slow. It takes too long to get to the first killing."

"So, it's a horror film?"

"Yeah."

"What kind of horror film?"

"You know...a horror film. There's a zombie that traps some people in an apartment after a bomb goes off near the town."

Oh, brother.

"So how long did it take you to shoot this and what did you shoot on—hi-def, film, what?"

"Well..."

Kyle started talking, his lips moving, words gushing out of him like water from a broken dam. Summer caught a few bits like "really cool," "special effects" and "Sundance Film Festival." But mostly she wasn't listening. She was thinking about Jack. And the more she thought about him, the angrier she got. He was really good last night and had given her a very happy ending. She had been struck by how handsome he still was when she first saw him in the booth at dinner. He was still lean, muscular, strong, and had a cool tattoo on his right forearm. She had even thought there was a remote possibility that they could rekindle their long extinguished flame. Perhaps have a long distance relationship.

And then he had lied to her face at dinner. And she suspected he had lied to her this morning on the doorstep outside her house. *It wasn't any meteorite that crashed out there.* Was it? If it was, why was he so cagey about it? But what the hell else could it be realistically? That's what she needed to know.

Kyle was finishing a thought, "...so if we can get this connection over at Lionsgate, I think we'll get some kind of distribution."

Summer nodded like she was tracking with him.

"Wow, that does sound pretty cool," she said. They fell silent and the sound of wet, sloshing tires on the road got louder.

"Hey, Kyle."

"Yeah?"

"I need you to do something for me."

The rains had dwindled as Jack drove south on the highway toward the spot they had been the day before. Linda had told him to keep driving another half-mile. He glanced down at the odometer, carefully watching the numbers count off tenths of a mile—3, 4, 5, 6—*Okay, pull over.* He eased off the highway and glided into the wet grass, then further off toward the forest wall and then beneath the edge of the trees. The car bounced, the old suspension grunting as it trundled onward. Jack glanced out the rearview mirror and saw that the highway was now eliminated from sight. He stopped the car and turned off the engine. Camouflaged. He was alone until something flashed in his rear-view mirror. Headlights. Linda's squad car hobbled next to him, rolling to a stop.

Jack climbed out quickly, and immediately noticed the sling cradling her right arm. *She should not be out here like this.*

"Hey," she said.

"Hey," Jack replied.

"Sorry about yesterday," she said. "I was in a lot of pain, and I was really short with you."

"It's okay," he said. "I understand. Are you okay?"

"Well, it's a fracture. Hurts like hell. It's going to take some time to heal up."

Jack nodded, but like a bloodhound turned his attention on the encircling forest. Sensing something out there.

"Jack, you want to fill me in here? What happened yesterday? You said something about seeing a picture of this thing?"

"Yeah, on Mars."

"Mars? The planet?"

"Yes. Someone at JPL contacted my Dad about Mars images that showed some kind of surface anomaly. I tracked their messages through email and found the images."

Linda glared at him. "And?"

"Something landed on Mars a few months ago with identical flight hardware to what we found out here...heat shield, aeroshell, parachute...and something else, something..."

He was at a loss. *How do you explain a thing like this?*

"Jack, please just tell me what you know," Linda said.

"It left tracks. Not like a rover with wheels. Different. It moved over the course of the two separate images that were taken by the Mars Reconnaissance Orbiter during several passes. It looked like...like an insect."

Linda frowned, contemplating what she just heard. She gently touched her gun, now holstered on her left side where she could reach it with her good arm. It was nerves.

"How big is this thing?"

"Not exactly sure," Jack said, "but it would have to fit inside the aeroshell we found. So I'm guessing five meters wide, three of four meters high."

Linda held on him, attempting to frame that up in her imagination.

"Fifteen feet wide, maybe twelve feet high. It's a big son of a bitch," Jack said.

"So is it mechanical, like a robot—or is it something else?"

"I don't know for sure," Jack said "But it's some kind of device. Maybe similar to a rover or a probe."

He darkened then, a quick glance off his right side, then back to her again. Making sure they were alone.

"There's something else," he said.

"What is it?"

Here we go.

"There's someone in the media—a reporter who I think is suspicious. She saw us getting out of the car yesterday and heading off into the woods together."

"Wait, Jack...who is it?"

"Summer Reyes."

Linda sneered.

"Yeah, I know her. She's not a reporter. She's a sensationalist, an opportunist, and a liar. She's perfect for the news business."

Jack averted his eyes. Linda deciphered it instantly.

"Wait...you talked to her, didn't you? What did you tell her exactly?"

"I didn't tell her anything, except that it was a meteorite out here and you asked me to come along and help find it. I told her it was consumed in the atmosphere and we didn't find anything."

"Okay, but why would she even talk to you in the first place?"

Jack shook his head, drowned by sheer incredulity at what he was about to tell her.

"We had dinner together last night."

Linda shifted on her feet, cocking her hips to one side. Had one of her arms not been bound in a sling, she'd have crossed them. Her eyes formed into straight razors.

"Really. What else did you do?"

Jack took a deep breath, steadying himself. In an odd way he felt as though he were about to spill this awful truth to his wife instead of an acquaintance he had known for merely a week.

"Summer was an old girlfriend. We had a very brief thing about ten years ago when I was visiting my parents."

Linda was unflinching, mannequin-like as he said it.

"You slept with her last night, didn't you," she said. "Ended up at her place? I knew something was wrong when you called so early and said you weren't at home!"

Jack pleaded, "I knew it was a mistake, I knew it was wrong! I just...I lost it yesterday at home. I was going through the boxes, I was seeing old pictures, I was breaking apart, I just wanted some normalcy and I thought maybe having dinner with a friend might help do that. But I had no idea what kind of a monster she had become in the last ten years and I knew I made a huge mistake. I'm truly sorry."

Linda looked away from him, disgusted. She glanced around aimlessly as though he didn't exist at all. She shook her head with no words capable of expressing what she wanted to say. Jack felt shame crawl on his shoulders. He had spent many a night with women in the past and never once felt this. This was different. Linda was different. What little chance Jack had of getting to know her better incinerated right in front of him, and he felt a sick weight in his stomach.

"Well, Jack—you really screwed the pooch, didn't you."

Great pun.

"Okay, we are done here. You go home and take care of your business. I'll call the sheriff and we'll begin a search and hope we find this thing, whatever it is, before Summer Reyes starts crawling through here with a camera crew."

Jack said, "I'm not going home until I find it myself."

Linda pivoted sharply on him.

"Not an option."

"I've seen this thing. I know what it looks like and I am the best person to make an assessment of what we are actually dealing with."

"I don't care, Jack! This is over! *There is no we, no us!* I cannot allow you to do this."

"Well," he said, "I'm doing this. You can come with me if you like, or I can do it alone. But I am not going to let Summer Reyes slither in here and blow this story into whatever sick, twisted tale she decides is best for her career."

Linda took a step toward him, and Jack instinctively backed up. She lowered her voice, carefully enunciating every syllable.

"Jack, as a deputy sheriff of this county, I am telling you to clear out of here and go home. Otherwise, I'll arrest you for impeding with a police investigation."

"Bullshit," Jack said.

Linda reached for her cuffs at the back of her belt.

"I'll outrun you, especially with that shoulder of yours," Jack said, taking another few steps back from her. He was ready to spring, and Linda knew if he took off running, she'd lose him. She also knew she had to contain this situation right then and there.

"You run, and I'll draw my weapon. I am not playing games, here, Jack!"

"Then you'll have to shoot an unarmed civilian in the back. You do what you have to do. But I'm going to find this thing and I'm going to find out what it's doing here. Because I don't think this is random. *This device is here for a reason.* And we had better know why."

They sized each other up, Linda x-raying Jack for a tell, Jack analyzing her body language. She concluded he wasn't about to back down. She also concluded that shooting him in the back was not such a great idea, either. Because even though the son of a bitch slept with Summer Reyes, he was the one person that could shed light on all of this insanity. And, dammit...she really liked him.

Linda said, "You listen to me...we'll go together right now, but you are still under my watch. If I feel there's a threat, or something's wrong, you do as I say. No arguing, no discussion. Got it?"

Jack nodded. "Got it," he said.

"Then let's get moving and find our visitor," she said. And they crept off into the woods that were gently rolling from a southwestern wind that was starting to push through the county.

Summer had wrapped up her piece at the convention center quickly. She had Kyle frame her up in camera with construction crews in the background of the shot, busily finishing up their work, clearing out the last of the debris and heavy equipment from the site. Donning a paltry smile, Summer gave everyone watching live a sense of excitement that the expansion would somehow bring in new events and new revenue to the city. Some of those new events, she added, might be a comic convention on par with the infamous San Diego Comic Con, an expanded auto show that normally came through town once a year and a clean energy trade show that was starting to make the rounds.

When Summer finished her report, she ditched the magic and told Kyle to chop-chop with breaking down the camera, tripod, and lights so they could get the hell out of there and make it back to Merriweather. Kyle grunted and moaned like he usually did when she rode him, but he was quick and got everything stowed back in the van.

Summer drove because Kyle was dull and still having a hard time staying awake. No way in hell was she giving him the wheel, even though she desperately wanted not to drive the van in this weather. The rains had stopped, but the roads were still like polished stone. One wrong pull on the steering wheel, or a hasty tap on the brake, and they'd be road kill.

Kyle yawned loudly and Summer rolled her eyes. God, this guy was annoying the shit out of her today, even more than usual.

"So, what is it you want me to do exactly? I forgot."

She wanted to punch him in the face. Badly.

"I want you to grab your small, portable camera from home, find someone and follow them."

"Why?"

"Because I think this person is covering something up and it might be a very big story."

Kyle groaned again and slumped in his seat like a kid who just got told they'd have to wait a little while longer before they got ice cream while Mom ran errands. Dear God, *was that what she was becoming—Kyle's mommy?* The very thought was revolting.

"Well, what if it's not a big story?"

"Then it's not, Kyle. Just do this, okay?"

"Yeah, but I still have to edit that piece for tonight."

"I'll do the editing. You go do this thing for me and then get your ass back to the station by six."

"Okay, fine. But you still haven't told me who I'm following and where to find them," Kyle snorted.

"The guy in the video, Kyle. Remember? He's the one who got out of the deputy sheriff's car? That guy."

Kyle perked up.

"Oh yeah, I knew when you flipped out over that shot there was something going on."

"I didn't flip out. You've never seen me flip out," she said.

"Oh I've seen you go bat-shit crazy, Summer! Remember that time during the fashion show thing in Indy with the chick from Top Model, you were..."

Summer threw him a glare, a *shut the hell up or I will murder you* sort of glare. Kyle backpedaled carefully into his usual conciliatory mode.

"So, um...where do I find this guy...what's his name?"

Summer said, "His name is Jack McAllister."

"Any idea where he might be?"

"Highway south, near the scene of the accident yesterday. I suggest you get your hiking shoes and an umbrella. He's probably in the woods in that area looking for something."

Kyle was pissed. A hike? In this weather? Really? For what? This was total bullshit. Summer was asking him to crawl up the ass of a dead rhinoceros here. So Kyle decided to tell her what she wanted to hear, then go home and play Xbox until 5:30, after which he could catch dinner at Steak N' Shake and then saunter into the station with nothing to report at 6:00. Yep, it was a good plan, he thought.

"And, Kyle...don't go home and play Xbox and try and put one over on me. I'll know if you do," she snapped.

Kyle snorted. "Wasn't planning on it, Summer."

"Yes, you were," she said.

Kyle suddenly realized that the real power Summer wielded over him was that she knew him too well. *Dammit!* Fine, he reasoned—he would go ahead and do this. He'd drive out to the site and have a look around for maybe a half an hour...but that was it. After that he would go home and play some Box. Summer could just suck it from there.

"Bring me footage, even if it seems like nothing," Summer said.

Kyle nodded and for the rest of the drive back to Merriweather, neither one of them said anything.

CHAPTER 27

JACK AND LINDA HAD BEEN hiking for twenty minutes beneath a prickly hush, bearing back toward the ill-fated camp where Dan and Monica had encountered it. Neither of them had spoken once, or so much as groaned or sighed. But while the muteness had created background tension in the air, it also gave Jack time to think and come up with some kind of plan once they found their mysterious visitor.

Based on the evidence they had, this device was incredibly powerful. It was also methodical. It appeared to be collecting samples from the ground, the trees and the leaves. *Yes, they must be samples,* Jack thought—*environmental samples, likely.* Why else would it gather material from the soil and the trees? And then there were those little holes in the foliage, the tiny dimples in the wood. Strange. Perhaps those were unrelated to the device. And since Jack was not familiar with this area, it was entirely possible that some local insect had been responsible.

But getting back to what they knew, and what Jack saw in the Mars images, begged the question: what were they to do if—more likely, when—they encountered this thing? Jack decided they would have to approach and observe by stealth. They would have to be invisible. Because if this thing was keen to their presence, and if it were hostile, Jack figured they would be in very deep shit.

Linda also had time to think while they ventured on. She was thinking about Jack and his tryst with Summer. She just could not believe it! He seemed so much smarter and classier than that! *God, he actually slept with her!* The thought alone was revolting on a number of levels. First of all, she was an old fling, which was an automatic red flag for any self-respecting man. Additionally, she was a super-narcissist who had no idea what it was like to be a human being and have some semblance of empathy for people other than herself. She was a monster and possessed a very dangerous kind of anger that if unleashed through her chosen profession, could lead to a panic in the town.

Most of all, Linda could not deny that she, on some level, felt betrayed by Jack. There was the obvious facet on the professional level, but dammit—*she really liked him*. He was extremely handsome, very bright, and deeply fascinating. Linda had dated a few guys after her very brief and failed marriage, and on the 'date-scale,' none of them made it to the halfway mark. There was something different about Jack, something wonderful. But then Summer Reyes happened, and all the wonderfulness seemed to implode into a million small, smoldering pieces of hot ash.

Linda was cut off mid-thought as she almost bumped into Jack who had stopped walking. He was intense, focused, panning the forest carefully with unblinking eyes.

Linda said, "What is it?"

Jack indicated she should be still a moment.

Jack said, "Listen."

They both stood motionless until the sounds of the forest were all that existed. Jack actually held his breath to subtract even the slightest noise from the air in order to isolate what he was hearing somewhere close to them.

Jack whispered, "Do you hear that?"

Linda wasn't sure, and thought perhaps she might be hearing a humming sound. But it was faint, ebbing in and out of range.

Linda replied quietly, "I think so. Not sure what that is."

Jack closed his eyes, listening even more fiercely. It was louder now, growing in volume and pitch, evolving from a strange susurration, escalating into a vibration in the air above them; a thrumming that sounded like a swarm. Like bees.

Shit! Had they inadvertently disturbed a beehive? Jack hadn't seen one and he hadn't heard anything that would tip him off to the presence of a large hive during their hike the last two miles. They both looked frantically about—left, right, up. Circling.

The air darkened and a black mist settled over them. No, not a mist, for it moved organically, undulating as loose fabric would in a strong breeze back and forth. A swarm. A very large swarm.

They both dropped low in the undergrowth, balling up, heads tucked down in anticipation of a million bees primed to blanket them and sting a million times. Jack's skin crawled with terror and Linda thought, *run in a straight line, run in a straight line away from the swarm!*

Oddly then, none of that happened. As intense moments passed, Jack recognized that the sound they were making—the humming—was not the same as bees or any other insect. The pitch was too high and it oscillated, producing variations creating whole note changes that glissaded up and down. A second tone grew from the first, creating an extraordinary harmonic pitch...like nothing they'd ever heard before.

Jack stole a hasty glance upward toward the swarm, now able to discern the tiny, individual parts of it. They were smaller than bees, maybe the size of common ants, maybe even smaller. And they didn't fly in a bobbing to-and-fro motion the way a bee or other common insect might. They hovered in what appeared to be some kind of formation. It was organized and under complete control. And that formation began to compress, tightening in the air until, to Jack's astonishment, it became a sphere...*a perfect sphere*, the size of a soccer ball, floating in the air some six meters above their heads.

"Look," Jack whispered.

Linda was hesitant, unable to shift even the slightest bit. She had just become aware that she was actually holding her breath.

Exhale.

Able now to pull up the stakes of anxiety, she wanted to see it for herself. The sphere, which hung motionless in the open air above them, was a perfect amalgam of the tiny individual bits. There must have been tens of thousands. No. More than that. Hundreds of thousands. They were not bees, flies, or bugs or any kind, and as a communal form they exhibited a nacreous quality. Perhaps even stranger were tiny bits of illumination that pulsed rhythmically across the surface of their sum, like tiny LED lights.

"Jack, what is this? What is it doing?" Linda cautiously breathed.

"I don't know, but...I think it's starting to move."

And it was. Slowly at first, then gradually faster, moving steadily away from them. Jack marveled that the globe held its form perfectly, despite the fact that it was made up of so many infinitesimal parts, which he suspected were sentient creatures of some kind. The orb floated away, moving effortlessly and in perfect contour. It was now fifty yards off from them, still moving, still a flawless globe. Feeling somewhat reprieved from imminent danger, Jack and Linda climbed from their lurking spot to get a better view of exactly where it was heading.

"Let's follow it," Jack said.

Linda hesitated, planted where she was.

"You think we should?"

"Yes, I do."

Linda tracked the sphere. It was heading toward a dense patch of braided forest growth. They were safe at the moment. No reason not to go a little further. She stepped out in front of him and began trailing very slowly after it.

"Follow me," she said evenly.

Jack fell in behind her and they deftly tailed the alien sphere that slowed measurably as it approached the taught, calloused screen. It stopped suddenly. Holding. Soundless. It shivered, palpitated, a pulse of light bleeding over its shell. The humming sound grew louder into a low, focused tone. All at once the tightly formed sphere disassembled, becoming a vaporous shroud in the air, once again a swarm of tiny dark things.

"What are we dealing with here?" Linda asked muted, cautious.

The swarm gushed forward into the ochre barrier of woodland growth, evaporating from site like an apparition. The sound of it drowned instantly, and all that was left was the song of nature—the gentle strokes of wind upon white oaks, the crisp sound of leaves hitting the undergrowth as they tumbled listlessly from the sky, the arias of crooning birds.

They looked at each other, the prosperity of their hunt fading. Now what?

Linda whispered, "I think we should..."

Abruptly, the earth shivered, the ground coming alive beneath tons of shifting alien weight. The air turned shrill with the sound of mechanical parts exploding to life. A massive silhouette lifted from the obstruction of vines and creepers, wreathed in dust and shade. Jack and Linda stood paralyzed, numb, as the device pushed into view on obscene, segmented legs wed of metal and cryptic, nonterrestrial materials. It crawled like a spider, dwarfing them beneath its shadow that spanned the width of a full-size swimming pool.

Dear Jesus, Jack thought, *we're going to die.*

CHAPTER 28

K YLE TROMPED THROUGH THE FRONT door of his one-bedroom house, soaking wet from the rain, hungry and pissed off. Mostly pissed off. He wiped his shoes on the little carpet there by the entrance then slammed the door shut behind him, locking it. Alone. Finally. He headed for the kitchen where he would grab something to eat. He pulled open the fridge that was immodestly bare save for the leftover Panda Express he'd had the night before. He always ordered double portions for that very reason. Inevitably he would need to eat, but find himself either too busy or just too lazy to actually cook something. It was so much easier to grab food on the way home, order twice as much, and then have it for the next day.

To his relief there were three beers left in the pocket of the fridge door. *Score*, he thought. He pulled one free, found the opener on the countertop and snapped the top off. He tipped the longneck to his lips and gulped half the bottle, the cold rocketing down his pipe, sending a shiver through him. It felt good, despite the fact he was wet and a little cold from the rains.

He quickly threw the Panda Express container into the microwave, ignoring all the radiation baked bits and chunks from hundreds of other meals fused to every surface of the little oven. Kyle figured if push came to shove, and it got to be too disgusting, he'd just go by another microwave at Target. Hell, they were like forty or fifty bucks, right? Yeah.

He finished heating the food, and then grabbed a plastic fork from a nearby drawer. He snatched the beer between his fingers and hustled everything to the living room where he sat in front of the big screen TV. He flicked it on for no other reason than to have some background noise and started eating. He glanced down at his Xbox 360 nested carefully beneath the screen.

Summer was such a bitch! And why in the hell did he let her treat him like a turd? Because...he wanted her. Badly. She was hotter-than-hot. Nuclear—off the charts. She was the ultimate fantasy, a woman who somehow materialized out of the pages of FHM, or maybe Playboy. And he was working with her—*for her*—at the TV station. At the beginning she seemed a little controlling, but nothing that Kyle wasn't willing to put up with since occasionally she would stare at him in a way that made him think there was a possibility between them...however remote. But after time, Kyle resigned to the fact that nothing in a million years was going to happen.

He finished off his food and then the beer. Slumped in his chair, staring zombie-like at the TV. Nothing on. Kyle glanced at the time. 11:50 a.m. He thought it through—*grab the camera, take a drive, shoot maybe fifteen minutes of nothing in the forest and then come back and play Xbox for a couple hours.* Then he could waltz into the station with something. Good plan.

He glided into the bedroom to grab his camera. He grunted once he realized his Final Cut Pro editing station with dual monitors had been left on, and that the latest cut of his hit film project was still open. He reached down for the mouse and made sure to save the project before exiting the program. Next he wormed his way around the bed toward the closet. With his big editing desk in here, there was little room for anything else besides the bed, which currently wore a snarl of dirty, cheap sheets and a comforter with holes in it. Yeah, it was a mess, but so what. It allowed him to edit late into the night, early into the next morning, until all he had to do was roll off the chair, onto his bed and fall asleep. It was efficient.

He slid open the closet door and found the camera bag. *Better check the battery*, he thought. He dropped the bag on the end of the bed and unzipped it. He pulled out his camera, a Panasonic HVX-200A. Now considered old school, the camera shot HD footage on P2 media cards. But it also had a Mini-DV tape drive. Kyle rarely shot tape anymore, but sometimes that softer, standard definition look was what he wanted. Kyle was an artist.

Despite its age, the thing was a workhorse, and in some ways, Kyle considered it his "lucky" camera. Things just seemed to go right when he shot with the trusty HVX. His zombie film was a breeze to shoot, his setup time effortless.

Quickly he checked the battery, which was at full charge. Outstanding! Then he checked the P2 cards and found them empty. Great, plenty of space to record! He also noticed a MiniDV tape still in the drive, unlabeled. It was probably a blank from the last shoot which was...he couldn't remember. Oh well, it didn't matter.

He had to get going so he could try and find this guy—what the hell was his name? Jack something? *The guy in the video.* Summer was interested in him for some reason.

He put the camera carefully back into the case and shouldered it, checking his pockets for car keys and his phone. *Ready to rock and roll,* he thought. A little rock and roll on the camera, and then straight back home for some Xbox and maybe another beer. After that he'd bang down a burger at Steak 'N Shake and then drift into the station with his footage. And hope that Summer didn't blow another rod when he showed her what was most likely going to be a bunch of useless, boring nature footage.

CHAPTER 29

NEITHER JACK NOR LINDA SO much as moved, breathed, or blinked as the machine decamped from its place of cover, torturing the ground beneath its prodigious weight with every step. In the wide open where they could see it clearly, it resolved an unthinkable leviathan, an enormous blend of machine and living, breathing matter. Biomechanical. Jack understood now what he had seen in the MRO Mars images from JPL, the strange insectile profile and the tracks in the Martian soil. It all made sense.

The six mastodon-sized legs were expertly, organically joined to a hexagonal body. As it moved, and the legs compensated for transgressions of the wild terrain, the body remained at an even tilt. Raised above the platform was a mast, a head, joined to the body by a stem, or neck. The head was an elongated, mostly featureless thing, hooded beneath armored skin that was blunt-edged and fanned at the back. All the more its appearance rung somehow profane—a nightmarish hybrid of insect and elephant. The head turned slowly on an azimuth toward what Jack guessed to be targets or points of interest. It had not seen them, apparently, and it pitched south, each step on the ground weighted like a pile driver.

Without any conscious thought involved, Linda felt for her gun at her left side, fingers shaking from the cortisol that had invaded her bloodstream. She simply could not believe what she was seeing. It was absurd, the kind of thing someone like Jack would dream up for one of his books—except it was real. The natural world she could see, touch, taste and smell evaporated in front of her. What was left, and what she was staring directly into, was a world torn open by something preternatural. She fumbled for her gun, her fingers powerless to free it from her belt. She took in a sharp breath, and it was that gasp that alerted Jack to what she was about to do.

He very gently, carefully drew her gaze toward himself. He shook his head cautiously, gesturing with his hands for her not to unholster her weapon.

"Wait. Don't," he hissed in a low, acute tone. "It hasn't seen us and it's moving away. Let's take it easy."

"Fuck easy," Linda said, still trying to free her weapon.

"Linda, please, just listen, it's okay. It's okay, it hasn't seen us."

From deep down inside, Linda drew on her training from those years back at the academy. She took long, deep breaths, and wrestled the anxiety to the mat, holding it there, pinning it. Her hand steadied, the adrenaline-induced tremors fading. Slowly. Slowly. Calm now.

Jack felt his own accelerated pulse beginning to ease. He had a momentary vision of her drawing the gun, pumping hard on the trigger, firing wild and senseless shots, alerting the enormous alien device to their presence, and then the two of them running as it charged after them like a furious locomotive, destroying the world behind them, overtaking them and killing them in the most horrible way.

"Better?"

"Yeah."

"Okay."

The device had moved on another ten meters and then stopped as it approached a large boulder, lodged snugly against an old tree, half covered in a shawl of forest ivy. It paused and did nothing, unmoving as though suddenly dead.

Linda said, "It stopped."

Jack said, "I think maybe it's looking for—"

A hum grew within the body and the entire platform lifted on those powerful legs. A dark limb sprouted repulsively from the underbelly. Vertebrae-like, it slithered from a concealed opening, bending and turning, carefully reaching, positioning itself over the flat face of the large stone. It reminded Jack of an elephant trunk. Not just in the length and size of it, but the way it hovered and probed its surroundings. It moved with deliberacy. And there was something on the end of it, another piece of metallic hardware that began to spin. It was hard to make out from where they stood, but they could hear the motion of it. Finally, after coming to a complete and perfect stop, the limb made contact with the face of the rock, and began...

"Drilling," Jack said, in a low voice.

"You sure?"

"Yeah, I think so. It's using some kind of tool on the rock. See?"

After several more moments of watching it, this seemed to be the case.

"It could be a drill, maybe some kind of abrasion tool."

"But what for?" she asked.

"For getting samples."

A high-pitched wail stung the air as the end of the limb pressed slowly into the rock, the sound dulling as it went deeper, then growing sharp again as the end of it cautiously withdrew. It eased away from the face of the rock, where now they could discern a spherical depression in the face of the stone. The limb swung carefully back beneath the body of the device, and glided soundlessly inside. An arcane mechanical murmur came from inside the body and then stopped. All was stillness.

Jack began to wonder—had this robot thing not detected or noticed them? *Or had it ignored them.*

"Now what?" Linda said.

Jack had a theory, and thought about how exactly he was going to try and explain it. And more importantly, how he was going to convince Linda that what he was about to do was necessary. As if picking up on this, she glared at him.

"What's the plan, Jack?"

He coagulated his decision because it was the only way to know.

"Trust me," he said, which Linda translated as, *I'm about to do something really stupid and I hope you don't mind.*

Jack crouched low and grabbed a stone that fit snugly in his palm. Before Linda could issue a syllable of protest, he threw the rock toward the robotic monster. It clacked loudly against the tree nearest the thing, bounced, and fell in the undergrowth beneath it.

"Are you insane?!" Linda hissed at him.

"Watch, just watch!"

There was absolutely no response from the machine.

"I don't like this," Linda said sharply.

Jack grabbed another stone.

"Jack—no!"

He threw again, this one hitting even closer than before, the sound a sharp, clear knock. Linda held her breath, her fingers going back toward her gun. Her breath shortened, perspiration forming on her forehead.

"Are you trying to get us both killed?"

"No."

The machine remained still and silent. There was no activity whatsoever. It was not paying attention to them…it *was doing something else.*

"I think," Jack hesitated, "I think this is a scout."

"A what?"

"A scout; a robotic geologist."

She was moderately incensed.

"How could you possibly know that? How could anyone know that?"

"I don't know absolutely, but it's what we would do exploring another planet. And it makes sense."

"Exploring another planet? Then…this thing really is from somewhere else."

"Alien," Jack said. "Yeah. Look at it. Does it look like anything we would build?"

And there it was in the simplest terms possible. No more ambiguity. A fact. An otherworldly device—a scout—had landed here and was doing some sort of environmental sampling.

CLING! Before Linda even realized it had happened, Jack had thrown a third stone. It had taken an oblique course, directly toward the body of the scout where it struck dead on. This time, Jack's heart froze, dropping a beat in panic. He hadn't actually aimed directly for it.

"Shit, Jack, stop!"

And still there was nothing. Not a goddamn thing from the robotic hulk. It rested. Silent like some derelict piece of heavy machinery.

"There's one last thing I need to do," Jack said.

"What?" Linda asked, annoyed. No, she was beyond annoyed. She was scared out of her mind.

Jack said, "I'm going to walk in front of it."

She scoffed.

"No way in hell you're doing that." She straightened herself, asserting a stronger stance.

"Yeah, I am," he said. "If something goes wrong, you do what you need to do, but otherwise...I expect to be back here in just a minute."

And without hesitation, he began walking toward the machine that lingered in some form of hibernation. Had Linda's shoulder not been injured, she would have gone after him to try and persuade him not to do this. If that didn't work, she'd have tried to subdue him, though based on his size and athletic frame he would probably not have gone down—not by her alone. But all of that disintegrated as Jack, now some twenty yards away from her, carefully approached the back end of the inactive scout. All she could do was watch.

As Jack got closer, the scout grew larger, smothering him beneath its size. As he closed on it, he got a much better look at the build of the legs. They were like pistons, robotic with complex hinges, joints and...something else. Intertwined with obvious metallic parts was something that looked softer and more organic, like muscle. These organic parts were married perfectly with nonorganic couplings and small tubes that raced all up and down them, all connected with the robotic parts in complete harmony. *Relays? Actuators maybe,* Jack thought.

He crept even closer and witnessed, in a state of quiet wonder, the organic parts of the mechanism pulsing—expanding and contracting. Breathing. Jack found himself buoyed in awe, sheer and total awe of this alien device that rested just a meter in front of him.

The distance it must have traveled to get here! The world on which it was built—what was that like?

He desperately wanted to take a few more short steps, reach out and touch it. And although caution mixed with anxiety pleaded for him not to continue, his distress rapidly abated in the light of this otherworldly encounter. He took those two short steps, reached out his hand, fingers extended, and touched the scout from another world.

CHAPTER 30

KYLE SLOWED HIS CAR WHEN he passed the spot he remembered from the day before. As he drifted toward the shoulder he saw absolutely nothing out here. No cars, no people—*nothing*.

It figures, he thought, fuming, acidic. This was a joke, a red herring. There was no reason for him to be out here with his own, personal camera.

Summer hates me!

Okay. Fine. He'd pull the car over and stop. He'd take a very short walk and shoot seven or eight minutes of footage—max. And after he acquired what was certainly going to be nothing more than some shaky handheld footage of wet forest foliage, he'd go back home and...

Something hit his eye, a subtle glint off the windshield of a motionless car snug in the overgrowth of the forest. Kyle hit the brakes hard, pulled deep along the broad shoulder and sank into the edge of the woods, instantly veiled from sight. He was twenty yards beyond where the other two cars were nested. He hit something and felt the front of the car buck upward and then drop with a sickening thud, the grunt of old, arthritic shocks following. Kyle groaned—just his luck—then turned off the engine.

He delicately exited his car. He picked up his camera and powered it on. As quietly as he could, he crept back toward the two vehicles, now getting a good look at them. One of them was a sheriff's cruiser, the other a dated maroon mercury. Kyle froze and listened closely for voices, damp footfalls, anything that might suggest someone was nearby. After a full minute there was nothing but the quiet spiel of raindrops randomly spotting through the forest canopy. He was alone.

Kyle lined up his first shot of the two vehicles in a dramatic sort of way, low angle through branches with dull throbbing backlight hitting the edges of the cars, creating a soft glow around them. *Kick ass*, he thought. And then another thought lodged in his mind. Since he was out here in the wild, he could get some footage for his horror film. Yeah! Some second-unit shots—pickups, detail shots—that might work well in the flashback sequence at the end of act one. Making lemonade out of lemons. This might not be so bad after all.

He noted the available record time on his P2 cards. Just over an hour of space. That should be plenty. Because all he might really find out here were a couple of people walking through the forest doing a whole lot of nothing. He drifted around the two cars and found multiple footprints, imprinted clearly in the soggy dirt. They bread-crumbed ahead, southwest, and then vanished beneath the leafy floor of the forest. Kyle began a careful hike, filming as he walked, now wondering if he could use this footage in a brand new film...maybe one of those "found footage" films. He was sure he could craft some kind of story out of this.

With every step Kyle became more and more confident that this was going to pay off for him in a big, big way.

Clifford Hawkins had woken up in the middle of the night with damp, clammy skin, his stomach turning and his pulse racing. The nausea was overpowering and he leapt from his side of the bed, sprang to the bathroom, and had just made it to his knees in front of the toilet as all of the contents of his stomach erupted out of him with all the ferocity of a cinder cone volcano. Mercifully none of it escaped the toilet bowl. As he knelt panting, grunting, he thought back to the leftovers he'd decided to have just six hours earlier. The chicken marinara had tasted funny.

Because it had been in the fridge for almost a week, you idiot, he thought. *Why the hell did you eat it?* Because his wife had been visiting her sister on the other side of town and he was just too damn lazy to cook something, or go pick something up. Never again, he thought, *never again.*

He had vomited the rest a few hours later and then finally managed to go back to sleep. He hadn't woken until his phone rang at around 11:00 a.m. It was Mitch calling from the office. As was his usual way of starting a conversation with some obnoxious or inane question, this time he led with a paranoiac drone in his voice.

"Sheriff, where are you? How come you didn't come in this morning?"

"Mitch, I got food poisoning last night and I'm still very sick. I'm not planning on coming in today."

"Then where is Linda?" Mitch asked.

Hawkins had to think a moment because his mind was still in a post-vomit haze. She had fallen in the woods on their escape from the storm yesterday. She had gone to the ER and afterward had called to inform him that it was a fracture, but she planned on being at her desk in the morning. Maybe she changed her mind.

"Mitch, she had an injury yesterday, remember? She went to the ER. I don't think she's coming in today, either."

Hawkins began again, his tone short and truculent.

"What's the emergency this time, Mitch?"

Mitch fumbled, "I called my brother-in-law in the Air Force to ask him more about their parachute systems."

"And?"

"From what he told me—and I did some pokin' around online about it—I'm not sure what we found was, um...Air Force."

"Did you tell him about what we found?"

Mitch hesitated. "No, no. I just told him I was curious, that's all. Sheriff, what are we going to do if it is some kind of spaceship out there?"

"Mitch, don't worry about it. Just get the usual business at the office taken care of and I'll be in later."

Hawkins quickly ended the call then turned his ringer off. He carefully lay back down in bed and closed his eyes. What the hell were they going to do about it, the spacecraft, or whatever it was? Hawkins felt his intestines clench, a gurgling fluid sound racing through his lower abdomen. It was too much to think about. The only thing he could comprehend right now was getting back to the toilet in time for the next and hopefully final round of this damn thing.

CHAPTER 31

J ACK, YOU DUMB SON OF *a bitch, you've killed us both!* The thought rang loud in Linda's head as she watched him touch the leg of the mechanized monster from an alien world. Had she any power to vocalize that thought, it would have come out as a cold, brassy judgment. But she had nothing to move those words into the air. She was anesthetized, and all she could do was watch, and pray.

As Jack held contact with the machine, it remained strangely dormant. Quickly he forced himself to put awe and wonder aside and examine this scout more closely and carefully, because something in him was certain he would not get this close to it again. This was his only chance for an examination.

All of the legs had the same biomechanical architecture and were capable of completely independent motion, as Jack had just witnessed during its crawl to this spot. He peeked beneath the belly of it where the serpentine limb with the abrasion tool had sprouted. The entire bottom had a gradual convex shape that reminded Jack of an abdomen.

There were twelve rounded conical parts that projected subtly from the surface. *Descent engines perhaps?*

Arranged around those parts were smaller, door-like features that rimmed the body, surrounded by metal slats. *Or vents?* Impossible to tell what their purpose was exactly.

Off center, Jack noticed a dark spherical thing that was nested into the body and slightly protruded. He found himself focused on it. And then, like the missing piece in the puzzle, something fell into place. The dark sphere looked solid, but it had a familiar sheen to it. And it was then that an array of small LED lights awoke on its surface, blooming in sequence counterclockwise over the entire thing. And then it fell into darkness.

The sphere, Jack thought. It was the amalgam of the swarm docked with the scout. They were part of it, able to disassemble into hundreds of thousands of tiny parts and then come back together as a whole.

Micro scouts. My God—if Dad could have seen this thing! If only he could have seen this!

Jack heard his name whispered from somewhere behind him. It was Linda. She had crept closer toward him.

"Jack, please...come back."

But he couldn't. Not yet. He was still touching it, in direct contact with it. Studying it. He glanced upward to the top of the deck, which was so high off the ground he could barely see it. But with the view he could afford, he made out more instruments, tubular arrays racing the circumference of the device. There was a dishlike attachment near the end of it that was surrounded by more arcane instruments that budded from the deck, all connected—all there for a reason.

Jack noticed more slots along the side of the scout, sealed shut. They too were there for a reason.

"Jack, please..." Linda's voice was pleading, urgent.

Finally he looked toward the mast. In an eerie way, from his low angle, it resembled an elongated skull, hanging umbrella-like over the deck. Similar to the build of the legs, and beneath the metallic parts, was organic matter that moved with some kind of a pulse. This thing was alive, but for some reason, inactive. Until finally, that head turned, pivoting slowly on its azimuth toward Jack.

It was looking directly at him now. Recessed beneath that large hooded cover was a terrible, dark countenance from a planet hundreds of billions of miles away. It was a face Jack would see again in the murky landscape of many all-too-real nightmares. Of machine and living tissue, it bore an expression cold and remote as the void of space in which it had traveled to get here. A biomechanical creature of singular intent...with no promise of what that intent was. There were glassy lenses—*or were they eyes*—set deeply in that stygian visage. They blinked, glistening, and regarded Jack as a lab technician might regard an old, long dead specimen in a Petri dish. Jack's skin crept, an injection of cold shock erupting down his spine, paralyzing him so he could not move or look away.

A focused beam of blue light fanned suddenly across Jack's face, sweeping over his features back and forth. Startled, he jumped backward, and noticed that his handprint was somehow visible on the body of the scout where he had touched it. And incredibly, it began to dissolve slowly, as if...as if the machine were ingesting it.

The beast suddenly moved, the sound of mechanized power roaring to life, those big legs adroitly stepping in sequence, bringing the body around at an angle, now facing Jack squarely, smothering him beneath its terrible shadow.

The sampling limb sprung upward from the bottom of the scout, uncoiling, arching itself upward like an angry anaconda right in front of him. Rings of razor sharp blades began to turn in sequence achieving power saw speeds. The abrasion tool hovered inches from his face. And just as Jack was certain it was going to eat right through his skull...the scout took four large steps backward, pivoted, and started away from him. It stomped another twenty yards south, then planted the whirring tool firmly into the base of a red maple where it began to drill a new sample.

Jack remained cemented in his spot and only then did he notice Linda just ten feet away, her gun drawn, hammer flat back, finger hugging the trigger, pointed at the empty space where the scout had just been moments before. They looked at each other in dumb disbelief. It was another full ten seconds before Linda lowered the gun and gently eased the hammer back into the stock, thumbing on her safety.

"Jesus, Jack," she wheezed.

"Yeah," he said.

Jack commandeered himself and was able to move again, urging Linda to follow him to a covered spot not far away. They could observe safely from there. They hurried to it and crouched low, noticing the scout drawing its sample from the tree, the acquisition limb rolling back under the deck where it slithered away into the body. The entire machine fell silent again, the life seemingly going out of it.

"I can't believe you just did that, Jack. You risked your life for nothing," she quipped.

"You're wrong," he said. "I got a very good look at it up close. I saw instruments, and what I believe were antennas. And the sphere we saw earlier was docked in the underbelly of it. The swarm we saw; I think those are micro scouts. Tiny individual machines that spread out and gather samples from a wide area. They collect back into a larger whole and dock with the scout where I'm guessing it ingests the data, the samples, and analyzes all of it."

"So this is a machine?" Linda asked.

"Yes and no," said Jack. "I saw what looked like organic tissue interconnected with mechanical parts. I think this thing is biomechanical—a living, breathing machine."

"So what in the hell is it doing here? And why didn't it just kill you?"

"I'm not quite sure how to take that," Jack said, half amused by the remark. She instantly realized what it must have sounded like.

"Sorry that came out wrong, I didn't mean to say that it should have—"

She stopped, corralled her thoughts and began again.

"What I mean is, it seemed deliberately uninterested in you. It didn't see you as a threat or an interesting specimen."

Jack chuckled. "That's a first. I've never been called a specimen before."

Linda grinned, then glanced back out toward the scout that was eerily inanimate. A tide of unease hit her all at once as Jack spoke, his voice hollow and haunted.

"There's a face in there, recessed under the hood of the mast. I looked right into it—right into its eyes."

Her neck bristled.

"It was empty, emotionless. But seeing it...somehow...I understood. It's not here for us. It doesn't care about us. That's what really scares me."

They heard a distinct snapping sound followed by a faint disturbance of leaves. And then a voice came from behind them. Low and trembling.

"What in the hell is that?!"

Jack and Linda spun quickly, now catching Kyle, half-crouched just fifteen yards away, pointing his camera toward the scout, the small red tally light blinking as it recorded everything.

Summer was hunched over the keyboard in Kyle's edit bay, organizing her shots in the Final Cut Pro bin for what was going to become her piece on the Indy Convention Center from earlier that morning. She began scrubbing the b-roll Kyle had shot before they piled in the van and started back toward Merriweather. She found the footage to be adequate. Not great. Not even very good.

He was slipping, she thought. His heart wasn't in it anymore, she could tell. He was becoming more and more distant and apathetic toward the work. He simply wasn't trying hard anymore to impress her. She knew it, and she knew all along what he really wanted and why he put up with all the shit she put him through. *Kyle wanted her.*

A small cube of ice tossed into an active shield volcano had a better chance of survival than Kyle had a chance of touching her body let alone having sex with her.

"Where's Kyle?" Walter droned from the doorway. Summer prickled and felt her blood pressure leap several notches. Without stopping what she was doing or looking at him, she said, "He's getting some b-roll footage for me, Walter. He'll be back later this afternoon."

"What's the b-roll for?" he asked brusquely.

What does it matter, you old fart? Go back to your damn office and leave me the hell alone! It's what Summer thought. And for a moment, she wondered if she had said it out loud. Mercifully, she hadn't.

"Follow up story on the highway incident from the other day. We can review it later if you like. I'm working on the copy for this afternoon."

Walter hesitated, and then finally said, "Okay." Without another word, he left her alone and walked off down the hallway.

Wow, she thought, tell him what he wants to hear and he evaporates. *Wish I had tried that years ago.* Oh well, back to business.

Summer kept foraging through her footage, and all the while her thoughts drifted toward Jack. What was he hiding? Why was he lying to her? And then it struck her like a ball peen hammer between the eyes. She was hurt— really hurt by what he had done. Summer would never allow herself to be hurt by anyone, especially a guy. But this was different. *Jack was different.* She finally had to admit to herself that she had strong feelings for him. Had them all along, even after ten years.

Get a grip and focus! That's when her thoughts shifted back to Kyle, and she wondered what kind of useful footage he would be bringing her later.

Dammit, she thought, *it had better be good footage...or else.*

CHAPTER 32

THEY ALL GAPED AT EACH other, dumbstruck from the shock, as the reality of the scenario grew vexatiously clear. Kyle was gawking saucer-eyed at the scout, while Jack and Linda glared incredulously at him. The scout was dead still and the air grew rich with the sound of insects and the panting of pre-storm winds. The sky was going marble grey.

"What is that thing?" Kyle asked, his voice amped with nerves.

"Who are you?" Linda asked pointedly.

Kyle kept the camera rolling, sweeping his shot from the scout to Jack and Linda where he took special note of Linda's uniform and the gun on her left hip.

"I'm a cameraman with local news, and I have coworkers and friends that know I'm out here somewhere. They'll be expecting me before the end of the day."

Okay, he's playing his hand, Jack thought. He looks scared out of his mind and completely unprepared, but he wants us to know that if there's any funny business, people are going to come looking.

"What's your name?" Linda asked firmly.

"My name is *big-friggin-trouble* if anything happens to me out here."

"Nothing's going to happen, just turn off the camera," Jack said.

Kyle noticed Linda take a half step closer to him.

"Tell me your name," Linda asked again.

"None of your business, deputy."

"It is my business," she said, and took another step toward him.

Linda saw this going only one of two ways: this guy would either cool and calm down so they could actually talk, or he'd bolt and she'd have to follow him and confiscate the camera. This was still a police investigation related to the death of a pedestrian, any way you sliced it.

"Don't come any closer, or I'll be putting all of this on the six o'clock news! It'll be the lead story, I swear it!"

Jack said, "Dude, just take it easy. And keep your voice down. You're yelling."

"I'm not yelling!" Kyle shouted. He took a deep breath and lowered his voice. "I know who you are—you're Jack McAllister. Summer told me all about you."

Summer. Linda scowled at Jack and he wondered if this thing with her could get any worse. He'd have to think fast and turn this around. He'd have to convince this guy that Summer was neither an ally or a friend and that she was using him like she would a piece of toilet paper. He'd have to try and forge some kind of alliance with, with—

"What's your name?" Jack asked.

It took a few moments, but Kyle finally responded.

"Kyle."

Good, Jack thought. *He gave us his name. Probably his real name since he was so jumpy and amped up.*

"Kyle, listen...whatever she told you about me is bullshit."

"Oh, yeah," Kyle sneered. "How would you know?"

"Because I know her. And so do you. She's got you on a leash, doesn't she? She runs the show, not you. Think she wouldn't lie just to get you to do what she wants? She is playing you like an iPod."

Kyle bristled, feeling a gush of resentment. Everything this guy was saying was true, but so what! If he acknowledged it, then he'd look like a putz—a weak, pathetic putz!

"Yeah, maybe. But I've got a job to do here. And this, this...thing you found. What is it? You tell me!"

Linda glared at Jack. He returned, putting the ball in her court.

"We don't know what it is," she said.

Kyle scowled.

"Really? How convenient. Guess I'll have to make something up for the broadcast tonight."

He began filming again, scuttling to his left to jockey for a different angle of the machine. He zoomed in, grabbing focus.

"I'll call it a doomsday machine, or a military weapon, or maybe..."

"It's a scout," Jack said.

"A what?"

"A scout. A probe. A robotic geologist."

Linda felt heat sprout in her shoulder followed by a dull throbbing. Pain meds were wearing off. *Damn! They were back in the car.* She felt an upwelling of panic as things were coming unraveled out here. And with such intense discomfort dawning, she'd have a hard time thinking clearly and making decisions.

"Really," Kyle snorted. "Where'd it come from?"

"I don't know," Jack said.

"Sure!"

"It's not from here, it's from somewhere else. But your guess is as good as mine."

Kyle chuckled nervously. *The nerve of this guy,* he thought. *Now it's some kind of alien device, something from another world? Ridiculous! Wasn't it?*

"You expect me to believe this thing is alien?"

The scout reactivated abruptly, lumbering backward a few long yards, then changing course, tromping onward through the woods away from them.

"Whoa, whoa! Shit!" Kyle yelled in astonishment, feeling the vibration of the ground beneath his feet. He was trying to grab a good shot, busy reframing and focusing. "Look at the size of it," he marveled.

Linda began to drift carefully toward him, watching her step. If she could get close enough to Kyle, she could grab the camera and put a stop to this. He'd be shut down. Jack noticed.

"So how did it get here?" Kyle asked, going telephoto on the legs of the machine as it elephant-stepped through a tangle of undergrowth, adjusting its path, turning, moving east.

"Not exactly sure, but it seems to have come down in a multi-staged landing configuration."

"What the hell does that even mean?"

Kyle spun his shot back toward them and spotted Linda getting close. He tensed and lowered the camera.

"Don't even think about it, deputy."

Linda fortified her stance, her eyes deadlocked with Kyle. But the pain exploded in her shoulder suddenly, racing down her shoulder blade and her back. She grunted audibly and winced.

"Kyle," she hissed, "I'm going to give it to you in plain, simple English, so even you can understand—this is my jurisdiction out here and you are interfering with a police investigation. There are consequences for that, Kyle. Think it through carefully."

"Kyle, I'd listen to her if I were you," Jack said.

Kyle rolled his eyes and huffed.

"Yeah, don't give me one of those bullshit morality speeches here, Jack! Freedom of the press trumps your morality any day of the week! We can report *what* we want, *when* we want!"

"And what exactly will you report, Kyle?"

"The truth," Kyle barked.

"Which is?"

"Whatever we say it is."

Jack said, "Deputy, how many people are there in this city?"

Linda said, "Fifty-one thousand people."

"Fifty-one thousand people suddenly find out that this device, or whatever spin Summer decides to put on it, has landed miles outside of town. What happens then, Kyle? Does everyone just go back to dinner? Change the channel? Go walk the dog before bed?"

Kyle averted his eyes, thinking. Then he said, "Maybe they leave town. They get out of harm's way because maybe this thing is a weapon of some kind. Ever think about that? If we don't tell them, keep it a big secret and something bad happens, who does that fall on?"

Jack nodded. "You're smart, Kyle. Smarter than Summer gives you credit for, I'm sure."

Linda said, "With just one phone call, we can mobilize emergency services and even the National Guard if necessary. We're not taking chances here, Kyle. This thing is a long way from town. But we've got to have at least some kind of an idea about what it is and what it's doing. And that's why Jack is here. He's been helping us figure this out."

Kyle stopped recording and lowered the camera.

"Okay, look, I'm not out here to bust your chops," he said. "I'm sure you've got good intentions and all, but this is my job. I'm here to find out what's really going on, and if what you've told me about...that huge thing is true, then this is a really big story. I mean, historically big! And I just can't leave here and pretend it doesn't exist. I'm sorry."

Linda's shoulder started to blaze from a pain deep inside, like someone twisting a screwdriver in the joint between her arm and her shoulder. It was noticeably stronger than it was just a few minutes ago and she knew it was only going to get worse. She'd have to go back to the car and get another dose of the prescription for the pain, otherwise she feared she'd faint and Jack would have to carry her out of here. And even as she thought this, a wave of nausea rolled over her.

I'm going to lose it out here, she thought, becoming alarmed.

Jack said, "Kyle, I could really use your help here."

He smirked. "Is that so?"

"Yeah, it is."

Kyle kicked a twig at his feet, "What do you want?"

Jack said, "The pain medication that the deputy needs for her fractured shoulder is wearing off and she's going to need to get back to her car. I need some more time to watch this thing, and I would like to borrow your camera so I can record its activities. A visual log of this scout's behavior could provide us with more critical information. You see that the deputy gets safely back to her cruiser, Kyle, and I'll be here with your camera. You can come right back and I'll hand it off to you. All I ask is that you allow me to take the tape, just for a while, to do some analysis."

Kyle glared at Jack, his face an empty mask.

Jack added, "Either that or we all leave now, together, and I take that camera from you myself, Kyle...don't think I can't."

"I'd totally sue your ass," Kyle sniped.

"I'm sure you would, but I'd do it anyway."

Kyle did inventory on Jack. The guy was bigger, more muscular, and looked like he would do exactly what he said he would do. Kyle would indeed sue him and try to get charges filed, but that would take time and money, and Kyle did not have money. He was flat broke and in debt. But most of all, Kyle's already fragile ego would be bruised. He'd be humiliated.

Linda hissed and stole a sharp breath.

"Jack," she said, "I can't stay any more. I'm going to black out here."

Jack said, "Kyle, you've got five seconds to make a decision."

"Fine," he said, "you win."

He flipped the camera over in his hands, pressed a button on the back of it, then handed it to Jack.

"There's an hour of tape in there, see it?"

Jack turned the camera over in his hand, noting the tape in the drive on the side.

Kyle lectured, "Battery is still good and it's already set up. Just point and shoot. Don't screw around with any of the settings. I've got it dialed in perfectly. Promise!"

Jack said, "I promise, I won't mess with anything. I'm just going to keep shooting a while. I'll be staying close to it, following it, so you should be able to find me since it's moving very slowly. You just make sure she gets back safely to her car."

Linda said, "Thanks, Jack. If I'm okay, I'll come back. If not, find me at the police station. I'll have to get with Hawkins on this."

Jack nodded and Kyle sidled up to Linda.

"Are you okay to walk?" he asked.

"I think so," she said and started off. Kyle walked along side her, then quickly glanced back at Jack who was holding his camera.

What the hell have I gotten myself into? Kyle thought.

"Thanks, Kyle," Linda said. "Thanks for doing this. I'm in bad shape right now."

"Yeah," Kyle said. "Sure thing."

Kyle thought about Summer, and how she would have killed him right there on the spot if she had seen him give his camera to Jack. And then he began to think about what he was going to do later once he got the camera back with the footage. The possibilities were staggering.

CHAPTER 33

MARION MCALLISTER SAT IN HER chair at the dining room table, looking at the pictures in a coffee table book about Arizona. Sometimes she read the captions, struggling to put the words together into sentences. Mostly she picked out a few words and struggled to form them, let alone speak them out loud. Her capacity for speech was unavoidably diminishing. It wouldn't be much longer—months, perhaps only weeks—before she'd be unable to so much as utter a syllable. Mostly she looked at the pictures, staring at them with a vague sense of fascination.

Cathy was rinsing the plates off after their breakfast and arranging them in the dishwasher when the phone rang. She hurried to the living room and grabbed the wireless handset.

"McAllister residence," she answered.

"Hello, is Jack available?" a voice asked.

"I'm sorry, but he's not here right now," she said. "I'm not sure where he is exactly. Maybe at the attorney's office or the bank."

But the truth was, she didn't have any idea where he was. She'd come in earlier than usual because insomnia had spent the night with her, and she decided that laying in bed just waiting for the damn alarm to start crying was time wasted. She'd gotten to the McAllister house at 5:50 a.m., preparing an extra bold pot of Starbucks coffee. It was a few hours later that she had actually tapped on Jack's bedroom door to which she got no response. An hour after that she knocked again and called him by name. Finally, gingerly, she opened the door, noticing that not only was the room empty, but the bed was still made. Jack had not come back home last night.

Cathy asked, "I'm sorry, who is calling please?"

"This is Sheriff Clifford Hawkins, ma'am. I know you've got your hands full there with Jack's mom, but I really need to get a hold of him. Somehow."

Cathy said, "Sheriff, since it's you calling, I can tell you that I don't think he came back last night. He's been gone since dinnertime. I'm kinda worried about him, to be honest."

Hawkins said, "Well, I wouldn't worry too much just yet. Jack is a sharp and resourceful guy."

Pretty lame answer, Cliff, he thought. The fact was, he was worried now. Very worried. Jack was missing and so was Linda.

"Sheriff," Cathy continued, "I have to be honest—he's been acting a little strange recently and it's not just because of what happened to his father. I think it's something else. I don't supposed you'd be able to tell me what he's been doing with you and your deputy the last few days?"

It was starting, he thought. People knew that something wasn't right. It was like a vibration in the air. And it wouldn't be long before the media knew something wasn't right and suddenly the whole thing would be rolling, then charging downhill with all the momentum of an avalanche with no way to stop it. And then fingers would be pointed, blame assigned, investigations and...*why didn't he just contact the mayor the moment they'd confirmed that some unidentified flight hardware had landed in the forest? Because it looked like a damn jet engine cover!*

Hawkins had to answer her.

"Ma'am to be perfectly honest, we're still trying to figure some things out ourselves. Wish I could be more specific, but I'm not able to at this time."

Cathy felt immediate resentment. He wasn't being honest with her about Jack—about anything. And here was Marion, alone now without her husband, and her son involved with a police matter that was some kind of a big secret.

Cathy said, "Sheriff, I really think Jack needs to be home to take care of his mother and all the business that has suddenly befallen this family. When you see him, would you please tell him that? And would you please release him from, from...whatever it is he's helping you with."

Hawkins felt the shame wash over him.

"Yes, ma'am, I'll do that. Thank you for your help."

"Yes, sheriff," she said, and hung up.

Hawkins tapped the END button to finish the call, then flipped through his phone book and once again dialed Linda's number. It rang five times and then ended up at her voicemail. *Damn*, he thought, *this is not like her. Something is really wrong.* He'd have to drive by her place and check on her...assuming that she was even there. And if she wasn't at home...then what? As he saw it now there were only a few ways this could go, none of them well. The worst possible scenario was that Linda and Jack had somehow found the mysterious visitor, whatever the hell it really was, made contact, and in doing so got themselves—

He pruned that thought and collected himself. The nausea was mostly gone. The liter of bottled water he had nursed over the last hour had provided miraculous results. He would get dressed and drive to Linda's place. If he failed to find her there, he would return to the police station and organize some kind of search in those woods that lay west of the highway. He'd have to hurry now because another storm was incubating in northern Kentucky, threatening to crawl north toward them. And perhaps worst of all, he would have to call the Mayor and explain everything. Especially why he didn't disclose all of this immediately after they had found the ravaged campsite and the pieces of the spacecraft. *Should have retired last year when you had the chance, Clifford,* he thought. Should have, but didn't.

CHAPTER 34

L INDA LABORED ANOTHER FEW STEPS, paused, folder over, and vomited yellow-brown bile. She dry heaved and then gradually, desperately got some measure of control back. She breathed shallow as little spots that looked like brightly rimmed amoebas were dancing in front of her and darkness began forming a vignette around her vision.

"Oh, God," she said, "Kyle...I think...I think I'm going to pass out."

Kyle started to panic.

"No, no, no! You're fine! Really, it's fine! We're almost there," he said, even though he had no idea how much further they had to go. He noted the sky. Time was running out. He'd seen enough angry low cloud ceilings to know they should be high-tailing it the hell out of here.

But no! He wasn't doing the smart thing—running for the safety of his own car—he was being a putz! He was escorting the deputy sheriff, who was on the brink of a pain-induced blackout, back to her car, after which he'd have to walk all the way back out here to redeem his camera from that asshole Jack McAllister!

Idiot—freakin' idiot! Why did you give him the camera? You should have just run like hell, or at least grabbed a rock and thrown it at him! You should have at least put up a fight!

If anything happened to that camera or the footage. *Shit.*

"How much further?" Linda gasped.

"I'm not sure, but we have to be close, we've been walking..."

She buckled and dropped to her knees, now putting her head between them.

"Kyle, this is it! I'm...I'm going to faint! You're going to have to carry me."

"What?! No, don't! Don't faint!"

"You have to call 911. Do you have a signal on your phone?"

"I'll just use your phone," he said. "Where is it?"

"Pocket," she said. She tried to reach for it, but her fingers were useless.

"Kyle. Please! Use your phone. What are you waiting for?"

Linda's vision tunneled precipitously into a sucking blackness with only a pin light at the end of it. And now that pin light was swallowed. The horizon banked left beneath her, the earth tumbling up toward her. Linda became a rag doll and collapsed on the ground at Kyle's feet.

Jack was getting the hang of the camera—focus, exposure, and zoom. He followed the scout another twenty yards, achieving a nice close-up shot of the sampling arm, which had contact with another tree, extracting a sample via the abrasion tool. It had climbed back into the body and the scout entered a cycle of rest. *But it wasn't resting.* It was either doing a chemical analysis on the sample it had just acquired or it was depositing the sample in some kind of cache for later evaluation. This cycle repeated twice more, the scout moving in an easterly direction, and then it stopped again, this time at the edge of a brief clearing. Jack kept watch of the time, and noticed that this last cycle of rest was the longest. The pattern that had emerged was over now. Something else was happening. And this became a point of concern for Jack. Planetary exploration required sampling and analysis and then finally a conclusion that would lead to—

"Jack! Jack!"

Kyle tromped into the area, his voice loud in the afternoon lull. His face was moist with sweat and his breath was labored and uneven as if he had just run like hell all the way back here.

"Hey, keep it down," Jack sneered.

"Sorry," Kyle said. "The deputy is back at her car now."

"Is she okay?"

"Yeah, she's going to be fine."

Kyle was swaying on his feet with nervous energy.

He said, "Dude, listen—it's getting late and I need to go back to the station otherwise Summer's going to know something is up. I gotta have my camera back. Right now."

Jack thought about all the footage he had just shot. He could have spent the rest of the day out here, observing the scout, taking pictures and video. But based on what he and Linda had observed earlier, and the footage he had just acquired, he would have enough information to at least form some kind of hypothesis about what the scout actually was, and what it was doing here.

Jack said, "I get the tape, remember?"

Kyle scowled and huffed, "Okay, okay! But I get it back! In the next twenty-four hours. Deal?"

Jack knew that would afford him plenty of time to make copies of the tape, review it thoroughly, and even make some notes. He was in the clear.

"Deal. Where's the eject button?"

Kyle said, "It's right behind the tape door on the side. Blue button with an arrow. See it?" He was fussy, swaying to-and-fro like a kid that desperately had to take a leak. "Do you see it?"

Jack found the button and pressed it. There was a dull whirring sound then a pop, and slowly the tape transport opened and Jack grabbed the tape, putting it immediately in his pocket. He closed the cassette door and then carefully handed the camera back to Kyle, who began inspecting it, starting with the body, then the base, the lens, and then the back.

"You didn't drop it, did you?"

"No, Kyle, I didn't drop it. You won't talk to Summer about this?"

Kyle shook his head, no. "I gotta go, dude."

Jack looked him in the eye.

"You said Linda was back at the car. Is she walking back in here, or is she driving back to town?"

"She didn't tell me that, she just told me to get lost."

He glanced down at this camera once more, double checking something. Then he turned and began a trot through the woods, vanishing from the area, leaving Jack alone with the unconscious alien scout. Jack tipped his gaze toward the sky that was a vaguely ominous slate-grey. He'd wait just another minute to make sure the scout wasn't going to be waking up and performing a new cycle. *He'd wait just one more minute.*

———————

Kyle ran like hell, his heart slamming against his ribcage as he leapt and hopped through the woods. He couldn't afford to get hooked on a fallen branch or root system at this speed, as he'd surely break something in his body, in addition to damaging his camera. Because now the stakes were high—*like to-the-moon-and-stars kind of high.* It began to sink in, as the trees and branches blurred past him, that he, Kyle Beck, had a chip in the big game now. And he decided right then in midstride that he would be cashing it that very big chip for the payoff. He stopped running in order to catch his breath, but also to check the files on his P2 high definition cards. Because the footage Jack recorded did not go to the MiniDV tape he had so confidently stuffed in his pocket.

Kyle brought up the playback for his media files via a small set of buttons and some menu options. The words ACCESSING MEDIA began flashing.

"Come on, come on," he hissed, glancing around in a paranoid circle as to make sure he wasn't being tailed. And then the thumbnails began to appear on the screen. The images were not only clear, they were high-definition clear! Kyle pushed the play button on the first file and there was the scout, in all of its beautiful, but frightening alien glory, crawling insect-elephant like through the forest.

"Jesus," he muttered. He stopped the clip and shut off the camera. He began running again, faster and harder than before. He was not going to the television station with this. *No way in hell.* He ran, and ran, ignoring the sweat, the cramp that stabbed him in his abdomen wall like a butterfly knife and the dull throbbing pain in his feet. He ran like a man possessed until he saw the vehicles and just beyond them the deep shoulder of the highway.

Kyle pivoted quickly, now spearing intently toward his own car. But for a brief moment, he nabbed a look at the deputy's car. Linda was not there. And he wondered if she would make it back, and if he should have carried her after all. But it was too late for that now. She'd be fine. *Wouldn't she?* Besides, Jack would probably find her. She was his responsibility anyhow.

Kyle threw open the door to his sedan and dropped quickly behind the wheel. He'd have to get home as fast as he could and download his footage; the *only footage* that existed of an alien, robotic device that was surveying their world for some, as yet, unknown reason.

Jack glanced at his watch, now realizing it had been ten long minutes since Kyle had gotten his camera back and hauled ass out of there, leaving Jack alone with the scout. He had been waiting for the machine to do something. Anything. Starting in the distance, then rolling into the immediate area was thunder. It was guttural, like the growl of a lion. The sky was angry, and Jack decided it was time to start back toward his car. He'd gotten firsthand visual information of the device close up and additionally a half-hour of footage that would provide even more data that would help better analyze the behavior of the scout. And that would ultimately help figure out what exactly it was—

She just told me to get lost.

It popped into Jack's mind. It was what Kyle told him Linda said (allegedly) after he (supposedly) saw her safely back to the car.

She just told me to get lost. It wasn't right. Linda wouldn't say that.

And immediately Jack was anchored to a terrible suspicion that Kyle hadn't gotten her safely to the car. He had left her somewhere along the way. He'd either done something to her, or she had fainted from the pain in her shoulder. Either way, the son of a bitch left her out here. Alone. Jack sprung away, leaving the scout behind, not even turning to look back at it. There was only one thing on his mind, and that was finding Linda. *If she's still alive.*

No! She's alive! He thought loudly, drowning out that other voice that seemed to come from nowhere. *I'll find her! I will!* Jack picked up the pace, rifling through the forest, faster still, ignoring the sting of low hanging branches that lashed at him as he tore onward. He looked carefully ahead for any sign of her. But with such dense undergrowth, it would be difficult, especially if she were laying flat on the ground.

"Linda," Jack called out as he went. Louder now. "Linda!"

Nothing. He slowed. He was heading in the right direction. But he couldn't see her. Had he passed her already? Was she somewhere back there, camouflaged by the undergrowth, her brown colored uniform and her red hair causing her to blend with the terrain? Panic began to fester, growing, spreading, getting stronger, tightening its grip on him. The heavens unleashed a warning then—an explosion of light followed by a world-shaking bellow of thunder.

Jack spun in every direction, his gaze bulleting frantically here and there. Nothing. *Nothing! Shit, Jack you've got to find her! There's no more time!*

Panic was smothering him.

"I'm going to find her," he said quietly. "I'm going to find her." Again, louder this time, "I'm going to find her." It was something in the sound of his own voice that he heard, a strength emerging in those words. It was confidence. No, not confidence, something stronger than that. It was faith.

"I'm going to find her. I'm going to find Linda!"

He glanced around once more to the left, to the right, behind himself, then back around toward... Something at his ten o'clock position, fifteen yards away, caught his eye. It was a wave of coppery looking—*was it hair*—blended with a gnarled root system from a large, nearby tree. Jack leaped toward it, toward her.

"Linda. Linda!"

She lay face down in the ground, knees curled up against her body, her left arm limp, twisted behind her back, her right arm still compressed in the sling. She wasn't moving. Jack leaned down toward her, examining her carefully.

"Linda? Linda, can you hear me?"

There was a moment of no response, but then...

"Jack?"

It was so weak and faint he barely heard it. And then she tilted her head toward the sound of his voice, and forced her eyes open so she could see him.

She said, "Where is Kyle?"

Jack gritted his teeth.

"The son of a bitch took off. Linda, can you move? Can you walk?"

She grunted, "Help me up. Very slowly."

Jack reached down and began to help Linda as she fought just to untangle herself from what looked like a terribly uncomfortable shape. She hissed as her slung shoulder fell into its normal position, knifing her with a deep, cherry hot pain. She cried out. Jack held her in his strong arms, keeping her steady as she climbed to her knees, then finally to her feet where she hung on to him fiercely.

"You want to try a step?" he asked.

Linda nodded, and leaning on him, took a step. Then another. Her next step was weak, her leg unwilling to support her. She felt the horizon start to tilt again.

"Jack. Jack, I can't. You're going to have to carry me."

Jack was already encountering a surge of adrenaline, and was sure he could do it.

"I've got you," he said, and lifted her in his arms with what seemed like little effort. He began walking as quickly as he could to the east, toward their cars and the highway.

Jack said, "Linda, I'm so sorry about this. I should have known. This is my fault."

Linda lifted her good hand and gently touched the back of his head, running her fingers weakly through his hair.

"No. Don't. Thank you for finding me. I would have been in serious trouble. Thank you." And she gently tucked her head into his chest, closing her eyes as though falling asleep.

CHAPTER 35

KYLE STORMED INTO HIS HOUSE, locked the door, bolted it, and drew all the curtains, including the tiny one that covered the shoebox-sized window in the bathroom. He dropped his phone on the Formica kitchen counter that only served to complement the dreadfully out-of-date cabinetry and appliances. The yellow shag carpeting in the adjoining living room did little to offset the ghastly wood paneled walls that resembled a set piece for an episode of "The Brady Bunch." But Kyle wasn't concerned. He'd do an upgrade on this place once he sold the distribution rights for his film. Or, hell...maybe he'd just buy a new place!

But this was not the time to be pondering such things. Kyle decided there was no way in hell he was going back to the TV station; not with the footage he had in his hands. What he had to do now was come up with a mound of bullshit to spoon-feed Summer. It would have to be good, because she didn't fall for such cheap trickery easily. She was perceptive in an almost supernatural way. She just knew things somehow. Or maybe it was just that Kyle was too easily read.

In any case, he'd have to come up with something ironclad because she would be calling soon, demanding to know where the hell he was and what he saw. He could choose not to answer the phone, or even turn it off, but she would see that as very suspicious. No, he'd have to answer and tell her that...

Summer, I just threw up. It's food poisoning. I stopped to get a sandwich on my way out, and I think the meat was bad. I've been puking my guts out for the last hour!

Not bad. Plausible. Realistic. And, as it happened...just in time. Kyle's phone began ringing.

He drifted toward it and saw Summer's name on the little screen along with a photo of her he'd swiped from the internet. It was a modeling photo, taken just a few years earlier when Summer had done a bikini shoot for an Indianapolis lifestyle magazine. Kyle had carefully cropped it so that her chest, which was poised to literally snap that very small bikini top apart, was centered beneath her blazing grin.

Kyle grabbed the phone and decided to wait another few rings, and then pick up, thus implying he was delayed in answering her call.

One, two, three...

Kyle tapped the ANSWER button and said weakly, "Hello?" Nothing.

"Hello?"

The line was dead. He missed the call. *Okay, she'll leave a voicemail and I'll call her back,* he thought. He waited another minute. There was no voicemail. Kyle felt his intestines clench.

Thinking fast, he decided to take the phone with him into the bathroom and hunch over the toilet. It would be more convincing, especially with the acoustics of the porcelain bowl in proximity to the phone.

He raced into the bathroom, and crouched square over the bowl of the toilet, seeing his faint reflection in the water. He waited another minute, hoping to get a voicemail. No dice. Should he call her back? Maybe. But it might seem suspicious. But if he didn't respond at all, she'd most certainly suspect—

The phone rang so loudly in the small space that Kyle almost dropped it into the toilet. It was Summer.

Okay, show time, he thought, and started breathing erratically for effect.

"Heh, heh…hello," he said, heaving.

Summer's voice was dry and even.

"Kyle, where are you? I need you back at the station. Right now."

"Oh, Summer, hey…um, I can't come in. I'm sick. I think it's food poisoning!" He coughed and heaved passionately, continuing.

"I stopped for a sandwich on my way out, and I think the meat was bad…"

Summer decapitated his act swiftly.

"Kyle, you are so full of shit! You're not sick. Now stop looking at porn, or playing whatever game you're playing on your Xbox, and get in here."

Kyle felt a pinned down anger surfacing. She never believed him. *Never.* Even when he was actually sick! Two years earlier he had gotten the flu, which had turned into bronchitis. He felt like he was going to die and Summer accused him of bluffing the whole time. Even when he coughed up a bloody piece of yellow phlegm the size of an egg right in front of her, she afforded him not one ounce of compassion or understanding. She accused him of faking it somehow.

Kyle said, "Summer, I'm not coming in! I told you, I'm sick! I'll be back tomorrow morning if I feel better!"

Summer said, "No—you'll be getting into your car right now and driving over here! Once you get your butt in the editing chair, I'll forget about this pathetic attempt to bullshit me and then you can tell me about what really happened out in the woods today. And I want to see my footage!"

Kyle glanced up at the sink, noting an almost completely full glass of water, perched there near his toothbrush. Thinking fast, he grabbed the glass and held it close to his mouth. He made the most convincing vomit sound he could muster and then poured out the glass of water into the toilet, trying for as much spill and splash as he could generate. He began heaving again, pretending to catch his breath.

"Summer, I am tossing steak and peppers right now! I gotta get off the phone!" He began the heaving sound again. Suddenly, the call was gone. She'd hung up.

Kyle had to stop and think about what that actually meant. Either she finally believed him after that very convincing heave-splash, or... It was the 'or' that worried him. Kyle climbed from his spot over the toilet and ran back into the living room to retrieve his camera from the coffee table. He raced back toward his bedroom and placed it on the desk where his editing system slumbered.

He sat down in his captain's chair and carefully removed the P2 cards from their slots in the back of the camera. He even more carefully slid them into the slots on a card reader that was connected to his computer tower by a USB cable. Small green indicator lights began to flash as the drive read the cards and the media contained on them.

Kyle grabbed the mouse in the same way a maestro would grab a baton, and began conducting his software. He launched the Final Cut Pro application. Once inside, he created a new project and named it X.

Hmmm, maybe a little suspicious, he thought. He quickly renamed it VACATION VIDEO 2009. Yeah. *Hell yeah, that would work!*

He slid his pointer to the IMPORT button, which opened another list of options from which he selected LOG AND TRANSFER. Slowly now, thumbnails of his media began to appear, small images of the scout clearly visible. Kyle selected them all and dropped them into the empty project bin.

This is it, he thought. No going back. Not now.

Summer's usual bravado was strangely missing as she glared at her cell phone, having hung up angrily on Kyle just a minute earlier. The little bastard was lying. She knew him too well to believe anything different. But this vexed her deeply. Kyle was a total wuss. *So why the act?* Why would he risk incurring her proverbial wrath?

Unless...*unless he shot something he didn't want her to see.* Something important, or even...

Quickly she gathered her phone and put it in her purse. She thought about something for a moment, her mind quickly assembling a plan. She stood up from her desk as Walter, who she now regarded as nothing more than a tumorous appendage of the station, was hovering in her doorway.

"You gonna have that cut for me soon?" he asked. "I gotta see something by five-thirty."

Summer said, "Maybe you can just push my piece to ten. No one really cares about this expansion anyway. And besides, Kyle has decided to call in sick."

Walter huffed. "Sick, huh?"

Summer said, "Yeah. I gotta run an errand. I'll be back in an hour. I'll finish the cut on this thing and you can decide if it's worthy of the six slot. Personally I don't. But I'll leave that up to you."

"You're being reasonable, Summer. You're scaring me. Anything wrong?" he asked.

"No, Walter. Nothing's wrong. I'll be back in an hour."

Walter nodded and slid out of the doorway and back down the hall toward his office.

It was starting to rain, the drops falling in an even shower—light, but getting stronger. The wind began bullying the woods, sending treetops swaying like waves on a sea. Jack was struggling to carry Linda. And although he could see the vehicles a mere forty yards up ahead, it was all he could do to stay on his feet. The cortisol had worn off and his augmented strength had receded. He was fighting now to keep Linda stable in his arms. He'd have to drive her to the ER immediately. She was seriously dehydrated and falling in and out of consciousness. The pain she felt must have been extraordinary, Jack thought. And it would only get worse since she had obviously taken another fall when she passed out...when Kyle had left her there.

That son of a bitch, Jack thought. She fainted right in front of him, and what does he do? He leaves her there in the middle of the forest, then comes back, lies about her being safe, then grabs his camera and runs. Little prick!

Jack decided that the next time he saw Kyle, he'd make sure the guy understood the ramifications of such treachery.

Jack finally reached his car, and ever so carefully, every muscle in his body protesting, put Linda gently on the ground while he opened the passenger door. He mustered every last bit of strength he had left, lifted her slowly back off the ground, then eased her into the front seat of the Mercury. He shut the door and dashed around the hood, dropping in behind the wheel, closing the door. He impaled the ignition with the key, and turned the car over, dropping it into gear. Linda stirred.

"Jack," she said, her voice hollow and feeble.

"Don't try and talk," he said. "I'm taking you to the ER."

She wheezed and coughed. "My car."

"We'll come back for it. Linda, just stay with me!"

Jack pulled out onto the highway, pounded over the big grass divider and sped north toward town, reaching 90 despite the rain that was dropping from the sky in tapestry-like waves.

"Jack," she said, "thank you. Thank you."

Jack reached over and took her hand in his. It was like ice; cold in almost the same way his father's hands were cold as he lay in the casket. Her eyes closed again. Jack bullied the engine of the car until it reached 100. They were running out of time.

Jack's phone rang. It was home. *Mom!* He answered quickly.

"Hello?"

"Jack?! It's Cathy! Are you okay?"

"Is Mom okay?" he pushed in return.

"Well, yes, she's okay...but we were worried about you."

"Don't worry about me. I'll be home later. Can't explain right now. Just hang tight with Mom. I have to go."

"But I don't understand what's going—"

Jack hung up.

CHAPTER 36

K YLE WALTZED INTO THE KITCHEN, grabbed a half-empty Starbucks coffee pouch from the cupboard, flipped open the lid of the coffee maker, and began dumping the grounds into the filter until it was nearly full. He'd need a full pot of this stuff at maximum strength to keep going all night. Yeah—this would be an all-nighter.

He'd spent the last half hour looking at all the footage, rapt on the stunning clips of the ominous alien machine. The footage was very good—excellent, in fact. Even the shots Jack had taken were well composed and in focus. Every frame was pure gold.

Now what? Kyle had to reason it out.

What are you going to do with this historical footage? You're not going to rush it to the station for the evening broadcast, and you can't just post it on YouTube—people will think it's fake. So—?

Kyle poured water into the coffee maker and turned it on, and as the brew began dribbling into the pot like motor oil, Kyle sadly realized that he had no idea about what he was going to do with this footage. No idea. Zip.

So he'd have to start thinking harder. Coffee would help. He'd go back to his room and look at the footage again. Often times Kyle got inspiration while scrubbing through visuals and experimenting with—

BOOM, BOOM! The thudding on the front door launched Kyle's heart straight into his throat and his pulse into orbit.

"Shit," he said under his breath. *Don't answer it. Don't make a sound, just turn and go back toward the bedroom.* BOOM, BOOM, BOOM! That angry knock again. It could only be...

"Kyle, open up! I know you're in there!" Summer's voice, despite being on the other side of the door, was sharp and ripe with anger. Kyle froze and held his breath, attempting a tomb-like silence. Long moments crawled by. *Maybe she'll go away? Weather's bad outside, surely she's not going to stand out there all evening?*

She pounded the door again, louder still. Relentless.

"Kyle, if you want to keep your job and have any hope of ever working at any station in Indiana, you'd better open this door!"

She's got me, Kyle thought.

And she did—she had him over a barrel. He desperately needed this job. Until he sold his film or could get a gig somewhere else, he had to have money coming in just to cover the cost of the rent and all the credit card debt.

Okay, easy now. Play it cool, he thought. *Play it cool.*

Gently, he went to the front door, unlatched the bolt and pulled it open slowly, creating a television-worthy reveal of the woman standing there on his doorstep: model-sexy stance with hands on hips, chestnut hair thick, long past her shoulders, exotic almond-shaped eyes unblinking, locked on him like lasers painting a target acquired for a bomb strike. He impulsively drifted out of her way so she could come inside, which she did, prancing into his living room as if she owned the place. She dropped her purse on the coffee table and then glared at the coffee pot in the kitchen.

"So, you were just puking your guts out twenty minutes ago and now you're making a pot of coffee strong enough to give a full sized rhino heart palpitations. Pathetic. Totally pathetic."

Summer grinned derisively. "Least you can do is make me a cup. I take cream, no sugar."

Kyle felt himself adrift in a haze that he had to swim through before he could so much as move. Finally, he snapped out of it and went to the kitchen where he retrieved an ACTION SIX NEWS cup from the cupboard and poured carefully from the pot, leaving just enough room for cream. He nabbed the Half & Half quickly from the fridge and carefully portioned it into the pitch-black coffee. He turned, startled, almost spilling it as Summer had closed the distance on him silently and was standing very close.

"Hope it's okay," he said sheepishly.

Summer took the cup from him and sipped carefully.

"Not bad, Kyle. You might have a career as a barista at Starbucks if I decide to fire you. I hear they have benefits."

Kyle cleared his throat and began carefully.

"Summer, I really wasn't feeling well earlier. See, I..."

"Kyle, be very careful. Thin ice."

The jig is up, dude, he thought. *Don't screw this up. Proceed cautiously.*

"Fine," he said, his expression hardening. "Why are you here, Summer?"

She took another sip of coffee, her eyes never leaving his.

"To find out what you're working on in your little cave back there," she said as she motioned toward the back of the house. "What is so spectacular that you would actually try and bullshit me with such a lame story, even after I gave you an assignment—an important one. It must be something incredible for you to take such a risk."

Kyle averted his stare from her, but it felt like she had tractor-beam eyes, because he was drawn back to her gaze, captured like mere prey.

Summer said, "You're working on porn, aren't you."

Button pushed, Kyle rolled his eyes and huffed, brushing past her toward the living room.

"I knew it," she smirked, "It's porn. Oh God, you're not starring in it, are you?" Her lower lip pursed in revulsion at the mere thought. Kyle had enough. He exploded, his voice loud, trembling with adrenaline.

"Goddammit, Summer, it's not porn!"

"Prove it," she demanded.

Checkmate. He could ask her to leave, but that would tender him jobless and her thinking, and probably gossiping to everyone she knew, that he was producing and editing porn. He resigned then to what he saw as his only option.

"Okay. Fine. But I want you to listen to me, Summer— and listen good! I went on your assignment today. I took my camera and I went out into the woods, and I saw something...something incredible."

Summer's iron stance began to wane. It was the shiver in his voice, the look of astonishment on his face. It was something she had never seen before.

"Oh, come on!" she balked. Kyle was unflinching. "Okay, Kyle, tell me...what did you see exactly?"

He hesitated, feeling the awe return; the same awe that had blanketed him when he first saw the alien scout. A chill washed through him and his eyes began to supernova, remembering.

"It's...it's impossible. No one would believe! But, the thing is real! It's really out there!"

Summer's nerves began to unbuckle slowly because Kyle was being honest. Something he saw actually amazed him, or scared him...or both. It was disturbing even for her. She'd have to get him back to earth, to calm him down and get him to spill it. She walked toward him, and reached out, touching his shoulders. She had never touched him before in any fashion for any reason.

"Kyle, easy. Easy now. Just calm down. Tell me what you saw. Please."

Slowly, she slid her hands up his neck, touching him gently, attempting to bring him to a rational state. Kyle was even more astonished, now acutely aware of Summer's proximity to him, inches from him, the feel of her soft hands and gentle fingers against his neck. He became instantly aroused and knew that if she glanced south, she'd see exactly what was going on. He couldn't let her know, it would give her even more power over him. *Picture something gross*, he thought. *Something nasty! Hurry!*

He strained to conjure something repulsive, something that would cause his body to stop responding to her touch—anything! But the harder he tried, the more he succumbed to picturing her in a variety of seductive positions, imagining what it would be like if she were to climb on top of him and...

"I'll show you," he said. "I'll show you—but you have to swear, Summer! You have to swear to God you won't say anything to another living soul! We can't tell anyone until we know what to do about it!"

Summer looked straight into his eyes, and in her lower periphery saw his very pronounced craving for her. She had him hook, line, sinker. Pretending not to notice, she got even closer to him, moving her hands now up toward his cheeks. Kyle could smell her. It was intoxicating and he felt a sudden and intense heat down there. *No, no, no,* he thought. *Don't, please! Not now!* Slowly, with nothing short of superhuman effort, he began to calm himself, his thoughts recentering on what he was about to show her. The heat sublimated down there and he felt himself wane and soften.

"Promise me, Summer. Not a soul."

Summer bled him a Mona Lisa smile.

"Not a soul," she said.

Kyle turned and began walking toward the bedroom. Summer went back to the coffee table to grab her purse, the slowly followed Kyle into the back of the house.

Clifford Hawkins had pulled into his parking spot at the station after having gone to Linda's apartment. He'd knocked on the door so many times he lost count and had waited there for fifteen minutes. Nothing. He'd dialed her number again, the call going straight to her voicemail, which meant it was turned off or the battery was dead. Linda was nowhere to be found.

Reluctantly he had gotten back in his car and headed for the station where he made it quietly to his office, hoping for a few minutes of privacy in order to clear his mind and decide what to do next. He'd have to find Linda and Jack, even if...even if they had been hurt or, God forbid, killed by the thing out there. Yes, out there—*somewhere*. They didn't even know for sure where, or for that matter, what exactly they were looking for. Jack did, but he was missing. This was turning into a big mess. They were losing control of the situation. *You never had control, Cliff*, he thought.

Mitch poked his head around the corner of the door, leaning into the office.

"Sheriff, you got a sec?"

Hawkins, not giving him a chance to launch into some paranoiac rant again said, "Mitch, we're going to need to organize a search, okay? Gather up the guys, same as before. We're going to need to go back out to the woods west of the highway."

Mitch bristled, "Weather's getting bad, Sheriff, there's a storm rolling in from—"

"Then you'd better grab your raincoat and boots. And check your ammo."

Mitch backpedaled momentarily.

"Yes, sir," he said low and evenly. "What are we searching for?"

"Gather the boys. I'll explain in a minute," Hawkins said.

"Yeah. Okay."

Mitch left quickly and the room fell quiet. The phone rang and Hawkins grabbed it quickly.

"Sheriff Hawkins."

Jack's voice was loud in the earpiece.

"Sheriff, this is Jack McAllister. It's Linda! I'm taking her to the ER at Merriweather Hospital!"

Hawkins stood suddenly, grabbing his coat. "Jack, what happened," he asked.

"Sheriff, we found it! We found the scout!"

"Wait, Jack—the what?"

"I have video of it! I can explain, but I've got to get Linda inside, I just pulled into the parking lot!"

"You said Merriweather Hospital?" Hawkins asked.

"Yes. We're here. Please hurry over. She's hurt, she's not...she...won't..."

The connection was disintegrating, Jack's voice daggering in and out. The call ended. Hawkins grabbed his things and left the building out the rear door. Mitch approached the door slowly, timidly, like a kid preparing to ask his dad permission to take the car for the weekend.

"So, the guys will be ready in..."

It was only then he realized he was talking to an empty chair. Hawkins was already gone.

———————

Jack parked in front of the emergency room entrance, ripped the keys from the ignition and ran inside, calling loudly for assistance. They moved quickly, removing Linda from his front seat and wheeling her into the building, through the big inner doors and down a long hallway into an exam room. Jack explained her symptoms and her shoulder injury, which the on-duty doctor had recognized from the day before.

"She was just here yesterday," he said. "I explained she wasn't supposed to move it or do anything too physical. What happened?"

Jack tried to explain that she had fainted while following up on an investigation, leaving out the part about the alien scout of course. Vitals looked good, but she was severely dehydrated. They had her hooked to the IV drip within seconds. The doctor assured Jack that she would be fine, but that for the time being she would need rest. Jack stared down at her, worried. Reaching out, he took her hand softly. She was asleep. Another voice materialized behind him.

"Is she going to be okay? What happened?"

Jack turned as Hawkins entered the room. He went to Linda's side, examining her carefully.

"Sheriff, she's going to be okay. The doctor was just here," Jack said.

"What happened out there, Jack?" he asked, then lowering his voice, went on. "You said something about finding it—*a scout*. What does that mean?"

The room they were in afforded no real privacy, as the door was merely a slip-away curtain.

"I need to talk to you privately," Jack said. And he slowly pulled out the Mini-DV videocassette from his pocket. "Any chance they might have an audio visual department here?"

CHAPTER 37

KYLE SAT IN HIS CAPTAIN'S chair while Summer leaned over his shoulder. When she first came into his room, the sight of it immediately smacked of a high school boy's den—an environmental disaster. The only thing missing were rock band tour posters and dirty underwear on the floor. His bed was unkempt and Summer guessed he probably hadn't laundered the sheets recently, hence the vague, musty odor about the room. She decided it best to not sit on the bed, on those adolescent sheets, but to stand over his shoulder.

She desperately wanted to give Kyle her unbridled opinion on his nauseating room, but she exercised an impressive measure of self-control and didn't, since apparently he had some universe-shaking, life-altering footage of something that was super-duper top secret. And if she pissed him off, he might change his mind. *This had better be worth it*, she thought. Being in Kyle's room, near his bed, near him, made her stomach turn.

Kyle took a deep breath, and looked up at her, his brow tight against his eyes in the most serious look he'd ever managed.

"Swear to me, Summer."

Summer said, "Kyle, I have sworn to you three times already and I'm not giving you blood. Show me or I'm out of here and you can consider yourself unemployed."

Kyle pulled up his Final Cut Pro project on his 24-inch program monitor, cued up the first shot of the scout and tapped the PLAY button. In living color, the mechanized behemoth stomped through the forest, on its way toward a sampling target. Summer chuckled, nervously at first, because she had no idea what she was actually looking at. Slowly, that changed and she leaned in closer to the image.

"Whoa," she said, "Is this animation? CGI? Kyle did you do this? It's phenomenal! Is this part of your horror movie?" For a moment—a very brief moment—Kyle felt awe from her, directed toward him. And if only he could claim himself the artist behind what she was seeing, he might gain her respect. But that was science fiction, and never to be.

Kyle didn't say anything. Instead he opened another clip, this one a long lens closeup of the scout as it crawled toward a tree, finally coming to rest as the sampling limb sprouted from its underbelly.

"Kyle...what am I looking at? What is this?" she asked intently, kneeling next to him, getting closer to the monitor, scrutinizing the image. Kyle turned and looked straight at her, his expression ominous.

"That is not CGI. It's real. And it's out there in the forest west of the highway."

"Bullshit," she said, testing him. Kyle was a rock and it sent a chill down Summer's back.

"No bullshit," he said.

"What the hell is it?"

"It's a scout, a...robotic geologist. I think that's what Jack called it."

Summer's eyes grew. "Jack? He was there? You saw him?"

Kyle said, "Yeah. He was out there following it, studying it. Saw the deputy with him, too."

Summer put it all together from there: the story about the alleged meteor, the accident on the highway, the way Jack had squirmed when she played the movie-pitch game at dinner the night before. She was pissed off at him. Big time. But that abated as she watched the footage, her focus centered on the moving mechanical hulk and how it looked so...unearthly.

"Where did it come from?" she asked.

"Don't know," Kyle said, "at least not for sure. But Jack said it was alien. It came down on some kind of landing system. Everyone thought it was a meteor."

Summer stopped him. "Wait," she said, "this thing is alien, as in from another planet? Extraterrestrial?"

"That's what he said."

"Is it possible this is military?"

"I don't think so."

"How would you know, Kyle?"

"Because I was there, Summer, I saw it up close with my own eyes! I watched it move. No way this thing was military. No way. This is not like something we would build. I saw living parts on it, like muscles or tissue. They were connected with the mechanical parts somehow. Scary stuff."

Summer glanced down at Kyle's desk, her eyes landing on the P2 card reader where she noted that the cards were still docked in it. Then she saw a small blue LED indicator light flashing on a removable FireWire drive as Kyle played the footage back. *The media is linked to that drive and also still on the cards*, she thought. *Okay, think Summer—think hard.*

"Kyle," she said softly, "who else has seen this footage?"

Kyle folded his arms. He was starting to feel in control of things. Just a little.

"No one. Just you."

Summer said, "Have you mentioned it to anyone since you got back. Anyone at all?"

Kyle scowled, "No, of course not. I'm not an idiot."

That's up for debate, she thought.

"What are you planning to do with it?" she asked in a matter-of-fact way, her tone shifting into business mode. Kyle sat very still. Thinking. He hadn't any idea what he was going to do with it and there was no big picture plan. And now he was going to have to admit it.

Kyle stammered, "I, uh, well...a documentary I think. Yeah."

Summer said, "Kyle, let me work with you on this. This is news, Kyle, possibly the biggest news ever reported. Think about that. Think about what this could do for our careers. You have any idea where this could put us?"

Kyle listened, particularly to the way she used the word *us*...but he kept his arms folded. The hardness on his face would let her know that he was not getting into the water with her...not yet at least.

"Kyle, we need to break this on the air. Tonight!"

Kyle shifted uncomfortably in his chair.

"I dunno, Summer, I mean...we don't know everything about this machine or what it's actually doing here."

"We don't have to Kyle, the story will write itself as we move forward. But we have to move forward on this. I'm proposing a partnership on this Kyle—an equal partnership—you and me, no pecking order. We write what we know for sure, then edit the piece, then I'll go on the air with it, giving you credit as the only cameraman in the world to have shot this amazing footage."

She jockeyed her stare for a read on him. He glanced at her for as long as he dared, then quickly looked back at the monitor.

Kyle thought about this, turning it over in his mind like an antique collector handling an extraordinary item in a pawnshop, over and over, considering it from every side, every angle. Was she really proposing a working partnership with him? And what could this lead to professionally and...*personally?* Finally, he cleared his throat.

"Let me think about it," he said, arms folded, that rigid look on his face as he stared at the frozen image of the scout on his monitor. It was then Summer realized she was going to have to act because in this moment, Kyle thought he had power for the first time in his life. And she could not, under any circumstances, let him—of all the people on the planet—have that power. Kyle sat motionless, rigid, having no idea what she was about to unleash on him.

After talking with the kindly nurse outside of Linda's room, the evening shift manager and someone in security named Duff, Jack and Hawkins were escorted to a small, closed conference room on the far side of the building. It was a shoebox with throbbing fluorescent light banks, a timeworn, particle board conference table and an audio visual rack complete with VHS, MiniDV and 8mm video decks connected to an antiquated TV monitor. Jack made sure the door was closed before he began powering up the rack. He removed the MiniDV tape from its case, powered on the small deck and then slipped the tape inside.

Hawkins said, "Jack, let me make sure I understand: this machine, this scout, you called it, is conducting some sort of environmental survey of our woods."

Jack said, "Yes. It's a robotic geologist. I've watched it acquire samples from trees and rocks and ingest them into its body, which I can only imagine houses some sort of chemistry lab."

"So once it's completed this survey, what does it do then?" Hawkins asked.

"Well," Jack began, "I can't be absolutely certain, but more than likely it's going to transmit the data about this environment back home."

"Back home," Hawkins said.

"Back to whomever sent it here," Jack said.

Hawkins sighed and rubbed his eyebrows, a weariness in his tone.

"Jack, I have to be honest, this is all very difficult to believe."

Jack found the power for the television and made sure the MiniDV deck was routed to it via an input selector switch.

"Trust me, sheriff, after you see this footage...you'll believe."

Jack pressed the play button and waited for the tape to thread. The drive engaged and the tape began to roll. Jack glared in pure astonishment at the screen, which was blank. He quickly stopped the tape to rewind it.

"Must be the end of the tape," he said. He tapped the rewind button, expecting the whirring sound of the cassette to begin. It stopped, unable to perform the function...*because the tape was already at the beginning.*

Jack felt a warm, sick feeling in his stomach as he began to fast-forward through the tape, through footage of the scout that should have been there. But there was no footage. The tape was empty.

"Oh, my God," he said, his voice shallow. He sped through the rest of the cassette which yielded only pitch black on the monitor. *Should have checked that camera more closely,* he thought.

"He must have been shooting to cards the whole time," Jack hissed. "Shit!"

"Wait," Hawkins growled, "where is the footage, Jack?"

"It's not here. The guy I told you about—Kyle—he...he must still have it on media cards!"

Hawkins stood still for what seemed like minutes, his expression teeming with contained fury. Jack looked him square in the eye.

"I'm sorry," he said.

Hawkins nodded solemnly. He pulled the door of the conference room open, turned quickly and walked away, the clacking sound of his shoes on the hard floor dissolving into a disturbing hush. Jack was alone in that very far corner of the building. He ran it over and over in his mind. He had to do something. *Something.*

He pulled his phone out of his pocket. No signal. He ran quickly down the hall, turning left, then right, then left again until he saw an exit up ahead. Jack stepped outside, coming under the merciful cover of an overhang as the front of the storm over Merriweather was erupting in the atmosphere, unloading heavy rain and fierce wind gusts. The signal on his phone came back, five bars full.

Jack found the number for Stephen Hunter at the Jet Propulsion Laboratory and dialed it. Listening as it rang, he heard it go to voicemail a moment later.

"Stephen, this is Jack McAllister, Richard's son. I found your number in my father's list of contacts. I didn't know whom else to contact at this point. Stephen, the anomaly that MRO caught on Mars...the images you sent my dad a few months ago...I know what it is. It's a device—a robotic scout. There's one of them here in Indiana. I've seen it up close. It's real. I need to talk with you, I have some questions and I need your advice. Call me when you can. Time's running out here. Pretty soon everyone's going to know."

Jack left his number and hung up quickly.

CHAPTER 38

K YLE KEPT HIS CHIN STIFF, his stare locked on the video monitor with *his* footage. He would not look at Summer. He wanted her to know by his cold, hard silence that things would play out on his terms, not hers. He would sit like this for as long as it took. *As long as it took!*

"Kyle, look at me," Summer said, her voice now smooth and velvety. Kyle thought, *no! Don't you dare look at her! Don't you look at her! She is not in control, you are! You are the man!* Slowly, Summer stood up from her motionless squat there by his desk. *Don't look at her!*

"Kyle, I know what you think of me. I see the way you look at me and I'm not stupid." She took a step back from him, making some distance so he would have a more complete view of what was coming next.

"I know that you want me, Kyle. You want me bad! Since day one working for me, you've wanted to have me."

Kyle felt his heartbeat accelerate, microbeads of perspiration about to form on his forehead. And then, the impossible happened. Summer unbuttoned the top of her blouse, her fingers drifting slowly to the next button, which she expertly undid as well.

"You can pretend all you want, Kyle, but we both know it's true. I saw what was going on in the living room. I barely touched you and you were ready to explode."

She unfastened the next button, a red bra peeking out from between her designer lapels. Kyle felt the heat surge back into his lower self. He closed his eyes in a desperate attempt to shut it out, to shut her out. In his mind he placed her away in a small dark concrete room with imaginary bars between them, the key in his hands. *No, he thought. She's not going to control me. She's not going to run the show!*

Summer said, "Kyle, I'm going to make you deal, right here, right now. You can have me. All of me. Anything you want, I'll do it."

Against all his summoned willpower, Kyle looked directly at her, meeting her eyes deeply. She pulled the rest of her blouse apart in one deft move, revealing the shiny Victoria's secret bra that scarcely contained her local Emmy-nominated assets. They were pressed tightly together, round and hard like cannon balls. Kyle consumed her with his eyes, and the resistance was over. The little place he'd built in his mind to keep her contained was ineffective. She had escaped. No, she hadn't escaped at all...he'd unlocked the door with that key and let her out.

"Well," Kyle said, his voice cracking like an adolescent boy, "I...yeah, I guess I've always kinda wanted to..."

"You should get on the bed," Summer said. "Now."

Wow, this is it, Kyle thought. *It's really going to happen! After all the daydreams, the late night fantasies, it was actually going to happen!* Kyle stood up from his chair and pulled off his shirt, revealing his pale and doughy upper body, spotted with an endangered and thinning forest of dark hair in the middle of his chest. Summer locked eyes with him, trying to avoid the sights beneath his chin. This was going to be harder than she thought. She'd have to become Meryl Streep, fast.

Kyle lay down on the bed in the middle of those cheap, ugly sheets. Summer tossed her blouse aside and Kyle took sudden note of her abs, which were sculpted in a symmetrical, semi-defined six-pack. Kyle imagined how many crunches it must have taken to produce such results. He also noted how toned her arms were. Long, pronounced biceps flexed gently beneath her skin while her shoulders bragged quietly with hints of striated muscle.

"Wow," Kyle said lying on his back, staring saucer-eyed up at her.

"You have no idea what you're in for," Summer said. "I go to the gym six days a week. Better grab onto that headboard. Trust me."

Without missing a beat, Kyle threw his hands up, grabbing the top of his headboard, which was as pedestrian as his sheets—made up of cheap metal bars and a magnesium pewter finish. He closed his eyes and a moment later, felt her crawl on top of him. Kyle beheld her as she arched her back, pushing her breasts out over him, her hands vanishing behind her back which he anticipated was so she could unfasten that bra and allow him to see everything. He closed his eyes again, feeling his heart race even faster, the heat in his body approaching a fever pitch. This was more intense than he had ever imagined it would be. This was beyond his wildest expectations. He tightened his grip on the headboard, feeling her lunge down on top him, grabbing his hand and...SNAP!

Kyle felt a cold metallic thing bite down on his wrist, a sharp clicking sound loud over his head. He threw open his eyes, greeted by Summer's beautiful face hovering there, stoic now. All pretenses gone. And it was then he saw a handcuff noosed tightly around his wrist, the other end anchored around the metal of the headboard, a stainless steel chain between them. And all at once he knew what was happening, reality melting on top of him like warm ice cream.

Summer climbed off him and he noticed she hadn't taken off her jeans. He should have noticed it before. *She left her jeans on.* She grabbed her blouse and slipped it on, carefully and quickly buttoning it back up. Kyle was thrown into the deep end of panic.

"Summer." He said. She did not respond.

"Summer, what are you doing?" he said, darkening his tone. Without a word, she finished final touches on her blouse and began lightly fixing her hair. Kyle raised his voice until it approached a roar.

"Summer, what the hell do you think you're doing? Stop screwing around!"

She glared at him dispassionately, turned, grabbed his mouse and saved a copy of his project to the desktop. Quickly then she closed the program and copied the project file to the FireWire drive which had the media files of the scout. Kyle pulled against the cuffs, feeling the metal biting into his wrist. He pulled against it, harder now, rattling the headboard and the frame of the bed. No dice, he realized.

"Summer, don't you do it! Don't you do it!"

She ejected the drive and the P2 card reader, quickly disconnecting them from the tower. She opened her purse and carefully seated them deep inside it along with the cables that were still attached.

"Kyle," she finally said beneath a sinuous grin, "when you first took the job with me, I told you to remember one simple thing...never trust anyone in this business."

Kyle felt paralysis hit, like someone had injected him with a potent nerve toxin. The room became foreign, the lighting surreal, sounds of the heavy rain outside like shouting voices. Kyle felt abruptly detached, as if watching this all play out in a movie to someone else—some other poor dope. He pulled again on the cuff, violently this time, the headboard rattling loudly, the bed frame creaking, a warm and sudden pain oozing through his wrist. And then the anger rose, exploding out of him like Mount St. Helens on a May morning in 1980.

"Summer, don't you dare leave you whore!"

His face was bright red, veins bulging in his neck and forehead like giant worms, sweat pooling on his forehead. Summer glared straight razors at him, the anger boiling over in her now, adrenaline spraying the inside of her like a sprinkler. *No way was this fat piece of shit going to have the final say in this,* she thought. Abruptly she found herself fast-walking into Kyle's kitchen where she pulled open drawer after drawer until she found a long, sharp kitchen knife, a carver.

She turned and pounded back down the hall, into his room and once he saw her holding the knife, he settled down, his eyes darting left to right, desperately searching for a way out. Summer approached the side of the bed nearest him, her knuckles white with pressure against the handle of the big blade, her hand trembling the slightest bit from the adrenaline.

"What did you call me?" she said, her eyes dilated, dark and dangerous.

Kyle swallowed what felt like a baseball lodged in his throat.

"I...I'm sorry. I didn't mean it. Summer, come on. Please." He was desperate now, staring at the edge of the knife that was hovering inches from of his face.

"Say one more word, and I'll dispose of your boyhood down there," she hissed, making a slashing motion with the blade toward his groin. Kyle pinned his lips together and nodded, his eyes beginning to tear up.

"Good," she said. "I'm glad we understand each other. You see, if you'd just kept your cool, I would have come back later out of guilt, pulled off every piece of clothing and done you with the handcuffs still on because I'm not completely unsympathetic and heartless. I would have done you, Kyle—to make it right. But no way that's happening now. *Not after what you called me.*" She backed away, lowering the knife, collecting her purse.

Kyle felt hot tears sprout in his eyes, becoming rivers that bled down his cheeks, the saltiness finally reaching his lips.

"Summer, please...I beg you..."

She backed out of the room, vanishing into the hall. Kyle listened closely as he heard her walk back into the living room, pulling the front door open, then slamming it shut behind her, leaving him alone with a leering, mocking silence.

Summer climbed into her car just as the raindrops turned to stone and the breeze became an angry gust. She pulled away from Kyle's place, no longer thinking about him, but about the media she carried in her purse. She would go directly back to the station, sneak in through the side entrance which was out of general sight. She'd take the P2 cards with the original media to her office and lock them in her desk. Then she'd take the FireWire drive to the edit bay, where she'd connect it with the Mac Pro tower. She'd lock the door and edit her piece.

It was her piece now. Kyle had forfeited his half of the deal when he had called her a whore. When it was edited, she'd call in Walter and once he saw it and realized how historical it was, he'd have no choice but to let her break it on the air herself. From there, Summer imagined this would take her to the very top at CNN. She'd write a book too and secure an astronomical advance. From there, well...the sky was the limit. She could have anything she wanted. Maybe even Jack McAllister...provided he came to his senses about her.

She pulled into the parking lot, her wipers barely able to keep the windshield clear. She settled into her assigned parking spot ten meters from that side door. If she tucked her purse against her body to shield it from the rain and ran like hell, she could make it. From there she could badge herself in and she'd be home free. Summer clutched her purse tightly and counted to three. She threw open her door and climbed out. She slammed her car door shut and dashed for the building.

Small hail carried in horizontally struck her in the face. She squinted and kept running, her jeans and blouse getting wet. It didn't matter, she thought. She could dry off in her office. She kept a towel in her—

The heel of Summer's boot split at the joint, breaking suddenly free. Her ankle twisted beneath her, her foot bending sideways. Summer fell, spilling almost face down on the hard, wet concrete, the hail beating down on her, pooled rain soaking into her clothes, chilling her instantly. Her purse toppled away into a puddle nearby with a sickening splash.

Summer's head spun, stars erupting in her vision like galaxies being formed in deep space. She was stunned. *What the hell had just happened? Her purse. The drives!*

She pulled herself off the ground, examining her palms. There were deep scrapes, blood beginning to ooze from the abrasions. The pain grew, but she shut it out and grabbed for her purse which was now soaked. She stumble-ran the last few feet to the door, panting, trying to gather herself. She felt inside the purse. It was wet in there.

Shit, she thought, *the drives!* She dug for her badge, her fingers eventually finding it. She pulled it out and slid it into the reader there next to the door. She heard the clack of the lock, and pulled the door open.

Summer made it to her office without being seen. She slammed the door shut, waited a few moments to make sure no one was coming. And then she felt it, bearing down on her like a brakeless, roaring freight train: weakness, helplessness.

Summer cried then. It was uncontrollable. The tears poured freely out of her, and she felt the sobs come next, heavy and in waves. She was suddenly overwhelmed, dangerously vulnerable, sensing herself flying apart. *Was this Karma coming to collect?* Was this the beginning of payback for what she did to Kyle? Was this payback for all the lousy things she had done to people in her life? *Lousy, horrible things.*

There was an old Summer from a long forgotten childhood that existed somewhere inside. But that Summer—the Summer who rode bikes, roller skated freely in driveways, and played with Barbie dolls—learned, through some painful experiences, that the world would not give her a fair shake. It would relentlessly beat her down unless she declared war on it and all the people in it. She had to become more than that person, more than human. It was the only way she could—

The door to her office banged loudly, startling her. "Shit," she hissed out loud. Walter's Lurch-tinted voice bled in from the other side.

"Hey, you in there? I need to see your Indy piece. Now!"

Summer took a deep breath and calmed herself, wiping the tears from her face.

"I got something a lot better than that, Walter," she said. "I need one hour."

From the other side of the door, he grunted and muttered something under his breath. Finally, she heard him walk away. She glanced at her purse and decided it was time to do this. Providing that the media was still intact.

CHAPTER 39

S TEPHEN HUNTER CROSSED MARINER ROAD and hurried up the stairs toward the glassy ingress of the Space Flight Operations Facility, or SFOF, at the Jet Propulsion Laboratory, ignoring a female deer that pottered by with her white-freckled calf close behind. Minutes earlier he had listened to a voicemail from Jack McAllister as he'd boarded the elevator from his office on the sixth floor of building 264, home to the Curiosity Mars Rover mission team which was a fusion of rover drivers, planetary scientists, support teams for specific rover instruments, software engineers, and tactical data personnel.

He listened to Jack's message while he rode the chrome-plated elevator down to the ground floor, ignoring the subtle shimmy of the carriage as it descended quickly. His head was swimming, not just because of what Jack had so passionately explained in his message, but also because of what was happening out there in the world, beyond the gates of the laboratory.

Stephen pressed his badge against the reader at the main door and a second later the electric bolt discharged, granting him access. He walked quickly, his arms swinging as he cut past the large reception desk and approached another sealed door. Badging the reader there, he pulled the door open, now entering the Mission Support Area, or as it was called on lab, the dark room—a cavernous space with large high-resolution data screens tiled all the way to the ceiling. Four rows deep in semi-chevron formation were squatting computer terminals. Normally vacant, save for landing events and other major operations, every console was manned. Grim faced men and women spoke with low, intense dialogue over headsets, shaking their heads.

Above them all on the big screens were animated representations of the large radio dishes all around the world that made up the Deep Space Network of Antenna's or DSN, showing data signals coming down from spacecraft and flight instruction data going back out into space. Among the spacecraft with data bins were Mars Reconnaissance Orbiter, Mars Odyssey, Curiosity Mars Rover, Cassini, Dawn, Voyager, and the Opportunity Mars Rover. None of the data from those missions was coming through. Something else was happening. On a large video display in the center of the room was a feed from CNN, a stern-faced anchor reading from pages in front of him, occasionally looking directly into camera.

Stephen glided to one side of the room, watching all of this intently as the DSN Tactical Downlink Lead, Kevin Brewer, approached. His headset was fitted tightly against the side of his head, his unblinking eyes wide, intense, and alert.

"If someone had told me this was even possible, I would have called him or her crazy," Kevin said, not looking over at Stephen.

"How many are there?" Stephen asked.

"According to CNN, there are seventeen...that they know of," Kevin said, glancing quickly over at another display which showed an active data stream which was labeled UNKNOWN.

"So who's doing this?" Stephen asked.

"It's them. It has to be," Kevin said. "They're hacking us, and our ass is up against the wall here. The data packs are full of this stuff."

"Where's it all going?"

"Wish I knew. Too early to tell."

Without another word Kevin evaporated from Stephen's side, hurrying now, entering an adjoining room through sliding glass doors, which held a panoply of flat screen monitors and computer towers, bathed in a low, womb-red glow. Stephen grabbed his phone and thumbed past a couple of screens before finding Jack's number. He hit the SEND button and waited.

As soon as Jack's phone rang and he saw Stephen Hunter's name on the display, he answered swiftly.

"Hello! Stephen, this is Jack."

Stephen said, "Jack, yes, it's me. I got your message. Had to listen to it twice to make sure I wasn't hearing things. So you've actually seen one of these things up close?"

Jack hesitated. *One of these things?*

"Stephen, wait...there are more of them?"

"You didn't know? It's on the news. There's a total of seventeen devices. Yours would make eighteen I guess, unless there are more that they don't know about yet."

Jack felt his breath escape, a surreal haze swim over him.

"When...when did they know? When did this happen?"

Stephen said, "It first came up on the ticker tape a few hours ago. Then it began to hit the desks at CNN, FOX, CBS...all of them. Now it's the lead story. They've got confirmations in Italy, Greenland, Kazakhstan, India, Australia, Argentina, looks like possibly the arctic biome, northern Canada. They're spread out like a net."

Jack dashed back into the waiting room where he saw Hawkins finishing a phone call, preparing to leave. He motioned desperately for him to wait. Jack ran to a television monitor and grabbed the remote that was lying on a table in a pile of old, molested magazines. He quickly switched from The Food Network to the news, now seeing the same grim-faced anchor on CNN who was narrating over a global map that had seventeen red spots spread out across it, indicating the approximate locations of the scouts.

Stephen said, "Jack, listen, I've got to get off the call now. They've got all of us here in SFOF working this because it looks like they've hacked the DSN."

"Holy shit." Jack's eyes grew large, staring at Hawkins, holding up his index finger, urging him to wait another moment.

Stephen said, "Washington seems to think it's some hacker somewhere trying to take advantage of the situation. You want my opinion? It's them. They're trying to upload all their data from these machines and send it home in one big data flow."

Hawkins ignored the TV, shrugged at Jack and started to walk past him, toward the exit.

"Stephen, I have to let you go. I'll check back with you later."

Stephen said, "I hear you, Jack. Good luck."

Jack ended the call and turned up the volume on the TV, almost maxing it out. The people in the waiting room jabbed him with looks of disapproval, which didn't last long once they realized what was unfolding. Hawkins stopped short of leaving the building when he heard the troubled voice of the anchor.

"...*Officials have no reason, at least at this point, to believe these areas were specifically targeted. But larger questions remains at this hour: what are these machines, where did they come from...and why exactly are they here?*"

Hawkins summoned Jack to the other side of the room with his piercing glare.

"Jack, who were you talking to on the phone?"

"Friend at JPL in Pasadena."

Hawkins scowled.

"Didn't we just have a conversation about this?"

Jack pointed at the TV screen across the room.

"Things have changed, wouldn't you say? Take a look at that map, sheriff. This is much bigger than just us now...it's global."

Jack's thought was cut short as the anchor on the television who was about to interview someone, transitioned to a live feed.

"*Sorry, we'll have to come back to you on those questions later. Okay, I'm just getting word that we have a live feed coming from an affiliate in Australia, just outside the Blue Mountains. We're going to go ahead and take a look at what's happening down there.*"

Jack McAllister, Clifford Hawkins, and everyone else in the waiting area of the ER watched the next several minutes of the broadcast together on the big screen in silence. None of them would forget it. It would become hooked in their memories like barbwire—sharp, tangled, digging in deeper over time, lacerating their peace of mind. It would stalk them in the day like a predator and wake them in the middle of the night, leaving them short of breath with tortured heartbeats, every last one of them.

And so it began as the camera went live to a pretty female reporter who stood in the densely wooded hills of Australia outside of Sydney. Behind her, perhaps by only twenty yards, was one of the machines, a scout, identical to the one that was perambulating the woods only a few short miles away from all of them in that waiting room.

CHAPTER 40

S UMMER DASHED TO THE EDITING room with the FireWire drive tucked carefully at her side. She shut the door, powered up the system and plugged in the drive. She waited, anxiously humming a little prayer under her breath, "Work, work, work, come on, come on..."

The drive powered up, but there was an audible clacking sound within the aluminum housing. CLACK-CLACK-CLACK. Summer watched the desktop screen of the computer carefully, agonizing every second while the drive tried to mount. It became clear after another thirty seconds that something was wrong with it. CLACK-CLACK. The drive's indicator light began flashing on and off as a tortured growl came from the device.

Summer hissed, "No, no, no! Dammit!" The drive was toast. She'd have to go back and grab the P2 cards and the reader and pray they still had their integrity and would—

The door flew open and Walter stuck his head in. Summer lost it instantly, exploding all over him.

"Goddammit, Walter, I'm working! I'll get you the Indy piece later!"

Strangely unaffected by her outburst, Walter simply said, "You need to come out here and see this." His face, which was in its normal state gloomy and expressionless, was intense and anxious. A production assistant from the station ran past him down the hall toward the studio. Walter left the doorway and hurried away, following the young man.

Summer rose slowly, hearing only the sound of a television feed over the big speakers in the studio down the hall. There were no other voices or sounds—no evidence that another human being was in the building.

What the hell is going on? she thought.

She inched carefully down the hall, approaching the studio, finding everyone—literally everyone—staring intensely at the station's 70-inch floor monitor. She hadn't seen anything even close to this since...since 9/11. She blended alongside them and watched.

The feed came in strong, the Australian reporter speaking clearly into her microphone, motioning behind her toward the robotic scout that slumbered in the midst of the woods. Summer felt the floor drop out from beneath her feet and she realized right then, inexorably, that her plan to own this story, one of the most historic of all time, was over.

The reporter spoke evenly, though just beneath her words ran a slow-moving current of tension.

"Now as you can see, this device appears to be resting. In fact, it hasn't so much as moved in the last hour. Earlier our cameras caught a spectacular view of this machine making its way down the arroyo, scaling this very challenging terrain, coming to rest in this spot."

Behind her then, something happened. The scout sank on its enormous legs, the elongated mast pivoting, then lowering and connecting snugly with the deck. The reporter turned abruptly toward it from the cue she was getting from her cameraman.

"Okay. Okay, it appears that something is happening. Something is happening now. The device is...changing."

The camera snap-zoomed in on the scout, focus becoming sharp. The slatted doors on its side opened slowly. More holes sprouted on the lower body, small, semi-spherical hatches recessing, opening like pores on skin.

"Something is definitely happening as we watch here to see exactly what—"

There came a deep, thunderous clap from the scout. A white, vaporous substance shot violently outward from those open vents, forming a ring-like wave, exploding through the area, spraying the reporter, engulfing her, obscuring her from the view of the camera momentarily. Her microphone was still active and they could hear her scream, a primal howl of shock and terror. The coughing was loud and strangulated. She gulped for air, desperate like a person drowning.

The woman lunged from the haze, her face leering suddenly, hideously into view of the camera. Her skin blistered, pockets erupting into craters of super-heated flesh that tore open, oozing blood which began to boil and steam. Her expression was a melting mask of horror, flesh liquefying, running with blood into rivers of viscous fluid down her cheeks that were slowly disintegrating. Her eyes ballooned outward and her jaw parted from her head grotesquely until mercifully the camera angle fell away, back into the white haze, the tortured howls of the cameraman peaking the audio.

The feed went immediately dead. Moments later they were taken back to the studio at CNN where the anchor sat hunched in his chair, his eyes clamped shut, his lower lip trembling reflexively.

"Dear Lord Jesus," someone said behind Summer as low weeping began to fill the studio. Summer turned and ran down the hall to the bathroom. She barely made it to her knees in front of the toilet as her stomach imploded into a tight ball, ejecting everything out of her ferociously. She vomited twice more before it ceased, and she slumped there in the bathroom stall, weeping uncontrollably.

Jack stood paralyzed in his spot as the people around him in the waiting area of the ER sobbed. A grade school girl with a ponytail and flu-like symptoms cried and buried her head in her mother's shoulder, while her mom, through a river of tears, held her tightly and said, "It's going to be okay, honey. It's going to be okay, Mommy's here." A young man who looked like he was fraternity material, prayed quietly under his breath.

A woman's voice rose loudly from a corner of the room, hysterical. "They're going to take out the cities next! They're invading!" Someone told her to keep her voice down and she snorted at them. "You don't know what's going to happen! This is going to be worse than 9/11!" Now someone else told her to shut up, nerves in the room slowly coming unbelted.

On the television now was aerial footage from a helicopter that was circling over a tree-rimmed glade somewhere in Canada. The narration followed as the camera zoomed carefully into the area where another scout rested in a similar configuration as the one in Australia—lowered, slat doors open, mast stowed on the deck. From the bird's eye view of the chopper, the changes that were taking place in the surrounding area were obvious.

"As you can see, the device below us has already issued some sort of a chemical cloud that has permeated roughly several hundred yards around it. And something is happening here that's hard to explain. The entire area around the machine is changing as you can see. Trees, vines, brush, the soil, everything within this radius of the chemical is becoming...I've never seen anything like it."

The moving image said it all. The entire landscape was turning a reddish-black color. Trees were bent impossibly backward on themselves, ruptured, while grotesque, needle-like growths were projecting out of them. Plants and shrubs were withered beneath a suffocating dark, epoxy-like substance. The soil itself was reacting to the change, hardening, splitting open, more of those terrible needles stabbing through it, sprouting everywhere.

And all at once it made sense to Jack.

"They're terraformers."

He let it slip unconsciously, the thought escaping on its own, now articulated in the open for everyone to hear.

Hawkins asked quietly, "What?"

Jack said quietly, "They've come to fundamentally transform our planet to an environment that's good for them, but deadly for us."

It made perfect sense: the scouts were sent here by terraformers to gather extensive data on the environment via the trees, the soil, the rocks, leaves, air, and from that prepare a chemical mixture that would react with those surroundings, transfiguring them at the most basic level into something hospitable for themselves. And Jack thought back to his intimate encounter with the scout, and what he thought he saw in that terrible face from so far away—*they weren't interested in us. They didn't care about us.* Because their operation was wholly environmental, and they knew that we would never survive the change. We would be mere collateral on the sidelines and of no consequence to what they were doing.

On the TV, the report changed locations and what they saw now was a canted mass of metal, a scout that had been destroyed. Four of the six legs had been torn from their joints, the deck crash-planted at an oblique angle where it fell, the mast twisted backward, smoke drifting lightly from it. Men with heavy green coats with the bold printed word, POLIZEI, in yellow, crouched fifty yards out, held rifles locked on the mechanical carcass of the scout. They all wore gas masks. A voice on the TV said,

"Now seeing these pictures from Germany, it appears this particular machine has been destroyed by police with standard issue firepower, apparently before it could launch its deadly chemical attack, perhaps bringing some hope that these devices can be stopped before this tragedy escalates any further."

Jack felt a hand tighten on his arm and he found himself being towed toward the exit of the building. Hawkins' grip was powerful, and although Jack was alarmed, he decided for the moment it was best not to resist. Hawkins led him outside where the rain continued to lash the parking lot. They were alone now.

He released Jack's arm and said, "Tell me exactly where it is."

Jack said, "Mile, mile-and-a-half southwest of the accident spot off the highway."

Hawkins lip tightened up, his eyes turning to iron.

"You stay here with Linda. And Jack, if she hasn't seen it already on the news somehow, you don't tell her. Not yet. Not till it's finished."

Jack said, "You're going to destroy it."

Hawkins said, "Yes. Right now."

Jack looked upward into the rain, thinking.

"Rain may have bought you some time, Sheriff. Those other locations that got hit were dry. This chemical they have...may be ineffective, or less effective, when it's wet like this. I can't state that as fact, just a theory."

Hawkins put out his hand for a shake.

"Jack, it's been a pleasure. In case we don't see each other again."

Jack took his hand and shook it firmly, feeling the finality of those words. Hawkins broke away, dashing to his squad car where he quickly piled in. He lit the engine and pulled out of the parking lot and back onto the dark streets of Merriweather. Jack watched him go another moment and then started back inside, back toward Linda's room where he found her sleeping, dreaming as her eyes moved briskly beneath her lids. He'd wait there with her in the quiet, and hope she'd sleep straight through the rest of the night.

Summer had been coiled on the tile floor of the ladies bathroom and cried for what felt like an hour. It had in fact been only five minutes, but in that brief amount of time, despite the shock, the vomiting, the sobbing, she was able to collect herself, calm her mind, and think about what to do next. The world had pivoted violently right under her feet, spun out of control like a centrifuge and all of her thoughts and plans had been torn away from her in the wake of that cosmic force. What would she do now? *What could she do?* The images of the woman reporter in Australia replayed in her mind, all the horrific details of her death vivid and sharp. It was like watching someone microwaved in a giant oven.

You always wanted to make a difference in the world, she thought. At the beginning that was true, though later it turned into a war, her career nothing more than a series of battles to be fought and won.

Do what's right, Summer. You can warn them. Do it now.

She climbed off the floor of the bathroom and walked back into the studio. Walter was wiping tears from his eyes, something Summer had thought was physiologically impossible as the man appeared carved from stone.

"Walter, I need to talk to you," Summer said.

He pushed the last tear off his cheek, sniffled loudly and attempted to blink away the redness in his eyes.

"What is it?"

Summer began, "One of those machines is just a few miles away from us in the woods southwest of town off the highway. Not sure exactly where it is right now, but I have footage of it from earlier today."

Walter frowned, and others in the studio began to close in around them. Michelle Hubbard, the evening anchor approached, carefully dabbing her mascara which had begun to bleed down the sides of her face from all the tears.

"Wait a minute...Summer, are you telling us that you knew something about this earlier today? That you actually got some footage of this, this...weapon?" Michelle said, her tone laser focused, intense and rigid.

Summer replied, "No, not earlier today! I just found out about it in the last couple of hours. I had no idea what it actually was, that's why I didn't say anything."

Michelle folded her thin arms like a praying mantis, pulling them tightly against herself, incredulity in her stare.

"Then how did you get footage of it exactly?" she jabbed.

Summer, normally the bully in the room, able to stare down anyone, struggled to make eye contact with Michelle, and she found it harder and harder not to break into tears while speaking.

"I...I didn't get the footage myself. Kyle filmed it this afternoon."

"Well, where is he?" Walter asked sharply.

Summer pulled up that last image of Kyle—shirt off, handcuffed to his cheap headboard, his face moist with sweat, eyes red and puffy from the rage, the crying. The betrayal. Summer felt a lump in her throat, her heart heaving from guilt that was slowly crushing her in its huge fingers.

"He's still at home...I can't explain right now...."

Do what's right, Summer! Do what's right!

She continued, "We need to warn people right now! I have the footage in my bay on P2 cards. If I can...I mean...if *someone* can do a quick assembly of the footage, or help me do it, we can break the story...maybe give people a chance to evacuate the area."

"Do the police know about this?" Walter asked.

"Yes, they've known since yesterday, I think."

Michelle walked right up to Summer, her arms still snug against her, her expression murky. Summer was sure she was about to get slapped, or spit on, and incredibly, she felt as if she deserved nothing less. If it came to that, she would accept it. But what occurred was far more bizarre. Michelle, who had never gotten along with Summer—never liked her to begin with—suddenly reached out, put her arms around her, and pulled her into an embrace, holding her gently.

Summer tore open, all of the emotions that had been damming up inside her bursting out. She wept and grabbed Michelle tightly as if for dear life. Michelle put one hand on the back of Summer's head, stroking her hair gently as she spoke softly to her.

"Summer, it's okay, honey. It's okay. Let me help you do this. We'll do it together."

Summer nodded softly, and the two of them began walking back down the hall toward the edit bay. Later that night they would break the story about the scout that had landed in the forest outside of Merriweather, an event that would be referred to as INCIDENT 18 (cataloguing their scout as the eighteenth confirmed device). All in all, the total number of devices found operational around the globe was twenty-seven by the end of the night.

CHAPTER 41

HUNKERED DOWN AT THE POLICE station, Mitch and the others stood dumbfounded around a wall-mounted TV, watching the news feed that was replaying the now edited and censored version of the Australian incident.

Mitch said, "Holy hell! Chemical weapons. WMD's from space!" Derek bit off half a Red Vine, chewing hard with nervous energy.

"So is that what we have in the woods—one of those robot things? We didn't actually find anything like that yesterday," he said, now cramming the rest of the candy straw deeply into his mouth. "And you said it was Air Force, Mitch."

"Shut up," Mitch said.

His phone rang loudly to the tune of "Sweet Home Alabama," at which all of them startled. It was Hawkins. He spoke without pause, calmly and evenly; the brass in his tone there to make sure Mitch knew not to ask stupid questions or skate into one of his paranoid rants.

"Mitch, I want you and the boys to pull together the heavy gear. That includes the masks for tear gas. I want the 12 gauges—all of them—and make sure all your semis are holding full clips. Load up right now and drive south on the highway, half mile past the scene of the accident from the other day. I'll meet you there. We're shutting down north and southbound lanes, so get some cars out there off the 5th Street exit. Do it now and meet me in twenty minutes."

Mitch hesitated, his voice unsure as he digested the information on the TV.

"Um...Sheriff, are we going after it?"

"Mitch, we are going to locate the device and we are going to destroy it with overwhelming firepower. If you've been watching the news, and I'm guessing you have, you know it can be done. No more questions. Load up. Meet me in twenty." And he hung up.

It was still raining when approximately twenty-five minutes after he had ended the call, Hawkins saw them driving toward him, slotting in together single-file, red and blue lights painting the wet pavement out in front of them, striking the raindrops stroboscopically in midair, turning them momentarily into small colored beads. They pulled hard off the road, tires sloshing in the wet grass and mud as they settled, the conical glare of hi-beams bathing the wall of trees. Mitch was the first to alight from his cruiser and he immediately ran toward Hawkins who stood fixed in the tall grass of the shoulder.

"Sheriff, we've got everything, but we're just not sure if—"

"No more talking," Hawkins said, giving Mitch a diamond hard look. "Gear up."

Mitch bit his lip, goggle-eyed by raw anxiety. He nodded tightly and jogged back toward his vehicle, gathering the gear and salvaging what little was left of his nerves. Within five minutes they had unloaded everything beneath the showery forest canopy, all of them conspicuously quiet as they checked weapons, flashlights and gas masks. They wore long raincoats with big block letters prominent on the back: POLICE.

They began their march to the interior of the forest according to the directions Jack had given Hawkins earlier. The rain was unrelenting, falling precipitously from that gunmetal grey sky that was roiling beneath a heavy ceiling of atmospheric instability. Hawkins had checked the Doppler on his phone before they left and saw what was headed their way: atmospheric wrath in the shape of a yellow ellipse with an angry red center that would inevitably drop on top of them like an anvil in less than two hours. No one wanted to be out in the open when a system like that fell. No one. They all stepped carefully, quickly onward, their high-powered LED lights hacking through the dense darkness of the wild.

The wind fingered the treetops as if merely passing the time before those fingers would curl into fists. Even as the rains fell harder, challenging their every step, they tracked onward, all the while building reserves within themselves for the impending encounter with the alien machine known as the scout, now unmasked on worldwide TV as a lethal mechanism from another world, capable of killing and destroying in the most unthinkable way.

Hawkins thought about Linda now, back in that hospital bed, dehydrated, falling in and out of consciousness. Weak.

Linda had been made of iron ever since she took the job. She had worked so hard and had proved herself worthy of the uniform every hour, every day. And now she was down. Hawkins couldn't shake the guilt that had managed to sink its razor-fine claws into him.

This was your fault, Cliff. You let it go a day too long. Should have called in the big guns the moment you found that parachute thing and the other part of it. But you hesitated—you hesitated and now look where you are. You may be a hundred steps from your own terrible death, Cliff. And—oh yeah—these young boys out here with you—toast. Their families will have something to say about that...won't they?

Hawkins realized that if he lived through this encounter tonight, he'd face the firing squad tomorrow morning when all of this hit the wires. Mayor Richard Kelley would read him the riot act and the city council members would go on TV one by one and decry his gross negligence in a time of national security. Hawkins began to ponder where exactly he and the wife could move after the whole mountain blew and their lives reduced to a small pile of smoldering ash. Maybe Florida. Hawkins cleared his mind, all of his senses refocusing now on what was just ahead as they weaved around a tight cluster of trees with low hanging branches and vines.

Hawkins was the first to see it, then Mitch, and then the rest of them. It materialized slowly from the gloom, like a vessel surfacing from deep, dark waters. Its very presence was dreadful, and they all felt icy hands grab hold of their hearts.

The scout sat still, centered in a hasty clearing of trees, padded by tall, moist grass that swayed serpent like and slow. Its hulking silhouette beneath the dimness of the storm-choked sky was alarming. But most troubling was the simple fact that it was so still and quiet. Dead? Or waiting?

They hung motionless for a full minute, assessing the machine. Hawkins crab-stepped a meter left to try and pinpoint targets on it, focusing on the legs. But the tall grass was creating a slow, undulating veil around the lower part of its mighty limbs, obscuring the joints of the lower half. And the cancerous storm above them had eliminated the late day sun, establishing a murkiness that resembled painful dark depths of the sea where sunlight suffocated to death. It was how they all felt standing there in the rain—tiny and fragile.

Hawkins gave a brief hand motion, a command that they should huddle close to him in order to hear and understand orders. Having served on the ground as a sergeant during Gulf War I, he understood all too well what happened when orders weren't followed or understood, most of all in the moments of battle when loaded weapons coupled with raw nerves and adrenaline met enemy fire.

"We are going to form a line, three meter spread, and open fire on my order," he said through his teeth. "We target the joints in the legs first to take out its mobility. After that we target the head, or whatever the hell that thing is on top. Keep firing until the son of a bitch is dead on its side." From the horizon of the southwest came a subharmonic growl that distilled into a ferocious call of thunder.

"Masks," he said. They all adjusted their gas masks, securing the seals.

Hawkins saw a bright flash in his periphery, a staccato pop of luminosity nearby.

Lightning, he thought. *We've been put on notice! We have to do this now. We cannot wait another minute!*

Immediately came another burst of illumination, and it was only then Hawkins realized it wasn't lightning—it was the flash of a camera. He spied a dim, hunched-over form, lurking toward the scout, closing on it through the tall grass like some curious, forest animal. Closer and closer. There was another flash, and the picture imprinted in their vision by that single strobe of light was of Derek Smith, holding out his phone, a mere two feet from the scout, snapping a picture of it.

Hawkins waved at him, furious, his nerves suddenly on total edge. *The stupid son of a bitch*, he thought.

"Derek," he seethed, "Derek get away from it! Get back here now! That's an order!" Through the gas mask, his voice was anemic.

Derek glanced back with a look on his face that suggested some supreme sense of satisfaction blended with a dose of adolescent carelessness.

"Just one more for Facebook," he said, and snapped the last photo he would ever take. What happened next came swiftly. Hawkins sensed it in those tiny cracks between moments where time somehow accordions and slows, where all at once everything feels like it's underwater.

A long, shrouded form materialized from the grass, as large as a fire hose, gliding like a snake, swinging upward. The sampling limb of the scout curled in the air just above Derek's head before it suddenly, and with brutal machine force, plunged into his chest cavity, exploding through his sternum like a shotgun blast through tissue paper.

The scout pitched upward, its giant legs unfolding with astonishing speed and agility, the machine now fully operational. That terrible, elongated head unstowed from the deck and immediately pivoted toward Derek, its cavernous alien eyes centering on his writhing form as it snatched him off the ground as a child would seize a small doll from a toy box. Derek hung miserably in the air, pinned to the end of the robotic limb, his arms and legs flailing, pin wheeling hopelessly as the howl of the scout's razor sharp abrasion tool, now buried in his heart, filled the air. He unleashed a soprano shriek, primal and enflamed that daggered the air above them all as if his soul and spirit were being mauled in the same way his body was. A high voltage burst of lightning overhead lit the world for a moment, burning that image in the backs of their eyes like a hot branding iron.

"Jesus Christ!" Mitch screamed as he lifted his shotgun, packing the butt tightly against his shoulder. His aim uncertain, he pulled the trigger hard, the enormous kickback of the weapon punching him, throwing him even further off target. He fired again reflexively, the round going wild somewhere in the ground, exploding a small stone and sending it straight to rock heaven.

Brett lined up his best guess for a shot, mashing the trigger down, the blast buffeting him, causing his aim to pull right and high, missing the scout which was now jinking evasively like a hunted animal.

The sky exploded above them in a furious flash, giving them all a glimpse of something tumbling through the air, falling toward them; a limp, multi-limbed shape. Derek's body struck the wet grass in front of them with a hideous, bone-snapping thud.

"Fuck!" Brett screamed, animal rage coursing through his body, his veins on fire, blood boiling. He pumped in another round with a loud clack, tilting the barrel for a shot at one of the big legs, steadying himself. It was getting harder to see anything as rain fell in a cruel downpour, drops streaking their gas masks, blurring their sights and disorienting them. One by one they tore the masks off, raindrops striking them directly in the face.

Hawkins steadied himself for a shot at the mast of the scout. The rain peppered his vision as he pulled the trigger, the round grazing past the big, alien hood, vanishing into the dark sky beyond it. As his vision atrophied beneath the downpour, the sounds encircling him became more fierce and tactile: the deafening discharge of guns, live rounds cutting the air loudly, the screams of the men fueled with primal pure rage, the drone of those otherworldly mechanical parts of the scout growling, the bitter howl of hostile winds pregnant with hard rain—a hellish sound tapestry.

The great metal beast lunged at them, moving impossibly fast, the ground whimpering beneath the pounding mass of it, its terrible multi-limbed profile becoming a nightmarish silhouette against the storm cloud ceiling. It charged them like a locomotive, imbued with terrible strength and speed, locked in an implacable charge straight ahead. The sight of it was so surreal, so fantastic that it seemed an apparition, like something from a movie and nothing more.

The shock alone caused every one of them a moment of tragic hesitation as the scout broke through their rank, trampling them like small insects. Hawkins stood helpless as several of the men fell beneath it, those giant piston legs stamping down on top of them, pulverizing them in the wet ground. Michael Brewer, the youngest man in his department, who had started work for them just three months earlier, took the worst of it as his head and shoulders vanished horrifically beneath the steel-hard foot of the machine.

Hawkins threw down his shotgun and grabbed his semi-automatic pistol. He was quick with the pistol and accurate. The machine was passing him, a mere few feet away. He couldn't miss. Hawkins unloaded his entire clip against the body of it, firing round after round like a man possessed. He bellowed now, feeling the rage explode inside like a bomb. And even after the last round had exited the pipe and the slide popped back empty, he kept pulling the trigger.

All at once he felt something strike him and the ground fell out from under him, leaving him, the world inverting. Hawkins suddenly realized he was in the air, tumbling and falling, a glass-sharp pain erupting in his side. He hit the ground and rolled, dark shapes slashing through his periphery, wet leaves and branches slapping him in the face. It all ended, and the last thing he saw as he fought to lift his head was the scout crashing through the deep woods like a berserk, super-powered Tyrannosaur, racing directly away from them. And despite his semi-addled mind, he knew it was heading due east toward the highway.

———————

The scout trampled quickly through the woods, slaloming the largest trees while snapping smaller ones that were in its path as if they were mere brittle twigs. All the while it began organizing its data from the last few days. Everything it had observed, recorded, ingested, and analyzed chemically in its onboard laboratory was being loaded into a memory buffer. Once it cleared this forest boundary, it could better find the signal it was looking for and from there, join the data stream and upload everything. The plan had been altered, the survey cut short. It was the primary species that occupied this planet—they had impeded with the survey and so corresponding aggressive and now evasive action was required. It was a complication to the mission.

Nevertheless, the scout would finish the formula it was preparing, find an appropriate spot for dispersal and deliver the mixture in aerosol form, just as the others were supposed to. The results of the change would be observed and properly analyzed for what would become a final mixture that would be delivered later by a vehicle that would detonate the combination in the upper atmosphere of this planet, thus allowing it to consume everything globally. This world, like others before it, would be irrevocably transformed, reborn and finally, repopulated. The scout moved effortlessly onward, searching for a suitable ground target for delivery of its compound.

CHAPTER 43

Linda woke suddenly from a dream with a loud moan and a desperate intake of breath. It startled Jack, who had been seated at her bedside in the small, antiseptic room. He touched her arm gently to let her know she was okay and that whatever dark dream she had just surfaced from, that it was over and that she was safe.

"Linda, it's okay. It's okay. It's me, Jack. You're all right," he said.

She glanced at him first. Her eyes then darted toward the tube fastened to a pronounced vein in her arm, then to the lime green privacy curtain hanging overhead that nicely obscured the nurse's station in the corridor, and then back to Jack. All at once she was alert and present.

"Jack, did you bring me here?"

"Yes."

"You carried me to the car, and then what happened?"

"I drove you back here and they helped bring you in. You were unconscious."

Linda thought it all through. She remembered Jack standing over her as she lay on the floor of the forest, then him lifting her and carrying her back to her car.

"What happened, Jack? What happened to Kyle?"

Jack lowered his head.

"I should never have trusted him. I should have taken you back myself the minute you were feeling faint."

She let that settle a moment—Kyle left her there after she had blacked out. She remembered throwing up, her vision tunneling downward into a great black abyss and the ground falling upward toward her and then nothing. So she'd been lying there, alone in the wet forest undergrowth for how long? Had Jack not found her, who knows how it might have ended for her? She was thankful, glad to be alive. Then she remembered something else.

"Jack, what about the footage you shot on his camera? What happened to it? Have you had a chance to look at it?"

Jack shook his head.

"No, I didn't get the footage. He duped me. I should have known. The tape was useless because the camera was instead shooting digitally to memory cards. He gave me the tape and took the cards, and the footage. I got nothing."

Linda put her head back on the pillow, now staring up into the fluorescent bank in the ceiling. She closed her eyes a moment and sighed.

"Well, I guess that's it. It's out. Everyone's going to know and we'll have to...Jack, what is it?"

Jack looked grim-faced. Hawkins asked him not to tell her what had happened unless she had somehow already seen it on the TV. She hadn't, and Jack figured if he was a better actor he could pretend it didn't happen. But the reality of it, the horror of what unfolded on worldwide television was too great. And in that moment he saw no value in keeping it from her.

"It's already out, Linda. The whole world knows about it."

She blanched instantly, her eyes flaring.

"What! How? How is that possible?"

Jack said, "We all watched it on the news about forty minutes ago. There are more of those scouts out there, a total of eighteen that they've confirmed in different spots around the world. It's hit all the newswires. And one of the scouts, the one in Australia...it, um...it launched some sort of..."

He couldn't bring himself to say it outright because he choked up reflexively, his eyes beginning to tear. It was the look on her face as it disintegrated from her bones, the shrill sound of her scream that rang fresh in his memory.

"Jack," Linda said, alarmed. "What's happened?"

Jack collected himself and began to describe everything they had seen, everything they had heard, all known information and even what he had heard from Stephen at the Jet Propulsion Laboratory some eighteen hundred miles away. Linda listened closely the entire time, her face ever so slowly becoming more focused, her posture in the bed stronger as she began to sit up. She faced him squarely.

"I want to see it."

Jack hesitated, his frown hard and severe.

"No, you don't."

"Give me my phone," she said.

Jack said sternly, "I'm warning you, this was a chemical attack and what it does to this woman is—"

"My phone. Get it," she said, unflinching.

Jack went back through the personal things they had brought in with her, located her phone, and reluctantly handed it to her. She took it carefully, and brought up the news on her web browser. Jack turned away from her and began to walk out of the room.

"Wait," she said, "where are you going?"

"I can't watch it again," he said. "I can't listen to her scream one more time."

And without another word he was gone from the room. Linda felt the floor drop out from under her, and for a moment thought perhaps she should heed his advice and put the phone away. But deep down she needed to know. She needed to see it happen—all of it. It would cement the truth in her, and she'd know, with all pretenses gone, what they were up against right here, right now. The signal was anemic in this tiny room, but she was able to connect, and pull up the now infamous video clip. Linda sat very still and played the clip from the beginning.

Hawkins laid very still, his eyes clamped against the big drops of rain that were spotting him, soaking through his uniform and hair.

You're hurt, Cliff, he thought. *No sudden moves, just take it slow.*

He began by moving his toes, then his feet. And then he moved his legs.

I'm not paralyzed, he thought. *I can get up.*

He carefully rolled onto his side and that's when the pain exploded in him like a bomb. He took a shallow breath, which immediately caused the pain to amplify. *Ribs*, he thought, *broken ribs*. At least that's all he hoped it was and not something more serious or internal. *You have to get up*. It took what felt like an hour for him to do it, but slowly, his throbbing side protesting every moment, he managed to ascend to his knees and then miserably to his feet where he rested a moment, steadying himself, now finally able to survey the scene around him.

A dozen yards away, Mitch was sitting in the mud silent, his eyes distant, rain running down his cheeks, blending seamlessly with the tears. Around them, the three others that had survived the encounter with the scout were gathering themselves slowly. And then there were the dead—seven to be precise—young men, all of them. Gone.

Tactical error, he thought. He'd assumed—wrongly—that based on what he'd seen on the news from Germany, this machine could be taken down with just a few men equipped with standard issue firepower. Tactical error.

Never assume anything of the sort under such extraordinary circumstances, he thought. *Cliff, you've slipped. You stopped caring and you were just riding out the time until retirement. You stopped caring because you were getting tired; tired of all of it.*

"We have to radio C.I.R.T.," Mitch said, his voice steady, his tone matter-of-fact. The C.I.R.T was Merriweather Critical Response Team, trained in special weapons and tactics designed to handle critical situations and emergencies. He turned and glared at Hawkins with something that reminded the elder man of a thousand yard stare. He'd never seen anything like it in Mitch who had played the part of a clown for so many years. This was the guy who would barge into conversations, pretend to know what the hell everyone was talking about and then be the expert in the room. And then there was the "C-Clamp" gag: Mitch would curl his fingers into semi-circles, creep silently up behind someone and then dig those calloused hard fingers deep into the armpits and squeeze as hard as he could. The result was a tickle that immediately turned painful. He'd laugh like a loon after the victim would twist-pull their way free from his grasp and then dart out of the room as quickly as possible thereby escaping retaliation. As Hawkins looked at him in the midst of the dreadful scene that surrounded them, that same obnoxious guy was gone, and Hawkins suspected, was gone forever.

Mitch said, "Sheriff, this thing is moving rapidly toward town. The forces back at the highway are inadequate. We have to mobilize the Critical Response Team. Right now." Hawkins agreed with him and said okay.

"Sheriff," Mitch said sternly, "there's no more time!"

I said okay, Hawkins thought. But that was just it...he couldn't speak and he hadn't said it out loud. He couldn't draw in the air necessary to support his voice let alone push the words out. He hunched over and Mitch became immediately aware of what was happening and he dashed over to Hawkins, examining his side. It proved nearly impossible to do in the murky dimness out here. But Hawkins' iron clenched jaw, the short, desperate breaths, provided enough information. Mitch grabbed his radio and mercifully found a signal. He called everything in, and it was done.

Quickly he turned to the others and spoke without missing a syllable.

"We need to get the Sheriff safely out of here. He's seriously injured so we've got to move him carefully. The storm is building over our heads and it won't be another hour before the worst of it is right on top of us."

He made direct eye contact with Hawkins who was breathing shallow which afforded him some relief from the pain. As excruciating as it was, even the slightest respite was welcome.

"Sheriff, are you able to walk?" Mitch asked.

Hawkins took a step, and then another, feeling his weight on his legs and feet. There was stability. The pain in his side seemed largely unaffected as he stepped. It was the breathing that caused the most severe pain. Hawkins nodded—yes, he could walk.

Carefully now, they all stayed close together and began to make their way through the forest, heading back toward town, where even now the men of the critical response team were assembling their gear and vehicles.

CHAPTER 43

J ACK HAD WALKED AWAY FROM Linda's room when his phone rang. Without looking at who it was, he answered.

"Hello?"

"Jack," Samantha said, "Jack are you alright?"

"Yes, yes I'm okay. Sorry about earlier, but I've been a little—"

"Jack, I don't know where you are right now or what you're doing, but can you please come home right now? It's your mom."

What now?

Jack said, "What's wrong with her?"

Samantha said, "We were turning channels on the TV and the news came on..."

He knew where this was going, and he was furious. *Why did they let her watch the news!* It would upset her. In spite of the fact that Marion was end stage Alzheimer's, she still reacted to intense stimuli: loud noises, unexpected visitors at the door, and sometimes movies if they were too violent or scary.

"Jack, I'm sorry, I didn't know! I had no idea! It's just so terrible! Marion's really upset. I can't calm her down. I need you here, Jack, please. She needs you!"

And all at once he realized that right then, more than anything, he needed to go back home and comfort his mom as best he could. Whatever happened next concerning the scout was not up to him. He had absolutely no control over it. Jack quickly ran back toward Linda's room, arriving just as she finished putting her uniform back on. She looked at him intently.

"What are you doing?" he asked.

"Someone from the department is coming for me."

All at once, Jack understood.

"They weren't able to stop it, were they?"

She adjusted her belt, radio and weapon, hardening up to fight the tears that might so easily come were she not back in her uniform. The conversation she'd just had with Kyle Smith from the department was dreadfully blunt: an attempt to take down the device with standard issue firepower had failed. Officers were apparently dead after the encounter and some were injured including Sheriff Hawkins. The device was moving quickly due east toward the highway—toward them. C.I.R.T. had been mobilized and this was now deemed a high-risk, high-danger situation.

"They've called out the critical response team. Actually they've called out everyone. The scout is coming toward us now, moving fast. I'm going to do what I can."

Jack locked eyes with her, a long look of understanding falling between them.

Finally she said, "Keep an eye on the news. If we can't stop it, then follow whatever instructions you hear once the emergency broadcasting system is activated."

Jack hesitated. "Did you watch it?" he asked. "Did you watch the video?"

She finished with the last of her uniform, not looking at him, not saying anything. She crossed the small room, preparing to leave. She reached out for him and they embraced, she grabbing on to him tightly. He held her very close.

"Hope to see you again, Jack," she said. And then she let go of him and was gone.

Jack made it home in less than ten minutes by way of streets that were eerily hollow and pooled with shadows, blanketed by the downpour that was a mere prelude to the big system that was about to drop like Thor's Hammer. In the distance he heard police sirens crying like wild wolves on the hunt—hungry for their otherworldly prey that was on the move, approaching them, preparing to fulfill its mission objective just like the other devices around the world.

Jack pulled into the driveway of the house. Lights were on inside. He pushed the big button on the garage opener, the weathered wooden door lumbering upward. Jack left the car and trotted quickly through the downpour, up the driveway, into the garage and through the door that deposited him directly into the kitchen. The moment he entered he heard Samantha's voice from the living room.

"Marion, honey, it's okay. It's going to be okay."

Jack breached the corner into the living room. Samantha was sitting on one of the hard wooden chairs that belonged to the dining room set. She was planted next to Marion who was curled in her big, soft recliner that nearly swallowed her small, fragile frame.

She was chanting, "No, no, no."

"Mom," Jack said, approaching her carefully and slowly as not to alarm her any further. Her trembling gaze fell on him, and he sank to his knees in front of her so they were joined eye to eye.

"Richard," she said. "Richard, help me."

Her eyes were wide and protuberant, distraught, appearing even larger by magnification of the prescription glasses she wore.

"Mom, it's me, Jack," he said, gently.

She quieted, glaring at him, trying desperately to recognize and discern him. Jack could only imagine what she was experiencing—rivers of thoughts and images passing through her mind, pooling here and there, drifting mostly, all broken into pieces, disconnected and dull.

He took her hand gently, feeling her skin that was week by week growing paper thin on her.

"Richard," she said. He was about to correct her, but instead didn't. He smiled at her, gently putting his other hand over hers. He spoke softly then, his eyes not leaving hers.

"Yes, honey. It's me," he finally said.

With what must have taken great effort on her part, Marion smiled just a little. It was so subtle, so fragile, but there just the same. Jack smiled warmly in return.

"It's going to be okay, now," he said.

"Yes," she said immediately.

He nodded kindly at her.

"Yes," he said.

Marion said it one more time. "Yes."

"I love you," Jack said.

"Yes, I know," she said in the most matter-of-fact way, nodding faintly. And Jack knew, at least for the moment, that she was going to be okay.

CHAPTER 44

THE SCOUT CRASHED ONWARD THROUGH the woods, moving even faster than before. It found this environment—this entire planet—a vile place that served no good purpose other than to support its indigenous life forms including the main species. That alone was reason to terraform and remold it into something much better. They had remote surveyed many hundreds of worlds and from those had identified the best candidates for the change. The scouts were sent ahead to do a more complete ground analysis. Only so much information could be captured remotely. Surface operations that included environmental studies were the only way to be sure the larger and more complex operation of terraforming would be possible.

And as of now, based on all the data it had acquired in a short span of time, the scout saw this place as a strong candidate for the operation. But it would have to hurry and finish the mixture, deploy it into the environment and catalogue the reaction. From there it would send that data back via the large stream along with the other scouts.

Up ahead were many lights, hues of red and blue, which blinked brightly through the trees. Forms took shape among the lights—small standing forms—the species. They were here to oppose the scout's activities. This was a complication, so it seemed, but the scout would finish the operation. Early if necessary. The species would be eliminated once the deploy happened. The mixture was almost ready. It was time.

The members of the Critical Response Team stood motionless on the paved shoulder of the highway in the rain, automatic rifles packed snugly into their shoulders, waiting, tense, gas masks snug on their faces. Flanking them some distance back were officers, hunkered down behind their cruiser doors—dozens and dozens of them, all waiting, all poised for battle. The winds rolled over them, gaining strength, the rains coming in diagonally. The sky discharged a massive flash, gunshot thunder instantaneous. Linda was on the edge of the perimeter, crouched behind a cruiser door, pistol firm in her good hand, peregrine eyes set open despite the hard falling raindrops.

She had been thinking about the video on CNN that she had seen, despite Jack's plea for her not to watch it. The images, the sounds, were now embedded in her mind, set on a nightmarish playback loop. She could hear the woman screaming, the pitch of that primal shriek sharp in her memory.

And the woman's face...*her face. No one should have to die like that! No one! No way this goddamned thing is getting through here*, Linda thought, rage surfacing in her bloodstream.

She'd empty her gun ten times and if necessary throw rocks after that until the damn thing was scrap metal. The death of the Australian reporter grew faint in her memory and then vanished all together. Linda entered a place of complete and enormous focus, her mind a closed steel trap. Nothing else was getting in there now. And that's when they all saw it, lurking just behind the wall of trees, towering in the dimness, the mast swiveling, camera eyes plotting its course. Inculcated with its primary objective.

Everything held tomb still for what seemed like minutes until it moved, exploding out from the forest like an express train, lunging at them, tremoring the ground beneath its trampling weight.

"Open fire," was what they barely heard beneath the roaring wind and thunder. They unleashed hell, every last one of them, fingers flat on their triggers. An explosion of muzzle flashes lit the highway stroboscopically in concert with the deafening fusillade. A hail of rounds struck the body of the scout all at once, tearing at its hull violently, nipping and then eating organic joints in the front legs which tipped and staggered, but battled for power and purchase. The scout rerouted power to its rear limbs, muscling forward further, closing on the front line of the team. They lightning-slapped new magazines into their weapons and fired relentlessly. Hundreds of rounds hit the scout, which slowed, its poise destabilizing, until those powerful front legs collapsed, the joints splitting open in a mess of metal and alien tissue, the platform tipping, falling canted on the wet road. *It was down!*

Linda stood from her cover, dried her gun into the hind legs that were still moving, pumping up and down, desperate for control. But they too were failing as another shower of rounds impacted them, tearing apart couplers, hinges and hoses, dark fluid jetting out of them like blood.

Suddenly her focus fell on the mast as the hideous alien head turned toward her and tilted upward. And at last she saw it—just as Jack had described it earlier—the face of the scout. It held on her with those horrible tunnel-dark eyes, draconian and heartless.

The legs were destroyed. The scout could no longer move, though its eyes, it seemed, were still tracking her, processing her...judging her. The firing ceased all at once and everyone held perfectly still, hearing only the sharp ictus of rain on the pavement. But Linda heard something else then—the scream of the woman reporter, like a siren in her head. It drowned out everything. Like an embedded shard of glass in Linda's memory, a phantom image sequence of the woman's gruesome death replayed, tormenting her. Over and over.

Linda felt herself go numb. She was empty, but for one thought.

Kill it. Kill it now.

She reloaded her weapon and started out solo toward the scout in a dead-walk, her stride mechanical like a terminator. The whole troop watched in astonishment.

"Cease fire! Everyone stay back!"

Linda didn't stop.

"Everyone back!"

The command from the C.I.R.T. Sergeant fell useless beside her. She couldn't hear the command. All she could hear was that tortured scream from nine thousand miles away. Linda raised her gun aiming directly at the face, at those cold, alien eyes.

Cease fire! Everyone back!

Linda fired into the lenses, round after round, still dead-walking a perfect line right up to the dying machine.

The scout watched her approach, trying frantically to assess its own integrity, furiously rerouting power to its backup systems, calculating some last ditch effort to save the samples and data. Its portion of this mission had failed, so it seemed. It would be unable to deploy the mixture and catalogue the results. The species here had interfered, and now one of them was attacking with a weapon, destroying the scout's visual instruments used for navigation and sample acquisition.

But perhaps all was not lost. There might be another way. And so it began to talk to its own systems, preparing a contingency plan.

Linda pumped through her clip until it was dry, the last few rounds tearing directly into those big lenses, splintering them, dissecting pieces of connecting alien tissue that surrounded them until any semblance of that terrible alien visage was gone. Dead.

The scout was dead.

She hung suspended in the moment with the slide of her gun already sprung open, the empty muzzle still pointed at the creature. Then, and only then, did she lower her weapon as sounds began to materialize around her and she heard someone screaming.

"Back away, deputy! Back away now!"

Linda carefully stepped back, shedding her trance, climbing out of it as if from an oversized coat. First thing she remembered after that was the glare of all the lights, the long shadows they cast on the wet pavement. And then she felt the pull—someone grabbed her good arm and was pulling her away from the detritus of the scout.

"Get back," the man from the C.I.R.T. had shouted while he held on to her tightly. She wrenched her arm from his grip, staring at him with green, fiery eyes.

"Don't touch me! I'm going!"

"Back to your cruiser, over there," he said in a brassy, military tone.

"I know where it is," she countered, and walked on, closing the slide on her weapon.

She was pissed, but understood that this guy, and all of them for that matter, were amped on a million volts. Linda let it go and walked away without saying another word...*because the scout was dead.* And that was all she cared about. It was the only thing that mattered.

What happened next, none of them actually saw. A black, semi-nacreous mist rose from beneath the body of the scout. Now moving swarm-like, it hovered momentarily there like fabric in the air above the dead scout before it glided away, dissolving into the forest wall, into the shadows.

CHAPTER 45

J ACK HELPED SEE MARION OFF to bed after they had played her a DVD of the movie *Singin' in the Rain*, starring Gene Kelly, Donald O'Connor, and Debbie Reynolds. Marion had always loved musicals and had herself been a singer and performer before she married Richard. She'd continued doing local theater and teaching voice after Amy and Jack were born, but most of her time was dedicated to being a mother of two very bright, ambitious kids. It was during the movie that Samantha urged Jack aside into the dining room so they could talk without Marion hearing the conversation.

"Jack, I'm so sorry about what happened. I didn't know," Samantha said, her voice shaky. "We were just watching the news and then that reporter was on live and it...it happened so fast, I couldn't change the channel."

"I understand," Jack said. "We need to keep her occupied with other things now. Hopefully by the time she's in bed, she won't remember it."

Samantha lowered her voice even further then.

"Jack, I know you've been doing something with the police here. Is that what's going on? Is it one of those things?"

The charade was over. Anyone could have seen the truth of it in his eyes. There was no profit it hiding it any longer.

"Yes," he said.

Samantha cupped her hands, covering her mouth as her eyes began to lightly puddle.

"Are they going after it?" she asked.

"Yes," he said, and he thought about Linda out there in the rain and wind—out there with the scout.

They had gotten Marion quietly off to bed, though the thunder that erupted from that angry system above startled her and made the process more difficult than usual. Eventually, they got her settled and comfortable in her hospital bed. Samantha volunteered to stay with her in the bedroom for a while and make sure she could actually fall asleep. Jack agreed and made his way back toward the living room. He decided to turn on the news. He had to know what was happening out there in the world, and more importantly, what was happening just a few miles away.

What if they failed to stop the scout and it was on its way into town to release its mixture? What if there's an order from the Emergency Broadcasting System and they had to evacuate?

Jack flipped from the DVD input to cable TV and immediately the story was clear: the latest device that had been discovered outside of Merriweather, Indiana, had been destroyed by a critical response team and local police. No pictures from the site had come in yet, but reliable sources, according to CNN, had confirmed the scout had been destroyed. And while this began to sink in, Jack heard his phone chirp as a text message appeared. It was from

Linda's number, and simply said: *We killed it. The scout is dead.*

Jack smiled, feeling an immense wave of relief fall on him. He quickly thumbed a response on the keypad: *Are you okay?*

Moments went by, and then minutes. Then ten minutes.

Finally, she responded: *Yes. I'll be okay.*

Jack crept gently into Marion's room to tell Samantha the good news. Moments later, his phone rang. Amy.

"Jack," she said anxiously when he answered, "I just saw it on the news. One of those devices was near you guys! Are you all okay?"

"Yes, we're fine. They destroyed it. It's all over."

And in saying it out loud, Jack felt even more convinced it was true. It was over, and they were going to be okay. He stayed up another hour to watch more of the broadcast. The stories coming in from around the world were the same. The devices were being terminated, and only a handful of them actually deployed their lethal aerosol. Mercifully it had only been the Australian reporter and her cameraman that had perished as a direct result of mixture. As the commentary went on, the sentiment became one of thankfulness and a sobering realization that things could have been worse...a lot worse.

Jack finally shut it off, exhausted. He drifted toward the guest bedroom, but passed the door and instead went into Richard's office. *The letter.* He went straight to his father's desk, opened the top drawer, and removed the envelope with his handwritten name on it. *Read it.*

Jack tore the envelope open slowly. Inside was a folded piece of yellow legal paper, which he carefully removed. At the top was a list: ATTORNEY, BANK, and INVESTMENTS, with phone numbers following each. The rest of the letter was hastily scratched on the canary paper in blue ballpoint pen; words precariously perched on the faint ruled lines as if they might fall off. The letters themselves were wavy from Richard's unsteady hand.

It read: JACK, TRIED TO CALL YOU AGAIN. DIDN'T HAVE A CHANCE TO TELL YOU IN PERSON—SORRY FOR BEING SO HARD ON YOU. GUESS I LEARNED THAT FROM MY FATHER. HOPE YOU'LL FORGIVE ME. FEEL LIKE A SCOUT, ABOUT TO SET FOOT IN A NEW WORLD AS YET UNSEEN. NEVER BELIEVED IN GOD, BUT HOPE THAT IF I WAS WRONG ABOUT HIM, THAT HE'LL BE KIND AND SHOW A STUBBORN OLD MAN SOME MERCY. PLEASE TAKE GOOD CARE OF YOUR MOM. KEEP LOVING HER. KEEP HER SAFE. SHE NEEDS YOU. TAKE CARE, JACK. DAD.

Jack felt himself choke up reflexively, and he sobbed freely for the first time in weeks.

CHAPTER 46

J ACK AWOKE SLOWLY FROM A valley of dreams he couldn't remember. He lay very still, thinking about what happened last night, thankful that he was waking up in a world where the scout was no longer a lurking, sinister presence.

We killed it. The scout is dead.

Linda's text message hung in front of him like a banner, those words weighted with absolute finality. But he wondered what the world might become in the aftermath of something like this. The truth was, it was not really over. For Jack it instantly brought up memories of the morning of September 12, 2001. The world had crawled from the fiery ashes of the attack into a motionless haze that never lifted or thinned. And Jack suspected that this morning, some eleven years later, the haze might just become more dense and opaque. He felt a heaviness enter the room, a weight slowly pressing down on him in the bed.

Jack's phone vibrated loudly on the cheap wooden nightstand as a call came in. He turned over quickly and squinted to read the name on the screen. Stephen Hunter. Jack answered immediately.

"Hello, Stephen," Jack said.

"Hey, Jack. Saw on the news about Indiana. Is everyone there okay?"

"Yes, everyone here at home is okay. What's happening out there? You get the DSN back under control?"

Stephen said, "On the record, yes. We were able to cut off the flow and gain control of the network, but not before a lot of data went up. Between you and me, there's more to it than that. I'm not even sure why I'm telling you this, maybe because of your dad."

Jack sat upright in the bed. "What is it?"

Stephen spoke in a lower voice. "We tracked the signal as it left. It terminated about seven minutes later."

"Terminated," Jack said.

"Yeah."

Jack knew instantly what that meant—or at least what it implied. Signals sent and received from the Deep Space Network traveled at the speed of light—186,000 miles per second. Multiplying that by the actual time a signal spent traveling allowed for a calculation of distance. To reach a rover on Mars, depending on the orbital distance of the planet from Earth, the travel time for a signal could range anywhere from 10 to 14 minutes. Stephen had said the signal terminated at 7 minutes.

Jack said, "When you say terminated, you mean—"

"Captured. Received might be a better word," he interjected. "You can do the math just like any of us here at the lab. That's inner solar system. That's our neighborhood."

All at once the implication grew claws and began burrowing.

"You think it's them? They're close?"

"Jack, I'll be honest—I don't know what to think. After what happened yesterday, I feel like we've all been sent back to kindergarten. I don't mind telling you we're all pretty unsettled here."

"Yeah, I understand," Jack said.

"Look, I'd better get going. We're going to be pulling some rough shifts here for a while. Take care of yourself, Jack. Sorry about your dad. He was a really great man."

"Thanks, Stephen."

"Sure. And hey, when you're safely back in Pasadena, let's get together for a drink or something."

"You got it."

"Okay," Stephen said, and hung up.

Jack opened the calculator on his phone and did a quick computation based on seven minutes travel time at 186,000 miles per second. The result was unsettling...78,120,000 miles.

That was closer than Mars was to Earth. In solar system terms, that distance was effectively in the neighborhood or just down the street.

They're close.

Jack shoved the thought away. *No, no...it didn't mean that.*

The signal terminated. It didn't mean that someone or something actually captured it. It could have also been an error. If the DSN had been hacked, who knows what kind of errors might occur once they got it back online. But just a week ago, if someone had told Jack that a biomechanical geochemist from a distant, alien world could touch down virtually undetected near a city with a population of 51,000, he'd have categorically dismissed it. So he couldn't entirely dismiss the possibility that they, *the terraformers*, had captured some of their data, and that they were close.

They'd want the missing data, he thought. *They'd not travel all this distance, come this close, and not get what they came for.* The implication of that settled on him like a lead vest. Slowly, he climbed out of bed and got dressed.

Marion was hunched at the dining room table over a plate of hot scrambled eggs. Cathy sat beside her, carefully feeding her small bites, all the while encouraging her.

"Remember to chew your food, honey," she said.

Marion stared at her. It would take several seconds until finally she'd begin to work her jaw and chew the portion in her mouth. This was part of the disease, and Jack knew that there would come a point not so far off in which she'd be unable to chew anything or even swallow. Cathy offered Jack a paltry smile. The anxiety and fear were shouting through her eyes.

"Good morning, Jack," she said, her voice hollow. "How is everything?"

Jack smiled in return as playing out a scene in a film.

"Okay. Things are okay. I'd just like to make sure that she doesn't see the news today."

Marion turned toward Jack, staring up at him, not recognizing him, not reacting in any discernable way, and Jack hoped it was a sign she'd forgotten about what she'd seen on the TV the night before.

"Of course," Cathy said, turning back toward Marion, wiping a small remnant of food from her lower lip. "We were worried about you, Jack. When you didn't come back home."

Jack nodded politely.

"So, were you...helping out on this thing?"

"Yes."

"Did you actually see—"

"Yes."

Cathy fell silent. She smiled at Marion and carefully gave her another, small bite of food.

"They've been saying all night that it's over. Is it, Jack?"

Jack nodded. "If that's what they're saying, then it's probably true. They know more about it than I do."

Cathy chuckled.

"I doubt that. You're Richard's son. Richard knew a lot of things. He saw things that other people missed."

It was true. Jack remembered when he was just a kid, hearing Dad talk about the Viking Mars Landers and how he was convinced that if they had only dug another several inches at their respective landing sites, they would have found the ice table. Many years later an observation by the Mars Reconnaissance Orbiter confirmed the presence of subterranean Martian ice in the mid latitudes of the planet, very near the equator, and in the very region that Viking 2 had landed.

To find ice that far from the pole of the planet would have likely reshaped the entire exploration directorate of NASA. Richard suspected, or somehow knew, all those years before, that the ice was there.

Jack's phone rang, and he excused himself from the room to answer it. He glanced casually at the screen, then felt tension when he saw the name on the call. It was Summer. He could ignore it and let it go to voicemail. But then he'd have to deal with it later. No, he was going to deal with this right now. Jack answered the call, glowering.

"Hello," he said in a moderate tone of ire.

"Jack? Jack, it's Summer." Her voice was small and weak, strangely so. He waited another moment before responding.

"What is it?" he said.

"I...I wanted to call and see if you were okay," she said.

What the hell kind of game is this now? he thought.

"Summer, what does it matter to you if I'm okay?" he asked.

"Listen, Jack, I realize that I've been...well, I wanted to say sorry about the other night, and I wanted you to know when we ran the story, I didn't mention you or use any of the footage with you in it. I didn't involve you in this."

"That's very big of you. So what do you want, a medal?"

She was quiet then for a few long moments.

"No. I just wanted a chance to say sorry."

Jack decided not to analyze or try and decode what was actually going on. He'd simply take it at face value and end the call.

"Okay, Summer" he said. "Now I really have to get going."

"I understand," she said. "Maybe some other time—later I mean—we could go have some coffee."

Jack rolled his eyes.

"I really don't think that's a good idea," he said. "I gotta go now."

Summer collected herself.

"Sure, Jack. I understand. Goodbye."

Jack hung up quickly.

Summer stood in her office, staring at her phone vacantly. She hadn't slept all night. She'd been at the station, helping to produce the story about the local scout, assembling the footage and writing the copy. In between her work on the story, she'd been watching the CNN feeds, reading the online pages from MSNBC, Drudge, FOX, ABC News, The New York Times, the entire spectrum of internet outlets for any further information on the other devices around the world. The amount of articles, blogs, and commentaries was staggering. And there was no doubt it would only multiply in the days to come.

She'd decided to call Jack and apologize after mustering the courage to do so, which was unusual for her. She felt strangely broken, shattered, as though when she hit the pavement coming into the station, something had happened to her soul. But that was just the opening. It was the video from Australia, the death of the woman reporter that really broke her down. It was that expression, that split second of realization that her life was ending in the most horrific way imaginable. And Summer realized in that moment—it could have been her standing there in the field, trying to get a story, when sudden death came for her. And she began thinking about her life, and the people in it.

She thought about Jack then, and how ten years earlier she had shoved him away just before he left for home, after their brief few weeks of uncomplicated fun together. At the time she used him as a toy, but deep down she was growing roots of feelings for him, and those feelings terrified her. All last night she had hoped there might be a chance, no matter how slight, that she could reconnect with him, and this time do it the right way.

There was a loud knock on the door of her office.

"Summer, it's Walter. I need to see you out here."

She was momentarily annoyed, but floated to the door and opened it. Her eyes dilated when she saw the two police officers standing there, stern-faced and frowning.

"Ma'am," said the first, "We need to speak with you."

"What did you do to Kyle?" Walter asked her, his face hard and fixed.

Two miles away, the swarm of micro scouts lifted from the forest floor, rising softly into the air like a cloud, hanging suspended near the top of the trees, thrumming in the morning air, assessing options. The mother scout had been terminated, preventing them from docking. If they couldn't dock, they couldn't transfer data. And on their own, they lacked any sort of antenna with which to move the data back home. But there was another problem concerning power. Without the mother scout, they'd be out of power and dead within a few weeks. They'd have to find someplace to unload the data before that happened; someplace it could be found and extracted later—a host device. And if that host had some source of energy, a low-gain beacon could be activated, signaling the others where to find it.

The micro scouts accessed information from the last few days. Having been joined to the mother scout, they were able to recall everything it had observed, processed and recorded. They sifted through data and images, ultimately identifying a suitable host that would offer a solution to this problem. *Because the data was the mission.* If the data could be preserved, the mission would be salvaged.

They would find this host—the one that made contact and had been scanned—plant the data, and when the others came, they could track it by the beacon, capture it, and extract the information. Nothing would be lost. This would work. The swarm ascended just above the tops of the trees and began to move softly, quietly ahead toward the chosen target, which would most likely be somewhere in the small town that lay just a few miles away.

CHAPTER 47

T HREE WEEKS PASSED LIKE THREE months, protracted and laborious. Jack had felt the weight of every day on his shoulders as the task of corralling Richard's estate, coupled with finding Marion a suitable place to live—or rather endure—her final chapter of Alzheimer's, seemed to swell. The heaviness was in the details of it all: life insurance forms, power of attorney issues, and beneficiary rules. Jack had figured the living trust that Richard had set up years ago would be simple to administer, but was surprised when it proved to be far more complicated. Unless an asset, whether it be physical or a bank account, was named in the trust, it would not automatically go into the trust. Some of Richard's assets like the house, the car, some paintings, and a savings account were designated for the trust. Other accounts were not. Some bank accounts had both Richard and Marion's name on them, others had only his. Since Richard had passed away, the power of attorney for him also went away, and this presented even more issues that Jack had to weed through with the bank, and with Richard's attorney, on an almost daily basis.

And back out in the world, three weeks meant people were trying to get back to their lives, to reassimilate into some sense of normalcy after all the scouts had been successfully terminated. Governments from all over the world muscled and sometimes bullied their way in to take possession of the remains of the scouts, making sure that no one but their militaries recovered all the remains and transferred them to secure and secret locations. It became Roswell on a global scale.

It took only a few short days for the media to begin politicizing the event, somehow tying the arrival of the scouts to political parties and failed policies of some sort or another. Liberals blamed conservatives and conservatives blamed liberals. Communists blamed capitalists, the Palestinians blamed Israel and the East blamed the West. Everyone had a finger to point and blame to assign, none of it based on reason or any empirical data, only knee-jerk emotional reactions and self-righteous crusades.

Finally came the theories that it was all about global warming: the scouts had arrived because of man's arrogance concerning the environment and they were merely benevolent planetary 'inspectors,' sent by a 'highly superior' race that was issuing some sort of intergalactic environmental report card, and Earth had most certainly earned a failing grade. It went on and on, the tenor of it all reaching a hard boil when finally Al Gore offered the governments of the world his services, which would include him contacting these intergalactic environmentalists, apologizing for the entire human race and somehow 'making it right.'

After a short while, Jack couldn't take it anymore. He stopped reading the online news and stopped watching all the late night broadcasts. He had to shut it out because it was becoming toxic, affecting his mood, which was already tenuous. Things were complicated and he found there was no time to mourn, no time to just cry or feel bad. Marion was getting worse. She was losing her appetite and losing weight. She was speaking a lot less and it was getting harder for her to walk. Whereas just a month earlier she would shuffle around the house with some help, now she spent most of the day sitting in her chair unwilling, or unable, to get up and walk.

They had to relocate her to a full-time care facility and their window of opportunity was shutting. Amy had spoken with Jack the week before and there had emerged a possibility at a place in Tampa near her home. She was going to follow up on it and see if they could get her on a waiting list for a room.

It was a Tuesday morning as Jack was piling papers on the floor of his dad's office for mass shredding that the doorbell rang. Jack ignored it and kept sorting. He heard voices down the hall, the rhythm of polite conversation, then footsteps that approached the office where he sat.

"Jack, someone here to see you," Cathy said from the hallway.

Jack huffed and tossed a handful of papers on the pile in the middle of the room that ascended into a mound that resembled a shield volcano. Annoyed, he finally glanced up to the doorway, now seeing Linda standing there. She looked great—better than great in dark jeans and a fitted, soft T-shirt.

"Hi, Jack," she said.

"Hey. How are you doing?" he asked.

"Shoulder is a lot better, healing nicely. Ditched the sling yesterday."

He smiled. "Glad to hear it. You look fantastic."

"Thanks," she said, her gaze falling on the pile of papers in the middle of the room. "How are you holding up?"

How was he holding up? Good question. One he'd not evaluated. The truth was, he had no idea how he was holding up. He felt like he was falling apart, yet was somehow able to keep hacking through the work day after day.

Jack said, "I'm taking it one thing at a time. Small pieces. That's about it. You can ask me again in another few months."

She shifted on her feet. "Are you going to be here that long?"

"I'm not completely sure," he said. "This is all taking a lot longer than I had expected."

A staccato silence fell between them.

Linda said, "Listen, Jack, I came by to thank you for pulling me out of woods. Literally."

Jack said, "You already did, but you're welcome. I'm just glad you're okay. How's the sheriff?"

"Resigned," she said, stiffening in her spot. "He'd been hospitalized with a couple broken ribs, and once he was able to leave and go home, he resigned. It's a big mess. We lost seven officers. Couple of them I considered friends."

Linda glanced down at the carpet.

"Sorry," Jack said. "Are you still a deputy?"

Linda said, "For now. County board has to appoint another sheriff, which is always a political ordeal."

She glanced back at him, looking directly into his eyes.

"Jack, I'm not even sure why I'm asking you this because I've been watching the news just like everyone else...but anything coming from you concerning all of this, I'm going to put some real stock in. Is it over?"

Jack said, "I'm not sure what you mean."

"Is all of this—this thing with the scouts—is it *over?*"

Jack thought about the conversation he'd had with Stephen Hunter just a few weeks earlier after it had all happened. The truth was, he had been thinking about it and the implications of it every day since. Jack held silent for a moment too long. He didn't want to bullshit her and he didn't want to scare her.

"I don't know," he said. "I don't know if it's over."

She held his stare carefully.

"Is that a gut feeling, a theory...or something more?" she asked.

"Yes," he said.

She nodded. "Is there anything else you can tell me?"

Jack spoke, his tone cautious, words measured. "Whoever sent the scouts didn't get all the data they needed once the devices were terminated. They'd likely have a cache or some sort of removable hardware that would store all the data from the scouts. I know...I mean, I suspect, that they'll come after it."

Linda said, "Invasion. Sounds like one of your books."

Jack said, "Yeah, it does."

Cathy, who had done her best to be polite and offer them some coffee, had interrupted. Linda graciously declined and informed her that she'd have to be leaving. Jack was annoyed, hoping to keep Linda around a little longer. He was growing feelings for her.

And what are you going to do about them, he thought. *You're leaving in a few weeks: back to Pasadena, back to your agent, back to work on the new book. What do you think could possibly happen here that wouldn't be problematic at best?*

They made their way toward the front door, but Linda stopped in the living room to say hello to Marion who was propped up in her recliner, in front of the *Andy Griffith Show* reruns on TV Land.

"Mom," Jack said, "This is Linda."

Marion held on the TV, apparently unaware that any of them were present with her in the room. Her eyes were more disconnected, her gaze more distant and cold. Linda knelt down next to the chair, coming eye-level with Marion, giving her a warm, compassionate smile.

"Hello, Marion," she said. "It's very nice to meet you."

Marion turned her head in the direction of Linda's voice, now seeing her face there.

"Oh," she said weakly.

"I'm a friend of your son, Jack. He's a wonderful young man, you must be very proud of him."

Marion nodded faintly.

"Yes. Yes." She said. And then she turned back toward the television, gone from the interaction.

"It was nice meeting you," Linda said. She stood up slowly and crossed the room toward Jack.

"I wish I could have met her a long time ago, before all of this."

"I think she would have really liked you," he said.

They walked to the front door, where Linda turned and said, "I hope I'll see you before you go back home."

"Yes," Jack said. "Definitely."

She took the steps down to the driveway, but paused before going to her car.

"Jack," she said, "I hope you're wrong about this...about them." And she walked quickly to her car, getting in behind the wheel and starting it. She looked at him directly one more time, and then glanced over her shoulder to carefully back down the driveway.

Had she not turned her head, she might have seen it, hanging suspended in the air over the top of Jack's house— a familiar dark swarm, shifting, rippling like fabric in the bright yellow daylight. It hung in the air another minute, then drew together in a tight, spherical shape, and sank behind Jack's roof, out of sight.

CHAPTER 48

I T WAS ALMOST 1:00 BY the time Jack had finished with another pile of papers that would have to be boxed up and driven to the secure shredding facility just a few miles away. He was alone in the house. Cathy had taken Marion to the eye doctor to pick up a new prescription. They'd be back home in an hour. Amid the quiet, Jack decided he'd load up the car with the 'to-shred' boxes, take them to the shredders, go grab a quick bite, and then come back and start all over again. And there were the clothes too, still in the closet. He'd all but forgotten about them.

Deciding to have a quick look inside, Jack scanned the clothes that hung bunched together on one side of the space, but noticed something else. On a waist-high shelf, not so conspicuously nested in with a row of shoes, was a gun: a .38-snubnose revolver. Next to it was a small box of ammunition.

So Dad had a gun. It surprised Jack, since he'd heard his father's anti-gun sentiments since he was a kid. Something had obviously changed his mind. Jack would have to do something with it. Pawn it maybe? Maybe. But it would have to wait. He carefully placed the gun and the box of ammo high on the top shelf, out of sight.

The wireless phone in the living room rang, the chime loud and sharp in the empty house. Jack trotted down the hallway, debating whether to actually pick it up. While still deciding, he answered the call.

"Hello?" Jack said.

A man's voice on the other end sounded pleasant, if not a little cautious.

"Hello, I'm looking for...Jack McAllister," he said.

"Speaking."

"My name's Tom Smith, I'm a realtor here in Merriweather. Friend of mine at the bank mentioned you and the situation with your parents. I'm sorry to hear about your loss."

Everyone was sorry.

Jack said, "Thanks. Yes, I was told you might be calling."

Tom said, "I hope this isn't a bad time."

"Actually, I'm about to run a few errands," Jack said, "But we can talk later today if that's convenient."

Tom said, "Sure, Jack, that's fine. I can try you later this afternoon. Oh...I did have one quick question for you. Someone at the bank mentioned that your dad had installed an emergency generator for the house. If you have a free minute, perhaps you could take a quick look at it and tell me what the make and model is? That'd be a nice bonus for any prospective buyers."

Jack said, "Yes, I can do that. Talk later."

"Okay, that sounds great. Talk then."

And he hung up.

Jack came out to the backyard from the rear door of the garage, squinting instantly against the loud, hard sunlight. Working in Richard's office was like being burrowed in a cave of sorts—those ancient brown plastic shades ate the slightest amount of illumination that dared to try and penetrate them.

The humidity was exceptionally thick and heavy today, and Jack felt like he was walking through a warm mist. Invisible insects buzzed loudly from all the trees that surrounded the property, a midday bug concerto in progress.

Jack swung around to have a look at the generator, which was squatting next to the edge of the house. He had every intention of walking over to it, kneeling to inspect the label affixed on the side of it, and making note of the printed specifications. But he never made it to the generator...because something else in the yard netted his attention.

Nested in the tall, moist grass was a dark, metallic-looking sphere. And almost instantly Jack recognized it...and knew what it was.

No, this was not possible. The scout was dead. It was dead! Wasn't this thing a part of it? What in the hell was it doing...

Jack didn't have time to interpret the thought any further, because everything happened so fast. All at once the sphere exploded outward into a dark, vaporous curtain of tiny, sentient, micro scouts. They encircled him in a loud, thrumming cloud that trembled with braided sinuosities and tiny vortices of rippling energy. He turned every direction, helpless, shrinking down in his spot as they pressed toward him, darkening the air, tightening in a haze around him, the sound of their biomechanical parts clicking and buzzing in his ears now.

Jack exploded off his feet, running toward the house, swatting at them. But he was disoriented. The house, which was probably only a few meters away, had been swallowed from view by the swarm, the sky above him erased.

Jesus, they're attacking me!

They stayed with him, swirling angrily, closing, their motions lightning fast and aggressive. Jack spun quickly and ran in a straight line toward the other side of the yard. Isn't that what you were supposed to do in case a swarm of bees were attacking: run in a straight line as far as you could? *Except these were not bees.*

The swarm imploded on him, making contact with his skin. It stung immediately, sudden gouts of pain like thousands of hot needles pricking his arms, shoulders, chest and back all at once. The heat was intense. He clamped his eyes shut, but not before witnessing them burrow into his skin, vanishing beneath it, making small, distended bumps that tunneled grotesquely through him just beneath the surface.

Jack felt them on his forehead and cheeks, the nerves in his skin flush with gruesome hot pain. He unleashed a scream, and immediately felt them rush into his mouth, gagging him, choking him, scurrying down the back of his throat and downward into his esophagus. They entered his ears, the sound of their tiny biomechanical parts, once merely a hum in the air, were now a deafening cry inside him. It grew into the wail of an otherworldly monster, pressing on his eardrums like the abyssal pressure of a deep-sea dive.

Jack fell on his side in the grass, thrashing wildly like an animal, trying to shriek, but unable. His thoughts were an incoherent mesh, broken and superjacent. But one managed to surface through the turmoil: *Get inside the house and call for help.*

Jack's airway unclogged suddenly, and he captured a shallow breath, and then another. Finally he was able to draw in a deep one. He coughed immediately, his lungs pounding against his chest cavity as they regained their flow of air. He lay very still then, coughing, gasping, regaining his faculties slowly, one at a time. He slatted his eyes open. They stung. Jack imagined it was what pepper spray probably felt like. He felt tears pooling there and that would help clear his vision, he thought.

He began to move slowly, pulling himself up to his knees, resting there another minute, coughing again and again.

"Oh, God," he managed, the sound of his voice resonating in his head, dull in his ears. Shit, his ears! He felt them inside his ears when they attacked, and now his hearing was dull. They hadn't eaten through his eardrums...*had they?*

He reached a trembling hand up to the side of his head, dabbing his finger against his earlobe. He felt something moist and viscous. Blood. *I'm not dying out here in the yard,* he thought. *I'm not dying now—not like this!*

Jack summoned strength he didn't know he had, and climbed painfully to his feet. He examined his arms, where he had seen (*or had he imagined it*) the micro scouts eating their way into him. The thought alone sent violent shivers through him. The skin on his arm was blistering and had turned a tint of salmon from trauma, and there were pinpricks of half-drying blood everywhere. It meant they *had* penetrated his skin...and that meant *they were inside him now.*

Jack felt a sudden detachment in light of that revelation, as though he was leaving his body, becoming merely an observer to someone else's nightmare. And for a moment he became someone else entirely, sitting in a movie theater at some remote, safe place, reacting along with the other moviegoers whom, after this horrific story was over, would all go home in the comfort of knowing that it never really happened.

Jack shambled back to the house, pulling open the door to the garage and making it inside. He went straight to the bathroom and without looking at himself in the mirror, turned on the cold water in the sink. He kept his eyes shut, cupped his hands and began throwing cold water against his face and then over his arms. The cold on his skin brought some relief. He splashed more into his face and his eyes, which were still burning. In the darkness of his own mind, he was finally able to think critically.

He could go the ER and get checked out. First thing they'd ask him would be what happened. *Indeed.* How in the hell would he explain what actually happened? And if he did try and explain, one of a few things would likely occur after that: they'd assume perhaps that he was crazy, delusional, stung by bees and having an allergic reaction in which case they'd give him some Benadryl and send him on his way. Or, if they thought he was telling the truth, would he end up in the care of the US military in some remote facility, quarantined in a metal and glass cage, studied, probed, and perhaps even dissected?

Okay, okay...get a hold of yourself, Jack! Get a grip...just wait...wait.

He heard the sound of the front door open and then Cathy's animated voice as she lead Marion back inside the house. Keeping his eyes shut, he reached out, feeling for the door handle. His hand swung clumsily around in midair until his fingers touched it. He pushed the door shut and locked it. He coughed again. It was loud and pebbly.

From outside the door he heard Cathy's voice.

"Jack, we're home. Are you okay?"

Jack steadied his voice and answered cautiously.

"I'm just feeling a little sick. I'll be okay."

"Are you sure? Is there anything I can do for you?"

"No, no, I'll be okay. Just see to Mom. Think I'll go take a nap. I just need some time to rest."

Silence answered from the other side of the door, and Jack could feel her hovering there. Cathy was a sweet woman who cared for people...sometimes too much. Sometimes it came across as smothering.

Finally, she replied, "Okay, Jack, sorry to hear it. If you need anything at all, just let me know."

"Sure. I will. Thanks, Cathy," he said.

He heard her footfalls moving back down the hallway toward the living room, and then her soft voice speaking to Marion, asking her if she'd like to relax and watch some TV. Jack continued to splash cold water all over himself. He hunched over the sink and breathed carefully and deeply, second by second purchasing more control over himself.

Unconsciously he stood upright, and opened his eyes, seeing himself in the mirror beneath the cruel light of three 60-watt bulbs. For a moment he didn't recognize himself: the trauma to his skin, the swelling, the freckles of drying blood, left him looking like a victim in a burn ward. And that's when he noticed, or thought he noticed, something in his right eye. He leaned in very close to the old mirror and pulled his bottom eyelid down, just in time to witness one of the last micro scouts crawling there in the soft of his eye. It quickly channeled into the moist, blood-red tissue, vanishing behind his eyeball. The nausea from shock took him, and all at once he dropped in front of the toilet and threw up.

Jack waited until he heard Cathy take Marion into her bedroom and close the door. The nausea had abated, and he was feeling more stable. His throat was raw and he was still coughing, though not as violently. He needed to drink water...a lot of water. *There were water bottles in the cupboard in the kitchen.* He'd slip into the kitchen, grab them, and then go to the guest bedroom where he would lock the door and ride this out. *Ride it out? This wasn't a flu, it was...madness.*

Jack left the bathroom, hurrying into the kitchen, pulling open the cupboard where he found a plastic-wrapped case of Kirkland water bottles. Jack tore the plastic apart and pulled four bottles out from the case, then grabbed two more, carrying them carefully in his arms. He made it to the guest bedroom and shut the door, then locked it.

Okay, he thought, *better start flushing out your system.* He screwed the cap off the first bottle and began gulping the water, finishing off the entire thing in just under a minute. He grabbed another one, snapped the cap off the top and began drinking. He got halfway through before he had to stop. He sat down on the bed and wondered why they had attacked him, why they had invaded his body. *And what exactly they were doing to him.*

CHAPTER 49

T HE DREAM BEGAN WITH THE troubling sensation of falling through vast open air in a pitch-black void. There was an explosion of sapphire light, a looming vast horizon, curved and gradient, tilting then stabilizing, resolving now into the curve of the earth, magnificent in view for only a heartbeat. It was swallowed by the dark, and the falling sensation changed suddenly as an opposing force struck like a giant fist. It was friction. Powerful. Crushing. This was no longer falling—this was deceleration.

A thunderclap of sound occurred—a shudder—and then the falling sensation began again, followed quickly by a turn, then a flip, and then more deceleration; forces of gravity at war with propulsion of some kind. And then it all stopped.

The dream dissolved instantly to the ground where Jack found himself running dangerously through the woods, his footing precarious in the undergrowth that grew thick with the root systems of trees, fallen limbs and long grass. It was dark, so dark that all he could see were dim impressions of objects as he ran past them. His legs were pumping hard, but his actual speed was in agonizing slow motion. But he ran, nevertheless, his heart thudding painfully, because *they* were out there with him, watching him, tracking him, appearing momentarily in the dark gaps between trees, moving expertly through the wild and very fast.

They're here! They're here! Run, run! His thoughts bellowed.

They were men perhaps, but he wasn't entirely sure. They stood and ran upright on two legs, their outlines not entirely distinct. He didn't know who or what they were exactly, but he was dreadfully certain that they were hunting him and if he did not run faster, they would overtake and capture him. He spun to look backward, and saw them closing, closing, one of them sprinting from its place of camouflage in the nearby trees. It was a powerful bipedal form, midnight dark, closing precipitously on him. Beyond was a terrible shadowy kaleidoscope of the others, their shapes shifting, shutting the distance on him. Indelibly closing.

Jack came out of the dream, lurching into the darkness of the bedroom, where for an instant he thought he saw one of them, ducked in the corner of the room, preparing to vault on him. He snapped on the bedside light, the darkness and shadows extinguishing instantly. There was nothing there. He sat still for a moment, only then feeling a warm tide of nausea overtake him.

Jack darted to the bathroom, closing the door and reaching the toilet where he clamped his eyes shut and allowed himself to be emptied. He hadn't eaten for the last twelve hours, so he wondered why it felt like food, or something solid, was dumping out of him and splashing into the bowl underneath him. It kept coming, almost absurdly, but he endured until it ceased.

He panted then, whimpering, *Oh, God, oh, God...*

He took a few desperate breaths and opened his eyes, glancing down into the toilet. Floating in the water was a black, swampy liquid. No, not liquid—tiny solid bits that looked like soaked coffee grounds.

But that's not what they were. They were micro scouts. Dead, it seemed.

Shit, they're coming out of me, he thought. *And they look dead. Deactivated perhaps.* Did it really matter? All that mattered to Jack was that they were no longer *inside* him. There they were—*where they belonged*—as far as Jack was concerned. He reached up and flushed the toilet, watching the mass of them spin into a swirling murky vortex and away through the porcelain throat of the bowl.

Jack felt relief coat him from his head to his feet. It embraced him warmly. He began to think that this thing was over—well and truly over. He could gulp down some more bottled water, eliminating the horrific taste in his mouth, lie down in the bed, turn off the light, and sleep this off like it was just a bad dream. Jack decided that was exactly what he was going to do. He also decided that when he woke in the morning, he'd not speak a word of this to anyone. *Anyone.* It was finished.

Jack crept soundlessly back into the bedroom and closed the door. He gulped down another half bottle of water and lay back on the bed. Very slowly he closed his eyes, feeling relief through his entire body. It wouldn't be long before he'd be back asleep. That would have been true, had it not been for a single word that fell into his mind as he turned off the light.

Why?

CHAPTER 50

THREE DAYS HAD PASSED SINCE the micro scouts had left Jack's body and he was healing rapidly. The swelling and discoloration of his skin had mostly abated and he had stopped coughing. The attack, the swarm—all of it began to thin behind him and fade as though it had been a dark dream and nothing more. The call from Amy that morning had brought Jack further relief as she explained that a room for Marion at the facility in Tampa had finally become available. They'd need to drop a deposit to hold it, but the door for Marion was now open. Amy would make the arrangements, fill out the paperwork and Jack would mail a check.

"I can be there in three weeks to move her," Amy said.

"It'll be great to see you again. How've you been holding up?" Jack asked.

Amy hesitated.

"I'm angry sometimes that he's gone. Sad. I can't sleep. I have dreams about him. The kids don't really understand what's going on with their mom, why I'm so erratic. It's hard."

"Yeah," Jack said. "It is."

They hung up, having agreed that in about three weeks, Amy would arrive and help Marion relocate. And it would be there in her new home that she'd go through the last few months of Alzheimer's. But not alone—not with strangers. Amy would be close by, visiting her almost daily.

Feeling energy, fueled by hope, Jack decided to leave the house before lunch, get some coffee, stop at the bank and of course run another box full of antiquated documents to their papery death at the shredding company. After that he'd come back to the house and break the news to Cathy that Marion was going to be relocated, and the person that she'd been caring for so closely for the last two years, would be gone. It would be a hard conversation, but a short one. Everything it seemed was lining up, and it would all be over very soon.

On his way to the Starbucks on 5th Street, Jack had passed a short convoy of Army National Guard vehicles including Hummers and Bradley Fighting Vehicles that resembled tanks. Since the scout incident a few weeks earlier, the presence of National Guard had increased and then, once the device had been secured and shipped out to God-knew-where, it had thinned. But they were still around, interacting with local government and law enforcement. Jack could only imagine what all of it must have been doing to Linda's workload. And he guessed that because he hadn't heard from her in several days, it was prodigious.

The phone call came as Jack was adding cream to his coffee. It was local, but he didn't recognize it. Since he'd been talking to people at the bank, the university, the doctor's office, he figured it best to answer.

"Jack? Hey, it's Mitch from the sheriff's office. Are you mobile?"

"I'm out running some errands if that's what you mean."

Mitch said, "Any chance you could stop by the station this morning? Just for a few minutes. Need to talk to you about something."

Jack said, "Is Linda there?"

Mitch said, "Not yet, but she'll be coming in."

Jack said, "What's this about, Mitch?"

"Someone here wants to talk with you about the scout."

Jack grabbed a lid for his coffee, securing it.

"Who exactly?"

There was the slightest hesitation in his voice that quickly regained footing.

"An agent from Homeland Security."

And in those few words, Jack felt the peace evaporate inside him. Mitch quickly interjected.

"Look, I already spoke with him. It's all routine stuff. He knows that you helped us out after the landing, but that's it."

Jack was irritated. "I wonder who told him that," he said sharply.

Mitch said, "Jack, please, it'll take three minutes. I didn't want to give him your home address."

"Thanks. That was big of you," Jack said sardonically.

"See you in a few," said Mitch, and hung up.

Jack met Agent Collins from the office of Homeland Security and instantly distrusted him. Perhaps it was the smug tide that ran beneath his half-grin, the acne-scarred ruddiness of his complexion, or the fact that his eyes seemed to be squinting relentlessly as though he were trying to detect a grain of guilt, real or imaginary, in every living being he encountered.

Jack suspected that the man was in his late forties and came from wealth. Parents likely put him through Columbia or Harvard where he studied political science or political theory. And although he fed freely at a trough full of money all his life, what he really wanted was power. The power to make people squirm beneath his uncalloused and perfectly manicured thumb. Jack also mused that Collins had probably tortured small animals as a child.

Yeah, Jack thought, *he'll be running for Congress in less than two years.*

They were together in an office halfway down the hall at the back of the building. Jack left the door open and he could hear Mitch and some others milling just a few doors down, the sounds of the station louder than usual.

"You're Jack McAllister. Pleasure to meet you," Collins said.

Jack nicely extended his hand for a shake, keeping his grip firm.

"You're a...writer? Book writer?"

"Yes," Jack said.

"What kind of books?" he asked.

"Science fiction."

"Cool. You don't live here?"

"No, I'm from LA. My father died and I'm here tending to his affairs."

Collins never blinked or showed any emotion whatsoever.

"Sorry to hear it."

Bullshit, Jack thought.

"Look, Jack, the reason I wanted to speak with you is because...well, I've heard that you were somehow instrumental in putting the pieces of this puzzle together and also tracking and locating the device."

Jack kept his tone even, his body language loose as he knew Collins was looking at every muscle twitch, every blink, listening to the inflection of every syllable, hunting for flags; anything that might cause him to think Jack was lying about something...anything.

"Greatly exaggerated, I'm afraid," Jack said. "I offered some guesses and theories, but the police department here put it all together."

Jack saw Collins left eye twitch the slightest.

He said, "Sure. Anyhow, I wondered if you might have any more information about all of this."

"All of what?" Jack said. "It's over."

Collins drifted toward the door of the office and eased it shut, closing the two of them in the room together.

"I'd rather you leave the door open," Jack said.

Collins examined him and then gently cracked the door open.

"Sorry, I was hoping for a tad more privacy, since what I have to say is confidential."

Jack decided right then it was time to finish politely and get the hell out of there.

"Agent Collins, I have no interest in confidentiality or anything more concerning this event. I have one thing on my mind and only one responsibility—my family. If you're looking for help, theories, whatever...I've got zip."

Collins pursed his lip and nodded.

"Sure, Jack. Sorry to bother you like this. I know this is probably the last thing you wanted to do this morning."

He pulled the door open and stepped aside. Jack nodded and made for the door when all at once Collins eased the door half shut and shouldered himself halfway between Jack and the outer hallway.

He said, "It's just that after having gone through all the parts of the device after it was recovered, it appears that a piece of it might be missing. It's weird I know, but we found an empty dock on the underbelly of the device."

Jack said, "Someone in your lab getting a pink slip then?"

Collins said, "No...no, I don't think so. We're pretty thorough. Damned thorough. It's not there."

Jack said, "What is it exactly?"

Collins said, "We don't know. That's why I was hoping you could tell me. I heard you got a close look at the scout. Real close."

Jack said, "You heard wrong."

Collins said, "Maybe I did...maybe I did, Jack. The guy seemed pretty honest if not a little anxious about it when I spoke to him. He captured some pretty spectacular footage of the device. I saw you in the footage there along with the deputy sheriff."

Kyle, Jack thought. *The son of a bitch.*

Jack glared at Collins.

"Look, Agent Collins, I saw the scout, but not as intimately as you're being led to believe. Way too dangerous getting so close to it as I'm sure you can judge by the footage. I'm sorry. I can't help you. And now I really have to get going. You see, my mother's dying from Alzheimer's and I have a very short amount of time to get her into a proper care facility before she can't walk, swallow, or breathe anymore. You understand."

For the first time Collins looked away from Jack, slashing his gaze back out the door.

"Sure. I understand. Sorry to trouble you. Wish you the best with your mom."

Jack nodded and brushed past Collins, walking straight out of the building, not speaking to Mitch or any of the others as he left. He wanted them to know he was pissed.

———————

Linda had just pulled into the parking lot and saw Jack exiting in a hurry, heading for his car. She parked quickly and alighted, grabbing him with a shout. He saw her, glanced back at the building to make sure no one had followed him out, then walked quickly to her.

"Jack, what are you doing here?" she asked, concerned.

"You didn't know?" he asked.

"No, I...what happened to you?"

She motioned to Jack's arm where, in the hard morning sun, signs of his blistered and pink skin were still scarcely visible. She saw it on his neck too, and just a whisper on his face. He was caught off guard.

"Oh...I was stung. Swarm in the backyard...not pleasant."

She considered him another moment, deeply concerned.

"Are you okay now?"

"Yeah...although I didn't need this today," he motioned back toward the station.

"What's going on in there?" she asked.

Jack said, "You'll find out soon enough. And I think I'd better leave."

He turned and started for his car, but held.

"Linda, there's something else I need to tell you, but not here...not right now."

"When?" she asked.

"Call me," he said, and walked quickly back to his car.

Linda entered the building from the side and immediately noticed Agent Collins floating around, peering into the offices running the length of the building. He turned then and noticed her for all the wrong reasons, undressing her with his imagination.

"You must be deputy Linda Craig," he said, his tone practiced and smooth.

Linda approached him, unsmiling.

He's going to give me the speech, she thought. *He fancies himself a big dog at Homeland but he's probably somewhere in the middle—no, lower middle. And he's already undressed me with his eyes,* she was certain. *Scumbag.*

"I don't know who you are," she spoke sharply.

"Oh, let me clear that up for you. I'm an agent from Homeland Security, and despite your attempt to keep us in the dark about your scout incident three weeks ago, we're kindly giving your department another chance to help us close out our stay."

Linda said, "Well, I'll be more than happy to help you close out whatever it is you need. The event was over three weeks ago and your vehicles are still buzzing around our town as if we're at war."

Collins said, "Deputy, surely you were aware that this whole thing became a matter of national security the moment that device touched the ground. Or perhaps you weren't. In any case, we've got some unfinished business and until I'm satisfied that the matter is adequately resolved, our vehicles will continue to buzz around your streets. We are looking for something. A component of the scout is missing, and I'm here to turn over rocks looking for it."

Linda asked, "What's the missing piece, Agent Collins?"

Collins said, "Not sure exactly. Hoping you could tell us since you got a closer look at the scout than most anyone."

"You've lost me, agent. Perhaps if you could be any more specific—"

"A sphere...some kind of removable hardware that was missing from the belly of the scout. We're certain because of the shape of the empty dock. Did you see anything like that on the device, deputy?"

Linda thought about the sphere instantly, the tiny parts of it that could disperse and swarm. Jack called them micro scouts. But the damn thing was dead. Linda herself had emptied her gun into that ghastly alien head to finish it off. Once the device had been removed by the team in the puffy, blue plastic suits and loaded meticulously into the back of an unmarked truck trailer with military vehicle escort out of town, there was nothing left, not so much as a bolt or washer.

Linda said, "Agent, I'd like to help, I really would. But if there's any part of the scout that was lost or missing, that'd be a problem with your cleanup crew or your labs, or whatever facility you've got the thing at now. You're welcome to go out on foot and search in the forest if you'd like."

She smiled benignly, eyes cautiously conciliatory.

Collins said, "You're tough, deputy. You'd fit in nicely at Homeland. You should consider a move up the ladder. There are some staggering benefits that come with that job."

Linda said, "I'm sure there are. Thanks." And she started off toward her office.

Collins said, "Oh, and I'll be staying at the Courtyard off College Ave. You should meet me there later and I can fill you in on our job opportunities."

Linda bristled, turned, and said, "Can't." She hurried off then, feeling him osculate her with his stare.

Collins hovered in the hallway where he decided he'd have to try another tactic in order to get her into his hotel room somehow. He'd finish up the day with some phone calls back to Homeland, and then punch out. After that he'd go get a few drinks, loosen up and put together some sort of strategy, because this magnificent red-haired babe was not going to be as easy as he first thought.

Linda reached her desk and was about to start going through her voicemails.

I was stung...swarm in the backyard.

Jack mentioned a swarm and being stung. Specifically it was the word *swarm* that carried some arcane weight to it. He wanted to tell her something, but hesitated. Had Mitch not jabbed himself in the doorway of her office she might have put things together and called Jack immediately.

"Hey, we've got a small protest going on over at city hall. They just showed up with signs and started screaming."

"What about?" Linda asked.

"Something about alien property rights and giving back the scouts...shit, I don't know," he sighed. "They're pissed off!"

Linda wearily grabbed her things and said, "Okay, let's take a walk." It was going to be a very long shift.

CHAPTER 51

WHEN JACK AWOKE FROM the dream, it was 9:00 p.m., and he came out of this one even more shaken up than he'd been before. The nightmare had ended in a dissonant strobe of sapphire and blood-red police lights beneath a curtain of rain rippled by the wind. It was a point-of-view looking upward through the lights, through the rain, directly at Linda. She was standing motionless in her uniform, glaring downward at him, her gun pointed directly at his head. Her eyes were empty like a doll's eyes, but wholly resolute in the verdict to pull the trigger on him. He pleaded, but the words came out mush, muted and incoherent. Now indelibly focused, her expression hardened into a seething mask of rage. She pulled the trigger on him repeatedly—again, and again, and again, the thunder of the gun deafening.

Jack woke up sweating in the bed sheets, only then realizing that a peal of thunder had in fact shaken the house, the sound of approaching southern winds swelling outside. He quickly turned on the light and grabbed his phone to check the time. *Shit*, he thought, *five hours!* He'd been asleep for five hours after the headache and fever started.

Earlier, Jack had been going through Richard's things, finding a box full of old notes his dad had made while at JPL. It was all math equations and crude sketches of orbits of planets and spacecraft. It was then that the headache started subtly, like slow pressure building behind his eyes, then growing until it became unbearable. And to his dismay he was running a low-grade fever.

Jack grabbed the thermometer which he'd placed carefully on the nightstand and checked his temperature again. He waited, certain it had climbed since he fell asleep. He removed the thermometer and read it: 102.1. It had been 99.3 a few hours earlier. Was it a flu, a virus...was it them...*or something they did to him?*

Jack sat very still then, thinking it carefully through. If his temperature went much higher, he might have to get to the ER. But with the National Guard prowling the city, Homeland loitering, if the doctors found something unusual about him, he'd be boxed up and shipped to a facility in the bowels of the earth somewhere and never heard from again. *Paranoia,* he thought for a moment...but only for a moment.

Agent Collins sat draped over the bar at a local brewery. He'd finished off an order of hot wings and was carefully working on his third sixteen ounce Sam Adams. Three hours earlier he'd called back to Washington, the Homeland office, and checked in with his boss, Richard Armstrong, head of the Intelligence and Analysis Division.

"Go Hoosiers," Richard had said sarcastically.

"Shit," Collins replied.

"Status," Richard asked.

Collins said, "Nothing...not a goddamned thing! Starting to think those assholes in bunny suits did lose the piece...if it even exists."

Richard backed off. "Well, you may be right. Wouldn't be the first time. Look, give it another day and if we're still coming up dry, you get yourself back here."

Collins said goodbye and thereby officially punched out for the day. He needed a drink. Badly. Not the hard stuff anymore. Those days were over for the most part. Beer was filling and would take the edge off. He found a brewery within walking distance of the hotel, which meant there'd be no embarrassing stops by law enforcement followed by field sobriety tests and breathalyzers. Collins could not imagine the humiliation and reprimand he'd incur if he were arrested while in the field. His career might not be over, but it'd sure as hell be stained.

And what if it was the redhead deputy that made the arrest, he thought. *That would be bitterly ironic.*

She'd likely see it as somehow poetic since it was obvious she didn't like him. Despite her controlled contempt for him, Collins found Linda extremely hot, even while in the uniform. He could see the trim, athletic build on her, and the tightness of her perfectly formed ass through those ghastly uniform slacks. Her thick coppery hair, lustrous green eyes and model-worthy cheekbones put her at the top of the "hotness" scale as far as he was concerned. And now he was having a hard time getting her off his mind.

That is until Summer Reyes walked into the room, and took a table not far from where he was sitting. And it was then he all but forgot about deputy Linda Craig.

CHAPTER 52

T HEY DETERMINED THAT THE ONLY way to recover the
missing data from Scout 18 was to undertake an
exceptional risk, but at this point in the mission, it
was the only way to ensure a complete data set. Without all
the data, further operations and more resources would be
expended and time—precious time—would be lost. They
would have to land, locate the data cache, and recover
everything from it. But the challenge of landing safely on
this planet, considering its very unpredictable atmosphere,
was enormous, as would be the ascent off the surface. It
could be done with the crew on board and the remaining
fuel—if they landed now. If they waited and began using
fuel for an extended orbit, they'd not have enough to get
back.

The local atmosphere at the last known location of Scout
18 was growing more and more unstable. There was no
more time to wait. With all of this in mind the crew
prepared for atmospheric entry and landing. Unlike the
scouts that relied on simple, multistage landing
architecture, this vehicle could in fact reach the surface

and achieve escape velocity from the planet without having to use any disposable hardware. An alarm sounded on a navigation console as the vehicle adjusted course, decelerating through the upper atmosphere of the blue planet.

———————

It had taken agent Collins less than five minutes to make his way over to Summer's table and offer her a drink. She initially refused but he quickly convinced her that she needed it. And in fact, she did. Summer had been arrested and gone to jail two weeks earlier after Kyle had filed the assault charges. She posted bail and was out, awaiting a hearing before the judge, which would take place in another ten days. Kyle had filed a restraining order against her, which aggravated the shit out of her because if she inadvertently ran into him somewhere, he'd glare at her and wag his phone in the air, his way of saying, *you're in violation of the order and I'm going to call the cops.*

Her reputation at work had gone straight down the toilet and her days there were numbered. She'd have to leave Merriweather and find work somewhere else, somewhere more understanding and forgiving of her now patchy personal life. LA perhaps. But then again, Jack lived there...*the son of a bitch.*

Summer volunteered none of this information to Collins who took the seat across from her with a slit grin that smacked of used-car-salesman-meets-corporate-drone. She accepted the drink he bought her with gentle good humor, taking sips in carefully measured amounts as not to get hammered and be at a disadvantage. He'd asked her about her work, and she told him she was a reporter on the local TV news.

"I was going to guess bikini or lingerie model," he said.

"Well," she replied with a mellifluous smile, "I've done some of that, too." And she straightened up in her seat, pushing her chest out slightly.

Collins began to burn on the inside for her. He could feel his heartbeat accelerate, heat between his legs, and an explosive urge to invite her to his hotel room right then and there.

"So what do you do for a living...what's your name?" she asked.

Collins loosened the collar on his shirt.

"I'm here from out of town, actually."

"Oh," she said. "Let me guess...sales."

"No, I'm in the business of national security."

She took a sip of her drink, her eyes never leaving his.

"I'm from the office of Homeland Security, Intelligence and Analysis department. I'm here because of your scout incident a few weeks ago."

Summer smiled humorously, figuring Collins was just another bullshitter from out of state, a married man on a business trip trying to impress any woman stupid enough to believe him.

"Can I see your credentials?" she asked, batting her eyelashes playfully at him, as if this were some kind of game.

Collins chuckled, then became abruptly serious. He reached into his coat and pulled them out. He flashed them to Summer, never letting them leave his hands. She'd seen similar badges when she did interviews at the state capitol some years earlier with a representative from Homeland.

The credentials in front of her were real. This guy was legit, apparently.

"So, Agent Collins," Summer said, "you guys cleared the scout out of here weeks ago. National Guard's still buzzing around and now here you are. Interesting. So what exactly is going on?"

Collins grinned again and leaned closer to her, his eyes drifting down toward her full lips.

"Well, that's classified I'm afraid."

"The c-word," Summer said.

"Don't say it like that," Collins grimaced.

Summer took another sip and grabbed her phone to check emails. Collins was losing her. *Shit. Can't let this one go*, he thought.

"We're looking for something related to the scout and coming up empty. I'll be going back to DC in another day unless my luck changes. I've been talking with the deputy here, but she's not very cooperative."

Summer said, "Linda, you mean? Yes, she's got an attitude."

Collins said, "Oh, I met this other guy. Fiction author here in town for his dad's funeral or something. Can't remember his name off hand."

Summer bristled and Collins instantly x-rayed her.

"You know him?"

Summer chuckled derisively.

"Uh, yeah. I know him. His name's Jack. Jack McAllister."

It was then that agent Collins saw the pieces falling together neatly, the dots interconnecting in opportune ways.

Collins said, "So then you must also know Kyle Beck, local cameraman."

Summer finished her drink.

"I have to go now," she said.

Collins intercepted.

"Wait, wait, Summer," he said. "Look, I spoke with Kyle and he volunteered some footage which I reviewed carefully. You probably already saw it, too. Am I right?"

Summer nodded—yes.

"Then you know as well as I do, that Jack McAllister and the deputy sheriff both saw the scout up close and in greater detail than anyone else."

Collins lowered his voice and leaned in toward her.

"We're looking for a piece of the device that's missing, and I think—suspect—that Jack McAllister may know something about it, but isn't talking. And I really hate it when people don't talk to me."

Summer considered agent Collins long and hard. The guy was smarter and more informed than she had initially given him credit for, and he had power. *But what the hell was she supposed to do?*

"He won't talk to me, if that's what you're asking," she grunted.

Collins listened patiently.

"You two have...something? I'm not here to judge, by the way."

Summer was beginning to burn inside, a very dangerous anger beginning to surface. *This son of a bitch was applying leverage.*

"That was a long time ago, but some people just can't let things go," Summer said. "Now Agent Collins, you have exactly five seconds to tell me what you want from me, after which I'll be going home."

Collins leaned in very close to her, his trained eyes focused and sharp despite the three beers he already consumed.

"I have friends in very high places back in DC. And if someone, such as yourself, might be looking for a career fast track in spite of a less than...spotless record..."

He let that sink in, and sink in it did.

"I'm listening," Summer said.

"I can make things happen. Big things. You know what I mean, Summer. That's my offer. But I need some help from you first."

"Name it," she said.

"I've got only one more day here and I'd really like to know where Jack is staying because I think he's lying to me. I'd like to put the squeeze on him. That, and..."

"And what?" she asked, even though she knew damn well.

Collins blushed.

"It's walking distance from here," he hummed. "What do you say, Summer? I'm good in a hotel room, if you know what I mean."

She imagined what it was going to be like. Collins was overstimulated and drunk, which meant it would be over quickly. He might even fall asleep afterward. She could handle him, she thought.

"Get me one more drink," she said, and then slowly ran the tip of her tongue over those very full lips. Collins called out loudly to the bartender, "Over here! Another drink!"

CHAPTER 53

THE SKY WAS BLACK GREY and the clouds were brewing, blistering, explosions of lightning firing through them like synapses across God's brain. The storm was not one of the worst to sneak up on Merriweather, but was ominously weighted with the possibility that it could choose to become a monster. And it was through the outer edge of this storm that the alien ship descended quickly, tobogganing its way toward the landing site, which was a clearing in the forest just a few short miles from the edge of town.

No one on the ground saw it coming as it remained shrouded within a fold of purling clouds. No one realized that when a purple-blue explosion occurred in between gauzy bursts of white lightning, it was in fact a low-grade energy pulse deployed from the ship to knock out the power grid, a tactical move meant to further cloak their arrival. Power outages during storms weren't uncommon, so most people who were still awake chalked it up to just another one of Mother Nature's tantrums and would light some candles and wait it out as they had many times before.

But Ronnie Talbot wasn't buying it. Because after the darkness had settled for fifteen minutes and things had grown tomb still, his dog, General, would not stop barking. And after the incident with the alien scout weeks earlier, Ronnie suspected that there would be a large-scale invasion soon. This was based on what he read in the conspiracy forums online and buttressed by a lifetime of general paranoia. Betsy Talbot gave Ronnie the look she usually gave him when she thought he was about to do something stupid. It was a look he had eventually learned to ignore.

Ronnie grabbed his shotgun from the closet by the front door, which was where he always kept it. That way, if trouble came knocking, it would take the brunt of a .12 gauge in the face.

"Ronnie, it's just a blackout," Betsy said, standing in the kitchen in her oversized robe and slippers, hair knotted back in a large braided ponytail. She was carrying a candle, which struck her face from below with hard light in an almost theatrical, horror movie way.

"This happens every time there's a bad storm, and every time you grab the gun and run outside expectin' to see government robots or aliens," she continued.

Ronnie was unamused and checked to make sure the gun was loaded. He reached back into the closet to grab an oversized flashlight.

He said, "General never barks and carries on like this! Never! I'm telling you, somethin' ain't right!"

They could hear the dog barking incessantly, growling as though he were losing his big doggie mind over something.

Betsy hollered, "Shut up, General! It's just the damn storm!"

Ronnie said, "Don't shout at General like that!"

Betsy glared at Ronnie.

"I'm going back to bed, Ronnie. Be a damn fool and do whatever you like." She turned and immediately disappeared into the blackness of the rear of the house.

Ronnie snarled and was preparing to give her a piece of his mind when he heard General howl in distress, yelping sharply. The dog issued a long, loud cry which was suddenly truncated as if....

Ronnie threw open the front door and bolted across his porch, down the steps and out into the open, facing the woods.

"General!" he called. "General!"

There was no sound but the wind from the storm breathing through the wilderness. A sick feeling exploded in Ronnie's gut like a bomb, a sudden and almost complete understanding falling on him like a cloak.

General was dead. Someone or something had just killed him.

"Goddammit! Goddammit, General, where are you?"

Ronnie snapped on the flashlight, stabbing it into the throat of the forest, brushing the beam frantically back and forth, painting the trees with pale, hard light.

"General," he said, his voice lower now, more cautious.

Ronnie lifted the gun, aiming the tip of the barrel toward the wilderness. It was awkward trying to stabilize the weapon while holding that big flashlight in his hands.

Ditch the light, Ronnie, he thought, *you can't shoot anything with a damn flashlight!*

Ronnie let the flashlight go, gripping the rifle now with both hands, stabilizing his aim, his finger stroking that cold, steel trigger. He crept in toward the edge of the forest, and that's when he heard it...a faint disturbance of branches and brisk footsteps, slashing left to right, then stopping instantly.

Ronnie swept his rifle in that direction and pulled the trigger, the round exploding into the husk of a tree, blowing bark into powder and punching a hole deep into its wooden guts. The sound was earsplitting and Ronnie's hearing drowned beneath a ringing so loud he could hardly hear himself yelling.

"See that! I mean business and I will shoot you dead! Now you best get your ass off my property!"

Ronnie jacked another round into the chamber, loud and fluid, making his point.

"Hear that?! Next one's goin' through your da—"

The ground vaulted out from under him, his back making hard contact with stones on the ground. Ronnie felt an abrupt, searing pain in his ankle, the instant sensation of hot blood escaping and running briskly down his hairy leg. He pulled angrily on the trigger, sending the round straight up into the air as if he were trying to shoot the clouds. The next thing he felt was the earth moving beneath him, but of course it wasn't...he was being pulled into the trees by something impaled through his ankle. He felt leaves and dirt sliding up under his T-shirt and sharp twigs stabbing him in the back as whatever it was that had a hold of him was moving faster now. It was like he was being towed behind a small pickup truck.

Ronnie fumbled with the rifle, now pointing it at the pitch dark, humanoid shape that was hauling him off like wounded game. He pulled the trigger to the dull clack of an empty chamber. That's when Ronnie got a good look at the long arms, the short, powerful legs and the elongated head of the thing that carried him. It had skin—no, not skin—armor maybe: plated, cold, strong, the eyes fixed and glassy, unblinking. *And Jesus*, he thought, *there was no mouth or nose!*

Ronnie shrieked as the trauma, the disbelief and horror of it all collapsed on top of him. He turned his head, looking upside down and back from where he had come, the sight of his house vanishing as this thing towed him further into the deepness of the forest. And it was there that it finally let him go, and vanished in a murky, scuttling blur.

Ronnie rolled over, face on the ground, huffing, battling for every shallow breath he could steal.

"Oh, God," he said, "Oh, God, oh, God, oh, God…"

Despite the ringing in his ears, he could hear it. Though dull and muted, he knew what it was. Breathing…inhuman, mechanized breathing. Ronnie saw it now, the shape surfacing from behind the tree on his left. That terrible dark outline was crouched, waiting, watching him bleed.

"You bastard," Ronnie groaned, "You bastard monster…"

It was the last thing Ronnie said before it charged at him unsympathetically, drawing a metallic instrument from its armor that lit up and began to spin like a drill, producing a mechanical shriek. The creature brought it downward straight through the back of his neck and deep into his spine.

The 911 call that came in from Betsy Talbot, amongst the myriad calls regarding the power outage, was wholly alarming.

"Nine-one-one, what is your emergency?"

"My name is Betsy Talbot, and I'm at…Oh, God…"

"Ma'am? Betsy? Where are you? What is your emergency?"

"I think it's in the house, I heard it come in through the back!"

"Betsy, did you say there's someone in your house? What is your address?"

"It killed Ronnie! Ronnie's dead!"

The operator heard a crash on the other side of the line.

"Betsy, can you get to a safe room somewhere in—"

"You bastard! You bastard!"

Another loud crash came from the phone, the distinct sound of wood splintering. Betsy shrieked. A new sound bled into the earpiece, a strange, filtered breathing.

"Ma'am, police will be there shortly. Ma'am? Ma'am?"

"You killed Ronnie! *You bastard! You bastard, you killed my Ron*—"

Her last scream was so loud the operator pulled the headset from her ear. She'd taken very bad calls before. But none like this.

CHAPTER 54

THE CLOUDS BLED A LIGHT rain as Collins and Summer exited the brewery along with the other patrons who had been enjoying their drinks when the power was cut. The entire street was erased, everything veiled below deep shadows, including the hotel. Collins realized then and there he would not be making it with Summer, the prosperity of his position faded. He was pissed. The anticipation he'd had for her was supernova hot and he was ready to explode. And now it waned, fading beneath his frustration. Summer felt momentary relief; she'd not have to ride this guy on a cheap bed after all. She'd find her car, excuse herself, and go home.

"Maybe next time you're in town," she said.

"Oh, come on," Collins protested.

"Hey, look," she said, "the power is out! Get it? We're not hooking up right now. I gotta get home."

People milled passed them, looking for their cars in the dark, grunting beneath the sprinkling rain. And that's when Collins decided he should finish business with her, but not here. If he could get her to drive him away, maybe toward

McAllister's place where he'd have to go anyhow, he could convince her to park somewhere off the road and then…

"Drive me," he said.

"Where," she asked.

"McAllister's place. Just drive by it so I know where it is. I'm going to have to visit him tomorrow."

Summer bristled.

"I really don't want to do that right now," she said.

Collins eased in toward her, lowering his voice. "Summer, if you do this for me, I swear I can help make things a lot sweeter for you around here. Or are you looking forward to spending the next few years on parole, leashed to some restraining order? I will hook you up with people at levels you cannot possibly comprehend."

Summer thought about it and decided that he may be right. She'd have to leave here eventually and then what? Maybe Agent Collins could link her with the real power players in this world.

"Okay. My car's over here," she said. "To McAllister's and then I drop you back off at the hotel."

"Sure," Collins said, his tone promising nothing of the sort.

Summer led him to her Prius and they quickly climbed in.

"You okay to drive?" he asked.

"I can hold my booze, Agent Collins," she said.

"Me too," he said, and they carefully pulled out onto the streets of the city that had been eaten by the blackness.

CHAPTER 55

LINDA DROVE THROUGH THE DOWNTOWN area in her cruiser, talking with Mitch on her radio. With the power amputated, homes and businesses would sometimes become targets for looting. It had happened a few years earlier during a severe power outage that lasted for nearly twelve hours. Within two hours after darkness fell, several businesses near the college were hit. There was some vandalism and a few cars were stolen. Linda remembered it well, and was out tonight to make sure things didn't get out of hand...as if they couldn't get any *more* out of hand. After the scout incident, the arrival of the National Guard and now the Homeland agent, things were tenuous. People's patience was running thin as military vehicles would frequently buzz down 5th Street and cause traffic to choke up around the downtown area.

Mitch's voice was choppy on her radio. "Spoke with the guy at Duke Energy. He said it was an overload caused by a lightning strike."

"Any estimate when we'll be back online here?" she asked.

"Negative," he said. "I'm on my way out to a call at the Talbots' place. Sounds like it might be serious."

"What was the call?" she asked.

"Sounded like someone broke into the house and attacked them. Not sure. I'll be there in a few minutes."

Linda didn't like it and felt an ethereal spray of anxiety.

"Hold on, Mitch. Don't go over there alone. Just give me ten minutes and I'll swing out there with—"

A woman darted out onto the road in front of her, waving her arms in the air, motioning for Linda to stop the cruiser. She slammed on the brakes, turned on the red and blue lights and alighted expertly, touching the handle of her gun.

"Ma'am! Ma'am, stop right there! Let me see your hands! Hands!"

The woman cried loudly, showing Linda her empty, trembling hands. She was wearing a bathrobe and pink slippers. Ashen faced, she pointed down a dirt driveway toward her house.

"Please help! They're in my backyard! I saw them hiding in the trees!"

Linda steadied herself, hand still on the gun at her side.

"Easy, ma'am, easy. What's happening here?"

The woman was frantic, her eyes huge and moist from tears.

"They're in my backyard, I saw them! They're standing there, watching me."

"Someone's in your backyard right now," Linda clarified.

"No, it's not...I mean, they're not..."

Linda lowered her voice to calm the woman.

"Who are they? What do they look like?"

The woman sobbed, struggling with the words.

"They look like monsters," she said.

Jack had gone outside to inspect the generator because strangely it had failed to kick in and restore power to the house. Marion was in her bed and unable to sleep. She was mumbling under her breath, words that neither Jack nor Samantha could make out.

"Stay with her," Jack had told her. Samantha agreed and lit a candle for Marion in the bedroom to try and cheer her up.

Jack stood over the generator with a small flashlight, having no idea what he was actually supposed to look for. The thing seemed dead and he had no idea how to fix it. Looked like they'd have to light candles and ride this out until the power was restored.

Jack turned off the little flashlight. But there was still a glow in his hand. *Weird.* He flipped the flashlight over, inspecting it closely. It was switched off...but the glow oddly remained, and Jack quickly realized it was not coming from the flashlight.

He spun his palm back over, now observing that the pulsing, scarlet radiance was coming from the back of his hand...from inside it, beneath his skin.

Jack closed his eyes.

This is not possible. I'm seeing things, he thought.

Perhaps the flashlight, having been turned on and off, was playing tricks with his vision. With his eyes still shut, he began hearing a tone that seemed to come from the middle of his head. It rose in pitch, then fell and recycled. Over and over in a loop. Jack opened his eyes and the strange crimson light was still in his hand, pulsing in synchronization with the recycling tone he was hearing. Slowly, inevitably, Jack realized what it was.

He grabbed his cell phone to call Linda because she was one person—the only one—that he could trust. But he didn't dial right away. Instead he observed that as he held the phone in his glowing hand, the display got brighter and the signal strength climbed to five unflinching bars. Jack put the phone down on top of the generator box and backed up. The display dimmed and faintly he noticed the signal strength drop to two bars. He picked it back up and immediately the display brightened, the signal strength spiking.

It's happening, he thought, and quickly dialed Linda's number.

Linda had called for backup and asked the frightened woman to stay with her by the cruiser. All at once they heard the snapping of large branches, the unsettling of leaves and brisk footfalls that seemed to shoot back and forth around the house. The woman took a jagged breath, her eyes enormous.

"Oh, my God. It's them, right over there!"

Adrenaline kicked in as Linda whipped her pistol out in front of her, jabbing her Maglite beneath the barrel, clicking it on, the beam now a small, focused searchlight playing the dark.

"Police officer," she called out. "Come out now where I can see you!" The woman began breathing loudly behind her.

Without taking her eyes off the void beyond the tip of her barrel and the reach of her light, Linda said, "Ma'am, I want you to climb into the back seat of my cruiser, close the door and stay there."

The woman instantly complied, sealing herself securely in the back of the car, peering cautiously out the reinforced glass. Another very loud crack came from the side of the house, and Linda's nerves constricted as she crept forward a step at a time. In concert with her eyes, the gun swept the scene right to left, then back again over the front of the house, then past the house, into the trees that formed a crown around the property.

"Police officer, I have my weapon drawn! Come out where I can see you!"

Cemetery stillness answered. It was then that fear began to coil silently around Linda, tightening on her like a strong chord, and a terrible revelation surfaced.

It's them. They've arrived.

"Police officer, come out where I can s—"

A fearsome, humanoid form vaulted off the roof of the house, running explosively away into the woods, followed immediately by another.

"Freeze!"

Linda expertly pumped off three rounds, which she quickly realized had missed the targets. They moved too fast. *Inhumanly fast.* And they had been cloaked there the whole time, watching her. Her skin crawled.

Linda's phone rang back in the cruiser. She stepped cautiously back toward it, her gun still tracking phantom forms in the pitch black around them. She glanced at her phone, noticing the low battery warning, but answered swiftly when she saw it was Jack calling.

"Hello? Jack?"

"Linda? Can you hear me?" he said loudly.

"Yes," she said.

"Something's wrong with me," he said. "They did something to me."

Linda thought she saw a standing form in her periphery, moving through the lightless void. Quickly she swept her gun in that direction. Nothing there.

"Jack, something's happening here, I think maybe—"

Jack interrupted her.

"Linda...the other day in the yard. It was the device from the scout, the swarm, the micro scouts. They attacked me. Did something to me. Maybe planted something inside me!"

Linda's head swam, unable to process what he was telling her.

"Jack, listen to me, I think they're here! I just saw...they moved so fast!"

Linda's phone chimed against her ear as the low battery warning flashed incessantly.

"Jack, my battery is going!"

"Linda, I think I might be...signal...my mom...somehow..."

"Jack? Jack!"

The call evaporated and Linda's phone shut down. Behind her on the road another squad car arrived, lights splashing on her mirrors. Linda leaned in to speak with the woman in the back seat.

"Ma'am, I'm going to leave you with this officer. He'll take care of you from here. It's going to be okay."

"Please tell me I'm not crazy. They weren't human, were they?" the woman asked.

Linda said, "You're not crazy."

CHAPTER 56

SUMMER CRUISED A TWO-LANE highway that would deposit them near Jack's place. They could do this quickly. That way she could have agent Collins back at the hotel in about fifteen minutes. And if the power came back on in the meantime, she'd make up some excuse not to sleep with him in that cheap hotel room. Even if the guy was going to make good on his promise about connections in DC, the hotel room was a turnoff, in part because it was on his terms, *not hers*.

"Do you think we could pull over a sec?" Collins said, "I'm feeling sick."

Oh God, she thought, *this guy is not throwing up in my Prius!*

"You're fine," Summer said. "We're almost there anyhow."

Collins fidgeted in his seat.

"So where is it exactly?" he asked.

"Half mile, then a left at Lariat road, a right on the next street, house near the end on the left," she said.

"You really know your way around," Collins quipped.

Summer kept driving.

Collins insisted, "Seriously, pull over, I'm going to be sick in your car."

Summer contained a huff and pulled over, brushing up to the edge of the trees, floating to a stop on the soft shoulder.

"Just take a few steps away from the car before you…"

Collins grinned, and in one deft move, pulled her keys from the ignition, pocketing them. Summer realized instantly what was happening.

"You're not sick. Give me the keys. We're not doing this."

Collins stared at her, his features dimly lit from the splash of the headlights hitting the ground outside. She looked at him for as long as she dared because there was a very mysterious anger in his eyes.

"Come on, Summer, you won't be sorry, I promise." Collins unfastened his seatbelt.

"No," she said.

"You want to," he said.

"No means no," she said.

"Saw that PSA myself, Summer. But we both know what kind of woman you really are. Don't play games with me."

Collins brushed his blazer off his hip, showing her the butt of his automatic pistol. She'd not seen it earlier when they were having drinks.

"You going to shoot me, Agent Collins?"

"That's not up to me, Summer. I suggest you climb over here on top of me. Right now."

Summer thought it through another moment, coming to a decision.

"Okay. But I'm not climbing over the transmission. Open your door and I'll come around."

Collins threw his door open and Summer hers. She unbelted herself, reached back and snatched her purse and then stepped out of the car, the sound of her clicking heels rapidly floating away into the dark. Collins grunted.

He swung out of the car, putting his hand on his gun, scanning for any sign of her. Summer was gone, digested by the dark that hung motionless on every side.

"Summer, come on!" Collins shouted. "Come on, don't jerk me around here!" He quieted and held his breath, listening intently.

Twenty meters away, crushed up against the side of a big tree, Summer held her breath and waited. She soundlessly peered with one eye back toward where Collins was standing outside her car. Her view was partially obscured by forest growth and smaller trees, which meant his view was shit. He'd not see her if she remained in this spot. But he might hear her if she so much as crushed a single leaf. Her cellphone was in her purse at her side, but she dare not try and make a call. It would be too loud and he'd certainly hear her voice.

Collins exploded, "Summer, if you don't get back here right now and take care of business, I will hunt you down and you will be very sorry!" To make his point, Collins pulled his gun free and chambered a round.

"I'm giving you ten seconds!"

Summer closed her eyes and began to think. She'd have to move, but if she did, he'd hear her and if he didn't put a bullet in her back, he'd surely chase her down on foot and then attempt to have his way with her. Summer was physically strong, and she could put up a good fight. But Collins was a stocky man, fueled with rage and alcohol. And he had a loaded gun. She opened her eyes and saw a piece of tree branch that oddly resembled a baseball bat just a few feet away.

"Nine, eight, seven...." Collins bellowed.

If she made a move for the branch, he'd hear her, but if she hesitated and he closed on her she'd not have enough time to—

"…six, five, four…"

If she could crawl over to it, she could grab it and—

"…three, two…."

Shit, shit, shit!

"…one!" Collins began to creep away from the car. He was coming her direction, one step at a time.

Move, Summer, she thought. *Move! Do something!*

She took a deep breath, preparing to crab-step her way over to the branch. But she hesitated. Because for some reason she had the distinct feeling she was being watched. Not by Collins, *by someone else.*

Directly behind her, a twig split, and Summer heard something else that sounded like breathing. Adrenaline drowned her, and she quaked, turning her gaze slowly backward, toward it, seeing the shape of it, comprehending almost fully the creature standing over her.

Collins heard her scream. It was shrill and rang like a siren in the pitch black. And then, all it once, it was lacerated.

"Summer!" he shouted, pointing his gun in the direction of the scream. From the same spot came sounds of branches snapping, stones and leaves upturned and thrown, followed by a sickening, bone-breaking thud.

"Summer," he called again, lower this time. A voice came from the black. Not a voice exactly, but a texture of sound that resembled words. Collins became acutely aware that someone else was out here, and they had done something to Summer. No—his mind countered—it's *your imagination.* He would back off.

"Summer, hey look...I wasn't really going to do anything. Summer? Summer?"

There was a distant roll of thunder. Collins lowered his gun. It was then that three of them materialized from the woods, running toward him.

They don't have faces. Collins realized it too late.

One of them struck him so hard he was crushed against the side of the Prius, putting an imprint of himself neatly in the door panel. His gun spilled away, clacking loudly against the pavement, skating beneath the car. He felt heat in the center of his chest. His breath was hard and shallow, his vision bubbling in front of him. He rolled over on his side, only catching a glimpse of their mottled forms scrieving into the growth on the other side of the highway, heading in the direction of Jack McAllister's place.

CHAPTER 57

LINDA HAD SEEN TO IT that the woman from the house was in the full care of her fellow deputy before she began making her way toward Jack's place. She was having difficulty grasping what had just happened and what was now likely unfolding. But she had the distinct impression that Jack knew exactly what was going on, and that he himself was in serious danger. He'd said that it was the micro scout swarm that had attacked him the other day. He'd said they might have done something to him. He'd also told her that the beings that sent the scouts might return to collect any of the data they were missing.

And now she'd seen them herself. They flew off that rooftop, ran impossibly fast through the woods, and despite the gloom, she could see enough to discern the features which were human, but not human at the same time. *This was all really happening.*

Mitch called in on the radio.

"Deputy, do you copy?"

"Go, Mitch. What's the situation out there at the Talbot place?"

"I got support here, I'm not alone, but shit...it's bad, deputy. Ronnie Talbot is dead. He was dragged a football field away from his house and...he's got a hole in the back of his neck."

"Gunshot," Linda asked.

"No, definitely not. But remember all those holes in the ground we saw when we were still looking for the scout a few weeks back. Can't believe I'm saying this...but it's the same kind of thing. Looks like he was drilled into."

Linda felt her stomach turn, knotting. Had Ronnie Talbot been sampled the same way the soil and trees had been?

"What's the situation with his wife?" she asked, even though she already knew the answer.

"Same kind of thing," he said, a quiver in his tone.

"Is the location secure?"

"Yeah, why?"

"Meet me over at the McAllisters' place."

"It'll take me some time to get all the way over there."

"Then you'd better leave now," she said and pressed down on the accelerator, bombing through a sinuous two-lane road, hemmed in by the wilderness which was coming alive with strong winds pushing north by the shoulder of the approaching storm.

CHAPTER 58

J ACK CREPT DOWN THE HALLWAY toward the door of his mother's bedroom in the dark, groping for, then gently palming the door handle and quietly turning it as not to startle her or Samantha.

"It's me," he said lightly as he eased the door open and glided into the room, which was dancing dimly from the candles Samantha had lit. She was next to Marion's bed, softly reading her a story from a children's book. Jack recognized the book instantly; it was one Marion had read to him when he was a little boy. In her state Marion had become as a child, and seeing her like this, listening to the book, Jack couldn't help but feel that life had somehow swung around in a great circle and turned upside down: parent had become the child, child the parent.

Samantha looked at Jack, a nervous smile painted on.

"What's wrong with the generator?" she asked.

"I don't know," Jack replied.

He approached Marion's stiffened form, crooked there in the hospital bed.

"Mom, it's me, Jack," he whispered. "Are you okay?"

She grunted, unable to turn and look at him.

Samantha said, "She's nervous. Kinda jumpy. I don't think it's the storm."

Jack leaned in toward Marion.

"Mom, are you okay?"

Marion wrestled with the words. "Nnn-no. No."

She coughed, her wary eyes fixed on the slatted window blinds.

"I...ju-ju-just," she stammered.

Through the window Jack heard a whisper of tall grass in the yard, the dim sound of crushed leaves and then the tones of the wind chime that hung at the corner of the house near the garage. Samantha spun her head quickly to the window then back toward Jack again.

"Is there someone out there?" she whispered.

A throaty growl of thunder sank into the ground, but underneath it they heard the sharp tempo of rapid footfalls rushing past the side of the house.

"Put out the candles and stay right here," Jack whispered. "I'll come back in a minute."

Samantha nodded, put the book aside, and carefully blew out the candles, abandoning the room to darkness. Jack took a long look at Marion's fragile form. Dim as it appeared, he leaned down and kissed her lightly on the cheek.

"I love you, Mom," he said. It came out organically. Jack supposed it was because something deep inside him was imagining that this might be the last time he would speak to her. Jack slid back out of the room and gently pulled the door closed. There was the sound again of the wind chime, followed by more audible footsteps. *Dad's gun,* Jack remembered.

Quickly he crossed into the office and went to the closet. He reached the top shelf feeling for the .38 snub nose, where he'd placed it carefully out of the way. He grabbed the small box of ammo, only then noticing that his hands were shaking. Fingers jittery, Jack loaded the weapon and thumbed off the safety. Carefully then he fingered open the plastic shutters to have a look out the window. The murky outlines of the trees were all he could see.

Jack moved back into the hallway and spider-stepped his way down the hall toward the front of the house. He held the gun in both hands, the tip of the barrel pointed directly ahead of him at the empty space of the living room which gradually resolved from the gloom. Jack felt heat in the back of his right hand as the strange, crimson glow returned, panting from dim to very bright. There was a loud, pronounced bump at the side of the house, the swishing of long grass beneath moving feet.

It's them! But how could they be here? It didn't make any sense! Even if they had arrived to gather lost data, why would they come directly to...? The glow in Jack's hand whispered the answer.

It was precognition then that caused him to look up at the large living room window. Veiled by thin, chiffon curtains, it stood, watching him. It was a sinister shape, diffused by the fabric, but Jack could make out the extended arms and the elongated head, like a great barn owl's head. Faceless but for two large, immobile eyes.

Jack pulled the hammer back on the .38, but never got the shot off. The attack was sudden and terrible, the glass shattering inward, exploding through the room like hundreds of shark's teeth. Jack felt the impact in his chest and he crashed backward into the drywall, crushing it. The gun slipped from his grasp and bumped on the floor. His vision spinning like a vortex, he spotted it for a split second, locking on it. He reached for it, his fingers tickling the handle.

All at once he felt himself lifted off the ground, hard digits grasping him, a strong hand clamped around his arm. Jack came face to face with the creature, realizing that it wore some kind of environmental suit, its features hidden behind a mask that provided protection and some sort of a breathing apparatus.

From his left, Jack heard Samantha. She was standing paralyzed in the recess of the hallway, her eyes huge, veins bulging in her neck as she screamed. The creature snapped its head toward her. In its hand Jack saw a device that came to life, illuminating suddenly, cracking loudly with purplish-white electric current. It was pointing the end of the device directly at her.

Jack seized the arm with his free hand, clamping down vice-hard on its wrist. Filled now with impossible, adrenalized strength, he twisted the arm upward where the device issued a sharp, bullwhip crack of energy into the ceiling. Jack crouched and dove forward, lifting the creature off its feet, carrying it across the room, smashing it into the opposing wall. The creature dropped momentarily on its knees, stunned. But it recovered quickly, climbing to stand. Jack kicked its front leg out from under it, grasping it by what felt like seams in its suit between hard plated pieces. Still unusually powerful, Jack heaved it backward where it punched through the drywall. It fell again, collapsing on the ground, its mechanical assisted breath labored and malfunctioning.

Jack raced for the .38, but saw Samantha still standing there, immobile.

"Get back in the room! Stay with Mom!" he shouted as the creature sprung at him. Jack fired a shot that tore one of the plates on the thigh of it. He fired again, but the round went wild, hissing past the creature, punching through the wall to the outside.

Thunder cracked loudly outside and lights slashed past the front window, the sound of an engine approaching. The creature grabbed Jack by the ankle and pulled his leg out from under him. He hit the ground hard, air escaping his lungs in one, huge gust. He couldn't breathe and felt himself being towed toward the shattered window. The creature was making noises now, textured grunts and clicks mixed with mechanical growling. Jack's vision was blurry, but he saw the glow in his hand, the gun in his fingers, and the outline of the creature beyond the tip of the weapon.

Jack pulled the trigger, the flash from the muzzle painting the room brightly. He heard an inhuman shriek and then felt his leg drop. He was no longer moving. The wounded creature had let him go.

Linda pulled into Jack's driveway, put her cruiser in park, and was about to climb out when the creature landed on her hood, compressing it, cracking against her windshield, spider-webbing the center of it. It writhed and rolled, now staring at her through the kaleidoscope glass. Linda shrieked, inches from the elongated, faceless thing that was pointing some kind of device at her.

She pulled her gun free, pressed the muzzle directly against the glass, closed her eyes and spun her face away.

She pulled the trigger and the windshield turned to razor-sharp powder.

The creature screeched, thudding violently against the roof of the car. It scuttled back over the trunk, leaping into the forest growth nearby, blending with it perfectly, becoming invisible.

"Linda? Linda!"

Jack came racing toward her cruiser as she climbed free with tiny bits of dusted glass in her hair. Some larger pieces had cut into her chin and blood was soaking into her uniform collar.

"Are you okay?" he asked. "Linda, are you okay?"

She was stunned, but shook it off, locking eyes with him, grabbing onto his shoulder for support. She noticed the .38 still clutched in his hand.

"Did you use that?" she asked, panting.

"Hit it twice, I think," he said.

And then she noticed the glow from his hand, cycling from dim to bright to dim again.

"Jack, what is this? What's happened to you?"

"I don't know how they did it, but they planted a tracker in me when the swarm attacked the other day."

"Why the hell would they do that? Why you?"

The sound of slashing wet grass, crushed leaves and twigs silenced them. Something was moving nearby. Then came the same sound off to their right side, followed by a scuttling directly behind them.

"Shit, they're all over us," Linda said.

They touched shoulder blades, fanning their guns back and forth over the dark.

"I don't know why this is happening," Jack said, "But I'm going to get the hell out of here. They're after me for some reason, which means if I leave they'll follow me away from the house! I don't want them anywhere near my family!"

Linda protested, "Not a good idea! They'll be on top of you within a minute! Get your mom and I'll drive you all to the station! We can bunker down there and fight with more manpower!"

Jack said, "No, listen to me, I'm going to take off in your cruiser! You take my dad's car. It's undamaged. Drive it to the station with my mom and Samantha! That will buy you enough time to—"

There was a purple flash of brightly charged current and a loud, hissing sound. Linda hit the ground hard, unmoving, and for all Jack knew in that moment, she was dead. He swiveled and fired the gun wildly into the trees until a bolt of that same current struck him in the back. Jack's vision tunneled quickly and he blacked out.

Linda forced her eyes open, despite the pain that was gnawing her entire body. From her periphery she saw two of them carry Jack away, their elongated arms slung beneath his shoulders. They vanished with him in the trees, heading south along a crude foot trail. It was only a moment later, despite her fierce resistance, that she fell unconscious.

CHAPTER 59

I T WAS THE UNFAMILIAR NOISE, the alien, overlapping sounds that bled slowly into Jack's subconscious. It grew into a lattice of bizarre mechanical noises crossed with a sub harmonic hum that was gently tactile beneath Jack's feet. The sound of the creature's otherworldly, mechanical breathing was floating around him, moving from one side of him to the other. He felt a cold hand press down on his right shoulder, then something like a metal cuff slide up and over his wrist, tightening. He sensed the same thing on his other wrist, then his feet. Jack was fully restrained against a hard surface, tilted on an incline.

He didn't want to open his eyes, didn't want to allow himself to see exactly where he was or what was about to happen to him. He could only imagine what sort of dreadful plan these creatures had for him—what they would do to him now that he was immobile. Jack heard a whirring sound that reminded him of the abrasion tool on the scout, and that's when he forced his eyes wide open. Nothing he had dreamed of had prepared him for what he saw now.

He was in a long, tubular space with a high ceiling. The walls looked like a mixture of hard material with softer, organic parts, couplers, and tubing that ran the length of the place. There were membrane-like sections that reminded Jack of the innards of a nautilus shell. The entire thing was a blend of organic materials and complex mechanical systems. It was as though the room itself were alive somehow. Jack had once been in the rear of a C-17 Military Plane at an air show. It was essentially a naked fuselage on the inside, meant for transportation and deployment of troops and field gear. This space appeared very similar when it came to overall function and purpose. Lining the walls were banks of arcane equipment and holographic displays that glowed with alien images, things Jack could not comprehend.

I'm inside their ship, he thought. *Are we still on the ground, on Earth?*

Based on his weight, the gravity he felt, he assumed as much. There were six of them in this space, each one busy at their consoles. When another one came into the ship, Jack turned and noticed the opening, perhaps fifteen yards from where he was cuffed down on a dark, metal slate. This one had just arrived, carrying a strange, cylindrical device in its hand. *There must be more of them,* Jack guessed. *They're waiting for the rest of their crew. But why did they bring me here?*

One of the creatures came toward him with a metal container, and placed it at his side. Once properly positioned, the box opened autonomously. Jack caught a glimpse inside of what looked like strange computer hardware, an illuminated display, and something else...something that moved, pulsing with organic life.

Jack panicked and slammed up against his restraints. This startled the creature and it quickly grabbed hold of him and thrust him back down on the slate. Jack felt something warm crawl around his shoulders, sucking on him, clamping him down against the surface, so much that he could now only swivel his head.

From inside the box, a moving limb uncoiled grotesquely, squirming, lifting serpent-like, a razor-fine needle thrusting outward from its amorphous, finger end. It hovered, swaying above Jack's right arm, then steadied.

"No! No! Wait," Jack pleaded out loud. "Wait!"

It slithered low over his arm, the needle aligning with a large vein that was bulging under his skin. And in the mere blink of an eye, that terrible needle thrust through the skin and connected with his bloodstream. The pain was immense and Jack howled in agony. The creature abreast of him jabbed something into the soft of his neck, and all at once his voice shrank and failed. Pins and needles danced across his jaw as numbness set in. He couldn't scream, or speak, or even whisper. The only thing he could do now was watch as the machine in the box that was connected to the limb-probe, now inside his arm, cast a holographic three-dimensional display in front of him.

What Jack saw next seemed so fantastic and impossible it caused him a long moment of troubled awe. And in it, he suddenly realized what they were doing. It explained everything; what the swarm had done to him, why they were tracking him and why they brought him here alive.

In bioluminescent blue, hanging in midair, was the model of a DNA molecule, represented in double-helix form. The model split apart down the middle and vanished from the display. What came next was a river of letters, flowing left to right, G, A, T, C, the encoded sequence of nucleotides: guanine, adenine, thymine and cytosine that made up genetic information.

A moment later came a ribbon of new data—binary code, ones and zeros. And now it appeared that a conversion was taking place as the G, A, T, C sequence blended with, and became: 01000111 00100000 01000001 00100000 01010100 00100000 01000011, on and on.

They're pulling data out of me, implanted somehow in my DNA by the swarm. All the missing pieces from the scout's environmental survey—they're downloading it!

The download from DNA continued as computer banks nearby gulped down the data stream. And Jack began to wonder what they were going to do with him once the transfer was complete. Once they had what they needed.

CHAPTER 60

LINDA MOVED HER FINGERS ONE at a time, then her hands. She felt her toes and swiveled her feet. She climbed to her knees and held there a moment, expelling the last bit of paralysis from her body by sheer will. The alien bastards had used some kind of taser on her. It hurt. Badly. But she pushed through it, now more stable with one foot on the ground and then the other.

Headlights swept over her, the sound of tires mashing wet leaves and grass as a car rolled to a stop nearby. Mitch climbed from the cruiser, noticing instantly her hunched over form and the pulverized front end of her car.

"Holy shit. What the hell happened?" he asked, helping her stand fully upright, quickly spotting the blood on her shirt collar.

"You're bleeding," he said.

"I'm fine," she said.

Samantha emerged from the house, her expression a perfect mixture of shock and anxiety.

"Jack? Jack? Where is he?"

Linda waved toward her, then spoke quietly aside to Mitch.

"You take her and Jack's mother to the station immediately and keep them safe until this is over."

"Until what's over?" he asked, pointedly. "Linda, what in the hell is going on here?"

"That's what I'd like to know," another voice said from the gloom of the nearby trees. Agent Collins stepped cautiously into the open where they could see him. He held his gun tightly at his side. Ready. Linda recognized him instantly.

She turned back toward Mitch and said, "Get them out of here. Just do it. Right now. And be careful. Jack's mother is late stage Alzheimer's."

Mitch nodded, then climbed up the steps to the front of the house where Samantha was still standing.

"Is Jack okay?" she asked again.

Linda said, "I'm going to find him. He'll be okay. Please go with the officer right away. He'll take you to the police station where you'll be safe."

Mitch urged Samantha back inside.

"Hi. Can you show me where Jack's mother is? Can she walk?" he asked gently.

"She has a wheelchair," Samantha answered, and walked with Mitch toward Marion's room at the back of the house.

Collins approached Linda, his face a mask of tension.

"What the hell is this, deputy Craig? Where's Jack McAllister?"

"You're from Homeland," Linda said. "Thought you boys had all the answers. You tell me."

Linda squared off with Collins; her shoulders set straight, jaw tight.

"I don't know exactly what's going on here, but I do have some theories," he said. "Namely that these creatures, beings, whatever the hell they are, have sent down some sort of small detachment to try and find something—something they didn't already get from the scout. They probably dropped in just ahead of the big storm, and my guess is they'll want to leave soon to avoid getting grounded and thereby exposed and perhaps vulnerable to an attack."

Linda smirked. "Nice theory. So why did they take Jack?"

Collins scowled. "They took him? Where?"

Linda brushed past him, grabbing her Maglite and aiming it onto the footpath she'd seen the creatures take earlier.

"Don't know. But I'm going after him before it's too late."

Collins said, "Deputy, if they got him—it's already too late. Now why don't you let this go and we'll come up with a plan for...*hey!*"

Linda had already pressed into the trees, the dim dance of her light the only evidence of her evaporating presence.

"Shit," Collins hissed and started after her, pitching into the dark, crawl-stepping quickly to keep up with her.

Linda would not accept that Jack was dead. *He's alive,* she thought. *He's alive.* She began whispering it to herself like a prayer.

"He's alive. He's alive. He's alive..."

Linda moved faster now, a straight arrow, leaving Agent Collins quickly behind.

CHAPTER 61

J ACK FELT THE ELONGATED NEEDLE of the biomechanical limb probe deeper into his vein. The very abrupt pain associated with it was enough to cause spots to detonate across his vision. Had his voice been of any use, he'd have screamed his vocal chords apart. But the numbness was still coating his lips, his chin, even the front of his neck and the top of his chest. Jack reflected for a moment on the mere fact that it seemed a miracle he was still alive. Though once this process was finished, his future was decidedly precipitous and uncertain. The data conversion from his DNA continued to surge across the display floating in front of him. *How much data could there be?* he thought. *How long am I going to be connected with this thing?*

The creatures were busy around him, some of them hovering over a console that was displaying the data stream coming from Jack. Others were working at what he thought might be the navigation system of the ship, as what he saw displayed there looked vaguely like star constellations. One of them crossed to another terminal, touching the panel that caused a low frequency shudder to crawl beneath the ship. *Propulsion systems?*

Jack observed the creature that had arrived with the cylindrical device connect it to a small, transparent chamber that rose from a panel. The cylinder spun and locked into place, the bottom opening. A dark, red-brown semiviscous fluid drained neatly into a small collector, about an inch long, that looked like a capsule. Blood. They had sampled someone's blood. The machine ingested it and began humming as it processed the sample. Now these creatures not only had broad data sets about Earth's environment, they had detailed data and samples of human DNA.

Jack's heart rate accelerated and suddenly, surprisingly, he thought to a time long ago when he was just a kid. He began to view, from what felt like a detached place, scenes from his young life: skateboarding, riding his bike, running with his sister through the waves in the afternoon at Santa Monica Beach. And then he thought about a pretty girl he liked in high school, seeing her face, her smile anchored in uncomplicated glee from a simpler time long passed. Then he observed his parents, Richard and Marion, young, happy, having a quiet dinner together with him and Amy at their home.

So this is what it meant when people said 'your life flashes before your eyes,' Jack thought.

God, please help me. Dad? I think this is it. I think they're going to kill me now. Help me if you can.

Jack heard a voice—not audible—but a feeling on the inside that formed strong, concise words.

"Look around and study the ship. You're connected to it. Their systems are complex, but as vulnerable as any you know. You can stop it."

Jack became focused then, looking carefully around the ship, gazing at each set of consoles and controls carefully. And deep down he felt the connection to the ship and its systems. On some astonishing, esoteric level, he was plugged into it. Jack's focus became enormous as he began to feel a tangible link with the hardware, growing stronger and stronger. He understood the ship. He understood them. And he knew that he had only a few minutes left before they finished with him.

Linda pushed through the woods, following nothing but pure instinct. She loped onward skillfully, floating over fallen branches and large, protruding root systems. Agent Collins struggled, stumble-running to keep up with her, which was nearly impossible. He'd fallen twice already, the second time gashing his knee on a branch that jutted at a dangerous angle from beneath the undergrowth. With every passing moment he longed for the soft leather chair in his office back in DC, the feel of the power behind his desk.

"Stop!" he called to her several times. "Deputy, stop! Slow down!"

Linda shouted back, "Why don't you keep up! I'm not losing Jack because of you!"

Collins fumed. He was at the breaking point. He'd never keep up with her—not like this. He'd have to lay down the law right then and there.

"Deputy, I'm ordering you to stop right now!"

Linda did stop and her blood boiled.

"Ordering me," she shouted back at him. "Listen asshole, I don't work for you!"

"My authority is the final authority, deputy!"

"Like I said, I don't work for you, Agent Collins. You're not the final authority! You're a public servant like me. Maybe it's time you start acting like one!"

"I will ruin you!" he howled.

"Do your worst," she said, and kept moving.

"You bitch! Do you really think you have any power out here? You're a bug under my thumb!"

Linda spun quickly, rage filling her. She was prepared to put her fist through the back of his head, but only then saw that Collins was pointing his gun at her.

"I'm an expert shot, deputy," he said, his voice a sinister drone. "I will put a bullet through your frontal lobe and you'll be a zombie before you hit the ground."

Linda said, "You're not really going to do this."

Collins answered, "Wake up! The world has changed, popped off its fucking axis! Anything can happen in the new world because it's people like *me* that get to make the rules."

Silence fell between them, but a sound not too far off became more pronounced. It was a low frequency tone, recycling, purring. Alien sounding. They both heard it.

"Listen," he said. "It's their ship. Now here's what I am going to do, deputy: I'm going to reach the ship before it takes off. I'm going to eliminate most of the crew, incapacitating two of them for study later. I'm going to disable the ship, then call my boss in DC and tell him I have the mother load. We're going to pull that ship apart, down to every nut and bolt, and make damn good use of the technology."

"What about Jack? What if he's on board?" she asked.

Collins shrugged. "Irrelevant."

Off to Linda's side, she heard something move.

"God, what a waste of a great body," he leered. "Goodbye, deputy," he said, his face emptying, now just the shell of a man. Linda closed her eyes, and Agent Collins pulled the trigger.

CHAPTER 62

THE BULLET PASSED SO NEAR the side of Linda's head that she heard the hiss of the projectile, felt the air torn in its wake, and only then realized she was still alive. A mere moment after that she knew why. One of the creatures had been close, watching them the whole time, camouflaged in deep forest shadows. She'd heard it move the moment before Collins pulled the trigger, and it had sprung on him, taking him down. And now she was hearing him scream beneath a tumult of twigs, stones, leaves, and earth. She drew her gun, scanning for the creature.

Dull, heavy thuds came from her right side and the screaming stopped. A mechanical howl clipped the air, followed by a wet sounding impact and a loud, sickening snap.

"Agent Collins!" she called out.

There was silence, then the rapid swish of footfalls, sprinting away into the dark distance.

"Agent Collins," she said one more time, sidestepping carefully toward the place where he'd vanished. She clicked on her Maglite and stabbed it in between the trees, the beam drifting, panning, and then finally finding a bleeding, curled up form on the ground. It was Collins, and Linda could make out what looked like a very deep hole going into the back of his neck. And there was a lot of blood.

Had she not heard the sound of the creature still out there, moving, pausing, then moving again, she'd have gone closer to inspect his body. But there was no time. She had to locate the ship and rescue Jack. Time was running out. The creature was still out here with her. *Keep moving,* she thought.

Just keep moving.

The sound of the alien ship grew, and Linda thought for a moment that she could see something through the trees in a clearing some seventy yards out; a large, looming, amorphous shape with a set of lights, alternating from red to purple to white.

Linda barreled on, moving faster still, stopping momentarily only to listen for sounds of the rogue creature that might cue her to its location and proximity. She couldn't hear it. Maybe it had gone past her and made it to the ship. No, it hadn't. No way. It was still out here. Tracking her. Closing on her. She could sense it traversing the dark, using the shadows as cover. She was absolutely certain of being watched at that very moment.

Nevertheless she pressed forward, using all her senses, arriving finally at the edge of the clearing where she got a fantastic view of something she had believed all her life to be a fantasy, cut from the cloth of daydreams and illusions, an enigmatic leviathan.

"Holy God," she whispered, taking in the mass of it, which consumed the length of the forest clearing. Fifty, sixty yards? Maybe more.

The low, tactile hum that came from it gave the impression that it was breathing—not merely a machine, but a living machine. Like the scout. It was hard to discern the exact profile of the ship, as most of it blended with the storm-choked darkness of the surrounding woods. That is until a flow of circuitous illumination bloomed across the hull, racing and dancing along its sides, over its top and back down beneath it where the red, purple, and white lights still pulsed. And in this astonishing moment, Linda thought instantly of the back of a great whale with a long, protruding dorsal fin growing spectacularly from it. She could only imagine other remarkable details that might be revealed were it beneath a bellowing midday sun.

Linda spotted the lip of the boarding ramp, still touching the ground. That was the way in. *Probably the only way*, she suspected. She wrapped her hand around her gun, unaware that the rogue creature had closed the distance on her, hiding the sound of its traverse beneath the drone of the great ship. It was ready to take her down.

Jack had become singularly focused and intense. He was sensing a tactile interaction with the ship, recognizing the terminals, the systems and what the creatures were busying themselves with. And in his mind, be began hearing commands. No, not hearing them exactly, as in a voice, but more like seeing printed words in his mind:

NAVIGATION SET. PROPULSION ENABLED, SET DEPARTURE AHEAD OF ATMOSPHERIC EVENT, LESS 5. DATA RECOVERY SUCCESSFUL. THERMAL TUNING ON STANDBY. FUEL STABLE, CONSUMPTION WITHIN EXPECTED RANGE. NO ADDITIONAL ALLOWANCES.

Jack thought, *They're lifting off in five minutes before the storm hits, otherwise they're grounded.*

No additional allowances. Jack guessed that meant no additional weight, since apparently their fuel consumption was still a finite amount. That meant they wouldn't be taking him with them. So they'd either let him go, or they'd kill him and throw his body out there in the woods.

They cannot leave, he thought. *They cannot take all this data back to their world.* And then another thought entered his mind, strong like the words that hit him earlier. "*You have to sabotage the ship. You're still plugged in. Control something.*"

Quickly, Jack centered his attention on a dark, dormant machine terminal eight feet away on his right.

Power on the terminal, Jack thought. *Power on the terminal. Power on the terminal. Power on the—*

The screen lit up suddenly. Coincidence? No! It worked! Jack began thinking harder. What would stop them from leaving? What would keep them here?

Thermal tuning. Ship temperature.

That was it. This vessel had physical limitations, which meant it was subject to the punishing temperatures encountered in space travel. It was something NASA spacecraft dealt with all the time: the differences between direct sunlight and opposing shadow could be as much as 500 degrees, especially in the inner solar system. Certain materials on the ship were designed to handle one extreme but not the other. Thermal tuning required a spacecraft to remain in a strict orientation so as not to expose the wrong materials to the opposing temperature. But what if these creatures had engineered a way around that? *What if?*

Jack decided there was no more time to question it. He had to try something. He sensed through the limb in his arm where ship temperatures were controlled. He looked quickly over all the displays, trying to locate the right one. If he could find it, he could think the command, and control it.

But Jack spotted one of the creatures staring directly at him, its glassy, non-organic eyes processing him. It studied him for several dilated moments, and then turned its attention to the terminal he had just powered on. The creature looked back toward Jack from behind that cruel, featureless mask.

It was thinking. Analyzing. It knew something was wrong.

Hurry, Jack thought.

Hurry!

CHAPTER 63

L INDA WAS OUT OF TIME and out of options. There was only one entrance into the alien ship and one way to get there. She'd have to approach head on and walk right into its throat, then somehow find Jack and get him out.

If he was still alive.

She gently, quietly pulled the magazine from her weapon, verifying that she had a mostly full clip. She clacked it back in, slid the pipe open, and carefully chambered a round. She'd go in, picking her targets carefully, her shots conservative and precise. She'd not waste a single bullet. It was time. She took a deep breath, readying herself.

The force with which she was struck felt like a runaway car. Linda's feet left the ground. Trees dashed past her, the sky tumbled, the lights of the alien ship spun. She made full contact with the ground. The impact stole her breath. She spun reflexively onto her back and then realized the gun was still in her hand. The shadow of the creature slithered around her, the sound of wet grass sloshing beneath its feet. She rolled left, inverting her point of view, now locking on its shape. She was barely able to make it out, but noted the puncture wound in its upper chest where she had shot it through her windshield back at Jack's place. This creature was already wounded. It remembered her. And it was going to make her suffer.

Linda pulled the trigger. The bullet took the creature square in the right shoulder. From beneath the mask came a dreadful howl, a demonic cry. It dropped, but clambered furiously back up, recapturing purchase on its feet. It closed on her, its sudden proximity alarming.

Linda rolled—just in time—as the creature slashed down at her with something in its hand, some kind of weapon, a razor sharp, metallic spur bristling with small denticle hooks along its length. The weapon came down, puncturing the soft ground next to her ear, tearing through the grass like wrapping paper. She turned her gun on the creature, but it struck her hand so hard the firearm broke from her fingers, tumbling ten feet away, landing in the grass.

The terrible spur weapon sliced down through the air. Linda curled in a ball, and it caught a piece of her hair, severing it instantly. She spun and kicked upward, catching the creature's thigh, then scissor-kicked backward, knocking its leg out from underneath it. It dropped, but quickly sprung back on its hands and knees. Rising.

And that's when Linda felt the end of a thick branch, brushing her fingertips. She stretched toward it and wrapped her hands around it, feeling its girth, the weight of it heavy as she lifted it. She climbed to her feet, now holding the big branch with both hands. The creature reasserted its grip on the pommeled handle of the spur weapon, about to unleash—

CRACK! The sound of the wood striking the metal façade of the creature's face was gunshot loud. The creature dropped, stunned. Linda swung again, taking it in the side of its head. She swung again, and again, possessed with supernatural strength fueled by a river of cortisol and rage.

The final blow caused the end of the stick to break off, and with it the mask of the creature disengaged and tore free from its suit. Small hoses that formed a breathing apparatus burst wide open in a fiery release of gasses that sent tubes hissing and writhing like angry snakes. The creature gulped desperately as all at once Earth air rushed into its lungs. From deep in its throat it unleashed a scream that sent Linda's ears ringing. But she saw it now clearly, the horrible face of the alien, its huge, black, almond eyes suddenly bleaching to white, bulging in their slatted sockets under a sudden change of pressure. There was no nose that she could discern, but the mouth was a horror of its own: a gaping maw, purple-pink with rows of sharp ochre teeth fitted tightly together.

Its neck distended, strange organs protruding beneath its skin as a flowing apron of bluish-purple fluid gushed from its throat. Linda jumped backward, her senses reeling with astonishment and revulsion. All at once it reminded her of the reporter in Australia. It was the shock, the hopeless agony in the eyes, *even in those dreadful alien eyes*, that Linda found herself remembering it, now hearing in her own mind the screech of the woman reporter on that terrible day so many weeks before.

The creature dropped on its side, its body seizing up, suffocating. Linda quickly spotted her gun and grabbed it. She circled the monster, lined up its head with her barrel, and fired the round that terminated its suffering. It wasn't that she felt compassion for the creature; it was that she couldn't listen to its gurgling, rattling, tormented breath any longer.

She looked toward the ship, now noticing that two more of the creatures were standing in the opening, looking straight at her. Linda raised her gun, sighting them in. There was no more shock left, no more fear or awe. She was wholly resolute and clear on where she was going and what she had to do. Stepping quickly, the gun pointed ahead as if it were an extension of her arm, she closed on them and fired expertly, the first creature's neck bursting into a sharp, purple mist. She would kill both of them within a few short seconds.

CHAPTER 64

I T WAS THE EXTRATERRESTRIAL SHRIEK from outside the ship that caused Jack, along with the alien crew, to hold still a moment. The creatures, sensing something was desperately wrong, began hurrying at their stations while two of them walked down the ramp toward the opening to survey what was happening outside.

Linda, Jack thought. *It has to be.* This was followed by the sound of gunshots; loud pops that clipped stridently off the deck of the ship. There were more screeches, otherworldly cries of pain.

Jack glanced at the holographic display in front of him. The data streams had gone. The download was complete. But the limb-probe was still inside his arm.

Think, Jack! Focus! You can stop them!

He glanced down at the restraints pinning him to the hard platform. He focused on them carefully.

Open the cuffs, he thought. *Open the cuffs. OPEN THE CUFFS.* Astonishingly, they loosened on him, parting, retracting back into the table.

The limb in Jack's arm twitched and he could feel the long needle receding through his vein, slowly crawling out of him.

They know, he thought. *They're going to disconnect me.*

Jack threw his attention toward a console he'd determined—*hoped*—controlled the ships thermal bias. He could sense the heating and cooling settings. And instantly he focused on the heaters.

Heaters on, set to full, he thought. *ALL HEATERS ON, SET TO FULL. OVERRIDE THERMAL PROGRAM. EMERGENCY—ALL HEATERS ON, SET TO FULL!*

The console responded. Incredibly, Jack saw what looked like gauges rising and falling, adjusting to his command. One of the creatures saw this and dashed to the terminal, but didn't make it before Jack thought: *LOCK TERMINAL. LOCK TERMINAL. OVERRIDE ALL CONTROLS. HEATERS TO FULL. HEATERS TO FULL!*

The creature scuttled over the terminal. Desperate. Unable to get it back under control. And within moments, Jack felt the air thin, then warmth engulf the space of the room, then heat begin to flow past him, sudden perspiration forming over his eyes.

Instantly the limb-probe shot free from Jack's arm, dotting him with blood as it withdrew. He climbed off the table. He was free, and they knew it. Swiftly, one of them grabbed its Taser weapon while the others were frantic at their controls as propulsion systems were overheating, the sound of the ship's drive now a keening, labored whine. A shudder passed through the hull around them and from outside there was a distinct clap of thunder. The storm would be on top of them in a minute. The chamber darkened around them, now painted stroboscopically by the displays that were chopping on and off. *Systems are starting to fail. It's all failing,* Jack thought.

The creature with the Taser jumped at him, the energy snapping dangerously in bolts. Jack dropped instantly behind the table he'd been pinned to, an explosion of light occurring over his head as the weapon made contact with the surface of it, a deafening crack from the discharge in his ear. He reached then for it, grabbing it near the handle, wrestling with the creature for a purchase on it. But the floor shook violently, and Jack heard what sounded like a large turbine engine starting up. Looking back he saw the ramp closing. And then he heard Linda's voice through all the noise, coming in through the closing gap of the ship entrance.

"Jack! Jack!"

"Linda," he shouted. "Get away from the ship! It's unstable!"

The creatures secured themselves into restraints as now the entire ship began to tilt. Jack grabbed on with his free hand to a piece of the hull for balance, but his hand began to burn as the surface itself was overheating dangerously. The creature with the Taser was still clamped to him with brute force. Jack fought to extricate himself, but exhaustion was swallowing him. He saw the ramp closing, felt the tilt of the ship increasing, the cry of the engines vicious.

LET GO. The words were immediate and unblemished as they formed inside him. The ramp was falling into a steep grade beneath him, closing, swallowing the outside world. There was a flashbulb pop of lightning beyond that shrinking gap, a clap of thunder following. The crew of the ship was in place. They were going to attempt an ascent. *They know the ship is overheating and systems are unstable,* Jack thought. *But they're going anyway.*

It was an act of desperation.

LET GO.

Jack let go of the hull, and using both hands, he grabbed the Taser, twisted it in one swift motion and pushed it directly into the chest of the creature that restrained him. He heard the weapon discharge, felt the bite of the voltage. The creature howled and Jack dropped precipitously, falling backward down the ramp, sliding on the hard surface, plunging now toward what was left of that opening.

Linda had felt the ground shudder just before the ship lifted impossibly off the ground. She dashed away, but threw her gaze backward toward that opening, hoping, praying that Jack would somehow make it out. And a moment later, she saw him plunge from it, dropping into the dirt beneath the ship.

"Jack!"

She ran then, back toward him, her heart pumping painfully in her chest every yard until she reached him. He was curled on the ground, unmoving.

"Jack," she said, touching him carefully, feeling for his pulse, which was strong.

"Jack, it's me!"

He looked up at her, his eyes narrow, blinking rapidly as the shock began to wear off. They were beneath the lights of the ship as it drifted over them, Linda's shape bathed in them, her outline angelic in the otherworldly glow.

"Linda," he said.

She touched his face gently.

"Jack, can you move? We have to get out of here!"

A low-pitched whine formed in the air above them, colliding with the sound of thunder from the storm. Jack marshaled all his strength, feeling the protest of his body, the vague sense of pain throughout. But he fought it until he felt his feet planted, balanced and sure. And together they ran toward the tree line as the howl of the ship in the air crescendoed to a treacherous level.

"Don't look back!" he yelled as they crossed into the woods, running onward, full tilt in a dead-straight line away from the clearing.

The world ignited as lightning struck the ascending ship, connecting with its drive that had already dangerously overheated. The blast of energy was like the death of a small star, pushing concentric waves of energy outward over the countryside. The resulting pulse struck Jack and Linda from behind, throwing them in the air, burying them against the side of a large tree. Lightning came down, torturing the ground, the atmosphere suddenly alive with millions of volts. There were loud cracks in the forest as pieces of the alien ship began to meteor down in a shower of torn and fiery debris. Jack and Linda heard the big pieces punching holes through the forest canopy, incinerated bits of detritus from the ship shelling the branches, leaves, and tall grass. They clamped their eyes shut, both of them saying quiet prayers.

It all continued for several minutes more until eventually it stopped. A minute later the rain began—a light, cool rain. They sat pressed together, holding each other beneath the showers for what seemed like an hour before climbing to their feet. Very slowly then, without saying anything, they walked back out of the forest. Back toward home.

CHAPTER 65

I N THE WAKE OF THE event, an unprecedented military presence descended on the State Forest where thousands of pieces of the alien spacecraft had strafed and pockmarked several square miles of the woodland. It was a massive operation, though kept veiled and fuliginous behind a bulwark of National Guard vehicles and troops. Local law enforcement were kept mostly in the dark as to the specifics of the operation and ordered to keep civilians in line. Lethal force was authorized should someone be found removing pieces of the spacecraft from the area. The media began descending like vultures, picking pieces of the story off the carcass of some eyewitness accounts and the commentaries of "experts," all too eager to share theories that covered the scale from conceivable to absurd. Everyone talked about how the world had changed and would never be the same.

During those surreal weeks, Jack became invisible, focusing all his attention on Marion and transitioning her to her new home in Tampa. The private room they wanted for her had become available and the day arrived that they would get her there via a flight out of Indianapolis International Airport. Jack drove his mother there and gently wheeled her into the terminal in her chair. They met Amy who had flown in a few hours earlier. She would take Marion back with her on an afternoon flight. They said their goodbyes in the cavernous space of the main terminal and Jack kissed Marion gently on the forehead before Amy rolled her away toward security. He felt almost certain it was the last time he would see her.

Back at the house, alone now, Jack listened to the silence at night as he lay on the small bed in the guestroom. Everything else in the house had since been donated or sold. The house itself was no longer a home, just an arrangement of wood, bricks and concrete. In his final few days there Jack thought about everything that had happened, but mostly he thought about his parents and what kind of place the world had become without them in it. In just a few more days, he would give a copy of the house key to the realtor, rent a car, carefully pack some of his parents' valuables including pictures, jewelry and notebooks with Richard's handwritten logs from JPL, and then drive 1,800 miles back to Pasadena. It would be a long, lonely trip.

When the phone rang and Jack noticed it was Linda calling, he answered immediately. They hadn't spoken since the incident. Despite the voicemail Jack had left her seven days earlier, he'd not heard anything from her.

"I wasn't sure if I was going to get to speak to you again," he said, his voice loud and tinny sounding in the hollow living room space.

"Hey, Jack. How are you doing?"

"It's quiet here. Empty. Mom's gone, settling into her new home in Tampa."

"It must have been hard to say goodbye like that."

"It was."

A beat fell between them, the warm sound of birds and humming insects outside buffering the silence.

"Linda," Jack started, "I was really hoping to see you one more time before I leave."

She hesitated.

"Jack, I think...I think it might be better if we didn't. I'm sure if we did, something might happen...something that would make both our lives a lot more complicated. You're going home. I'm staying here. This is my home."

Jack felt an ache in his heart, the weight of her words settling on him.

"I'll be coming back. Bringing Mom here for burial next to Dad," he said. "Maybe soon. I don't know how much more time she has."

Linda said, "I guess we'll see each other, then."

Jack said, "I guess we will."

CHAPTER 66

I T WAS DECEMBER 23ᴿᴰ, A moist, cold evening in Pasadena. Jack was at home, sitting on the couch, watching something on the Travel Channel, a half-empty beer in front of him on the coffee table next to the remains of a pepperoni pizza. He had packed his suitcase earlier as to avoid having to do it late that night. Everything was ready for his trip to Tampa where Marion was living in a cozy facility that provided hospice care for her around the clock. It had come to that point just two months earlier when she'd gotten an infection and ended up in the hospital. Miraculously she bounced from the worst of it, however it became clear that her body was shutting down, and she'd not withstand another infection like it. Comfort care was going to be vital in these last days. But she was still hanging on, and Jack decided to visit her over Christmas, see Amy and the kids, and take one last break before getting back work on his book that was now overdue.

It was just after 9:00 p.m. when he got a text message from Amy. It simply read:

MOM. 911.

Jack had seen this once before, and it had proven to be a close call, not the end. But somehow he knew—this time—it was different. This was it. He called Amy and got her frantic voice on the line.

"Jack," she said, "I just got a call from the hospice nurse who's with Mom right now. She's going...*she's going right now.* I'm driving over there, but I don't know if I'll make it before she's gone. Can you please call her?" Jack took the number from Amy, hung up and dialed the hospice nurse who answered immediately.

Jack said, "This is Jack McAllister, Marion's son. What's happening? Is she going?"

The man's voice was solemn. "Yes, I'm sorry, she is."

Jack said, "Will you please put the phone to her ear."

"Yes, of course," the nurse said. After that Jack heard his mother's breathing on the phone—hollow, labored, rattling in her throat.

"Mom. Mom, it's me, Jack. I love you, Mom. I love you. You were a great mom; you took good care of Amy and me when we were kids. It's okay to go now. It's okay. *We love you.*"

Less than three minutes later, Amy called him back.

"Jack, I'm here with her now. She's gone. God, she's still warm."

Marion looked miniature in the casket, Jack thought. She'd been five-foot-one her adult life. The age and Alzheimer's had shrunk her, and as she lay there in the soft, pale fabric, she appeared even smaller than he'd remembered her being just a few months earlier. It was a short reception that morning in the same chapel they'd been in seven months earlier for Richard's service. It felt absurd somehow, if not a wholly ironic.

It was 10:30am on New Year's Eve, and in just a half hour they'd be graveside for the internment, putting Marion to rest directly beside Richard. Twelve months earlier, New Year's Eve, Jack was at a party in Encino with friends and people in the "biz," partying early into the next morning. He thought about this as they drove south toward the cemetery following the hearse. What a difference from twelve months ago...as if the whole planet had inexplicably tumbled from its fragile axis. And in some ways—*in many ways*—it had.

It was biting cold beneath the wintery grey sky that hung like a tarp from horizon to horizon as they all sat on folding chairs in the grass near Marion's casket. Richard was six feet directly below them, and in just a little while, she would be down there right beside him. Jack stood before the group to say a few words, trembling from the cold, stamping his feet lightly as he spoke.

"Thank you all for coming out today. I doubt there's anything else I can possibly say that hasn't been said already. I guess the only parting thought I can offer is...Dad, Mom...I miss you both very much."

The service ended, and as people were pulling out, Jack spotted the sheriff's car rolling gently along the pavement, coming to a stop nearby. Linda climbed from the car, walked straight to Jack and embraced him. He held her tightly.

"I'm so sorry I didn't make it earlier. It's New Year's Eve—busiest day of the year for me. Got a long shift."

Jack said, "It's okay. Thanks for coming by. It means the world to me."

"I can't believe it's been...what...five, six months," she said.

"Yeah," Jack said. "Whole world's changed."

"Well, I try not to read the news anymore."

"No," Jack said, "I meant this."

He tipped his hand toward the grave where the internment crew was preparing to lower Marion into the ground. Linda took it in for a long moment. They stood silently together in the cold winter air as their breath danced visibly out in front of them.

"Are you in for the night?" she asked.

"Yes. I won't be celebrating this one. Pulling out first thing in the morning," he said.

Linda nodded.

"Unless..." he added cautiously, "you had some time later, after your shift. We could get late night coffee."

She bled a half smile.

"I'm with someone," she said, blushing ever so slightly, something Jack had never seen her do before. He nodded and smiled.

"Lucky guy," he said.

She nodded and they stood together another minute before saying goodbye for the last time, driving their separate ways.

That night Jack dreamt of Richard and Marion together—young, vibrant and alive. They were walking in a beautiful garden.

Jack called out to his father and asked, "Dad! Dad, where have you been?"

Richard turned to him, his youthful expression beaming, and said, "The most wonderful place you could never imagine." And then he said, "Jack, I'm proud of you. You're going to be okay."

Jack awoke in tears and lay in the bed until his heart steadied and he wasn't crying anymore. He slid off the mattress and drifted toward the window, pulling the curtains back softly to have a look at the sky.

Overhead, through a gap in the cloud cover, a deep black heaven with diamond bright stars shone magnificently. Light burst suddenly in that space as a small meteor knifed through the upper atmosphere at impossible speed. It sprouted a fiery tail with warm orange core and a deep blue mane. It hung brilliantly for mere moments before it was consumed, vanishing then as though it had never existed.

THE END

ACKNOWLEDGMENTS

This book is for my parents, George and Monte Tozzi, who passed away in 2011. Not a day goes by that I don't think about both of them with great fondness and affection.

I give my love and utmost thanks to my wife, Nina, for encouraging me as I sometimes felt adrift on a sea of words and ideas, wondering when I'd land ashore, and where that shore might be.

To my beta readers who gave me such valuable feedback, I sincerely thank you for being so constructive. Nina Tozzi, William Snyder, Shalene Petricek, Lisa Battig, John Bucholtz, Paul Sansone, Beth Martin, Brett Stimely, Tiffany La Belle Smith, Stephanie Hurd Lievens, Kristin Amundsen Cubanski and Sean Hinchey.

Copyeditor/proofer, Kristen Tatroe, thank you.

All my friends at JPL/NASA

To others in my life that have in some way inspired and/or encouraged me, I give special thanks. Brett Stimely, Marc Scott Zicree, Ray Bradbury, Sean Hinchey.

To my family, Nina, Alyssa, Katy and family, Jennifer and family, Paddy Paws.

And to God from whom all blessings and creativity flow.

www.ingramcontent.com/pod-product-compliance
Lightning Source LLC
Chambersburg PA
CBHW072107250626
47159CB00007B/2334